mojo: (mó•jō), noun

1. personal magnetism; sex appeal
2. a magic charm or spell
3. a town in Louisiana with a surplus of peculiar inhabitants and powerful voodoo dolls

syn. exhilaration

Sentence: *Finding your mojo means rediscovering love . . . and yourself.*

Author's Note: For those of you who read *In Deep Voodoo* and were expecting a sequel titled *Voodoo or Die*, I hope you will forgive the retitling of this book to *Finding Your Mojo* to better match the story that the sequel turned out to be. Thanks very much for your continued support—I hope you enjoy the book!

By Stephanie Bond

Finding Your Mojo
In Deep Voodoo
Whole Lotta Trouble
Party Crashers
Kill the Competition
I Think I Love You
Got Your Number
Our Husband

STEPHANIE BOND

Finding Your Mojo

AVON BOOKS
An Imprint of HarperCollins*Publishers*

AVON BOOKS
An Imprint of HarperCollins*Publishers*
10 East 53rd Street
New York, New York 10022-5299

ISBN-13: 978-0-06-082107-4
ISBN-10: 0-06-082107-8
www.avonromance.com

First Avon Books paperback printing: November 2006

Printed in the U.S.A.

10 9 8 7 6 5 4 3 2 1

Acknowledgments

Thanks to my editor, Lyssa Keusch, for inadvertently sparking this idea with an offhand reply to my suggestion that a secondary character in a previous book have her own story. The comment went something like, "I'm not sure Gloria is the best name for a main character." To which I replied, "Well, maybe that's not her *real* name." Thanks to my critique partner, Rita Herron, for being my first reader as the manuscript unfolded. Thanks, too, to my husband, Christopher Hauck, for patiently listening to the story bits as they unwound in my head. But most of all, thanks to those of you who read the first book in this series, *In Deep Voodoo,* and have emailed me through my website to say you can't wait to get back to Mojo, Louisiana. Welcome back—I hope you enjoy your stay!

Stephanie Bond
www.stephaniebond.com

Chapter

1

Gloria Dalton juggled her purse, a briefcase, and a cup of coffee as she struggled to unlock the door to her new law office. Her sweaty palm slipped on the doorknob as she questioned for the hundredth time her decision to leave New Orleans and relocate to the nearby small town of Mojo to take over the practice of a dead man.

"I can do this," she murmured. "This time will be different."

All signage for the not-so-dearly departed Deke Black had been replaced with gold lettering spelling out Gloria Dalton, Attorney-at-Law. Her name across the large plate-glass window facing the parking lot for the Charmed Village Shopping Center was especially satisfying, and something she had envisioned in her mind's eye since she was a teenager.

Admittedly, she had visualized a different name . . . one ending with Riley. She smiled indulgently at the unbidden adolescent memory, then told herself it was only natural that she think of Zane Riley. Leaving the New Jersey town, where she'd met her first love, in the middle of the night without saying goodbye had been a traumatic event for a sixteen-year-old, and she would forever associate moving with leaving him.

Fourteen years and over a dozen moves later, she was accustomed to picking up her life and moving it, but this was the first time she felt good about it. Ménière's syndrome of sudden vertigo and nausea, which had plagued her since she was young, had worsened in the frantic, overstimulating environment of New Orleans, where simply standing among a sea of bodies could trigger a feeling not unlike seasickness. Mojo was by far the smallest town she'd ever lived in, but the experience would be good for her, physically and mentally. She just might make friends here . . . make a life for herself . . . stop looking over her shoulder . . . find her own mojo.

Her new law office shared the strip mall with other local businesses, including Primo Drycleaners, Tam's Electronics, Lewis Taxidermy, S&C Upholstery, Quinto's Sub Sandwiches, and the Looky-Loo Bookstore. Some of the storefronts were already decorated for the holidays, but none had opened yet for the Monday workday.

Gloria jiggled the stubborn key and sloshed coffee on her new peach-colored blouse. So much for her first-day outfit, which she'd agonized over. Muttering a curse, she set down her load to free her hands.

That was when she noticed the burgundy-colored gift box topped with a gold bow sitting on the sidewalk next to her door. She smiled, thinking how welcoming the residents of Mojo had been. She'd expected them to be more resistant to outsiders, especially an outsider taking over a local man's business—a business that meant she'd be delving into the lives of people who came to her for help. Legal issues had a way of bringing out a person's deep, dark secrets.

Which is why she intended to stay on *this* side of the desk.

After a bit more wrangling, she managed to unlock the door and walked inside, where she was assailed immediately by the cold air. Penny Francisco, Deke's ex-wife, whom Gloria had represented in the divorce before he . . . er, *died,* had warned her that the office was infamously cold.

Shivering, she went back to pick up her coffee, purse and briefcase, thinking she'd return for the package after she got the heat rolling. Despite the chill, though, December in Louisiana was warmer and nicer than most places she'd lived. She didn't miss the snow of Wisconsin or the rain of Washington or the wind of Kansas.

She walked through the reception area; glancing at the desk of the paralegal she'd inherited with the office, she nursed misgivings. Steve Chasen had his own nameplate, coffee station, and reserved parking space in front of the plate-glass window, closer to the door even than her own space. The man was certainly . . . ambitious. And a bit arrogant, although he'd proved to her that he knew Deke's files and clients and could help her get up and running quickly.

Penny had warned her that Steve was difficult, and although at one time Penny had suspected him of murdering his former boss, Deke, her fears had proved to be unfounded.

So, with the murder suspicions put to rest, Gloria had hired him. It wasn't as if she was going to have her pick of paralegals in such a small town.

The half-empty box of fund-raiser chocolate bars sitting open on his desk looked tempting. She hadn't had breakfast, and she was sure Steve had bought them with the office petty cash fund—the man seemed to have dipped liberally into the cash bag since his former boss's demise, but in this case, Gloria didn't mind. The chocolate bars being sold to raise money for the families of the victims of Mojo's Instruments of Death and Voodoo Museum had even made their way to New Orleans: The depravity that had gone on in the museum under the noses of good people in a small town had shaken even the residents of the big city thirty miles down the interstate, which was *known* for its teeming corruption.

But she'd save the treat for later—she needed something substantial in her stomach to give her energy to get through what promised to be a long day.

Gloria proceeded to her own office, newly decorated with light maple and glass furniture and sleek chairs to reflect her own taste. She unloaded everything on her desk and inhaled deeply in satisfaction. The first day of the rest of her life seemed a little clichéd, but somehow it seemed so appropriate today.

She was ready for a change, and in the wake of the scandal of the voodoo museum, Mojo also seemed primed for transformation. Not to mention the fact that it would give her a chance to be near one of the largest missing persons identification efforts in history.

She had a special affinity for the missing. Technically, she was one of them.

On the way out of her office, she stopped to adjust the thermostat up a few degrees and headed to the bathroom to try to clean up her blouse. While she dabbed at the coffee stain with a wet paper towel, she heard the chime sound for the front door.

"Use cold water," a female voice yelled, "or you'll set the stain."

Gloria frowned and stuck her head out of the bathroom. Blue-haired Marie Gaston, Penny's right-hand employee at the health food store, stood in the reception area smiling, holding the burgundy gift box in one hand and a brown paper bag in the other. "Penny sent you carrot muffins for breakfast. Welcome to Mojo!"

"Thank you," Gloria said, walking forward to take the paper bag. "That's very kind of her to think of me, and of you to bring them. But how did you know about the? . . ." She gestured to the stain on her blouse, remembering that Penny had insinuated that Marie might have some ESP abilities.

Marie's mouth rounded, as if she realized her gaffe, then she pointed to the front door. "I noticed some spilled coffee, and when I heard the water running, I put two and two together." She held up the gift box. "This was out front, too."

"Thanks," Gloria said. "I was coming back to get it."

"Your window looks great," Marie offered. "There's something very . . . *permanent* about it."

Gloria admired it again from the inside. "Thanks—I like it. And I guess that means I have to stay at least long enough to pay off the fancy lettering job."

"Are you getting settled into your own place?"

"Yes," Gloria said, wary of sharing her new home address. She had rented a house from the Gallaghers, just down Charm Street, near Goddard's Funeral Chapel, and even though she'd changed the locks, she hadn't had a chance to arrange for all the security features that would help her sleep at night.

Old habits died hard.

"The Gallagher house is really nice," Marie said.

Gloria raised her eyebrows in surprise.

"Uh, moving van in the driveway gave it away. You'll find out soon enough how fast news travels in a small town." Marie extended the burgundy box. "Someone must have left you a welcome gift."

"Let's see," Gloria said, taking the box and setting it on Steve Chasen's desk. She lifted the lid and frowned as she rooted around in the tissue paper. Her hand touched something solid, and she withdrew a voodoo doll, dressed in dark strips of suit fabric, obviously meant to be male . . . and obviously meant to be in pain, considering the fact that a long pin stuck out of the doll's stomach.

"Uh-oh," Marie said. "Not another one."

A finger of unease trailed up Gloria's spine. Two months ago, Deke Black had been found stabbed to death a few hours after Penny, his ex-wife, had stabbed a voodoo doll as a joke. Even though the flesh-and-blood murderer had been caught, many people still believed there had been some kind of supernatural connection between the doll and Deke's demise.

And the maker of that doll had never been identified.

"Why would someone leave this voodoo doll for you?" Marie asked.

Gloria lifted her shoulders in a slow shrug. "I have no idea."

Then she looked up, and her lungs stalled to see a white car bulleting toward the newly gilded window. She grabbed Marie by the arm and yanked her backward. They raised their arms to protect their faces just as the car plowed through the window in a crashing cacophony of shattered glass and splintered wood. The car stopped just inside the reception area, but a man's body projected through the windshield and landed with a thud faceup on Steve Chasen's desk.

Which seemed only fitting, considering the man *was* Steve Chasen, his body bloodied and deathly still.

"Oh, my God," Gloria murmured through her fingers, her body wracked with shock and disbelief.

"Wow," Marie whispered. "I didn't see *that* coming."

Chapter 2

Gloria stood rooted to the floor, the coffee stain on her blouse a moot point, considering the fact that her shoes and clothing were coated with dust and bits of glass. She blinked and sputtered to clear her eyes and mouth, trying to absorb the horror of a car sitting in her reception area and the fact that her paralegal was badly injured . . . at best.

"Call 911!" Marie shouted, rolling into action as she rushed over to the man.

With her heart in her throat, Gloria reached for the phone on the desk next to Steve, the handset bizarrely untouched. When she realized that she was still holding the silly voodoo doll, she tossed it to the floor. With shaking fingers she punched buttons on the phone and brushed dust from her face and arms while she waited for a connection. After what seemed like hours, the operator answered. Gloria explained as calmly as possible that a car had just driven through the front of her office and a man was badly injured.

"Send an ambulance to the Charmed Village Shopping Center in Mojo—they'll see the car."

"Is the victim breathing?" the operator asked.

"Is he breathing?" Gloria asked Marie.

Marie looked up and nodded. "Barely."

Gloria exhaled in relief, then told the operator.

"Is there a pulse?"

Gloria asked Marie, and the young woman placed her fingers on the side of his neck. "No."

"No," Gloria told the operator, tamping down her panic.

"Is the victim bleeding profusely from an open wound, such as the site of a major artery?"

Gloria winced and looked. So much blood, it made her legs weak. Yet despite the numerous cuts on the man's face and head, nothing appeared to be spurting. "I don't think so."

"Do you know how to administer CPR?"

She did . . . she had performed it to no avail on her father years ago . . . the night she and her mother had fled. "Yes."

She handed the phone to Marie, then swept bits of debris from Steve's chest. After locating his breastbone, she positioned her stacked hands just below and leaned her weight into depressing his chest for thirty hard, fast pulses. As she counted, bad memories came rushing back, the sticky, crimson blood, the gaping black bullet hole in her father's neck. She banished the images to the back of her mind, reminding herself that *this* man's life was at stake. When she stopped to check his pulse, she was perspiring from the effort.

But beneath her fingers, a faint rhythm vibrated. "His heart is beating," she said, her arms trembling. Blood trickled from a long cut on the back of her hand that she hadn't noticed before.

She heard a siren in the distance. Suddenly she realized that the front door was impassible with the nose of the car wedged into the front wall. "Marie, go out the back door to flag down the ambulance and show them where to come in."

"We hear a siren," Marie said into the phone, thanking the operator before she hung up. "That's actually the police, not the ambulance," she told Gloria.

Gloria raised her eyebrows.

Marie looked as if she'd been caught. "Uh . . . they sound different. That'll be the new chief of police—today's his first day on the job."

Gloria nodded. New because of the upheaval in the police department over Deke Black's murder and the subsequent discovery of the horrible things that had been going on at the Mojo Voodoo Museum. The town's main tourist trap had been a trap, all right, in the most depraved sense of the word. With two live witnesses recovered and an untold number of persons dead, the museum had been closed and the governor had sent a task force to uncover the extent of the criminal activity that had occurred within the walls of the creepy old mansion. The new chief of police had his work cut out for him.

And now this to deal with on day one.

"Steve has to make it," Marie said. Tears clouded the young woman's eyes, and Gloria wondered how close Marie was to the injured man. Before Gloria could ask, Marie disappeared in the direction of the back door, which opened onto a narrow paved lane lined with trash Dumpsters for the respective businesses along the strip.

Gloria checked Steve again, alarmed to find that his breathing had grown more shallow and his face had turned a deep cherry red. "Hang in there, Steve," she murmured, squeezing his hand. She'd seen a man die before, and it still haunted her. She didn't want to watch this young man's life slip away, too.

She wondered what could have made him accelerate into the window—a heart attack, or some other sudden medical condition, such as an aneurysm or a stroke? Or had he been distracted by something and accidentally depressed the gas pedal instead of the brake? He had seemed like a fastidious person, but everyone made mistakes.

In an attempt to comfort him in his unconscious state, she smoothed a hand over the fine brown tweed of his jacket, stopping when a memory stirred. Her thoughts were so jumbled that she couldn't reconcile the disjointed impressions for several seconds. Then, with her heart clicking, she stooped to retrieve the voodoo doll from the debris on the floor. She held it against Steve's jacket. A strip of the same brown tweed had been wrapped around the stabbed doll. Fear gripped her lungs and squeezed.

A connection was impossible . . . wasn't it?

She dropped the doll and yanked back her hand, her fingers tingling. The noise of Marie returning brought her head up and around.

"An ambulance is on the way," Marie said.

A tall, darkly uniformed man followed her, removing his hat as he entered. He scanned the scene before them and made his way toward Steve Chasen, casting his slate-gray eyes on her with a nod.

"Ma'am," he said curtly, and she noticed abstractly that living in the South had softened his Northern accent.

A buzzing noise sounded in her ears, and little spots of light danced before her eyes as her brain registered exactly whom she was seeing.

Zane? *Zane Riley?*

Chapter

3

This man couldn't be Zane, Gloria thought, her senses going haywire. Her mind was playing tricks on her. But he had the same gray eyes . . . the same square chin . . . the same tall, athletic build, the same thick dark hair, cropped closer now, and shot with silver near his temples. His job, she thought vaguely, must be stressful for him to be turning gray prematurely. And his expression was . . . sterner. She might have attributed the flat line of his mouth and his hardened jaw to the situation at hand if not for the furrow between his eyebrows that seemed permanent.

"I'm Zane Riley," he bit out, erasing all doubts.

She took a step back, gouging the corner of the desk into the back of her thigh. His appearance was so surreal that she was swamped with fear and confusion, as if she had stepped into another time dimension.

"I know," she said on an exhale. At his surprised look, she gave herself a mental shake. "That is, I *heard*, that the t-town has a new chief of police."

"And you're the new attorney," he said with disinterest, bending over Steve.

"Yes," she murmured. Of course he wouldn't recognize her. If he remembered Lorey Lawson at all, he remembered her as a blonde, not a brunette, with stick-straight hair, not spiral curls, and blue eyes, not green. Having lush curves, not compact muscles that she'd honed through kickboxing. Wearing brightly colored clothing, not the browns and beiges that had become her staples. And speaking with a heavy Jersey accent, not the generic pronunciation she had perfected with a diction coach while she'd attended law school in Arizona.

"Ms. Gaston said you administered chest compressions," he said, feeling for a pulse and seeming satisfied. "You probably saved his life."

Between the shrill siren of the ambulance arriving and the fact that Zane Riley was looking at her and talking to her, gooseflesh raced over her arms and shoulders. A shudder overtook her, and she had to cross her arms to get a grip on her emotions. "I . . . did what anyone would do."

She stepped aside as the ambulance workers rushed in and checked Steve Chasen's vitals, then transferred him to a gurney, hooked him up to oxygen, and swept him out of the shattered room.

"I'm riding in the ambulance," Marie announced.

"Is there someone I can call?" Gloria asked.

"I'll check his wallet for emergency numbers and

call on the way if I find any," the young woman said, then rushed out.

"You'd better get out of here, too, ma'am," Zane said, touching her arm. "The roof might have been compromised."

He was studying the ceiling, unaware that his casual touch had practically set her on fire. She noticed that he wasn't wearing a wedding ring, and she wasn't sure how that made her feel. Then he looked at her.

"I'm sorry, what was your name again?"

She panicked—did he see past her carefully contrived disguise? She averted her gaze. "Gloria," she mumbled. "Gloria Dalton."

He gave her a tight smile. "Ms. Dalton, I need to ask you some questions about Mr. Chasen and the accident."

"Okay," she said, immediately nervous at the thought of spending time with him. "Let me get my purse and briefcase. I'll meet you outside."

"I'll phone a tow truck," he offered and walked back through the hallway with her. His long stride came back to her in a rush, the way he moved next to her, walking a half step behind, as if to protect her. She closed her eyes briefly to will away the ache that settled in her chest. Her mind whirled with a thousand questions—what happened next?

At her office door she veered off and walked woodenly to her desk. She put her hands on the back of her chair and leaned forward, gasping for air. She'd dreamed of seeing Zane again, but deep down, she had known it wouldn't happen, had known it *couldn't* happen . . . not when her safety was still at risk . . . along with anyone else who knew her true identity.

"Ms. Dalton, are you okay?"

Zane stood at the door, his shoulders back and his face creased in professional concern, as if he didn't need another unwell person on his hands.

"Just a little shaken up," she said, straightening. *Over seeing you again.*

"I don't mean to hurry you," he said in a voice that clearly indicated he *did* mean to hurry her, "but I have a lot to get to today."

"Right," she said, a little surprised at his brusque behavior. He seemed to have developed a hard crust over the years, which was natural, she conceded, especially considering his line of work. "I'll be right there."

She picked up her briefcase and purse, still reeling. When she'd driven the short distance to work this morning, she couldn't have imagined what a turn her life would take. What were the odds that she and Zane would wind up in the same small Louisiana town at the same time?

And poor Steve Chasen—when he'd left his house, he couldn't have imagined how his short commute would end.

As Gloria made her way back to the hallway, she remembered the voodoo doll. Glancing toward the rear door, she saw Zane on his cell phone, his back to her. She picked her way to the desk, where she stooped to recover the bizarre gift. A brisk breeze blew through the gaping hole in the wall, kicking up dust and small pieces of debris. The car sitting in the lobby looked positively cartoonish.

Beneath the edge of the desk lay a Hartmann briefcase, presumably Steve's. From it spilled folders with names on them—clients, no doubt. Steve had told her he'd been working from home to sort Deke's files. Gloria removed the folders and stuffed them into her own briefcase. She shouldered her bag and hefted Steve's briefcase in one hand. Then, with her heart thumping, she retrieved the grotesque little voodoo doll and the crushed burgundy gift box it had come in.

She walked outside just as Zane was putting away his phone. "The tow truck should be here soon. Does one of those briefcases belong to Mr. Chasen?"

She nodded and handed him the Hartmann briefcase. When he looked at her, she was struck all over again with disbelief that after all these years of wondering what had happened to the quiet, handsome, good-hearted teenager she'd fallen head over heels in love with, he was standing a mere arm's length away.

Her hands itched to touch him. Her skin felt too small to contain her emotions.

"Can you tell me what happened?" he asked, pulling out a notebook.

My father was murdered and my mother and I were hustled away in the middle of the night, given new identities, and told to forget the lives and the people we'd left behind.

"Ms. Dalton," he said sharply. "I know this has been a great shock to you, but I have to get your version of what happened while it's still fresh in your mind."

His irritation helped her focus. "I don't know what I can tell you other than I looked up and saw the car coming toward the window. Marie and I barely had time to react."

"You were both standing in the reception area?"

"Yes."

He whistled low. "You are one lucky lady."

His observation put a sheen of perspiration on her upper lip. She had never considered herself particularly lucky—in fact, just the opposite. But at this moment she was feeling . . . *charmed.* And mystified.

"Did you notice if Mr. Chasen braked before impact?"

"It seemed to me that he sped up, but it all happened so fast, I can't be sure."

"Did he have any medical conditions that you were aware of?"

She shook her head. "I'm sorry—I really didn't know Steve Chasen very well. I came to town to interview him, and we've talked on the phone several times. He oversaw the delivery of the new office furniture and supplies while I tied up loose ends in New Orleans. Today would have been the first day we worked together."

He closed his notebook. "Probably had a heart attack—he's young, but I've seen it happen."

Zane's own father had died of a heart attack at a young age, she recalled with a pang of sympathy. She pressed her lips together and looked away—how would she be able to live in the same town and pretend they were strangers to each other? Zane Riley had been the cause of her metamorphosis from shy teenager to sexually aware young woman. They hadn't made love during those stolen hours in his bedroom while his mother had worked, but they had done everything short of it. Those intense, erotic sessions of learning every inch of each other's bodies had fueled her fantasies for years afterward.

She clenched her hands and realized she still held the box and the voodoo doll. "Zane—" She blushed furiously and cursed her lapse. "I'm sorry—I mean, Chief Riley. I don't know if this has anything to do with . . . anything, but this was waiting for me when I arrived this morning." She removed the voodoo doll and handed it to him.

He took the doll, then gave her a disapproving glare. "Is this some kind of joke?"

"No," she said, feeling warm around the collar. "I mean, maybe. I don't know who left it, or why, b-but the brown fabric looks like the fabric of the jacket that Steve Chasen is wearing."

He raised his eyebrows. "So you're telling me that this voodoo doll caused the accident? That's nice, Ms. Dalton—how would you propose that I write this up on a report?" He dropped the doll back into the crumpled box.

She frowned, irritated that he'd made her out to be the village idiot. "But—"

"Stop," he said, lifting his hand. "I've read all the stories about what happened in this town over the past few months, and I refuse to believe all that voodoo garbage." His mouth twitched downward. "Accidents happen and sick people do horrible things on their own, not because someone stuck a voodoo doll and made it happen."

His phone rang, piercing the tense moment. "Chief Riley," he answered, his condescending gaze raking over her.

Gloria's skin tingled under his obvious disdain. Between being knocked off balance by his appearance and revealing the voodoo doll, she probably did come off as someone who was a notarized-form short of being committed.

He snapped his phone shut, then sighed. "That was the hospital. Steve Chasen went into cardiac arrest en route. He was dead on arrival."

She covered her mouth. "Oh, no."

"I'm sorry, Ms. Dalton, really I am. And I'd appreciate it if you kept this nonsense about a voodoo doll to yourself. One of the reasons I came to Mojo was to restore faith in the law enforcement around here. I can't do that if you get everybody stirred up over a bunch of black magic baloney." He leaned in, his eyes challenging. "Do we have an understanding?"

Behind her fingers, she nodded mutely.

He made a rueful noise, then suddenly reached forward and took her hand.

She inhaled sharply at his touch, her senses jarred, then she realized he was scrutinizing the forgotten cut.

"You'd better have this looked at," he said. "It's a deep cut."

"I'm okay," she said hurriedly, trying to pull her hand away from his unnervingly familiar touch.

But instead of releasing her, he removed a snowy handkerchief from his back pocket and wrapped it around her hand. She stood mesmerized, thinking how his long, gentle fingers had matured into the hands of a man accustomed to dealing with emergencies and carrying a weapon. Tiny jolts of electricity shot up her arm. He had no idea what he was doing to her.

He gave her hand a pat, then he nodded toward the tow truck that was pulling in. "Let me have a word with the driver, then I'll take you to the doctor's office."

It was a statement, not a question. She watched him as he strode away, his broad shoulders set in a line that said he wasn't a man who would suffer fools . . . especially fools who believed in voodoo. She closed her eyes briefly, trying to calm her whirling mind. How was she going to handle this . . . *proximity?* Maybe if she played the resident kook, Zane would give her a wide berth.

Then she stared down at the voodoo doll that someone had left, unable to believe that Steve Chasen was dead . . . and unable to shake the feeling that no matter how improbable, there *was* a connection between the two events.

And if so, it still wouldn't be the strangest thing that had happened today.

She massaged the headache that had mushroomed behind her eyes. An hour ago, her life had been simply messed up. Now simply messed up looked pretty damned good.

A dead paralegal and a resurrected boyfriend. What was it that Marie had said?

Welcome to Mojo.

Chapter 4

"I could have driven myself to the doctor's office," Gloria murmured to Zane's profile. She sat as close to the door of his cruiser as was humanly possible, in case she had to throw herself from the moving car. She was self-conscious about any mannerisms that might inadvertently give her away.

"I thought you might get more attention with a police escort." He gave her a little smile, as if it was an effort to make his mouth work that way. "Maybe you'll be in and out more quickly—I assume you'll want to supervise your office being boarded up."

She winced. "That reminds me—I need to call my landlord, Mona Black."

"The mayor is your landlord?"

"The man's practice I'm taking over, Deke Black, was her son."

His jaw hardened. "From what I've heard, he wasn't the most upstanding guy."

"No," Gloria agreed. "He represented the voodoo museum on legal matters and was aware of the goings-on there, but no one is sure of the extent of his involvement. His ex-wife, Penny, knows he was no saint, but she believes he was murdered because he was on the verge of exposing the situation."

"Penny's the lady who runs the health food store across from the pink Victorian?"

"Right—The Charm Farm." She gave a little laugh. "But the pink house is a bit of a sore spot for Penny. She and Deke renovated the Victorian. When they split up, his girlfriend Sheena moved in and had it painted, um . . . that color. Sheena still lives there."

"She's the lady who runs the tanning salon?"

"You've met her?"

"Oh, yeah."

Gloria bristled. Of course the busty blonde would go out of her way to meet the handsome new chief of police—not that it was any business of hers who Zane associated with. He'd obviously been with dozens of other women over the years not to have noticed anything about her that was remotely recognizable. She rerouted the subject. "The girl with the blue hair, Marie Gaston, works for Penny."

"Ah. And Penny hangs out with B. J. Beaumont."

"Yeah—they met a couple of months ago, when he came to town working on a missing persons case."

"That's what led him to the voodoo museum."

"Right—and why the governor asked BJ and his brother Kyle to be on the task force."

"You seem to know a lot about the people in this

town to be new yourself," he commented, a curious note in his voice.

She squirmed under his interest, even if it was only casual. "I represented Penny in her divorce and when the police questioned her about Deke's death. I got to know a few people around here."

"Is that why you moved here?"

"Partly," she said, not wanting to mention her Ménière's attacks. Zane had been with her once when she'd suffered an attack in high school—it might jog a memory. "I was tired of practicing family law in the city. My workload was about eighty percent divorce settlements. I thought that practicing in a small town would allow me to do more things."

"To find yourself?" he asked with a little smile.

She nodded, transfixed by his lopsided smile and by the irony that she'd landed in the one town where now she couldn't possibly be herself.

"I know what you mean," he said vaguely, as if he, too, were on some kind of personal quest. "Where are you from originally?"

Caught off guard, she hesitated before offering her practiced answer. "Wisconsin."

His eyebrows went up. "You don't sound like you're from Wisconsin."

"That's because I've lived all over." That, at least, was the truth. "What about you?" she asked, a glutton to hear the mundane details about his life that were burned into her permanent memory.

"I grew up in a small town in Jersey," he said.

You played receiver for the Dillard Hill Diamondbacks. You were a straight-A student in math and biology. You drove a battered blue Ford Tempo that leaked oil. And the sound of your laugh took my breath away.

"But I've spent most of my adult life in the South," he continued.

"Do you have a family?" she asked, digging her fingernails into her thigh.

"Not of my own," he said, his voice rueful.

The news made her chest squeeze painfully—partially because she remembered that he had wanted his own family someday, and partially because she'd been half-hoping for a wife and kids to put emotional distance between her heart and his body.

"My mother is still up North," he said. "And my sister is married and has two boys. They're great." He smiled the first smile that reminded her of the old Zane, a smile that made his gray eyes flash like silver.

Little Lisa, she marveled—married with two children. Zane's sister had been a pesky eleven-year-old when she and Zane had dated, conspiring to interrupt their make-out sessions whenever they'd been at Zane's house pretending to study.

"How about you?" he asked.

She looked down at her loosely wrapped hand. "No. No family." She tried to laugh. "There's something about handling divorces that makes a person think twice about settling down." And there was the little issue of struggling to trust a man while simultaneously lying about her entire background.

"But you came to Mojo for a change, didn't you?"

She turned her head to find him studying her. It was the first indication that he'd noticed her as a woman rather than a resident in need of his services.

The realization sent a lump to her throat and a thrum of desire to her stomach. It was impossible to look at Zane and not remember him as she'd known him—young, cocky, and achingly sexy.

The softness of youth had passed from his face, leaving sharp features, and the cockiness had been replaced with confidence. And heaven help her, the man was still sexy enough to make her forget her name.

Her new name, that is.

She hadn't felt like Lorey Lawson in years, but one look into his gray eyes and she was sixteen all over again, with heaving hormones driving her to distraction. With a jolt, she realized he was waiting for a response. What had he asked her?

"Um, yes . . . I did come to Mojo for a change." She cast about for a segue out of dangerous territory. "The town itself seems poised for change."

"More like being forced to change," Zane said, his voice taking on a hard edge. "It makes a person wonder how something like what went on at the museum could have happened under everyone's noses."

"The people arrested were trusted members of the community," she offered.

He scanned the quiet streets of the picturesque town, slowing before driving around the town square. Children ran around the giant Christmas tree that had been erected in the center of the square, old men sat on park benches eating sausages, and women carried colorful shopping bags.

"It looks so innocent here," he observed. "But chances are there are still people walking the streets of Mojo who should be behind bars."

"But the investigation is continuing, right? Isn't that part of what the task force is doing?"

"Yes." Then Zane shook his head. "But that museum is a four-story crime scene. The team has a monumental task ahead of them."

"So," she said as casually as she could manage, "what brought you to Mojo?"

His wide shoulders lifted in a slow shrug. "The job sounded interesting. I wanted the chance to work closely with the task force. Did you know that over twenty thousand people were reported missing last year in this country?"

She blinked at his intensity. "I . . . guess I've never thought about it."

He pulled the car to a stop in front of the doctor's office and turned off the engine.

Suddenly panicked, she said, "You don't have to go in." She jumped out and retrieved her briefcase. "I'll get a cab back."

"I'm here," he said abruptly, emerging from his side. "Might as well meet the town doctor. I can write up the report on Steve Chasen's accident while I wait."

She manufactured a wobbly smile. They walked up to the door where a faded sign announced Dr. Jonas Whiting, M.D. Zane looked down and frowned, then used the toe of his black boot to disperse red dust on the concrete.

"What is it?" Gloria asked.

"Brick dust—an old voodoo myth says to spread it in front of your door to ward off evil spirits." He shook his head as he held open the door. "Don't tell me even the town physician buys into this stuff."

"It seems harmless," she said, surprised by how

defensive she felt about the townspeople and their beliefs.

"It's not harmless if it creates hysteria or prevents people from taking true security precautions."

He seemed so intent that she remained silent. She walked under his arm, reminding herself that she shouldn't be looking for ways to engage him in conversation or challenge him—the more distance she put between herself and Zane Riley, the better.

At least until she could figure out what to do.

The most obvious choice was to hightail it back to New Orleans . . . no, she'd have to move farther away from Zane. Knowing he was only a few miles down the road would torture her. No one would question her decision to leave, considering what had happened this morning. She wrapped her good hand around the injured one—it was really throbbing now.

The doctor's office was a little on the shabby side, full of mismatched chairs and odd tables cluttered with dated magazines, and nearly empty. A wiry, quiet-looking woman when Gloria didn't recognize sat on the chair and appeared nervous when they walked in. Her gaze darted to Zane and froze, then she looked down, fingering the pentagram earrings that swung from her ears.

The receptionist, a chubby, effervescent brunette wearing an inspiring amount of makeup and a badge that read Brianna, was on the phone—a personal call, from the sound of it.

"When? Are you sure? Is he okay? Omigod, are you sure?" She glanced up and raked her gaze over Zane and his uniform. "I'll call you back," she said into the mouthpiece, then banged down the phone and flashed an inquisitive smile. "Hi, there."

Gloria smiled and opened her mouth to speak.

"Hello," Zane said, leaning in. "I'm Chief Riley, and this is Gloria Dalton. There was an accident at Ms. Dalton's office involving broken glass, and her hand was cut. I thought the doctor should take a look at it."

Maybe it was the pain in her hand or the aftermath of the accident or the frustration of being so close to Zane, but Gloria's anger spiked at his controlling attitude. "Chief Riley," she said tightly, "my hand was cut, not my tongue."

He glanced at her in surprise, then frowned briefly. "I'll wait over there."

"Thank you."

When she looked back to the receptionist, she saw that Brianna's purple-shadowed eyes were wide, surrounded by tarantula lashes. "You're the new attorney, aren't you?"

"Yes, I am."

"And that's the new chief of police?"

"Er . . . yes."

"And the accident he was talking about was the car driven clean through the plate-glass window down at the Charmed Village Shopping Center?"

"Yes."

"Is Steve Chasen really dead?"

"I'm afraid so. Was he a friend of yours?"

"Nah, my friend Melissa used to date him, and he was kind of a butthole." Then she blanched. "But I'm sorry that he's dead."

Gloria coughed lightly. "Is the doctor available?"

"Yeah—he's giving Elton Jamison a shot of steroids for a rash. Ms. Davidson there is waiting for an anti-inflammatory for her knee, but I'm sure she won't mind if you go in next, seeing as how you're bleeding and all."

There were certainly no medical secrets in Mojo.

"Have a seat and fill this out," Brianna said, handing Gloria a form attached to a clipboard. "Here's a pen."

"Thanks," Gloria said, her stomach churning. Forms made her nervous—a paper trail of information that could be cross-referenced against other information and possibly used against her. She preferred asking others to fill out forms.

Thinking how surreal the day had been, she opted for a seat a couple of chairs down from where Zane had planted his big body. The lady with the knee problem—Ms. Davidson?—was staring at her, and she realized that her clothes and hair were covered in dust from the debris of the crash. She gave the woman a wan smile, then turned her attention to the form.

The first part was fairly uncomplicated—name, address, phone number. Under Date of Birth, she listed the date on her new birth certificate, the one that the witness protection program (not so fondly referred to as WITSEC) had provided her. She truly had to focus when she wanted to remember her original birthday.

Under the Sex column, she was tempted to write "long overdue" but sighed and checked the box for female.

She glanced at Zane under her lashes, conceding

that today was the first time in a long time that she'd felt female, that she so vividly recalled a period in her life when she had given and taken physical pleasure with abandon, before she had assumed a clandestine identity and tucked into herself. Plus, there was nothing like death to make a person feel alive. She attributed some of her new self-awareness to the shock of the accident and the palpable pain in her hand.

Emergency Contact. Gloria wet her lips—her former boss in New Orleans? Her landlord? At moments like this, she felt so alone. She'd give anything to know where her mother was.

After living and relocating together many times, the last contact Gloria and her mother had had was eight years ago, after someone had broken into her mother's home in Arizona. She'd called Gloria to tell her that she was leaving WITSEC. Her mother had felt that Gloria would be safer if they broke off contact altogether. Gloria hadn't been given any choice in the matter, hadn't been able to say good-bye in person. And since her mother had also broken contact with their handler, a U.S. marshal named George O'Connor, Gloria had no idea what had happened to her, if she was dead or alive.

It was like a cancer, slowly ravaging her heart.

She wrote down Penny Francisco's name and cell phone number as her emergency contact. After checking a few boxes attesting to her general good health, she handed the form back to Brianna, who was on the phone again.

"No, he's dead, I tell you. Because his boss is here and just told me so." She covered the mouthpiece long enough to say to Gloria, "You can keep the pen—I sell Lucky Lady cosmetics and my phone number's on there. Give me a call if you ever want a makeover. I have just the thing for those dark circles under your eyes."

"Uh . . . okay."

Brianna turned her attention back to the phone and made a token attempt to lower her voice. "I'm serious, she's standing right here in front of me. Her hand got sliced when he plowed through the window."

Gloria returned to her seat, thinking she might have made a big mistake by moving to a place where everyone knew everyone's business. She sighed and lowered her head in her hands—she couldn't get her mind around the fact that Steve Chasen was dead. And that Zane Riley was alive, sitting a few feet away.

"Here you go," he said, his voice startling her.

She lifted her head and looked at the form Zane extended to her.

"Report for your insurance claim."

She smiled in gratitude but froze when his hand brushed hers and she realized he was staring at her intently. "What?"

He shook his head. "For a second, you . . . reminded me of . . . someone."

Her heart skipped a beat and her breath stalled in her lungs. Her mouth watered with longing to tell him who she was, but her handler had prepared her for moments like this. For hours they'd rehearsed what she would do if she crossed paths with someone who'd known her in her previous life, and what could happen to her if she wasn't convincing.

She forced air into her lungs and a smile to her dry lips. "I get that a lot—I guess I just have one of those faces."

A slight frown crossed his face, then he nodded.

"Ms. Dalton?"

Gloria turned her head to see a sandy-haired, pleasantly handsome man in a white lab coat smiling at her and holding her form. Another man, presumably the unlucky fellow with the rash, ducked his head and walked toward the exit.

"Yes," she said, standing.

"I'm Dr. Jonas Whiting. Come on back and I'll take a look at your hand."

Zane's radio crackled, and he answered it. "Three-car pileup on the exit ramp," a staticky voice said. "You'd better get out here, Chief."

He glanced at her.

"Go," she said. "I'll be fine. And thank you for the ride."

He stood and nodded curtly. "Call me if you remember any details about the accident." Then his mouth twitched downward. "Any *logical* details, that is."

Gloria frowned at his implication, but he had already turned and was halfway out the door. She stooped to retrieve her briefcase, where she'd stowed the voodoo doll that he had so thoroughly dismissed. She didn't believe in voodoo either, but neither did she believe in coincidence.

Although it was an almost inconceivable coincidence that she and Zane had wound up in the same place at the same time.

The thought that she might not like the brusque,

cynical man that Zane Riley had turned out to be slid into her mind . . . and she couldn't understand the disappointment that accompanied the notion. It wasn't as if they had a future. Or even a present.

Only a past that she had to pretend she didn't remember.

Chapter 5

"That's about as good as I can make it look for now," Elton Jamison said, standing back and jamming his hammer into the tool belt that dragged the waistband of his grimy jeans down to alarming depths.

Gloria looked at the town handyman, vaguely wondering what kind of a rash he had, where it was, and if it was contagious, before looking back to the patched-up storefront of her office.

A network of two-by-fours and sheets of plywood replaced the once-gloriously gilded window. The door frame had been salvaged and repaired. The rough, unpainted hollow-core door didn't offer much in the way of curb appeal, especially since Elton had spray-painted Lawyer Here on its surface in black.

But it was operational, and at least the supporting structure hadn't been compromised.

And he'd spelled *lawyer* correctly.

She manufactured a smile, conceding that the day's events were catching up to her. "That's fine, thank you, Mr. Jamison."

"Folks around here call me Elton," he said, scratching his belly through his shirt.

"Okay . . . Elton. What do I owe you?"

"I'll settle up with Mayor Mona," he said, then turned to watch a long black car pull into the parking lot. "There she is now."

Gloria's pulse kicked up a notch as the tall, severe woman parked and climbed out of her car. Mona Black gave her the creeps.

"Good grief, what a mess," the woman said, stepping over debris that Elton had stacked in piles. "It's a wonder that someone wasn't killed."

Gloria raised her eyebrows at the woman and felt obligated to say, "But Steve Chasen *was* killed."

Mona gave a dismissive wave. "I meant someone besides him." She put her hands on her hips and sighed. "What's the total, Elton?"

He scratched his man boob. "I need to do some figurin'. I'll get it to you tomorrow or day after."

Mona nodded, then looked at Gloria. "Has all this scared you off yet?"

What an odd choice of words. Gloria moistened her lips. "No. I mean, it's not as if any of this was planned, right?"

"Right," Mona said, then gestured to Gloria's bandaged hand. "You okay?"

"Fine. Dr. Whiting cleaned the cut and gave me a few stitches."

"Good. Well, I guess you got your first case."

"Pardon me?"

"I'm suing Steve Chasen's estate for damages to my building," Mona said. "Can you take care of that for me?"

"Uh, sure," Gloria said, flummoxed by the woman's callous behavior. "Mona, do you know anything about Steve? Does he have family here?"

"Not that I know of, although I didn't know him very well."

"I understood that he'd worked for your son for a couple of years."

"Yes, but the extent of my acquaintance with the man was when he answered the phone."

"If it turns out that he doesn't have family, I'd be happy to make the funeral arrangements," Gloria offered. "It seems like the least I can do."

"You should check with the new chief of police," Mona said. "He'll probably be the one to track down the next of kin."

"I've met Chief Riley," Gloria said, wondering if she was destined to keep crossing paths with Zane. "I'll . . . check with him."

"You let me know if you change your mind about the lease," Mona said, walking back toward her car. "No one would blame you if you left, you know."

Gloria stared after her, perplexed . . . although hadn't the same thought crossed her own mind?

"Death is a bad omen for business," Elton offered.

"Thank you, Mr. Jamison, for pointing that out."

He scratched his underarm. "Folks around here call me Elton."

The headache that had been drilling at her temples all day jackhammered its way to her frontal lobe. "I'm going home, Elton."

"You moved into the old Gallagher house, didn't you?"

She sighed—did everyone know where she lived?—then nodded.

"Here's the key to the lock I put on your new door," he said, handing it over. "I'll throw all this stuff in the Dumpster, and I'll be back to fix everything proper when the supplies get in."

"Thank you," she murmured, thinking that some things were easier in a small town. In the city, she'd have to wait for building permits and all sorts of paperwork delays.

"Just watch your step around town, Ms. Dalton."

She frowned. "What do you mean?"

"Bad omen," he muttered, then stooped to begin picking up the building debris.

Gloria squinted at the strange, pot-bellied man and glanced at her watch—6:00 p.m. The day had evaporated. What she had hoped would be a joyous new beginning had instead turned into a nightmare of an ending for Steve Chasen, made even more sober by the fact that people in town seemingly dismissed the young man's abrupt passing. On her way to her car, she pulled out her cell phone and dialed directory assistance to be connected to the police department.

"Mojo Police Department."

"Chief Riley, please."

"Just a moment."

After more than a few moments' wait, Zane's voice came on the line. "Riley here."

She closed her eyes against the surge of emotion his voice triggered. "Chief Riley," she said carefully, remembering that her handler had said that some people might be able to recognize her voice without the distraction of her altered appearance. "This is Gloria Dalton."

"Hello, Ms. Dalton," he said, sounding preoccupied. "I hope your hand is okay."

"Yes, thank you, just a few stitches. I'm calling to see if you were able to contact Steve Chasen's family."

"He didn't have any that we've been able to locate. I didn't find references to relatives in his briefcase or wallet or in his car. Do you know if he had a cell phone?"

"Yes, he did."

"Have you seen it?"

"No."

"That might be our best bet. Would you be willing to go with me to his house tomorrow and help me look through his personal affects?"

"I . . . don't think I'm the right person for that job."

"You're his boss."

"But I barely knew him. Surely there's a friend—Marie Gaston seemed to be acquainted with him."

"No offense, but she doesn't seem like the most stable person to me. Plus, I'd feel more comfortable if a legal-type tagged along just to cover me."

"Okay," she said reluctantly, already looking forward to and dreading the time with him. "Were the doctors able to determine what might have happened?"

"Since he went into cardiac arrest in transit, the theory is that he had a heart attack just before the crash. Makes sense, considering what you said about him accelerating into the window. Is the front of your building secure?"

"Yes, I'm leaving now, and the handyman is cleaning up."

"I'll send an officer by there to keep an eye on things throughout the evening."

"Thank you," she murmured, soaking up his voice.

"Just doing my job. Is there a number where I can reach you tomorrow?"

She hesitated, then gave him her cell phone number, reminding herself that the less mysteriously she behaved, the fewer red flags she would raise.

"I'll see you tomorrow, then."

"See you tomorrow," she said, then slowly disconnected the call.

So casual, as if it were perfectly normal for her to be having a conversation with Zane after a fourteen-year absence. She drove to her rental house in a daze, holding herself rigid, like in the days when she and her mother had first fled their New Jersey home and she'd been afraid to move, afraid to speak in case she'd draw undue attention to them. . . .

Her gaze flew to the rearview mirror, expecting to see a car driven by a masked, dark-coated figure, like the man who had kicked down their front door, shot her father before he could stand, and calmly told her mother that if she testified in a racketeering and money laundering case against Bernard Riaz, someone would come back and finish off her—and her kid.

Instead, the man in the car behind her appeared to

be fixated on his comb-over—and the infant car seat in the back took the edge off the sporty lines of his black car.

She flipped on her turn signal, pulled into the driveway of the little bungalow she'd rented, and hit the remote control to open the garage door. The movers had left just enough space between the unpacked boxes for her to pull her Honda inside. Only after she'd parked carefully and the door was down behind her did she loosen her steely grip on the steering wheel.

Steve Chasen's death was a grim reminder that no matter how far she ran, she couldn't escape the terrible randomness of violence and mortality.

And apparently, she couldn't escape Zane Riley.

With her mind going in all directions, she dragged herself from the car and entered the laundry room, flipping on lights as she walked from room to room in the small house, threading her way through stacked boxes to the only spacious room in the house, the master bedroom. It was there that she already spent most of her time, in the little sitting area that she'd made comfy with a tapestry chair, ottoman, and a small rolltop desk, where she sat when she brought home paperwork. She set down her briefcase, then stepped into the bathroom and turned on the shower.

While the water warmed, she stripped off her dusty clothes and put them in a bag to take to the dry cleaner. She kept moving, wiping off her shoes and removing her simple jewelry, to keep her body occupied. But when she stepped under the warm water, she leaned her head back, let the water wash over her face, and gave in to the day's events—seeing Steve

Chasen's body flying through the air and seeing Zane Riley walk back into her life.

She had imagined what it would be like to see him again, but in her mind, it had always unfolded like a Hallmark movie—they would be reaching for the same postcard in a gift shop in Paris and their eyes would meet and he would instantly know who she was. All the yearning and heartache they'd each experienced since being ripped apart would evaporate. And they would live abroad, moving around to stay under the radar of the thugs who pursued her and her mother.

It was a fantasy that she'd clung to in the dark of night when horrific visions haunted her, threatening to rob her sanity. She sighed, pursing her lips under the water to receive a kiss from the warm, gentle flow, imagining Zane's mouth upon hers, extracting a promise never to leave him again.

Suddenly the water ran cold, shocking her out of her dream world, reminding her that being with Zane would always be a fantasy. When their eyes had met, he'd barely taken note of her, much less recognized her, a compliment to her handler's advice and her own years of practice.

Truly, she thought as she stepped from the shower and toweled off, seeing Zane again had been the ultimate test, and she'd passed with flying colors.

And while a small part of her felt proud of her success in making herself over so convincingly, a small part of her had been overjoyed when Zane had told her that she reminded him of someone.

She glanced at herself in the mirror. "Zane, it's me," she said, testing the words on her tongue. "Lorey."

But she wasn't Lorey, at least not anymore, she conceded as she surveyed her reflection. Short, springy dark curls above a lean face, her skin stretched taut over high cheekbones, an unremarkable nose, and a slightly pointed chin. Green contact lenses covered her pale blue irises, and cosmetic dentistry had changed the look of her teeth so that even Lorey Lawson's dental records couldn't be tied to Gloria Dalton.

She leaned her head forward and frowned at the reflection of the center part in her hair—her blonde roots were starting to show. She'd need to dye them soon.

It was only when she was nude and someone was very perceptive that her hair color was questionable. Her body hair was still as pale as the hair on her head had once been, betraying her as a natural blonde—she drew the line at dyeing her pubic hair. A female U.S. marshal had told her matter-of-factly simply to wax it off, but the advice had seemed ridiculous in absence of a physical relationship.

She sank her teeth into her lower lip, noting that she no longer had the figure of a nubile sixteen-year-old. Kickboxing, yoga, and a high-protein diet had transformed her full curves into trim, toned muscle that Zane might not find as physically appealing. She ran her hand over her flat stomach and realized that she hadn't eaten anything all day—she should have, she thought ruefully, grabbed one of those chocolate bars from Steve's desk this morning when she'd had the chance.

And she'd give anything for one of those carrot muffins that had gotten lost in the melee.

Shivering against the chill in the air, she hurriedly pulled on sweatpants and a long-sleeve T-shirt. The hardwood was cold beneath her bare feet as she padded to the kitchen, but she hadn't yet found the box with her house shoes, or even her socks for that matter. The unpacked cartons taunted her; she dreaded opening them, trying to find new places for everything and deciding what to keep, what to toss.

You could just leave everything packed, her mind whispered. *Call a moving truck, disappear in the middle of the night again. No one will miss you, no one will care.*

No one would blame you if you left, Mona Black had said.

Pushing aside the disturbing thoughts and decisions that faced her, Gloria opened the refrigerator to see if it would yield a passable dinner. Eggs, a portobello mushroom, and a half gallon of milk equaled a decent omelet and enough nutrition to make up for her abysmal diet today, which consisted of exactly three cups of coffee.

She carried the omelet and a glass of milk to her bedroom, turned on the television for background noise, and settled into the comfy chair. After a couple of bites, she relinquished the plate to her ottoman, which doubled as a TV tray, and pulled her briefcase to her lap.

Using her thumbs, she unlocked the closures and opened the briefcase until the hinges caught to prop it open. The voodoo doll lay on top, now dusty and a bit misshapen from having been trampled by the EMTs. But the pin was still imbedded in the doll's stomach, the macabre face punctuated with stitched X's for eyes to suggest death.

She'd gotten only a glance at the voodoo doll that Penny Francisco had stuck with a pin before her ex-husband Deke had wound up stabbed to death, but the size and general appearance of the dolls seemed similar.

Who had left the doll by her door? If the material was from Steve Chasen's jacket, how had the person gotten it? And had the doll somehow foreshadowed Steve Chasen's death?

She frowned at her own thoughts, Zane's reaction to the voodoo doll branded into her brain. It was ludicrous to think that there was a connection . . . wasn't it? Who would want Steve Chasen dead—and why?

She bit her lip, wondering how one disposed of a voodoo doll—it didn't seem right to simply toss it in the trash. She stood and looked around her bedroom for a safe place to stow the doll, and her gaze landed on her lingerie bureau. She slid open the top drawer, cheered, as always by the colorful contents. What she couldn't wear on the outside for fear of standing out in a crowd, she made up for underneath. Vivid silks, shiny satins, downy velvets, diaphanous chiffons—she had a lingerie collection to die for.

That no man had ever seen.

If ever there was a safe place, it was her lingerie bureau.

She smirked and laid the voodoo doll inside on a pillow of filmy fabric, then returned to her briefcase. Her mind raced with unanswered questions about Steve Chasen as she picked up the client folders that she'd removed from his briefcase. The first one was labeled Ziggy Hines. She opened it, impressed by the first-glance detail of handwritten notes, phone transcripts and . . . photographs?

Gloria frowned at the color candids taken from a

digital camera, the date and time stamped in the corner. The photos were taken in sequence, showing a barrel-chested, dark-haired man that she recognized as Ziggy Hines, a famous chef of New Orleans, kissing a buxom girl who didn't appear to be old enough to have a drink in his restaurant.

Gloria flipped back to the phone transcripts and realized that the recorded conversation was between Ziggy and an unnamed person who threatened to "reveal" his relationship to a certain underage woman unless Ziggy ponied up a thousand bucks.

Gloria blinked—was the unnamed person in the conversation Steve Chasen? And had he been blackmailing Ziggy Hines?

With her heart beating faster, she picked up the next file labeled Guy Bishop, the fellow who worked for Penny Francisco, she recalled. His folder held photos, too—of the X-rated variety. He and another man. Gloria closed the folder, feeling like a voyeur.

Her eyes popped when she saw that the next folder was labeled Mona Black. But curiously, the folder was empty. And before she could give much thought to the implication, her attention was caught by the name on the last folder:

Gloria Dalton.

She gasped and dropped the other folders in her haste to open the one with her name on it. Inside, there was a single sheet of paper with a handwritten note: *Contracted for info on L.L.*

Her heart stood still in her chest. L.L., meaning Lorey Lawson? How could Steve Chasen possibly have known about her past? Did anyone else in Mojo know the dead man's secrets? And—she gulped air—if he had been moonlighting as a blackmailer, could his death have been more sinister than a simple accident?

Gloria pivoted to stare at the lingerie bureau where she'd stored the voodoo doll dressed in the same cloth as Steve Chasen's coat, its stomach pierced with a long pin. Her heart jump-started with a jolt.

She was no voodoo expert, but this was all starting to look suspiciously . . . related.

Chapter 6

After a sleepless night, Gloria admitted that, her speculation about the voodoo doll aside, the cryptic note in Steve Chasen's files about "L.L." could mean that her cover was blown. She had no choice but to contact the U.S. marshal who was her handler. She used her cell phone to dial a message service, then punched in the five-digit code that connected her to George O'Connor's voice mail.

"This is Gloria D.," she said as calmly as she could manage. "There's been a complication with my move. Please call me back at your earliest convenience."

She hung up and expelled a sigh—it was the first time in her second life that she'd had to make such a call. Before, the relocations had been triggered by her mother's paranoia, real or imagined, and twice by the marshals, whose mysterious "sources" had told them that Riaz was zeroing in on their whereabouts. She had no idea what to expect; meanwhile, she'd try to maintain a normal schedule and keep her eyes open for anything unusual.

Such as the appearance of a voodoo doll.

Or a car plowing through the window.

Or the *re*appearance of an old flame.

The thought of Zane made her groan inwardly. She'd spent the night wrapped around a pillow, reliving every second of their unexpected reunion, agonizing over the fact that he was *so* close. She could pick up the phone and tell him everything if she wanted . . . if she dared. Or she could manufacture an emergency and have him summoned to her home to explain everything in private—that she hadn't wanted to go, that he must have known as much from the brief, vague good-bye letter she'd left with George to give to Zane.

She willed away the images of Zane; as incredible as it seemed, she had more important things to worry about for the time being. With her nerves singing, she dressed in a gray pantsuit, anticipating spending most of the day cleaning the interior of the office lobby and looking for more clues as to what Steve Chasen might or might not have known about her. She needed to get her hands on Steve's briefcase, which she'd handed to Zane—the idea of Zane, and possibly others, finding out about her identity in such a haphazard manner made her knees weak. And going through Steve's personal belongings in his home suddenly had taken on a new urgency.

When Gloria stood, the room tilted. She held her breath, remaining perfectly still in an effort to circumvent the vertigo and an onset of a Ménière's attack.

Please, not now, she prayed.

She'd suffered from the disease since the age of fourteen, but luckily her bouts of vertigo, nausea and vomiting had been few and far between, and controllable with medication. Only a couple of times had the attacks been severe and enduring enough to force her to bed until the fluid in her inner ear corrected itself. But the memory of those incapacitating experiences had remained with her.

When the room righted, she took a calming breath and walked slowly to her purse. She found the prescription bottle of Meclazine, discovering she was down to the last dose of her last refill. She'd have to go back to see Dr. Whiting and get a new prescription.

Retrieving a glass of water from the kitchen with steady precision, she downed the pills while trying to keep her head as level as possible, then sat quietly to make sure the vertigo didn't return before she walked to her car. Being behind the wheel when an episode struck would be truly dangerous, and driving during an attack was impossible.

One car through a storefront this week was enough.

A few minutes later she was feeling better, and she made the short drive into town with no incident. On a whim, she drove past the Charmed Village Shopping Center, glancing at her boarded office front to make sure that all seemed quiet, then proceeded along Charm Street to Penny Francisco's health food store. She was craving female conversation and hoped to be able to ask a few discreet questions about Steve Chasen while she was there.

The Charm Farm sat in the shadow of the looming Archambault mansion, former home of the Mojo Instruments of Death and Voodoo Museum. Penny, whose organic vegetable and herb garden extended to the mansion's property line, had been instrumental in uncovering the sadistic goings-on at the mansion. The spirited redhead herself was sweeping the stoop under the rounded burgundy awning that topped the front door. She waved at Gloria and met her at the car.

"I was planning to visit you today—are you okay? I was in New Orleans all day yesterday and didn't hear the awful news about Steve until I got back last night."

"I'm fine," Gloria said, emerging from her car. "How's Marie?"

"Mysterious," Penny said with a frown. "I was under the impression that she didn't like Steve Chasen, but she's really shaken up."

"It was a terrible thing for her to witness. Did she happen to mention anything else . . . strange?"

"You mean the voodoo doll?" Penny nodded, then jerked her thumb toward the door. "Marie's inside. Why don't we have a cup of tea?"

"That sounds wonderful."

On the way to the door, a commotion on the other side of the street in front of the pink house caught their attention. Sheena Linder, in all her busty, salon-tanned, white-blonde glory, was tottering after a younger blonde woman dressed more demurely, who was striding away from the house, her body language agitated.

"Wait, Sis, come back!" Sheena yelled. "I'll handle everything—it'll be all right, I promise!"

Penny shook her head. "It's always something over there."

"I'm surprised that Mona Black still allows Deke's girlfriend to live there," Gloria murmured.

"It's a strange relationship," Penny agreed. "But I try not to notice." She angled her head at the three-story Pepto-Bismol-hued Victorian that had once been her home and smiled. "It doesn't even look as pink as it used to."

Gloria gave Penny credit for a good attitude after all the bad blood between her and her dead ex-husband's mistress. Of course, in a town as small as Mojo, it seemed a little ridiculous to maintain a feud with people one saw every day. Eventually, the desire for cordiality overrode a grudge.

Except possibly where Steve Chasen was concerned. If the contents of the files he maintained on Ziggy Hines, Mona Black and Guy Bishop were any indication, there were plenty of grudges to be had in this little town.

A chime sounded as they walked through the door. Marie Gaston stood behind the smoothie counter, dipping her finger into an orange-colored concoction. She glanced up as they walked in and her eyes immediately clouded. "Good morning, Ms. Dalton."

"Please . . . call me Lorey."

The women squinted at her. "I didn't know you went by Lorey," Penny said.

Horrified, she realized her gaffe and tried to cover it with a little laugh. "My tongue isn't working so well this morning—I meant 'Gloria,' of course. How are you, Marie?"

"Okay, I guess. Still a little shaken up. I keep expecting Steve to walk in, asking for his morning smoothie."

Still reeling over the slip of her tongue, Gloria took a seat at the bar. "Did he come by every morning?"

"No, but most mornings he did, even if it was only to harass Guy."

Harass him was right, Gloria thought. Steve probably wanted to remind Guy that he had dirt on him.

"What did Chief Riley think about the voodoo doll?" Marie asked.

"Not much," Gloria admitted. "In fact, he dismissed it as a prank." Then as nonchalantly as she could manage, she asked, "Do either of you know if Steve had any enemies?"

"Enemies?" Marie frowned. "Not that I knew of. No friends either, but no enemies."

"He kept to himself," Penny added. "Deke thought highly of him as an employee . . . but then again, Deke didn't always exhibit the best judgment, à la Sheena Linder." She smiled. "How about chamomile tea?"

"Chamomile sounds good," Gloria agreed, smothering a yawn.

Penny scooped a diffuser into a pale green blend of leaves, then lowered it into a mug and added hot water from a stoneware teapot. "Are you thinking that someone left the voodoo doll for Steve?"

"It's possible."

"You mean, as some kind of warning?"

Gloria shrugged. "That would make more sense than implying that the doll had something to do with the accident . . . wouldn't it?"

Penny glanced at Marie. "Can you think of anyone that Steve would have crossed?"

Marie shook her head. "No one comes to mind."

The door chimed and a happy whistling tune pierced the air. From the pictures in Steve's files, Gloria recognized the thin, attractive, bespectacled man who appeared as Guy Bishop—although admittedly he looked different with his clothes on.

Penny introduced them, and he smiled wide, seeming to be in a happy mood. "Nice to finally meet you, Gloria."

Gloria's gaydar went off, and she wondered vaguely what a small town like Mojo had to offer a homosexual man in terms of lifestyle. Was he still closeted? "Same here," she said. *From one closeted person to another.*

"Gloria just asked us if Steve had any enemies," Marie said. "Do you know of anyone, Guy?"

He sobered and shook his head. "No. And why would you ask something like that? I mean, Steve's death was an accident, wasn't it?"

"Sure it was," Marie said quickly. "But someone left a voodoo doll by the door of the law office, and Gloria thinks it might have been meant for Steve, as a warning of some kind."

Guy frowned. "Another voodoo doll? You'd think everyone in this town would have learned a lesson, considering what happened with Deke."

"Did you keep it?" Marie asked.

"Yes," Gloria said reluctantly.

"Maybe you should look up Jules Lamborne," Penny suggested.

"Who's that?"

"An old woman who goes around town making strange projections," Marie said.

Penny glanced at the blue-haired woman sideways. "You should talk." Then she turned to Gloria. "Jules knows something about those voodoo dolls, I just feel it."

"It was probably a coincidence," Gloria said, choosing her words carefully. "But it does leave me worried that someone had a problem with Steve. Did he have a reputation that I should know about?"

Guy barked a laugh. "Steve? A reputation? I hate to speak ill of the dead, but the only reputation that Steve had was for being the most boring, unlikable person in town. Ask Marie, he had the hots for her."

Gloria looked at the young woman in surprise. "Oh?"

Marie frowned at Guy. "Even if that was true, Steve knew that I already have a boyfriend."

Gloria didn't miss Penny's eye-roll. "Don't get started on the incomparable Kirk, the rich pilot/physician/big-game hunter/humanitarian."

"Don't forget that he has a Mensa card and hobnobs with royalty," Guy added.

Gloria looked at Marie. "Does your boyfriend live near Mojo?"

Penny and Guy guffawed, and Marie crossed her arms in defiance. "Kirk has homes all over the world."

"What she means," Guy said, his voice heavy with

sarcasm, "is that she's never met this superhero in person."

"We have a long-distance relationship," Marie clarified.

Penny removed the metal diffuser from the mug and slid the steaming tea toward Gloria. "Lemon and sugar?"

"Just lemon, please."

"How about a muffin?"

"That sounds good, especially considering I didn't get to eat the ones Marie brought to me yesterday."

Penny looked at Marie. "That was nice of you."

"I knew you would have if you'd been here," Marie murmured, clearly distracted.

The door chimed again. Gloria sipped the hot, aromatic tea from the mug, reminding herself she should do everything in her power to keep her nerves calm until the Meclazine fully kicked in.

Then she turned her head to see Zane Riley walking in with B. J. Beaumont and a third man she didn't know, and her pulse skyrocketed. So much for staying calm.

She held her breath, wondering if, in the hours since she'd seen Zane, he'd figured out her secret. When his gaze fell on her, however, his curt nod was void of anything personal.

Her disappointment was acute.

BJ, on the other hand, walked up behind Penny and nuzzled her neck, oblivious to the audience. She swatted at him. "What are you up to?"

"No good," BJ said mischievously, then sobered and gestured to the other men. "This is Zane Riley, he's the new chief of police, and this is Cameron Phelps, he's a member of the missing persons task force. Zane and Cameron, this is my main squeeze, Penny Francisco, her right and left hands, Marie Gaston and Guy Bishop, and this is another new resident of Mojo, Gloria Dalton."

"We've met," Zane said shortly.

"Yes, yesterday," Gloria murmured, mimicking his all-business demeanor, when inside her heart was thrashing in her chest. Would she ever get used to seeing him in the natural course of a day?

You can't get used to it, a voice in her head whispered. *You have to find out if your cover has been compromised and if so, be ready to walk away . . . again.*

Cameron Phelps, whose sandy-colored hair was clipped in a military crew cut with a few waves on top, swept a friendly smile over the group. "Nice to meet everyone." Then his gaze lingered on Gloria in appreciation before he nodded. "Ma'am."

She blinked in surprise, then noticed Zane looking back and forth between them.

"So, Cameron," Penny said, "where are you from?"

"Most recently San Diego," he said, his voice deep, his speech precise. "I was on a team that was successful in developing a missing unidentified persons database for the state of California. I'm here to collate all the information from across the country on unidentified remains that have been found and marry it to the database that BJ and Kyle are building on persons who've been reported missing."

"That sounds like a mammoth task," Gloria said.

"It is," Cameron admitted, "but technology and

DNA have come a long way, and having the resources behind this project will make all the difference."

"We're lucky to have someone with Cameron's credentials on this project," BJ said. "Once this national matching system is in place, hundreds, maybe thousands, of missing persons cases could be solved overnight."

A memory stirred in the back of Gloria's mind—she recalled that when her mother had broken ties with the program and assumed a new identity, her handler had told her that if something ever happened to her mother, it was likely that she wouldn't be identified because her records were confidential. The eight years of silence suddenly screamed like a siren. Was it possible that her mother's remains were logged into this very database, never to be identified?

"What happens when a person is reported missing?" Guy asked no one in particular.

"That's the problem," BJ said. "Up until now, missing persons cases have been reported locally and handled locally."

"Which means," Zane interjected, "that if the person crossed or was taken across a state line, the chances of finding the person diminished considerably. And the more jurisdictions crossed, the lower the chances of the case being resolved."

Penny made a rueful noise. "You sound like you have a personal stake in this, Chief Riley."

A muscle jumped in his jaw. "Years ago I filed a missing persons report that was never solved, so, yeah, I guess I do have a personal stake in this."

Gloria froze, feeling as if a spotlight had been illuminated on her fake curls.

"Who went missing?" Marie asked.

Penny elbowed her. "Maybe that's private, Marie."

"It's okay," Zane said. "It was a girl I was friends with in high school. One day she and her family simply disappeared, and I never heard from her again."

Gloria was paralyzed. Her head buzzed at the surreal moment, feeling as if all her lies were tattooed on her face. She felt so conspicuous, sure everyone in the room would notice.

"That's so romantic," Marie said dreamily. "Maybe you'll find her someday."

Zane's expression closed, as if he had exposed too much of himself. "Meanwhile, there's plenty to take care of here. BJ, Cameron, let me know what I can do to help the task force." He turned to go, then stopped and settled his gaze on Gloria. She swallowed hard, relieved that the others were engaged in conversation.

"Ms. Dalton, will you be in your office today?"

She untied her tongue. "Y-yes."

"Then I'll be by to pick you up later this afternoon for that matter I asked for your assistance with?"

She nodded and watched him walk out the door. Her senses were on tilt, and she couldn't blame it on vertigo.

Zane had reported her missing all those years ago?

And he was still looking for her?

Chapter 7

Gloria left the health food store on wobbly legs, slid into the driver's seat of her car, closed the door, and rested her forehead on the steering wheel. How had things gotten so complicated, so quickly? By coming to Mojo, she seemed to have inadvertently plunged herself into a soul-sucking vortex created by the intersection of a voodoo doll, Steve Chasen, Zane Riley, the missing persons task force, and her own cloak-and-dagger personal history.

Her cell phone rang, rousing her from the funk that threatened to overtake her. The caller ID screen read Private. She connected the call. "Hello?"

"Gloria, this is George O'Connor. I got your message. What's wrong?"

The U.S. marshal who had handled her and her

mother's involvement in WITSEC from the beginning was succinct, as always. "George, a man I hired to work for me died in a car accident yesterday. When I went through some of his things I discovered that he might have been blackmailing local residents over domestic issues, and I found a folder he was compiling on . . . me."

"What was in the folder?"

"Just a handwritten note that said 'Contracted for info on L.L.' "

George made a rueful noise. "You said the man is dead?"

"Yes, he died on the way to the hospital. But obviously he was working with someone."

"Sounds like it. And I'm afraid this is especially bad news considering that Bernard Riaz was just released from prison and granted a new trial."

Gloria inhaled sharply to hear the name of the man responsible for her father's death. "What? Why?"

"Based on findings that the DA suppressed evidence in the original trial. Unfortunately, without your mother to testify again, the government's case to retry Riaz is shaky. I don't suppose you've heard from her?"

"No," Gloria said tightly.

"And you wouldn't tell me if you had?"

"I . . . don't know. And when were you going to tell me about Riaz?"

"I'm sorry—I've been swamped."

Gloria's eyes widened. "You've been swamped? My father's killer is on the streets and you've been too *swamped* to tell me?"

He sighed. "I'm sorry, Gloria. I swear I was going to call you, which is why I was so surprised to hear from you. If your cover has been compromised, then these two things could be related. You could be in real danger if Riaz's people are looking for you to try to get to your mother."

She swallowed the fear that lodged in her throat. "What should I do?"

"Give me the name of your dead employee and I'll see what I can find out about him."

She told him Steve's name, then recited the address and Social Security number that she'd gotten from Steve when she hired him.

"Give me a couple of days to look into this," George said. "Meanwhile, see if you can find out who this Chasen fellow might have been working with, but be discreet. And if you hear from your mother, call me. For both of your sakes."

At the warning in his voice, Gloria's lungs contracted. "Good-bye," she murmured, then disconnected the call. Only then did she realize that she hadn't mentioned that she'd also run into someone who'd known her in her previous life . . . but if George told her to leave town when he called back, seeing Zane again would be a moot point.

With her senses on alert, she drove the short distance back to the Charmed Village Shopping Center and parked in front of her law office, whose boarded-up front looked bleak and unwelcoming. Further down the sidewalk, a young man was unlocking the door of Tam's Electronics. She'd found the receipt showing that Deke had purchased the office alarm system from Tam's. Grasping at the chance to do something productive, she locked her car door and headed to the electronics shop first.

When she walked inside, the fluorescent tube lights overhead were coming on section by section, revealing row after row of small electronics and accessories: cell phones, portable stereos and MP3 players, handheld electronic games, cameras, radio-controlled toys, and office equipment. Near the entrance sat a photocopy machine for three cents a page—an unheard-of price, which probably explained why Deke hadn't gotten around to repairing the photocopier in the law office.

But apparently Deke had been so preoccupied with his divorce, his mistress, and the goings-on at the voodoo museum that he'd ignored a lot of things—including the fact that his paralegal had been blackmailing his clients . . . although it was possible, and perhaps likely, that Steve Chasen had seized the illicit opportunity to make money only after Deke's death.

Upbeat, funky music flowed into the space via overhead speakers, and a few seconds later, the young man whom she'd seen unlocking the door strolled into the showroom, wearing draggy jeans and an overlong shirt. He was pinning on a nametag that said Mark when he looked up and saw her.

"I didn't hear you come in," he said in the drone of a half-awake teenager. "Can I—I mean, *may* I help you?"

"I'm Gloria Dalton. I took over Deke Black's law office just a few doors down."

His eyebrows climbed high. "Wow, I saw the car sticking out of your window when I got to work yesterday. I heard that the guy didn't make it."

"That's right," she said. "Unfortunately, Steve died on the way to the hospital."

"Wow. What happened?"

"The doctors think he had a heart attack. Did you know him?"

"Nah, not really. He came in a few times to buy stuff for his phone and stuff. Bummer about him dying and all."

"Um, yes. Listen, I know that your company installed the security system in the office—could someone come down to see what needs to be done to repair the damage caused by the accident?"

"That'll be Elton," Mark said.

The itchy man must have been the only guy in Mojo who owned a hammer. "He's doing the repairs on the office. Do you have the specs for the system on file?"

"Yeah, we keep all that stuff. I'll give Elton a call if you want. He can let us know what parts we'll need to order."

"Yes, thank you. And do you service our copier as well?"

"Yeah, I'll call the tech and have him come out." Mark gestured to a display on the counter. "Wanna buy a candy bar for the victims of the Mojo voodoo museum?" He winced. "Sorry, but my boss is making us ask everyone who comes in the door or he docks our pay."

She thought of the half box of candy bars on Steve's desk that had been ruined and bought a couple of the chocolate bars, then asked Mark to help her select an antenna booster for her cell phone. Afterward, she walked down to her office, surprised to see a woman tying a small black bow on the door. When the woman turned, Gloria recognized her as the mousy woman from the doctor's office yesterday—the one with the foot problem . . . or was it her knee?

"Hello," Gloria said tentatively.

The woman gave her a shy smile. "Hello, Ms. Dalton. I'm Diane Davidson. I saw you yesterday at Dr. Whiting's. I hope your hand is okay."

Gloria flexed her hand in the taut bandage. "It's better, thanks. It was generous of you to let me barge in front of you after you'd been waiting."

Diane nodded demurely, her eyes furtive as she gestured toward the bow. "I hope you don't mind—I thought I should do . . . something to mark Steve's passing."

"No, that's nice of you. Did you know Steve?"

"A little. I saw him around town, and he seemed like a shy, lonely young man."

Hm, one person's difficult and unlikable was another person's shy and lonely. "Would you like to be notified if there's a memorial service?"

"Yes, please." The woman fidgeted, then said, "Actually, I wanted to talk to you, to see if you needed help. I lost my teaching job earlier this year, and then I worked in the museum gift shop until it . . . was closed." Her eyes went wide. "I had no idea what was going on there." Then she straightened. "But I'm a good worker, and if you need an assistant until you can replace Steve with someone more qualified, I'd like to be considered."

Gloria warmed to the woman, whose pale eyes hinted at past trials and tribulations. She seemed like a genuine person. Gloria's gaze moved to the Wiccan jewelry the woman wore.

Diane's hand flew to the pentagram pendant at her neck. "I won't wear my jewelry if it bothers you."

"No, it's fine," Gloria said. "Why don't we go in and talk?"

She unlocked the door, to be greeted by the uncanny coldness of the place and the dust and debris from yesterday's accident and repairs.

"I can clean this up for you," Diane offered quickly.

"I was planning to clean it up myself," Gloria said, "but I could use a hand." The phone rang, splitting the quiet air. "Excuse me."

She walked over to the phone sitting on Steve Chasen's desk. Trying not to remember his body landing there, she picked up the receiver. "Hello?"

"Is this the law office of Gloria Dalton?" a man asked.

"Yes, it is," she said, chiding herself for not answering more professionally. "I'm Gloria."

"Is it true that there was a voodoo doll involved in the death of the man who was killed in the accident yesterday at your law office?"

Gloria blinked. "Who is this?"

"Daniel Guess, with the *Post*. Just confirming a tip that before Steven E. Chasen," he said, apparently referring to notes, "drove through the window of your law office, you received a voodoo doll of his likeness."

Zane's remarks on not stirring up rumors about voodoo when the town was trying to recover from its bad reputation went through her head. She didn't want to be the one who brought unwanted attention to the situation. On the other hand, she didn't want to lie. "I don't have a comment, Mr. Guess. Please don't call here again unless you have business to conduct with my office. Good-bye." She set down the receiver and heaved a sigh.

"Trouble?" Diane asked behind her.

Gloria hesitated. "A reporter, trying to make something sinister out of Steve Chasen's death." She scrutinized Diane Davidson, in a quandary as to what to tell the woman about a job. Depending on what she found out about Steve Chasen's blackmail file and what her WITSEC handler told her, she could be leaving town abruptly.

The phone rang again, and Diane walked toward it. "Let me answer it." She picked up the receiver. "Gloria Dalton, attorney-at-law, how may I direct your call? Hold, please." She punched a button, then looked up. "It's Sheena Linder. She'd like to come in and get your advice on a legal matter, if you're open for business."

Gloria's eyebrows shot up—was she? She looked around at the chaos and conceded that until she had the chance to look through Steve Chasen's things or until she heard from George, she had to have something to occupy her mind. "Tell her yes, if she can come by tomorrow afternoon."

Diane pressed the button beside the blinking light. "Ms. Linder, would tomorrow afternoon work for your schedule? Two o'clock it is." Diane returned the phone to its cradle and smiled at Gloria. "I could work for you on a trial basis. I should be frank—I need a job."

Gloria bit her lower lip, then nodded. "Okay, I'm not sure how things are going to shake out around here, but we can give it a try." Gloria extended her hand, and Diane stared at it before clasping her hand, gently at first, then more firmly. To Gloria's discomfort, moisture gathered in the woman's eyes. "Thank you," she said.

"You're welcome," Gloria said, hoping she wasn't setting up the woman for disappointment. Then a memory chord vibrated in her mind. "Davidson . . . why am I thinking that I ran across a client file with your name on it?"

"You did. I was fired from my teaching job because the school board accused me of being a witch."

"A witch?"

Diane nodded. "I never mentioned the Wiccan religion while I was in the classroom, but a parent saw me wearing my pendant off-hours, and that's all it took for the rumors to start flying." She smiled. "Actually, according to the stories, *I* could fly."

Gloria crossed her arms. "You can't be fired on the basis of your religion."

"I know—the school board manufactured a charge about my performance record and budget cuts. I came to Deke Black to see if he would help me to get my job back, but in the end, he wasn't willing to take the case."

The sense of justice that her mother had instilled in her rose to the surface. "Did you find another attorney?"

"Not yet," Diane said, her voice hopeful.

Gloria realized she'd walked right into the woman's

plan and laughed. "Once things settle down, I'd like to hear more about your situation."

"Okay. For now, I'll make an Open sign for the door and start cleaning up in here."

While her new employee busied herself with a broom, Gloria took the chance to look through Steve Chasen's desk but found it amazingly . . . empty.

The drawers contained a few office supplies, a Mojo phone book, and a flyer about the fund for the families of the victims of the museum. The items on the top of his desk—a Rolodex, a pencil holder, a notepad—had been strewn during the accident, but again, no personal knickknacks, no photos. A two-drawer metal file cabinet sat next to the desk, but it contained blank forms and boilerplate agreements that Deke had apparently used often in his practice. In the office's assets that she'd purchased from Deke's estate, only one computer had been listed—the dated model in her office, which she had no intention of using except to extract client records on an as-needed basis.

She frowned and pushed to her feet. Whatever Steve had been doing on the sly, he didn't appear to have left a paper trail at work—which eased her fears only a tiny bit.

A knock preceded the front door opening. Gloria looked up to see Zane standing there, his shoulders spanning the door frame. Her heart bumped against her breastbone when his gray eyes landed on her. Suspicion lingered there, as if he didn't trust her but had to.

"Ready to go?" he asked without preamble.

Gloria hesitated to leave her new employee alone.

What did she really know about the slight Diane Davidson, who looked between her and Zane as if she suspected something was going on between them? Then Gloria consoled herself with the knowledge that the desk and file cabinet in her office was locked, and that the computer was password-protected. What harm could the woman possibly do? She was becoming paranoid about everyone around her.

In fact, distrust seemed to runneth over in Mojo.

She told Diane she'd be back shortly, then retrieved her purse and briefcase and met Zane at the door. How ironic that he was looking for her and she was standing close enough to smell the spicy scent of his aftershave. He had no idea who she was, yet she could tell him that he'd gotten the scar on his chin while catching a pass during the homecoming game of her sophomore year.

"Are you feeling well?" he asked with a little frown.

"Just a touch of dizziness," she said. "It'll pass." She made her way to the cruiser, but he beat her there and opened the door for her. She slowly slid inside, thinking that riding shotgun with Zane was becoming a habit. She fastened her seat belt, then looked at the steely profile of the man next to her, dismayed when her heart swelled to bursting.

Her mother had told her that was why the witness protection program had been especially hard on her—because Gloria was a creature of habit.

Which, when it came to Zane, meant only one thing where her single-minded heart was concerned: *uh-oh.*

Chapter 8

"Wasn't that the lady from the doctor's office?" Zane asked as he pulled out of the parking lot.

"Yes," Gloria said. "Her name is Diane Davidson."

"Davidson? I know the name. She's filed a stack of vandalism complaints."

"Vandalism?"

"Apparently someone's been targeting her house for graffiti."

"She practices the Wiccan religion—I guess that doesn't sit well with some locals, considering she was fired from her teaching job."

"I could see why that would spook folks who are tired of all the hocus-pocus in this town."

Gloria frowned. "She seems like a nice lady."

"But you barely know her." He lifted his eyebrow. "Are you always so trusting?"

"No," she said honestly, "but I feel like I'm a pretty good judge of character." Except when it came to her paralegal, she thought, squirming. "Have you found out anything else about Steve?"

"No. I'm assuming he didn't have a will on file at the law office?"

"No, I checked." She swallowed. "There was nothing . . . *relevant* in his briefcase?"

"No." He jerked his thumb toward the backseat, and she turned to see the briefcase lying on the seat. "It was empty, except for high-end merchandise catalogs. Your employee had good taste—in fact, that's a pricey briefcase for just toting around catalogs."

"I removed a few client folders from his briefcase before I gave it to you," she said in the dead man's defense. No need to raise his suspicions about Steve Chasen until she found out what she needed to know.

"So how do you like the Gallagher house?"

She pivoted her head. "Does everyone in this town know where I live?"

"Probably," he said smoothly. "If you're going to stay in Mojo, you'd better get used to people knowing your business. I've been here a month and people know what kind of underwear I wear."

"Boxers, white or blue," she said. A split second later, she realized her lapse and nearly swallowed her tongue.

His eyebrows flew up. "You already heard, huh?"

"I . . . uh . . ."

He gave her a wry smile. "I drop off my laundry at the cleaners, and next thing I know, people in line behind me at the grocery store are mentioning my unmentionables."

She manufactured a smile and shifted in her seat, trying to recover from her unbelievably sloppy blunder. She was going to have to be careful; a few hours around Zane and all her careful training was forgotten—she'd regressed to her former life without a second's pause.

"I didn't mean to embarrass you," he said.

"You didn't," she said quickly. Great—he thought she was a prude. Ironic, considering he was the only man who'd ever made her body respond with a simple glance or a brush of his hand. She turned to look out the window so she could clench her jaw for strength. The situation was so bizarre that she had to choke back a hysterical laugh.

"I think this is the address," Zane said, then pulled into the driveway leading to an unremarkable but pretty brick ranch house in a pleasant-looking neighborhood.

Brown leaves had accumulated in the flower beds, where a few evergreen bushes offered peeks of color. Gloria wondered distractedly if she'd be around in the spring to see the flowers in the beds around her rental house come to life. She had entertained thoughts of looking for her own place by then, but now . . .

She glanced at Zane's profile. Now everything had changed.

Reminding herself not to tilt her head at a severe angle that might trigger another Ménière's attack, she carefully emerged from the car. From a distance,

Steve Chasen's house looked surprisingly abandoned a mere twenty-four hours after his death: The curtains were drawn, curled leaves and a few sticks had caught on the doormat, two bundles of newspapers lay at the foot of the steps.

Zane stopped at the mailbox at the end of the driveway and retrieved a handful of envelopes, fliers and catalogs. When they reached the steps, he scooped up the rolled copies of the *Post,* then handed the bundle to her while he unlocked the door with a stainless C initial key ring that she assumed was Steve's. The wood door stuck, so Zane put his shoulder into it until it swung inward. He stepped in first, swiping his hand along the wall until he found a light switch.

When the lights came on, Gloria gasped. She'd expected to find bachelor furniture in a dreary décor, not sleek designer furniture surrounding a wall-mounted plasma television. The tinted-glass cabinets on either side held an impressive collection of stereo equipment. In the corner atop an L-shaped wooden desk sat a twenty-inch flat-screen computer monitor, with two CPU towers, printers, scanners, and an array of other top-of-the-line peripherals.

Zane released a low whistle. "How much were you paying this guy?"

"Not enough to afford these kinds of toys," she murmured. "Maybe he's living on a trust fund."

"Or maybe he was simply living beyond his means."

Gloria swallowed. Or off the proceeds of his blackmailing scheme? She held up his mail. "Should we go through it?"

"Can't," he said with a frown. "Got to get a court order to open his mail. But if we find something that's already open and looks like it's from a relative, we can take a peek. Let's look around."

She followed him from room to room full of luxurious furnishings: pool table, baby grand piano, rice-carved four-poster bed, a mahogany armoire stocked with crystal decanters and bottles of expensive liquor. Zane stopped next to the telephone. "There's a message."

Gloria's heart sped up. He pushed a button, and a male voice came on the line. "Hey, man . . . I got what you want, and it's good. Call me."

She swallowed hard. Was it the voice of the man contracted to get "info" on her?

"It's a Baton Rouge area code," Zane said, then picked up the receiver and dialed the number.

"He didn't really sound like a friend," Gloria said quickly, while memorizing the number herself.

"He's the only lead we have at the moment," Zane said, then frowned. "Line's busy."

Gloria exhaled. "Let's see if we can find an address book on his desk," she said to distract him. She was sweating as they went back to the living room, wondering what they might find and how Zane might react if he stumbled onto any of Steve's research regarding her. Questions swirled in her head as to who Steve's "informant" might be: Who knew her past, and how had Steve connected with the person?

Zane located a black address book on the desk and flipped to the *C*'s. "No other Chasens listed," he murmured, then turned to the front. "And no one listed under the emergency contact." He glanced at the computer. "Maybe he keeps his contact list online."

Panic infused her chest as he pushed the button to boot up the machine. Crazily, she considered confessing on the spot, but she reminded herself that if Zane knew who she was and thought she was in danger, he might endanger himself trying to help her. Confession was a last resort.

His cell phone rang, and he answered while the computer screen flickered on and icons began to appear on the digital desktop. "Riley," he said, then frowned. "Okay, I'll be right there." He put the phone away. "Sorry, but I have to go back to the office for a meeting with the task force."

She gestured toward the computer. "I can stay and look for a family contact on his computer. I'll call a cab to get back to the office."

He worked his mouth back and forth. "How about if I come back in an hour to pick you up?"

"That's fine, if it isn't too much trouble."

He made a rueful noise. "I just want to be able to make the notification of next of kin as soon as possible. I've searched Social Security and DMV records, and there's no relatives listed anywhere in his files."

"Maybe he's an orphan."

"Maybe. If I can't get away, I'll send one of my officers to pick you up."

She nodded, eager to be alone with Steve's computer, but nursing guilt over the trust Zane was placing in her hands. He leveled his gray gaze on her, making her lungs constrict painfully. Electricity crackled in the air between their bodies. Tense seconds ticked by, and pressure built in her muscles as she held herself rigid. Any questions she had about their enduring physical chemistry were erased.

Or was she reacting from fear of being revealed?

She wavered, crazily hoping he would suddenly recognize her and she could fall into his arms and . . .

And what? Pick up where they'd left off . . . as kids? A lump lodged in her throat as the enormity of the chasm between them began to sink in.

Confusion clouded Zane's eyes—he was aware of the magnetism between them but apparently didn't want to act on it. A muscle worked in his jaw, and his lips parted, as if he was going to say something.

Gloria waited . . . one second . . . two . . .

Zane averted his gaze and cleared his throat. "Let me know if you find anything."

She maintained a tight smile until he turned and his wide shoulders disappeared through the door. When it closed behind him, she expelled a noisy sigh, puffing out her cheeks. That had been close.

Breathing deeply to regain her bearings, she waited until she heard his car engine start. Then, with her nerves jumping, she sat down at the computer keyboard. As soon as she hit a key, though, a box for a password popped up.

Gloria muttered a curse, then began trying common preset passwords like *test, password, changeme,* and various forms of Steve's name. She followed up with days of the week, months of the year, the name of the town. Nothing worked. The only good news was that if she couldn't get in, chances were no one except a hacker could, and she suspected that the police would utilize other means to find Steve Chasen's next of kin.

She sat back in the chair. Maybe she was safe from whatever information he had contracted on her. Then she glanced toward the phone—unless Steve's informant decided to cash in on the blackmailing business himself.

She went through the desk drawers and CD storage cases but didn't find anything of note except receipts for groceries, a haircut from The Hair Affair, and a twelve-week package at Sheena Linder's tanning salon. In one drawer she found a stash of snacks, including a couple of the fund-raiser chocolate bars, which she assumed he'd removed from the box on his desk at work. And, surprisingly, in a top drawer, she found a picture of Marie Gaston, a black-and-white photo of her standing outside, looking away from the camera, her hand cupped over her eyes. It was a close-up, but Gloria noticed something in the young woman's hand on the edge of the photo. Squinting, she brought the photo closer—a broom?

Then she recalled seeing Penny sweeping the sidewalk in front of the door of the health food store. It seemed that someone had captured Marie unaware . . . almost as if she had been under surveillance.

Gloria bit into her lip. Had Steve taken the photographs in the files she had at home—and this one—or had he hired someone to take them? And did Marie know that he had been spying on her?

She returned the photograph, then opened a large lower cabinet to find an industrial-sized paper shredder with blades that looked powerful enough to shred a cardboard box. The bulging plastic bag beneath the blades helped explain why Steve's personal files were so clean.

Tamping down pangs of guilt, she went into Steve's bedroom and opened his closet door. Clothes—*nice* clothes. Designer, many with the tags still attached. And stacks of shoe boxes, all brand names. But there were no boxes of files, no secret paperwork. She opened an armoire to find more state-of-the-art television and stereo equipment. The drawers revealed nothing except his preference for porn magazines—he appeared to be into soft-core bondage.

She bit down on the inside of her cheek. Was it possible that Steve Chasen had been involved with the atrocities that had taken place in the voodoo museum?

A crashing noise from a far room jerked her head around.

Her pulse pounded in her ears—it sounded like a window had been broken. A burglar? Or perhaps someone whom Steve had been blackmailing, who'd had the same idea she'd had about finding files now that Steve was dead?

Throat convulsing, Gloria made her way slowly to the hallway, then paused when no other sound seemed forthcoming. Maybe it had just been an errant baseball, or a tree limb that had blown against the window. She crept to the living room and picked up her purse, pulling out a can of pepper spray that was so old she wasn't sure it would even work. Dubiously armed, she inched her way toward the hallway and the room from which the noise had come. It was a bedroom, if she remembered correctly, a catchall for boxes of upmarket merchandise like DVD recorders and video cameras. As she neared the closed door, she held her breath, listening for any sound that would send her in the opposite direction at the speed of light.

Hearing none, she put her hand on the doorknob and turned it slowly. Just as she pushed the door open, a pile of boxes went tumbling to join the one that had fallen next to the window with the broken pane. Gloria shrieked as a howling black furball raced toward her, streaked through her legs, and disappeared down the hall. When her vital signs returned to normal, she sagged in relief.

Apparently, Steve Chasen's next of kin was a cat.

She walked into the room to examine the broken window. Cold air whipped through the hole, which was easily large enough for a person to climb through. When she turned, she spotted three large clear bags of shredded paper. Whatever Steve had been up to, he certainly had covered his tracks.

With her mind running in circles, she walked back to the kitchen, searching closets and drawers until she located a plastic bag and duct tape. The cat had apparently found another hiding place, because she didn't see it when she made her way back through the house.

As she temporarily repaired the hole, she realized wryly that she wasn't having much luck lately with windows.

And neither was Steve Chasen.

She backtracked to the living room, calling, "Here, kitty, kitty," and making noises that sounded like a clucking chicken, she realized wryly. Animals were not her thing—she didn't want the responsibility or the aggravation. She didn't understand people who were pet-crazy, and God knew she'd seen plenty of those when it came to divorce settlements. Some couples fought more over custody of their pets than custody of their children. She'd considered it a low point in her career when she'd negotiated a visitation schedule so that a man could see a pet terrier that his ex-wife had brought into the marriage.

A low, throaty growl sounded from beneath the desk. She leaned down to see a pair of narrowed eyes glowing at her.

"Are you hungry?" she asked, then walked to the kitchen. In a far corner sat an empty stainless steel bowl that she hadn't noticed before. A cabinet revealed a stash of canned gourmet cat food—apparently Steve Chasen's expensive taste extended to his cat. When she mounted the can on a countertop can opener and pushed the lever, the black cat appeared at her feet before the noise stopped, obviously trained to associate the mechanical sound with an impending meal.

"Hello there," she said dryly. The cat was an enormous male with long, black hair, large paws, full whiskers, and a red leather collar. She carried the food to his bowl and spooned it out. The animal attacked the fishy-smelling chow, making short work of it and licking the bowl. Then it looked up at her expectantly.

"More?" she asked, then opened another can and watched as he devoured it as well, albeit more slowly.

Moving gingerly, she squatted and reached her hand out to the big feline. He retreated at first, then sniffed her fingers and licked them with his rough tongue. Seemingly satisfied, he nudged her hand with his head, then rubbed the length of his body against her knee and began to purr. She gave a little laugh. "Nice try, but you can't come home with me—I don't do pets. But I'll try to find you a good home."

As she filled his bowl with water, the phone rang, shattering the silence and jangling her nerves. She walked to the phone, and when she saw it was the same number on the screen as the one Zane had called earlier, her heart lodged in her throat. After four rings, the message kicked on.

"It's Steve, I'm not here, leave a message." The tone sounded, then the same male voice came on the line as before. "Hey, man, if you're there, pick *up*. Where the hell are you? You're not answering your cell phone either. I got the information you wanted on the girl."

Panicked that the "girl" was her and that she'd never get to the bottom of what was going on, she yanked up the receiver and croaked in her lowest voice, "I'm here."

"Man, you don't sound like yourself."

"Sick," she mumbled, which was true—her stomach was churning so hard that she was nauseous.

"Ah. Well, I got the information you wanted on that lady lawyer."

She made a big show of coughing and hacking like someone who was on their deathbed, and succeeded in scaring the cat. "Tell me," she wheezed.

"Gawd, you sound like shit, man. Maybe this'll perk you up—the woman, she's using an alias. Her real name is Lorey Lawson. You're not going to believe this—"

"I changed my mind," Gloria said in her fake man-voice.

"Huh? You changed your mind? Are you shittin' me?"

"No," she croaked. "Changed my mind, don't wanna know."

The guy's laugh was incredulous. "You can't just change your mind, dawg. I could get into big-time trouble over this." He made a disgusted sound. "Whatever, but you still owe me five grand, got it?"

"Got it," Gloria said, and too late, she realized that she'd forgotten to use the fake voice.

After a few seconds of silence, the man said, "Who the *hell* is this?"

"Steve is dead, so forget about the contract."

She slammed down the phone, her breath coming in great heaves. The man had no idea who he'd been talking to, yet she felt completely exposed. A car pulled into the driveway, and she looked out to see Zane emerging from his cruiser.

Gloria grabbed her bag, her heart racing. What if the guy called back while Zane was standing there? Steve's cat got tangled in her legs as she hurried toward the door. When Zane opened the door, she tripped and practically fell into his arms.

He caught her, steadying her. "Whoa, did you find anything?"

Her face flamed from the awkward predicament and the touch of his hands—and the overwhelming urge to stay in his arms. She straightened and pulled away. "Just a cat," she said, then shooed Steve's pet back inside. "I fed and watered him. I'll try to find a home for him."

"You don't want him?" Zane asked.

"Uh . . . no. I'm not much of a pet person." She pulled the locked door closed behind her and started walking toward the car. "I really need to get back to my office."

"Are you okay?" he asked, opening the passenger side door of his cruiser. "You seem . . . spooked."

She managed a little laugh. "The cat knocked over a stack of boxes and broke a window—it nearly scared me to death."

He hesitated, as if he didn't know whether to believe her. By the time he walked around and slid into his own seat, she realized she needed to do something to prevent him from calling the number on Steve's recorder. "Oh, and that guy called again," she said lightly.

"What guy?"

"The guy on the recorder. I answered, thinking he might know Steve, but as it turns out," she said, making up the lie as she went along, "Steve had just asked him to find a piece of computer equipment for him."

"So he didn't know him personally?"

"Um, no."

"Another dead end. Well, we still have a couple of days before the medical examiner finishes the autopsy."

"Of course," she murmured, recalling that an autopsy was automatic in a sudden death or following an accident.

"Maybe by then we'll know more about the mysterious life of Steve Chasen," Zane said.

Gloria glanced at Zane under her lashes, hoping that he was wrong. She also tamped down her guilt for wanting Steve Chasen—and her secrets—to be buried. The sooner, the better.

Chapter 9

"I have to stop by Dr. Whiting's," Gloria told Diane Davidson, "so I'll be closing the office a little early today."

The woman looked up from sweeping, her face creased in concern. "Is your hand still bothering you?"

Gloria smoothed her fingers over the bandage, which looked a little worse for wear with all the cleaning she'd done, and frowned at the black cat hair stuck in the tape. "Uh, no."

The woman's chin dipped. "I didn't mean to pry."

"It's okay. I just need a prescription, actually." Gloria felt a pang of compassion for the woman, who was covered in dust, her hair damp around her forehead, her face pink from exertion. "Diane, why don't you go home? You've done miracles today—thank you."

Diane ducked her head. "I'm glad to help."

"Maybe tomorrow we can get down to business." On impulse, Gloria removed a duplicate door key from a ring and handed it to Diane. "In case you arrive tomorrow before I do."

Diane smiled. "Remember you have Miss Linder coming in at two o'clock tomorrow."

"Right," Gloria said, wondering who the litigious woman wanted to sue now. According to Penny, Deke and Sheena's affair had begun after he'd agreed to take on one of Sheena's many personal injury claims.

But a case was a case, and if she intended to stay in Mojo, she'd better get used to handling all kinds of legal issues.

If she intended to stay.

As she waved good-bye to Diane Davidson and locked the door, she was suddenly very glad that she'd hired the woman—she liked her. Diane was quiet and thoughtful and seemed to anticipate Gloria's needs, answering the phone with just the right tone and fixing coffee the way Gloria liked it. The woman seemed so appreciative to be there.

It felt good to be able to help someone. Gloria bit into her lip. Even if the situation was short-lived.

She checked her cell phone to see if George had called. She'd left him a message with the phone number of the person who'd called Steve's house to see if George could zero in on the guy Steve was working with. Nothing yet, but surely it wouldn't take long to trace a phone number.

Her mind clicked like a meter as she drove the short distance to the doctor's office, parked, and stepped over the sprinkling of brick dust to walk inside. The reception area was empty. Brianna, sporting a white dust mask over her mouth and nose, was spraying a layer of Lysol over the furniture. She looked up, then lowered the mask. "Well, hello there. Gloria, right?"

"Right."

"Did you decide you wanted that free makeover?"

"Uh, not yet, thank you. Actually, I was hoping I could see Dr. Whiting if he hasn't left for the day."

"He's not doing any more exams today."

"I just need a prescription."

Brianna perked up. "Oh? What for?"

"If you don't mind, I'd rather talk to the doctor."

Brianna frowned and picked up the phone, then punched a button. "Gloria Dalton is here—she needs a prescription but won't tell me what it's for . . . okay." She hung up the phone, then flashed a tight smile. "Dr. Whiting's office is at the end of the hall."

Feeling the young woman's scrutiny as she walked away, Gloria took a deep breath before knocking on the doctor's door.

"Come in," he called.

She turned the knob and Jonas Whiting stood, extending a smile. "Ms. Dalton, how's your hand?"

"It's fine," she said, surprised to see him without his white coat, dressed in jeans and a striped button-up shirt. "I came by to see if you could write a prescription for me."

"Painkiller?"

"No—Meclazine."

He frowned. "For vertigo?"

"Ménière's."

"Ah. How long have you suffered attacks?"

"Since I was fourteen, but luckily, I've had only a couple of bad episodes."

"Any hearing loss?"

"No, thank goodness."

"And are you symptomatic now?"

She nodded. "Just occasional dizziness, but I'm out of medication."

He gave her a smile as he reached for a prescription pad. "I can fix that." She registered the fact that he was a nice-looking man, but her attention was drawn to a small purple cloth pouch hanging around his neck from a leather cord, peeking through the vee of his shirt where the top button was undone. "If you don't mind me asking, what's that around your neck?"

His eyebrows went up, then he touched it with his hand. "This? This is a *paket kongo*—it's a healing charm."

The back of her neck tingled. "You believe in voodoo?"

"Sure." He tore off the prescription and handed it to her. "A lot of my patients take great stock in voodoo. I use all the tools at my disposal to help my patients feel well."

She fingered the prescription. "Thank you. Dr. Whiting, do your beliefs extend to voodoo dolls?"

His expression sharpened. "Why do you ask?"

She weighed her words. "Someone created a voodoo doll of Deke Black before he was murdered—I just wondered if you knew who it might have been."

"No. And Deke's murder was solved. Why would you want to reopen that wound?"

"I don't," she said quickly.

His mouth tightened and he crossed his arms. "You can get that prescription filled at Webber's pharmacy just a couple of doors down."

Feeling dismissed, she nodded her thanks and backed out of his office. She seemed to have pushed a button with her question about the voodoo dolls. Did the good doctor know more than he was willing to tell?

As Gloria walked back into the reception area, Brianna took a break from her Lysol fog to lower her mask and extend a little pink gift bag. "Here you go—some free samples."

"Thank you," Gloria murmured, taking the bag. "Brianna, are you by chance a cat person?"

She scrunched her nose. "Allergic. Why?"

"Steve Chasen had a cat that I'm trying to find a home for. It's a black male, and he seems friendly."

Her eyes widened. "A black cat? Good luck trying to find a home for it around here, seeing as how superstitious everyone is." Then she gave a little laugh. "Hey, you might try Diane Davidson—she's a witch, you know."

Gloria frowned. "Diane is working for me now."

Brianna's eyebrows flew up. "Really? Wow, good luck with that. Listen, if you want, I'll ask around and see if anybody wants the cat."

"That would be great—just call the law office if you find someone who's interested."

"Will do. You're going to love that moisturizer I put in there for you. It plumps everything up."

Gloria gave her a tight smile. "Thanks."

Outside she walked the few feet down the sidewalk to the drugstore, mulling the new details that she'd learned about the people in Mojo today—Steve Chasen, Dr. Whiting. Were the two of them connected somehow? If Steve had had a heart condition, he might have seen the doctor for it. Too late, she realized she should have asked Brianna—the woman certainly would have spilled her guts.

Webber's drugstore was one of those little stores that was lost in time, full of dusty, obscure products like sock suspenders, Beta-to-VHS videotape converters, and yellowed greeting cards with sappy verses. She dropped her prescription at the counter, then roamed the aisles looking for necessities she hadn't yet been able to find among her packing boxes—paper towels, soap, razors.

She paused at the basket of City of Mojo, LA, back scratchers featuring a rather wicked-looking black claw on the end, then picked up one of the odd souvenirs. Strangely, it reminded her of the last conversation she'd had with her mother before she'd dropped out of WITSEC and disappeared.

As a teenager, Gloria had realized that her parents had been distant, and she'd suspected that they'd stayed together because of her. Her mother was an intellectual, who had married a blue-collar guy whose rough edges had never smoothed. Their marriage had grown more tense when her father had agreed to testify in a federal case against the man that he and her mother had both worked for, who had turned out to be a hard-core criminal. Her mother had become enraged, saying he was putting them all in danger. He'd said he was working with federal marshals about getting them into WITSEC, that they could move and start a new life with the money the government was promising to pay as a "bonus." Her mother had said absolutely not . . . and that was the night the man in the black coat had come and taken her father's life.

Her mother had reluctantly testified against Bernard Riaz, but Maggie Lawson had never fully trusted the WITSEC program or the people who ran it.

Years later, with several moves under their belt, Gloria had asked her mother if she missed her father. Her mother, who now went by the name Miranda Dobson, had hesitated, then smiled. "You know what I miss? How your father used to scratch my back. People who've never been married don't know what they're missing. Now when I get an itch, I have to rub myself against a door frame." She had looked at Gloria, brushed her daughter's hair behind her ear. "Find yourself a good man, honey, forget about this debacle with the feds, forget about your father, forget about me. Live your life."

Gloria, twenty-two at the time and newly graduated from college, never saw her mother again. Her mother's home was broken into that night. She called Gloria the next day to say good-bye, that she was leaving WITSEC, and that Gloria should go on with her life. Frantic, Gloria pleaded with her to reconsider, but Maggie had become disenchanted with WITSEC and had convinced herself that as long as her life touched Gloria's, Gloria was in danger. She had simply dropped out of sight.

On impulse, Gloria added the back scratcher to her shopping basket. If she relocated again and changed her name, she'd have to get rid of it, along with anything else that might reveal where she'd lived. But for now, what could it hurt?

In the hair care aisle, the boxes of dye featured pictures that were slightly old-fashioned. The expiration dates were still good, however, so she picked the one that best matched her chosen hair color.

When her prescription was ready, she paid for the items and walked back to her car. From where she stood, she could see the sign for Ted's Diner on the square, which suddenly sounded like a better option for dinner than a trip to the grocery. Besides, she had fond memories of a certain small-town diner in New Jersey, where she and a gray-eyed boy had fallen in love over shared burgers and chocolate malts.

She walked across the square, admiring the lights of the Christmas tree, thinking what a strange little melting pot the town was, and that she would truly miss it if George told her she had to move. She sighed, conceding that what she would miss was Zane Riley—could she leave him hanging, always wondering about the girl for whom he'd filed a missing persons report?

Behind her, the scrape of footsteps sounded. She turned her head, but the gloom of dusk revealed nothing. The twinkling lights of the tree cast a changing pattern of shadows on the ground, which disoriented her for a moment. She stood still, willing away another attack of vertigo, latching her gaze onto the horizon as a steady point of reference. The sun was sliding away, leaving fiery trails of thin, blood-red clouds hanging in the chilly December sky. A shiver of foreboding traveled up her spine, but she blamed it on all the bizarre coincidences of the past few days and hurried on to the diner.

When she walked inside, the person who had been dominating her thoughts, Zane Riley, was the first person she saw sitting at the counter. He was still in uniform and having a cup of coffee. She considered leaving to avoid another awkward encounter, but at that moment he looked up and saw her. He tossed a few bills on the counter, then picked up his coffee cup and walked toward her.

Her stomach fluttered as he neared—the emotions colliding in her chest forced her to look away to collect herself. She couldn't continue to revert to a sixteen-year-old every time the man was nearby.

"Hi, Ms. Dalton," he said.

"Hello, Chief Riley." Would every encounter with him be predicated by the gut-clenching question, *Does he know?* "Please, call me Gloria."

"Okay. Call me Zane. I need to talk to you about Steve Chasen," he said, his face solemn.

She swallowed. "Steve? What about him?"

"Well, actually, it affects you . . . Gloria."

Chapter 10

Even as Gloria strove to keep an outwardly calm appearance, the muscles in her legs bunched in preparation for a quick getaway in case Zane confronted her with the truth about herself.

"How could information about Steve Chasen possibly affect me?"

Zane gestured to an empty booth. "I assume you came to eat. Why don't we sit?"

She walked stiffly to the booth with red bench seats and a white Formica tabletop and slid inside. Ted appeared at the table to take their order. She asked for a salad and baked potato, and Zane ordered a piece of pie to go with his coffee.

Gloria eased a bit—surely the man wasn't going to confront her about her past over a slice of pecan pie?

When Ted walked away, Zane sipped from his coffee and leaned back in the bench seat opposite her. "About Chasen . . ."

"Yes?" she prompted.

"I made a few phone calls and tracked down his previous address in Richmond, Virginia. His parents are deceased, and he was an only child."

Blowing on her coffee helped to hide an exhale of relief that his news wasn't about her, but she did feel a pang of compassion for Steve Chasen. "That's too bad. Any extended family?"

"No. Which brings me back to your offer to arrange a memorial service—are you still willing?"

"Of course."

He gave her a little smile. "That's nice of you. I'll tell the folks at Goddard's Funeral Chapel to give you a call when the body is released."

She nodded and tried not to think too much about "the body." "Without a will, I assume his belongings will be placed into probate, then auctioned to satisfy his creditors, if he has any."

"You'd know more about that than I would."

"I was wondering if I could borrow the key to his place," she said, thinking she'd like to have more time to go through Steve's "things." When his eyebrows went up in question, she added, "To feed the cat, of course."

"I'll have a duplicate made and drop it off. I think I can trust you." His eyes crinkled at the corners, and she managed a smile despite the gumbo of guilt and desire that swirled in her stomach.

Ted returned with their orders, and Gloria began to eat her salad despite her sudden loss of appetite.

The sense of déjà vu was almost overwhelming: How many times had Zane sat across from her eating pecan pie and making her squirm with his intense eye contact? Except when they had been young, it was likely that their hands or legs would have been entwined beneath the table. A different time, a different place, and she was a different person, yet the sexual energy crackling between them was familiar . . . and dangerous.

She saw the sudden desire lurking in his eyes, shrouded by surprise and propriety. Gloria dragged her gaze away—Zane didn't understand what was happening, but she did, and she had to be the one who kept a cool head. It was so tempting to blurt everything, but where would that leave them? Her, running, and Zane, vulnerable, especially considering George's info about Riaz being out of prison. And then a horrible thought struck her—was it possible that Riaz and his men would track down Zane, thinking she'd be keeping tabs on her old boyfriend?

"How's your hand?" he asked, breaking the tense silence.

"Fine," she said, flexing it. "Just a little stiff."

"How are the repairs coming along on your office?"

"We have everything cleaned up inside, but the handyman is waiting for supplies before he can begin work on the outside."

A young waitress stopped next to their table and flashed a shy smile. "Excuse me, would you like to buy a candy bar for the families of the victims of the voodoo museum?"

"Sure," Zane said, reaching into his pocket. "I'll

take two." The girl thanked him and left the milk chocolate bars on the table, which he pushed toward Gloria. "Take them, I've got these things coming out my ears."

She laughed and pushed them back. "Me, too, and I don't even eat chocolate."

"You don't eat chocolate?"

She shook her head—she'd changed her diet as drastically as she'd changed her appearance.

"Are you diabetic?"

"No . . . I just try to avoid sweets."

"You take good care of yourself." He flicked his gaze over her. "It shows."

She blushed furiously, tongue-tied.

"I indulge occasionally," he said, gesturing to the pie. "But my favorite is—"

"Dark chocolate," she finished for him, nodding.

He squinted. "How did you know that?"

When she realized her gaffe, she froze, her mind racing for an explanation. "I . . . just . . . thought—"

"I guess it's not that unusual," he said with a laugh, lifting his coffee cup for another drink. "And don't get me wrong about the candy bars—selling them is a nice gesture, but the entire population of Mojo is going to be in a sugar coma."

His grin was so genuine, his expression so unexpectedly unguarded, that she was struck speechless as old feelings crowded her chest, taunting her with what could have been, tempting her with what could be now.

"Gloria," he said. "Are you . . . seeing anyone?"

She picked up her water glass and took a deep drink, then set it down. "No, not . . . currently."

The corners of his mouth turned up as he sipped from his coffee cup. "Is there an ex-husband in your past?"

"Not a husband."

"But someone serious?" he pressed.

She nodded, realizing that if Zane thought she was still hung up on someone from her past, it might help her keep him at arm's length. He didn't have to know it was the memory of him that she kept tucked in her heart.

"I know what you mean," he said, his eyes touched with sadness.

With a jolt, she realized that he might be talking about her—or, rather, Lorey. She knew she should change the subject, but the temptation to dredge up old feelings was irresistible. "You're referring to the person that you filed the missing persons report on?"

He nodded. "It was a long time ago, but it stuck with me."

It stuck with me, too, Zane. Her thighs warmed at the memories that suddenly seemed so fresh, so real. Desire stabbed her low and hard, and she realized with dismay that her relatively short time with Zane had been the most sexually satisfying phase of her life.

And they hadn't even made love.

"Surely you've had relationships since then," she murmured.

He pursed his mouth and nodded. "Yeah, I've known some really nice women, some I even grew attached to. Thought about settling down once or twice."

The faces of pretty, hopeful women flitted through

her brain, and she felt an unexpected pang for their loss. "So why didn't you?"

He splayed his hands and made a rueful noise. "When it came down to making a permanent commitment, I knew I'd constantly be torn between my family and my job. In the end, I always moved on, literally. I guess I've always felt this nagging sense of having unfinished business and it's left me . . . restless."

"I understand," she said, her leg accidentally bumping his under the table, sending a vibration of awareness straight to her feminine core. Her chest ached with longing to end the suffering for both of them, but the consequences of a confession loomed like a black cloud. It would solve a few problems but create so many more.

When his eye contact became too powerful to ignore, she glanced at her watch. "I didn't realize it was getting so late. I need to get home." She waved for the check, busying herself with her purse.

"Are you still unpacking?" he asked.

"Yes."

"Me, too," he said. "Don't you hate moving?"

She glanced up. "You have no idea."

The waitress came by with their check.

"I've got this," Zane said, gesturing to her half-eaten meal and his empty plate.

"No—" Gloria started to protest, but he'd already paid.

He smiled. "Consider it a very small thank you for all that you're doing for Steve Chasen. You don't have to, you know."

She smiled through her guilt and suddenly needed

to get away from Zane, the man who left her feeling so disoriented and so conflicted. "Thank you for dinner. Goodnight."

"I'll walk you to your car," he said, starting to rise.

"I'll be fine," she said quickly, holding out her hand to dissuade him. "Finish your coffee."

"Okay," he said, studying her warily. "I'll get that key to you sometime tomorrow."

She nodded and fled, releasing a pent-up groan of frustration when she walked outside into the cool air. Closing her eyes, she hit the palm of her hand to her forehead. What was she thinking, asking Zane about the past? What good could possibly come of it? Weren't her emotions tangled enough without making things even more complicated?

She sighed and gave herself a mental shake, then hurried to her car, shivering in the cold in her thin jacket. At the door of her Honda, she hit the keyless remote. But just as she reached for the door handle, a dark shadow fell across the pavement near her. She turned to see the outline of a man standing there, and she cried out, fumbling with the door handle in alarm.

"Ms. Dalton, I didn't mean to scare you."

She stopped, still leery, her heart pumping furiously. "Who are you? I can't see your face."

The man stepped up into the light. Thinning hair, stocky build, casual, but neat, clothing. "I'm Daniel Guess, from the *Post*. I called you the other day to ask you about Steve Chasen's death."

She frowned. "I remember."

"I was hoping you would talk to me in person."

"There's nothing to talk about, although I'm very sorry about Steve's death."

He took a step forward and leaned in. "Were you the one who found the voodoo doll?"

Her throat constricted. "Who told you about the voodoo doll?"

"Does it matter?"

"It might."

"So you do think it has something to do with his death?"

She scoffed. "Of course not—I'd just like to know who's playing a prank."

"Were you scared?"

"N-no."

"I know you're aware that another doll bearing the likeness of Deke Black was stabbed just before he was murdered last year, because you represented his wife in that investigation, didn't you?"

"His ex-wife," Gloria corrected.

"Is this doll similar to that one?"

"I don't know. I don't know anything about voodoo, Mr. Guess."

"Was the doll you found fashioned in a likeness of Mr. Chasen?"

"I didn't notice." Too late, she realized she'd just admitted to seeing it.

"What did it look like?"

She opened her car door. "That's all I have to say."

"Was it stabbed?" he persisted. "Where is the doll now?"

"That's *all*, Mr. Guess," she said, raising her voice an octave.

"What's going on here?"

She turned to see Zane striding up, his expression dark.

"You must be Riley, the new chief of police," the reporter said, flashing a smile. "I'm Daniel Guess with the *Post*."

"What's your business with Ms. Dalton?" Zane asked, ignoring the man's attempt at friendliness.

"We had a report that a voodoo doll was found shortly before Steve Chasen's car accident."

"Is that so?" Zane asked.

"Yes, and Ms. Dalton here confirmed it."

"I didn't," she cut in. "I told you I had nothing to say."

"Sounds to me like you're wasting your time," Zane said to the man.

The reporter narrowed his eyes at Gloria. "I should warn you—I always get my story."

Zane stepped closer to the man, leveraging his considerable height advantage. "And I should warn you—get the hell out of my town before I arrest you for harassment."

The reporter lifted both hands. "Just trying to do my job."

"Do it outside the city limits," Zane said, jerking his thumb in the direction of the interstate. "*Now*."

The reporter frowned but backed away. He stopped at an SUV close by, then grinned. "Hey, if you want to get rid of me, maybe you should make a voodoo doll." He laughed, then climbed into his vehicle and drove away.

Zane's mouth tightened as he watched the tail-lights disappear. "Are you okay?" he asked her.

Gloria nodded. "He just scared me when he first appeared, that's all."

He frowned. "Gloria, it's not good for the town for you to tell stories about that voodoo doll you found."

Anger sparked in her chest. "I wasn't telling stories!"

"Then how did he know about it?"

"I don't know—he called me yesterday and started asking questions. I told him I had no comment."

"Who could've tipped him off?"

She lifted her hands in a shrug. "I don't know—Marie was there, it's possible that she called him. Or that she told someone who called him. You said yourself that it's hard to keep a secret in a town like Mojo." Then she angled her head. "And it could've been the person who made the doll, did you think of that?"

"All the more reason to keep it quiet if we have some voodoo kook looking for a headline," he said hotly. "It's probably just a copycat."

"But quite a coincidence, wouldn't you say?" she asked lightly.

He moved to stand in front of her, his eyes challenging. "I don't believe in coincidences."

So how do you explain this? she wanted to say. *Me and you, after all these years, standing here, inches apart. Coincidence?*

In the space of an exhale, the atmosphere changed from irritation to stimulation. Zane stared into her eyes, confusion playing over his face.

Longing coiled tightly inside her, squeezing her lungs painfully. Then suddenly, like an animal springing on prey, she kissed him. A big, open-mouth, where-have-you-been kiss that took both hands. He seemed surprised at first but caught up quickly and lashed his tongue against hers.

She sighed into his mouth, reveling in the familiar tastes and textures that she had tried to forget, but hadn't been able to. God, she wanted to lap him up. His arms encircled her, and he pulled her against his long, hard body. It was as if she'd never left, as if she'd traveled back in time, to a love that transcended tragedy. The lonely years melted away, as if they never were. There was only Zane.

A loud bang sounded near them, wrenching them apart and sending adrenaline surging through her tingling body. Gloria's head spun as she tried to identify the noise that she'd heard before—fireworks?

But when Zane pushed her to the ground and covered her body with his, murmuring, "Stay down" in her ear, she realized what was happening and where she'd heard the noise before—in her living room, the night her father had been killed.

Dear God, someone was shooting at them.

Chapter 11

Gloria had imagined a time when Zane would be lying on top of her again, but she hadn't imagined that she would be facedown in the cold grass with the wind knocked out of her, wondering who could be shooting at them—and why.

"Are you okay?" he said in her ear.

She gasped for breath but managed to whisper, "I think so."

"Don't move."

She felt his weight roll off her, and out of the corner of her eye, she saw him crouching next to her car, talking low and fast into his radio. She heard the scrape of metal against leather and realized he'd drawn his own weapon. Her heartbeat pulsed in her ears as she resisted the urge to pull him back to the ground. The thought of him being shot sent a scream to hover at the back of her throat.

Was some lunatic on the loose? A fugitive? A fight in Caskey's Bar across the square that had moved outside? The square had been practically deserted except for her and Zane.

Although, admittedly, a parade could have moved through while she'd been kissing him and she wouldn't have noticed.

Then a cold, hard possibility hit her—had one of Riaz's men tracked her down? Fear curdled her blood, fogged her brain.

She heard Zane moving stealthily away, which only terrified her more. What if Zane was injured or killed because of her? A siren approached, and from the sounds of feet pounding and murmured voices, she assumed that Zane and his officers were canvassing the area. Her mind spun with horrible scenarios, all of them involving Zane's spilled blood. It wasn't fair that she'd just found him, only to have him ripped away.

After several agonizing minutes, she lifted her head gingerly, wondering if a night-vision scope was aimed at her head. Better hers than Zane's, she decided. Raised voices sounded a few yards away, followed by what sounded like a scuffle. She pushed to her feet to see Zane and two other uniformed officers surrounding a scraggly bearded man. Homeless? Transient? He lifted his hands in surrender, and an officer removed a large pistol from the man's coat pocket.

She squinted in the dim light to see if she recognized him. He looked more like a mountain man than a hit man for Riaz, but those people were masters of disguise.

Just like the members of WITSEC, she acknowledged wryly.

She watched as the man submitted to being handcuffed and was led toward a squad car yelling, "I didn't do anything wrong!" Zane strode in her direction, casting a long shadow, backlit by the signage of the businesses in the square that stayed open late: Ted's Diner, Sheena's Forever Sun Tanning Salon, Benny's Beignet Shop, and Caskey's Bar.

She was so glad he was okay that she nearly wept with relief. When he stopped in front of her, she resisted the urge to pull him close and reassure herself that he was unharmed. "What happened?"

His expression was hard to make out in the darkness, but his shoulders were set in a taut line. "That's Jimmy Scaggs, a local. We're not sure, but we think that he discharged a pistol accidentally."

She frowned. "I know that name from the Deke Black murder."

"Yeah. He's been in trouble with the law here and there, and he has a tendency to threaten hunters that go near his property. Just from talking to him, I don't think he meant any harm, but we're taking him down to the station to question him and maybe let him spend the night. He swears he didn't discharge his gun . . . but he's rambling about finding a body in the woods."

Her eyes rounded. "A body?"

Zane sighed. "Except he can't remember where." He made a gesture to his head that indicated he thought the man was addled, or perhaps under the influence of drink or drugs. "It could be nothing, but we'll check it out."

"Did he explain why he had a gun?"

"He has a permit to carry a concealed weapon, says he uses the .45 for hunting deer." He shrugged. "It's still deer season in this parish, so his story makes sense."

More sense than the paranoid conclusions her mind had leaped to. Gloria expelled a pent-up breath and reminded herself that she needed to relax lest she trigger another Ménière's attack.

"Are you sure you're okay?" Zane asked. He shifted, and the light revealed the concern on his face.

"I'm fine," she assured him, almost giddy from the ebb of adrenaline throughout her system. The memory of her guerilla kiss warmed her cheeks, and in the silence that ensued, she had the feeling that he, too, was remembering their intimate contact.

He reached up and pulled a leaf from her hair. His smile made her chest expand with emotion, and she realized with dismay that she was well on her way to falling in love with Zane again. "Thank you," she murmured.

"For what?"

"For . . . protecting me."

"Glad I was here," he said quietly, then they lapsed into silence again. Unsaid words clanged in her head so loudly that she was afraid he would hear them. Finally, he shifted his weight. "I guess I'll see you around."

Since her tongue had lodged in the roof of her mouth, she could only nod.

He opened her car door and she lowered her body inside, hoping he couldn't sense how mortified she felt over her brazen behavior. When she pulled away from the square, she looked in the rearview mirror, noting that he watched her drive away, his hands on his hips, his shoulders squared. Had he found something familiar in their kiss? Was his mind working furiously, trying to put the pieces together? When he closed his eyes tonight, would his subconscious link the pieces and jar him from a sound sleep with the truth?

Or had he filed away Lorey, his high-school sweetheart, in a compartment in his mind that was guarded even from his subconscious?

As she drove slowly along Charm Street, her mind went to Daniel Guess and the potential problem he presented. If he suspected that Steve Chasen's death was anything other than accidental, he'd keep digging into the dead man's life. A good investigative reporter could probably get his hands on phone records, and it would be only a matter of time before he found the guy who was in cahoots with Steve's blackmailing scheme.

Then a thought floated in her mind—who better than a reporter to sell info to someone like Steve? She chewed on her lip, wondering if Daniel Guess could have been the person on the other end of the phone today . . . and the person firing at her in the square?

To keep her from revealing his extortion scheme?

By the time she arrived at her rental house, a headache had descended. With her nerves jumping, she entered the dark house, turning on lights in rapid succession. When she stopped to listen, the creaky noises of the house settling in for the night were barely audible over her heartbeat, pounding in her ears. Gloria paused in the kitchen long enough to scoop a handful of ice into a dish towel as a makeshift ice pack for her head.

On the way through the living room, she winced at the stacked boxes that would sit unopened for another day. On the other hand, unpacking the boxes before she heard back from the U.S. marshal seemed like a futile effort. One box in particular caught her eye, though, and stopped her. It was a small moving box marked KEEPSAKES, holding items that she had salvaged from the hit-and-miss packing job that the marshals had done for her and her mother when they'd had to leave Schilling, New Jersey, so abruptly.

She picked up the box and continued on to her bedroom, gasping when she saw her reflection. Her face was smudged with dirt, her clothing was askew and grass stained. She frowned down at the pale gray pantsuit—at the rate she'd been ruining clothes, she'd have to buy a new wardrobe before the first of the year.

If she stayed. . . .

After a quick shower, she changed into soft cotton pajamas and downed a dose of Meclazine from the new prescription that Dr. Whiting had written for her. She scanned the label thinking that if Zane got wind that the doctor was a proponent of voodoo, the men would likely exchange words.

Gloria pulled the box of keepsakes onto the bed, then burrowed under the covers, leaned against the headboard, and set the ice bag on her throbbing head. When the coolness began to settle the pain, she lifted the lid on the box and surveyed the jumbled contents.

The lone female U.S. marshal had apologized when the moving truck had arrived at their new home in Wisconsin. She'd explained that anything that had connected them to their previous life had been destroyed—photos, yearbooks, letters, and anything with the town or family names on it.

Gone were the notes and cards that Zane had passed to her between classes and for special occasions, the engraved locket he'd given her with their pictures inside, his sterling ID bracelet that he'd removed links from so it would fit her wrist.

Gone was her diary that detailed her burgeoning love for Zane. Gone were all the photos of the two of them together—in school, at his football games, sitting under the one tiny shade tree in the backyard of her house.

If she closed her eyes, she remembered those moments—no one could take away her memories—but it had broken her heart all over again to lose the photos. It had been like losing Zane twice. The marshal had told her that not having reminders of her previous life would help her move on, but Gloria still believed that having reminders of her previous life would have been soothing.

There were days when she could almost convince herself that she'd never been Lorey Lawson in Schilling, New Jersey, that she'd never fallen in love with a gray-eyed boy, that her father was still alive. It had been tempting to believe . . . but she'd felt as if the comforting lies dishonored her father and her love for

Zane, so she'd stubbornly branded them on her heart.

From the box she pulled a small bean bag dog that had once worn a collar that had said Schilling Summer Carnival. She was grateful that the marshal had taken the time to remove and discard only the collar instead of the entire toy. Zane had won it for her at a game where he'd shot wooden ducks in profile with a toy rifle. It had been one of those hot summer nights when they hadn't been able to stop touching, hadn't been able to get close enough to satisfy the sexual energy vibrating between them. On more than one occasion, Zane had pulled her behind a tent to steal a kiss and to palm her heavy breasts. She would stroke his erection through his jeans, and only the threat of being caught would force them apart. They would run back to the crowd, hand in hand, laughing and burning for each other.

Gloria's breasts tingled now, as if Zane were lying next to her. They hadn't made love—Zane had agreed they should wait until she was older. But so many times she'd wished they hadn't waited, so she could have had the memory of Zane's body connected to hers, to warm her on those endless lonely nights after she and her mother had fled.

She reached back into the box and withdrew the Baby Giggles doll that her father had given her the day she'd started kindergarten. "She'll be your friend until you make new ones," he'd said.

Gloria's eyes teared at the memory. Her father hadn't doled out hugs and kisses as generously as some other fathers had, but she'd never doubted that he'd loved her. Gloria lifted the doll's arm, triggering a chorus of giggles from the electronic box lodged beneath the doll's yellow dress and cloth torso. Gloria smiled at the familiar noise, comforted anew.

From a small box she removed a necklace with a heart medallion that her mother had given her after they'd been relocated, to cheer her up. But stubborn and miserable, Gloria had refused to wear it. Tears at her selfishness clouded her eyes as she fastened it around her neck. It was of nice quality, and her mother had probably done without something in order to buy it.

When she dipped her hand into the box again, her fingers touched soft, fuzzy yarn. Zane's scarf. She lifted the dark green scarf from the box, recalling the dozens of times she'd opened her front door to find Zane standing there, his cheeks pink from the cold, the scarf wound around his neck. He'd left it in her bedroom several times, and when she'd found it inside one of the boxes that the marshals had packed, she'd been overjoyed to have something of Zane's, if only accidentally.

Gloria pressed the scarf against her face, the scent of Zane long gone but fodder for her imagination. God, how she'd loved him. The current emotions colliding in her chest seemed dangerously familiar, but she told herself it was impossible for her to be in love with a man she barely knew. These . . . *feelings* were simply nostalgia for a period in her life when she had been happy . . . and normal. Before she'd been ripped away from everything she'd known. Yes, she had loved Zane, but if their romance had been allowed to develop without the interference of WITSEC, wouldn't it have run its course and wouldn't their relationship have eventually ended?

She draped the scarf around her neck and leaned her head back. No doubt the traumatic events surrounding her departure and the fact that she hadn't gotten to say good-bye had stoked her feelings for Zane even higher. Falsely higher?

Gloria pressed her lips together. Was it possible that, in the weeks and months and years following that harrowing evening, she had idealized her romance with Zane, that she had taken a teenage crush and exaggerated it into more than it had actually been? And had Zane done the same thing?

It stuck with me, he'd said about her disappearance. Had it kept him from forming attachments to other women?

A strange gurgling gong sounded through the house, startling her. It wasn't her phone, she realized as she jumped to her feet, sending the ice pack to the floor with a plop. Was it the doorbell? She'd never heard it chime, although it made sense that a house this old would have a creepy-sounding doorbell.

As she walked carefully toward the front of the house, her mind raced. Who would be visiting her? Penny? Marie? She swallowed hard. Someone with more sinister intentions? She stopped at a hall closet and removed one of the items that she hadn't left for the movers but had transported in her car—a .38 semiautomatic handgun, loaded.

In the long, boring hours of their seclusion in the hotel after leaving Schilling and before being relocated to Wisconsin, George had taught her about handguns and encouraged her to buy a weapon for self-defense and learn how to use it. Later she had taken his advice and now was, in fact, a pretty good shot, although she realized that putting holes in a silhouette at a handgun range was a lot different than putting holes in a real person.

The doorbell gonged again, raising the hair on her arms. Glad that she'd extinguished the lights in the small living room, she held the gun down and crept slowly into the room. A part of her reasoned that anyone who intended to hurt her would simply break a window or force their way inside, but the marshals had warned her that many career criminals had gotten wise and traded in their gangster, headline-grabbing tactics for more low-key methods of accessing their targets: ringing doorbells, posing as a shopper, walking up to ask for directions.

In other words, the killers looked like ordinary people.

With her pulse thumping, she stopped at a side window and parted the heavy curtains a fraction of an inch, glancing toward the front stoop. The outline of the man revealed in the dim streetlight did little to relieve her anxiety—what was Zane doing here?

She sighed and pushed the gun into the pocket of her pajamas. She considered going back for her robe, but her pj's were of the full-coverage variety.

And it wasn't as if he hadn't seen everything she had anyway. Seen, touched, kissed . . .

She ran her fingers through her damp, flattened hair and conceded that she couldn't do anything about the rat's nest. Steeling herself against his effect on her, she turned on the outside light, then unbolted the front door and swung it open. "Hello."

Zane looked up and shifted awkwardly. "Hi. I was driving by and thought I'd check to see if you were okay." Then he gestured to her clothing. "But I can see that I disturbed you."

"No," she said quickly, fighting a flush, wondering if she'd ever get used to the fact that she could actually see—and touch—him. "And I'm fine, thanks. Just doing some reading. In bed," she added unnecessarily and wanted to kick herself.

"Are you having problems with your heat?"

She frowned. "No. Why?"

"That's some pretty strange reading gear." He grinned and reached forward to lift the end of the fuzzy dark green scarf—*his* scarf—that she'd forgotten she'd draped over her shoulders.

The moisture left her mouth as her mind raced for an explanation. She gave a little laugh that sounded false to her own ears as she removed the scarf and stuffed it into her pocket, displacing the gun, which fell to the floor with a thud.

They both stood there staring at the gun, and all she could think was that she was so damned grateful it hadn't gone off and killed or maimed one of them. Gawd.

Zane cleared his throat. "Do you always sleep with a gun?"

"Uh, no," she said carefully. "But a woman can't be too careful."

"Well, you could be a *little* more careful in handling a semiautomatic," he said, bending over to retrieve the gun. He removed the clip and saw that it was fully loaded. A check of the chamber revealed another round inside. He raised his eyebrows, then handed it back to her. "Do you know how to use this thing, Counselor?"

"Yes," she said, her voice curt as she took the handgun from him.

"And I assume it's registered?"

She bristled. "I abide by the law, Chief, but you're welcome to check."

"No, I believe you." Then a wary glint came into his eyes. "Although I have a feeling that you're not being completely honest with me about something."

Gloria decided to lob the subject back into his court. "Did you get to the bottom of the shooting?"

"Maybe. Scaggs is still rambling—we're going to let him sleep it off in jail. Meanwhile, his gun had been fired recently, and his shooting hand tested positive for gun powder residue. Without the slug, we can't be sure, but looks like he's our man."

She nodded, relieved at the explanation. The silence stretched between them, and Gloria wondered what he must think of her for throwing herself at him like she had. A flush started at her ankles and worked its way up her body. "If that's all, Chief, thank you for coming by." She moved to close the door, but he held up his hand.

"There was one other thing."

Her breathing stalled. "Yes?"

"Back in the square, when . . . we kissed. I want to apologize."

So he regretted it? "Apologize for what?"

"It was highly unprofessional, and I'm sorry if I made you uncomfortable."

His words rankled her feminist sensibilities. "Chief Riley, you make it sound like you took advantage of a schoolgirl. As I recall, I initiated that kiss."

He frowned. "Look, I'm just trying to do the right

thing. Besides, you're an attorney, you understand the position that I'm in."

Her mouth tightened in anger. "You're afraid I'm going to sue you for improper conduct, is that it?"

He lifted his hands. "All I'm saying is that it won't happen again."

She gasped at his audacity, then narrowed her eyes. "You're right—it won't happen again." Then she stepped back and slammed the door in his face.

Frustrated and knowing she was overreacting to his backward apology, Gloria groaned aloud at the ridiculous, impossible state of her life. And Zane—how dare he apologize for kissing her when all she wanted from him was . . . more, dammit.

Chapter 12

The next morning Gloria parked in front of Primo Drycleaner's, which sat at the opposite end of the strip mall from her law office. With great effort she dragged herself from her car. Only the slight sedating effect of the Meclazine had helped her get a few scant hours of sleep after her confrontation with Zane. If not for Sheena Linder's appointment this afternoon, she might have opted to close the office for the day and sleep.

Try to sleep, if her mind would stop replaying scenes with Zane—past and present—to torment her.

Heaving a sigh, she retrieved an armload of clothes from the backseat—her dust-covered clothes from the first day and the grass-stained clothes from last night.

A bell tinkled as she walked into the dry cleaner's.

A beautiful young woman wearing a colorful head wrap was in conversation with a wizened old woman wearing overalls and leaning on an ornate cane. They both looked up, the young woman smiling, the old woman frowning.

"Hi," Gloria said. "I'm—"

"You're the new lawyer," the old woman cut in, pointing her cane.

"That's right, I'm Gloria Dalton."

"I'm Cecily Knowles," the young woman said. "And this is my aunt, Jules Lamborne."

The woman that Penny had hinted might know something about the voodoo doll. "It's nice to meet you," Gloria said pleasantly.

Jules squinted and lifted a bent finger. "You can't *cacher* here, missy."

Gloria blinked at the woman's accusatory words. "Pardon me?"

Cecily laughed nervously. "Aunt Jules, why would Gloria be hiding? Please forgive my aunt. She gets confused sometimes."

Jules sniffed. "The only person confused is the lady lawyer."

"That's enough," Cecily chided, then turned a sad smile back to Gloria. "We heard about Steve Chasen—we're very sorry."

"No, we're not," Jules said sharply. "That man was spreading poison around this town."

Gloria's pulse picked up. Did the old woman know something about Steve Chasen's blackmail scheme? "What do you mean, Ms. Lamborne?"

"You'll learn soon enough," Jules muttered, then headed toward the door.

"Ms. Lamborne," Gloria said, then weighed her words when the old woman looked back, waiting. "Someone left a voodoo doll by the door of the law office the morning of Steve's accident. Penny Francisco said you might know something about it."

A light came into the old woman's eyes, but she shook her head. "Not me, although I'm not surprised." Jules leaned forward on her cane. "Folks spend all their time bein' scared of them dolls, when they should be grateful."

"Grateful?"

"Grateful for the warning of what is to come. Not everyone gets a chance to make things right." Jules gave her a pointed look, then left. Gloria stared after the old woman, her skin prickling. How bizarre that she'd accused Gloria of hiding.

"Sorry about that," Cecily said brightly. "My aunt is one hundred and nine years old—the oldest person in the whole state."

"Really? She's a very interesting lady."

"Yeah. But sometimes she uses her eccentricities to scare people, to make them think she's a witch or something." Cecily gave a dismissive little wave. "Don't pay her any mind. Now, what can I do for you?"

Gloria piled her clothes on the counter. "I seem to be having some bad luck with my clothes since I arrived. If you can't get out all the stains, I understand."

Cecily smiled as she sorted through the clothes. "I enjoy a challenge. Is the day after tomorrow soon enough for you to pick them up?"

"Yes, that's fine." Gloria moistened her lips. "From

your aunt's comment, I gather that Steve Chasen wasn't a popular guy."

Cecily shrugged. "I really didn't know him very well, but he wasn't overly friendly. He brought in his clothes a couple of times, but he complained about everything—the way I folded his shirts, the way I creased his pants. I finally told him he should find another dry cleaner, and he didn't come back."

"Is there another dry cleaner in town?"

"No—the nearest competition is in the city, but I guess he decided it was worth the drive. Whatever. For all I know, he could have been a nice guy who had hang-ups about his clothes."

"That's generous of you."

The woman crossed herself. "It's bad luck to speak ill of the dead."

The door behind them opened and Guy Bishop walked in, carrying a laundry bag. "Hi, Cecily . . . Gloria."

"Hello," Gloria murmured, noting the man's body language seemed tense as he handed a yellow pickup ticket to Cecily.

"Guy, I tried everything, but I couldn't get the stain out of your white dress shirt."

"That's okay," he said with a dismissive wave, then he gave a little laugh. "I'm sure I spilled tea or something on it at the shop." He gave her a flirtatious wink that made the young woman blush, and Gloria wondered if the man was bisexual, or if he was being coy. She moved toward the door to leave, but when Cecily turned around to the carousel of clothing hanging behind her, Guy smiled at Gloria.

"How are the repairs to your office coming along?"

he asked as he pulled shirts from his laundry bag and heaped them on the counter. The shirt he placed on top had dark stains around the cuff—the health food store was indeed a messy place to work.

"We're waiting for supplies," she said, "but hopefully, Elton can get started soon."

He nodded, then cleared his throat. "Any news on funeral arrangements for Steve Chasen?"

He seemed to be going out of his way to act casual. "I told Chief Riley that I would arrange a memorial service after the body is released."

"When will that be?"

"I'm not sure, probably today or tomorrow. I'll be happy to let you know when things are finalized."

"Thanks," he said. "You can reach me at the store."

He was either being conscientious, or he was eager to see the blackmailing Steve buried. "I'll be in touch. By the way, would either of you be interested in taking in Steve's cat?"

Guy shook his head. "I'm not a cat person."

"My landlord doesn't allow pets," Cecily said. "Sorry."

"That's okay. See you soon."

When Gloria walked out, she smothered a yawn and checked her cell phone in case George had left her a message, trying not to read anything good or bad into the fact that he hadn't gotten back to her yet.

Although the tension was killing her.

On her way to her car, she walked past The Hair Affair beauty salon. The door opened and Marie Gaston emerged, waving. "Good morning, Gloria."

"Good morning," Gloria said, pleased to see the smiling blue-haired woman.

Marie's expression turned to concern. "I heard about the shooting last night in the square—are you okay?"

"I'm fine, it just shook me up a little. The police arrested a man they think accidentally discharged a firearm."

"Jimmy Scaggs—I heard. He packs a gun with him everywhere since he started harvesting black truffles to sell to Penny at the store."

"I heard something about that. It's rather amazing that he can grow them here. And doesn't he use a dog to find them?"

"Yeah. And the fungus is worth so much money, he's paranoid that someone is going to find the place where he grows them." She smiled. "I'm glad you're all right. And by the way, I think you and the chief make a great couple."

Gloria blinked. "Excuse me?"

Marie covered her mouth. "Is it supposed to be a secret?"

A frown pulled at Gloria's mouth even as panic bloomed in her chest. "Chief Riley and I are *not* a couple."

Marie smiled. "Okay, I get it. Don't worry, mum's the word."

Gloria bit down on the inside of her cheek and decided to change the subject. She was half afraid to think about Zane, just in case Marie *could* read her mind. "Marie, Steve Chasen had a cat that needs a home. Do you know anyone who would be interested?"

Marie made a rueful noise. "Steve loved that cat. I have dogs, so I can't take him. But be careful who you give him to—there are a lot of bad people around here who might take in a black cat for some wicked purpose of their own."

Gloria winced. "I hadn't thought of that."

"Sad, huh? I love this freaky little town, but it certainly draws more than its fair share of weirdos—present company excluded, of course."

Gloria managed a little smile, although she'd felt nothing *but* weird since she'd arrived. She said goodbye and walked to her car, glancing around the quiet street and quaint homes situated just outside the shopping center.

A stiff wind picked up dead leaves and scuttled them along the ground, sending the nearly naked trees lining the sidewalks shuddering like frightened beings. She dipped her chin and pulled the collar of her coat around her neck to ward off the chill. What kind of strange wind blew through Mojo that attracted people with dark pasts, who had something to hide?

People like her?

Shivering, she swung into the seat of her car, then glanced back to the storefronts. Guy had exited the dry cleaner's and was holding an armful of clothing under plastic bags. He and Marie were deep in conversation—a heated conversation. Gloria leaned forward for a better look.

Judging from the way Marie shook her finger, Guy appeared to be on the receiving end of the woman's ire. An angry expression crossed his face, and he said something, his eyes blazing. Then he turned to stalk away, but Marie shouted something at his back before walking in the other direction.

Gloria frowned. What was up between the two of them? Were *they* hiding something?

Was it possible she'd moved to the one place where everyone had just as many secrets as she did?

Chapter 13

The argument between the odd couple who worked for Penny—the blue-haired woman with the clandestine superhero boyfriend and the sexually confused man who might have been blackmailed—stayed on Gloria's mind as she drove to the other end of the shopping center and parked near the boarded-up entrance of her law office. From the turned Open sign, it was obvious that Diane was already in the office.

Gloria smiled wistfully. It would be a shame if she had to leave; so far the woman was perhaps the best employee she'd ever had. Gloria pushed open the door to be greeted with the aroma of good coffee . . . and the enthusiastic barking of a rather large blood-hound. Gloria shrieked when he jumped up to plant two dirty paws on her coat and bathe her face with big slurpy licks.

Not unlike the way she'd attacked Zane last night, she conceded wryly.

"Down, Henry," Diane commanded, hurrying in from the hallway.

The dog reluctantly obeyed, and Diane dragged him away by his collar. "I'm so sorry, Ms. Dalton. I hope you don't mind—it's just for the day. He belongs to a friend who's in a little trouble. Henry here is still recovering from an accident and has to be fed his medicine regularly."

Gloria felt her muscles tense in frustration as she removed her coat and dusted off the telltale paw prints. "Diane, it's inappropriate to have an animal in a law office."

"I know," the woman said gently, "but it's just for today—he won't bother anyone, I promise. He doesn't bark, he sleeps most of the time. You won't even know he's here."

Gloria crossed her arms, wavering at the pleading expression on the woman's face. "Well . . . I guess we aren't exactly swamped with clients. What kind of trouble is your friend in?"

"His name is Jimmy Scaggs. There was a misunderstanding last night in the town square."

Gloria's eyebrows flew up. "The guy who shot off a handgun? I was there."

Diane gasped. For the first time, her face hinted that she was older than she looked. "I had no idea—were you injured?"

"No, but he took ten years off my life."

Diane made a distressed noise. "I'm so sorry, and I know Jimmy is sorry, too. He was upset—he said he found a man's body in the woods and was trying to find Chief Riley."

"I heard. Is it common to find bodies lying around in the woods in Mojo?"

Diane's cheeks turned pink. "No. Jimmy's a little eccentric, but he's a good, honest person."

The woman was obviously smitten with the man, Gloria realized suddenly. And when a person is in love, they overlook a lot of things. She knew that much from handling divorces for so many years. She looked at the dog with velvety, elephantine ears. "So this is the mighty truffle hunter."

As if he knew she was talking about him, Henry looked up at her and barked once in affirmation.

"One day," Gloria said, holding up her finger to the dog. "You can stay for one day."

Diane's face erupted into smiles. "Thank you." The phone rang, and she answered. "Law office of Gloria Dalton. Yes, who's speaking? Daniel Guess?" She looked up at Gloria.

Gloria's first instinct was to refuse the call, then she changed her mind and said, "I'll take it." She carried her coat and briefcase into her office, then yanked up the receiver. "Mr. Guess?"

"Call me Daniel," he said smoothly.

"Mr. Guess, I thought that Chief Riley and I made it clear last night that Steve Chasen's death was a tragic accident and nothing more."

"I was just calling to see if you were okay, Ms. Dalton. I heard that there was an incident after I left last night—a shooting?"

A finger of alarm trailed up her neck. "How . . . how did you hear?"

"Police scanner. No self-respecting reporter would be without one."

"You must not have found the incident interesting enough to come back and do a story."

"Not when I heard Jimmy Scaggs's name. The kook is always shooting at someone—he shot at me when I tried to get an interview about his alleged truffle farm."

Gloria smiled at the mental picture of Daniel Guess turning tail and running through the woods while an unstable man fired warning shots. "Surely, Mr. Guess, there's enough news in New Orleans without you trying to stir up something in little old Mojo."

"Nice try, Ms. Dalton, but you can't get rid of me that easily. Besides, one of the most shocking stories of the year came out of little old Mojo. The question is," he said, his voice dipping to taunt her, "are you trying to protect the town, or are you hiding something?"

Gloria's throat convulsed, but she strove to maintain a steady voice. "Good-bye, Mr. Guess."

She banged down the phone, wondering if the man knew something about her or if he was simply pushing her buttons to try to get her to say something that she would regret.

Gloria downed her cup of coffee, rolled up her sleeves, and threw herself into her files, so happy to be distracted from her own personal crises that she barely paused when Diane floated in and out to refill her mug. She scribbled notes on filing a suit against

Steve's estate on behalf of Mona but idly wondered how much of Mona's motivation lay in the fact that Steve had been blackmailing her. Had he extracted a lot of money from Mona? And what secrets had he threatened her with? Did the absence of information in her folder mean that Mona and Steve had reached a mutually acceptable agreement, or had Mona somehow turned the tables on Steve and forced him to abandon his plan?

Setting aside the disturbing thoughts, she called several of Deke's former clients and made appointments to finish work in progress: wills, deed changes, property closings. Tedious work to other attorneys, but soothing and *normal* to Gloria, who was accustomed to couples threatening to smear each other's reputations and tear their children in half.

A couple of Deke's clients had already secured another attorney, but most of them were happy to allow her to tie up loose ends. She finished a few projects and dropped them in her out-box, along with invoices that, if she had to leave town, she would never collect on, she admitted wryly.

On the other hand, until George told her to leave town, she had to conduct business as if nothing was wrong. She had savings to live on for a while, but she couldn't push revenue too far into the future in case . . .

In case things worked out, she thought desperately, knowing how much of a long shot she was betting on.

Just before 2:00 p.m., Diane buzzed her office and announced that Sheena Linder and her sister Jodi were there. Gloria told Diane to show them in, then stood and took a deep breath—Penny Francisco referred to her ex-husband's shack-up honey as a lot of things, "Litigious Linder" being among them because of the habit the woman had of suing for personal injury.

Apparently, the income from personal injury suits supplemented her revenue from her Forever Sun Tanning Salon, which, judging from the orange-ish hue of many Mojo residents, must be doing pretty well.

As the door opened, Gloria reminded herself to remain objective. Sheena's sister Jodi had been rescued from the horrors of her captors at the voodoo museum due in large part to Penny's curiosity and ingenuity, and Sheena had publicly thanked the woman whose husband she'd stolen. Maybe the incident had humbled her.

"Get away from me!" Sheena screamed at Henry, who stood with his nose imbedded in her crotch.

"Diane," Gloria said, a warning note in her voice.

Diane murmured apologies and dragged the dog away from Sheena's privates.

"I'm sorry about that," Gloria said, stepping to the front of her desk. "Please come in."

Sheena, now in a huff, was dazzling in her pink-and-black tiger-striped Lycra dress and pink stiletto heels, her bared teeth blinding against her too-tan skin. Her sister, dressed more demurely in loose jeans and a sweater, held her head down, her long blonde hair secured in a ponytail, her pretty face pale and devoid of makeup.

Gloria introduced herself and asked the women to have a seat.

Sheena posed herself in one of the guest chairs, while Jodi eased into a chair and proceeded to make herself as small as possible. Gloria remembered from the newspaper accounts that the young woman was only nineteen. At the moment she looked older than her years, and anxious.

"Would you like a cup of coffee or tea?" Gloria offered.

"No, thanks," Sheena said crisply. "We're kinda in a hurry."

Apparently, she spoke for both of them, Gloria decided as she took her own chair. "Okay. What can I do for you?"

"As you know," Sheena said, "my sister was subjected to unspeakable acts in that horrible voodoo museum."

Gloria shot a sympathetic look toward Jodi, who had tensed and refused to make eye contact.

"Yes," Gloria murmured. "And I'm so sorry for your ordeal."

Jodi's gaze flickered up, wary.

"Any-hoo," Sheena said, "we've been approached by a ton of Hollywood producers offering to buy Jodi's story, and we're having a heck of a time trying to make sense of it all."

Gloria's pulse spiked in surprise and, God help her, curiosity. "I'm no literary attorney, but I'm familiar with contract law and can at least help you narrow down the offers. How many do you have?"

"Forty-three," Sheena said, then she swung a pink gym bag to the top of the desk with a thud. "I brought copies."

Gloria unzipped the bag and stared at the mound

of papers. "Okay. But before I get started, I need to know—what are you looking for?"

"Money," Sheena said.

"Privacy," Jodi said at the same time.

The sisters glared at each other, and Gloria cleared her throat delicately. "It seems that the two of you have slightly different objectives."

"Completely opposite objectives," Jodi said. "I don't want to be the subject of some cheesy movie of the week."

"It won't be cheesy," Sheena said. "Honey, I'm gonna write the screenplay, so it'll be nothing but class all the way." She used her three-inch-long pinkie nail to pick something out of her teeth, then flashed a cajoling smile.

Jodi sent Gloria a pleading look—the young woman was in quite a predicament.

"Jodi," Gloria said carefully, "the unfortunate fact is that your story was widely covered in the media and, because of the extensive exposure, is considered to be in the public domain. A television or film producer doesn't need your permission in order to do a movie about your ordeal." She steepled her hands on the top of the desk. "If you don't sign a deal, they're likely to just make up the details for the sake of shock value for their audience. Your best bet might be to form an alliance with a producer that you feel will be the most fair, and who will give you as much control as possible over the way the story is told."

"Told ya," Sheena said, bouncing her foot.

"That said," Gloria said with a little more inflection, "no one can compel you to share your very personal and traumatic story."

A frown crossed Sheena's face. "But with the kind of money they're offering, we—I mean, *my sister*—will be set for the rest of her life."

"A class suit has already been filed against the owner of the museum and the people involved," Jodi said.

"Those people are in jail!" Sheena shrieked. "What little money they have will be eaten up in their own criminal cases! The most you can hope for is a couple of hundred dollars from those crummy chocolate bars that me and everyone else in town is hawking!"

Jodi's jaw hardened. "Money isn't going to make up for what happened to me."

Sheena seemed to soften as she reached over to touch her sister's arm. "Of course it won't, honey, but telling your story might be therapeutic. And if you have money, at least you don't have to worry about looking for a job right away. You can recuperate—you know, travel and shop!"

Jodi shook her head. "Sheena, you know if somebody pays me a lot of money for my story, our kinfolk are going to come out of the woodwork with their hands stuck out."

Sheena scowled. "You let me take care of those leeches."

The younger woman hesitated, pressed her lips together, then glanced at Gloria. "You'll help us?"

Gloria smiled. "I'll do everything in my power to help you reach a decision that's right for you."

"And I don't have to sign any of those papers if I don't want to?"

"Absolutely not."

Sheena clapped her hands. "Great, so we're in business!"

Jodi frowned.

Sheena gave a dismissive wave. "You know what I mean." She stood and pulled the stretchy neckline of her dress lower. "We'll wait for your call, Ms. Dalton, but time is of the essence—we need to strike while the iron is hot. Any day a killer whale could save a kid or something and knock Jodi right out of the headlines."

Gloria conjured up a smile. "Yes, Ms. Linder. I'll be in touch."

She escorted the women out into the reception area, and Sheena cocked her hip toward the boarded-up window. "Too bad about Steve Chasen—he was a good customer at the tanning salon."

"There will be a memorial service soon," Gloria offered.

Sheena sniffed. "I didn't know him *that* well." Then she angled her head. "You're not expecting me to refund the money for his unused tanning sessions, are you? Because he signed a contract that said no refunds, even in the event of death."

Gloria blinked. "Er . . . no, I don't believe anyone is expecting a refund."

Sheena squinted at Gloria. "You could use a little color yourself—God, you're pale for a brunette. Is that your natural hair color?"

"Yes," Gloria lied, touching her curls. Suddenly she panicked, then manufactured a laugh. "I mean, I cover my grays, of course."

"Hm. Well, I wouldn't mind if you wanted to use the rest of Steve's sessions."

"I, er . . . thanks."

"Zane said you haven't been able to find any next of kin yet."

Gloria blinked. "Zane?"

"Chief Riley," Sheena said, licking her pink, pouty lips. "We're on a first-name basis. In fact, I'm going to write him a part in the script. With those bedroom eyes and those bedrock shoulders, he'll be perfect on the big screen."

Gloria pursed her mouth. "You think?"

A sly smile slid across the woman's face as she lowered her voice conspiratorially. "Oh, honey, I *know.* Of course, he'll have to put in some time on my casting couch, if you know what I mean." The woman curled her lip and made a growling noise.

Gloria pasted a tight smile on her mouth and was spared answering by Jodi clearing her throat insistently.

Sheena straightened and jammed enormous sunglasses on her face. "We'll expect to hear from you soon. Toodle-loo."

The women left, and Gloria stood at the open door, watching them, unable to stem the spark of jealousy at Sheena's stunning curves. They would turn any man's head.

And Zane was definitely a man.

At their car, Sheena made a movement to hug her younger sister, but the woman stiffened and drew away. Gloria felt a pang of sympathy for both of them. Sheena seemed to want what was best for her sister, but perhaps she wasn't the best at showing it. Jodi, on the other hand, appeared to be so emotionally wounded—understandably—from her ordeal that she seemed to have collapsed upon herself.

Gloria had an idea of what the woman was feeling. Her own ordeal paled in comparison to what Jodi Reynolds had experienced, but she knew what it was like to withdraw from human interaction, to be suspicious of everyone she encountered, to wish for life to be the way it once had been . . . before she knew that there were evil people in the world.

The urge to counsel them billowed in her chest. Some of the most satisfying moments in her career had been when a referral to a family counselor had resulted in saving a marriage versus processing a divorce. Her boss had once chastised her that they didn't make money on reconciliations, but Gloria hadn't cared. Maybe when she next met with Sheena and Jodi, she would recommend someone for them both to talk to.

She had started to close the door when another car pulled into the parking lot. An attractive man who looked vaguely familiar emerged. When he smiled at her, she remembered meeting him at the health food store.

"Ms. Dalton," he said amiably, walking up with a folder under his arm. "I'm Cameron Phelps—BJ introduced us the other day."

"Yes. Hello, Mr. Phelps," she said, extending her hand.

He took it and held on a second longer than necessary. "I was hoping you could process some paperwork for me. Do I need an appointment?"

"No," she said, acknowledging that he was a very

appealing man—especially when he smiled. She couldn't help but compare it to the permanent frown on Zane's face. "Come in, Mr. Phelps."

"Call me Cameron," he said.

She nodded. "Cameron, I'm Gloria. Please excuse our mess—there was an accident a few days ago."

"I heard. I'm sorry about your employee."

"Thank you." She introduced him to Diane, who nodded pleasantly. Suddenly a baying howl sounded from the bathroom.

Diane squirmed under Gloria's raised eyebrows. "I figured he wouldn't bother anyone in there."

Gloria turned an embarrassed smile back to Cameron, who was fighting a grin. "Why don't we continue in my office."

When they were both settled, she clasped her hands on her desk. "What can I do for you?"

"I'm getting divorced."

"I'm sorry to hear that," she murmured.

He lifted his hands. "Me, too, but . . . it happens. With my job, I travel all the time. My wife said I was too involved in my work."

"Your work with the missing persons database is extremely important . . . and admirable."

A small smile lifted the corners of a very nice mouth. "Thanks, but I guess she has a different point of view."

"Is it an amicable split?"

He nodded and placed the folder on her desk. "I just need to sign the papers. They look okay to me, but I thought I should run them by a lawyer, and BJ said that you used to be a divorce attorney."

"Family law," she corrected with a smile, "which included many divorces."

He shifted in his seat. "It's none of my business, but why would a woman like you want to move from New Orleans to a small town like Mojo?"

She fidgeted with an ink pen. "Just looking for a change, I guess."

"Do you have any family nearby?"

She thought of her mother, and a pang of sadness barbed through her heart. "Um . . . no."

Cameron looked sheepish. "I didn't mean to pry—that was my way of asking if you're married."

"Oh." A flush warmed her cheeks. "No, I'm not married."

He gave a little laugh. "I guess I'd better get divorced before I start dating, huh?"

To cover the happily awkward moment, she reached for the file. "I'll be glad to take a look at the forms. When do you need them back?"

"No rush," he said, standing. "Sometime in the next week if you can manage it. I'll be working with the task force for at least the next month—there's still a lot of work to be done."

"Are you making any progress?" she asked, rising to follow him to the door.

He pressed his lips together in hesitation. "Guess it'll be public soon enough—two missing persons on the database have been matched to DNA found in the museum."

She winced. "I know that's comforting news for the families, but so tragic. And more bad press for the town, I'm afraid."

He gave her a wry smile. "Yeah. Are you starting to doubt your decision to move here?"

You have no idea. She opened the door and preceded him into the reception area. "How can I reach you when your paperwork is ready?"

"My cell phone doesn't work here, so until I switch service, I'm staying at the Browning Motel. You can leave a message for me there." Cameron locked gazes with her and leaned an inch closer. His mouth opened, as if he wanted to say something else, but Diane's subtle throat-clearing caught Gloria's attention. When she turned, Zane was standing there, filling out every inch of his tailored navy blue uniform, looking back and forth between Gloria and Cameron.

She jerked back guiltily, then felt foolish because she had nothing to feel guilty about—she hadn't been involved with Zane for a long time now.

And as far as he knew, they'd *never* been involved.

"Hello, Chief," she said cheerfully.

Instead of responding, he held up a key, then placed it on Diane's desk. "As promised. See you later." He glanced at Cameron. "Phelps," he added with a nod, then strode out the front door, allowing it to close with a bang.

Cameron gave her a quizzical look, then said good-bye.

After he left, Gloria nibbled on her thumbnail. The man's open interest in her made her wonder: If she moved again and changed her name, was it possible that she could find a nice guy to settle down with? Could she force her brain to compartmentalize her life, to shut off the piece that she was supposed to forget and simply move forward?

Diane cleared her throat again. "That young fellow seems to like you."

"I'm handling his divorce papers."

Diane stood and murmured, "I meant the other one." Then she turned to walk toward the bathroom and a whining Henry.

Gloria frowned, wondering what had led the woman to the conclusion that Zane Riley *liked* her, considering his abrupt behavior.

Of course, she *had* slammed the door in his face last night.

Scooping up the key Zane had left, Gloria called, "I'm going to feed Steve Chasen's cat. I'll be back soon."

Unless I just keep driving, she thought hysterically.

Chapter 14

Gloria unlocked the door to Steve's house, flipped on a light, and called out to the cat in the stillness. "Here, kitty, kitty."

The house was cool and quiet . . . deadly quiet. She gripped her purse tighter, drawing comfort from her .38 tucked inside, then sat down in front of Steve's computer and tried a few more passwords to get in, none of which worked. There were no phone messages, which relieved her tension a bit. Maybe the man who'd called would simply go away.

She spotted the stack of unopened mail and bit into her lip. Then she reached for it and sorted through, staring at the return addresses. When she got to his cell phone bill, she hesitated, then ran her thumb under the flap and withdrew the statement.

A federal offense, but then again, she had federal contacts.

Steve Chasen used his cell phone heavily. There were lots of calls to the Baton Rouge area code. She refolded the bill, intending to take it with her.

Her stomach growled, and she regretted skipping lunch. Remembering Steve's drawer of snacks, she slid it open and rooted through the bags of chips, Little Debbie cakes, and candy bars, settling for one of the fund-raising candy bars being sold all over town.

This was definitely not on her high-protein diet, she thought wryly, but she needed a quick energy boost.

She tore away the white Thank You! wrapper and began to munch on the candy bar. At first, the fantastic sweetness of the milk chocolate tasted strange on her tongue, a testament to how long it had been since she'd eaten chocolate. But its effects were almost instantaneous, the rich, gooey thickness on her tongue delivering sugar, caffeine, and other mood-altering stimulants into her system.

She sighed, remembering how Zane used to tease her about her chocoholic ways. He'd always bought her chocolates for special occasions, saying he had a vested interest in helping her maintain her curves. She smiled at the memory, chewing slowly to prolong the pleasure. When the first candy bar was gone, she fished the second one from the drawer and ripped off the wrapper.

What the hell—it felt good to let go . . . to indulge. She couldn't remember the last time she'd done something just because it felt good. Maybe she couldn't have Zane, but she could have empty calories.

She had just wolfed down the second bar when the black cat appeared at the door leading into the hallway, his ears perked, his whiskers twitching. He sniffed the air, then trotted to her and rubbed against her pants leg, leaving a layer of dark hair. She grimaced, thinking she hadn't yet unpacked her lint brush.

Not that it mattered, considering the fact that she'd dropped bits of chocolate all over her beige jacket. She wiped at them, smearing them and making matters worse.

Gloria sighed. It didn't take ESP to know that another trip to the dry cleaner was in her near future.

"Come on, cat," she said, dropping the candy wrappers into the trash and licking her fingers. Feeling flush with carbohydrates, she walked into the kitchen with the cat trotting behind. Gloria noted with a twinge of sadness the dishes that Steve had left in the sink, the bananas in a stainless steel bowl that were turning brown and drawing gnats. Evidence of a life interrupted. No matter how conniving the man had been, he hadn't deserved to be cut down at such a young age.

On the other hand, if he'd lived, how many lives would he have tried to destroy?

Her thoughts kept darting back to the voodoo doll and Jules Lamborne's words about it being a warning. Had someone merely been trying to scare Steve?

Or was magic truly afoot in this strange little town; could someone have foreseen his accident?

She pursed her mouth . . . or even *caused* it?

The cat yowled his impatience.

Gloria frowned down at him. "This is why I don't

have pets. I don't need something else complicating my life. How about someone taking care of me for a change?"

He began to lick himself.

Rolling her eyes heavenward, she opened a can of cat food and emptied it into the dish. When the cat attacked the food, she sighed, hoping she could find someone soon who was willing to take in a black cat. He *was* rather . . . regal, she admitted begrudgingly, with his shiny black coat, prominent whiskers, and red leather collar. Then Gloria squinted at something hanging from the collar.

Was that . . . a *note?*

The breath froze in her lungs even as she tried to convince herself that perhaps Zane had been here and left it for her. She crouched down, but as she reached for the scrap of paper, her hand shook because she knew the idea was next to ludicrous. This could not be good.

She removed the paper from the cat's collar and unfolded it. In neat capital letters was written: I KNOW ABOUT L.L.

Her throat convulsed, and she crumpled the note in her fist. Apparently Steve's partner in crime was picking up where Steve had left off. She jumped at a ringing noise that sounded near her foot, and she lost her balance, falling back on her injured hand and grimacing in pain.

Her cell phone. She rolled over and dug it out of her bag, her heart thudding like a bass drum. The screen read Private Call. What now? After punching the connect button, she said, "Hello."

"Gloria, it's George."

"Hi, George," she said, trying to sound cheerful, as if she could influence the direction of the conversation. She didn't need any more bad news. "What's up?" Slowly, Gloria pushed to her feet and looked around. Was it possible that whoever had left the note was still in the house?

"First of all, I traced the number you gave me to a phone booth in Baton Rouge."

She sighed. "That doesn't help much."

"Sorry. I also ran a background check on the Chasen guy, but I didn't find anything to connect him to Riaz."

She turned her attention back to the phone and exhaled. "But that's good . . . isn't it?"

"It doesn't mean that Riaz hasn't sent someone looking for you and your mother. The dead man and his partner might not be connected to Riaz, but they could have inadvertently tipped off someone in his organization. Riaz's men have scattered, and one of the witnesses who refused protection is missing." A frustrated noise sounded over the line. "If you know where your mother is, Gloria, now's the time to say so."

"I don't."

"Have you heard from her since she left WITSEC?"

"No," Gloria said, then closed her eyes. "But . . ."

"But what?"

"But . . . if you want to look for her, you might start in New Orleans."

"Where you've been living," he bit out. "So you *have* been holding out on me."

"No, I haven't," she said evenly. "I don't know

where my mother is, but she always talked about living in New Orleans, how exciting it would be."

"Is that why you moved there?"

Gloria gave a little laugh. "Yeah. I had this fantasy of walking into her one day at a festival on Jackson Square."

"But you never did?"

"No." She blinked back tears. "I'm afraid that she's . . . dead."

"Why do you say that?"

She inhaled deeply, then exhaled to calm her thoughts. "I guess because some days I'd rather think she's dead than to think that she's alive and doesn't want to see me."

"You know she left to protect you, Gloria. Your mother always worried that Riaz would find her someday and would make her pay for testifying against him. And she knew that if he found the two of you, he'd use you to get to her."

He was right—her mother was protecting her the best way she knew how. But it still hurt. . . .

"Gloria, I wasn't supposed to tell you this, but the night that someone broke into your mother's home in Arizona, she was beaten up pretty bad."

Gloria's heart clenched. "Was she okay?"

"They left her for dead. She was terrified, didn't want you to see her like that. That's why she took off—she was afraid the men would come back."

Gloria swallowed past a lump of emotion—and if the men had found her mother, no one would be the wiser. She could have died a brutal death . . . alone . . .

"Are you there?" he asked.

She sniffed mightily and forced herself to think.

"Yeah, I'm here. In fact, I'm at Steve Chasen's house and his cat just brought me a message."

"What?"

She told him about the cryptic note. "What do you think I should do?"

"I wish I had something concrete for you on Riaz, but I don't. To be on the safe side, I think you should relocate. Especially considering that some strange things are going on in that little voodoo town of yours."

Gloria pinched the bridge of her nose in an attempt to ease the pressure building there. "But I just moved."

"Have you unpacked?"

"Not entirely."

"Then it'll be easy for you to go somewhere else."

She shook her head. "And change my name . . . again."

"To be safe, yes."

"Safe?" A bitter laugh escaped her throat. "You told me fourteen years ago that I'd be safe, George, if I changed my name and forgot the life I left behind. But I've been looking over my shoulder ever since, and I haven't seen my mother in almost ten years." She covered her mouth with her hand to choke back a sob before regaining her composure enough to talk. "Don't patronize me, George."

"Gloria," he said, his voice gentling, "we do what we can. With all the new homeland security measures, we're stretched thin. And your mother dropping out of the program has complicated matters even more. My advice is that you relocate. You can't possibly be attached to this Mojo place in such a short time."

Zane's face materialized in her mind—could she leave him again, leave him with yet more unanswered questions?

"Gloria? Is there something you aren't telling me?"

A touch on her leg startled her until she realized that the black cat was rubbing himself against her again, twining around her legs. She put a hand to her head. "Well . . . it's hardly worth mentioning, really."

"I'm listening."

A false little laugh bubbled up and out, sounding more like a hiccup. "As it turns out . . . I mean, I had no idea when I moved here . . . and he just moved here himself to be the chief of police—"

"*Who,* Gloria?"

"Zane Riley—a boy who went to my high school in Schilling."

"Did he recognize you?"

"No. How could he? I don't bear any resemblance to the way I looked then."

"Wait a minute—was this guy a boyfriend?"

She swallowed. "Sort of . . . yes. He was my boyfriend when I . . . left. I gave you a letter to give to him." She inhaled. "But you didn't mail that letter, did you?"

Ten seconds of silence passed. "It was too risky. And better for everyone to make a clean break."

She bit down on the inside of her cheek to stem a wall of frustrated tears.

"Do you still have feelings for this man?" George asked.

"I . . . didn't say that."

"Gloria, this is bad. If he recognizes you, your cover will be blown."

"Zane wouldn't do anything to hurt me."

"Not purposely, perhaps. But all it takes is for one person who knows you to tell one other person, who'll tell someone else. And this guy might get it into his head to try to protect you, Gloria, but he can't. No matter what kind of supercop he is, he's no match for Riaz's men. We went over this a thousand times during orientation. You can't tell *anyone* your real name—that's how it all begins to unravel."

Funny, but she was already feeling frayed around the edges.

A sharp rap on the front door brought her head around and her heart to her throat. She slipped to the kitchen window and peeked outside to see Zane's cruiser sitting behind her car. "I have to go, George."

"Okay. Let me know what you decide to do."

She disconnected the call and walked toward the front door, the cat tangling in her legs just as Zane was walking inside. His expression was dark.

"Diane Davidson said I could find you here," he said without preamble.

"I was feeding the cat," she said, shoving her phone and the note into her pocket. "Is something wrong?"

"The ME's office in New Orleans just called."

"Has Steve's body been released?"

"Soon, but there's a problem."

"What kind of problem?"

Zane looked grim. "Steve Chasen's death wasn't an accident—he was murdered."

Chapter 15

Gloria felt her jaw loosen as Zane's words sank in. Something about Steve being . . . *murdered?*

"*What?*" She shook her head in confusion. "*How?*"

"He was poisoned. The ME found cyanide in his stomach—he thinks it was in a candy bar he ate."

Her eyes rounded. "A candy bar?"

"As in the fund-raising candy that's being sold all over town."

"Oh, my God." Her mind reeled at the pointlessness of the man's death.

A muscle jumped in Zane's jaw. "We don't know yet if someone was targeting Chasen, or if it's some sort of product tampering. The media has been asked to run emergency warnings wherever the candy is being sold. My officers are already going around town and bagging all that they can find."

Her hand flew to her mouth, still humming from the sweet buzz of chocolate. "There were two candy bars in his desk drawer. I ate"—she swallowed hard as her cheeks warmed in embarrassment—"both of them."

Alarm flared in Zane's eyes as he grabbed her arm. "You ate two of the fund-raising candy bars? When?"

"Just . . . now," she said, brushing at the bits of chocolate smeared into her lapels.

"Are you feeling okay?"

She touched her rolling stomach. "I . . . don't know. I'm upset."

"Sit down," he said, guiding her to the couch while reaching for his phone. "I'm calling the EMTs."

Gloria's heartbeat thudded in her ears as she sank into the couch, comforted by Zane's presence as he sat next to her on the edge of the couch. A hysterical laugh bubbled in her chest—surely the first candy she'd eaten in years couldn't be poisoned?

Death by chocolate?

Zane's voice sounded calm when he was connected to the EMTs, but his worried gaze was locked on her. "I have a possible cyanide ingestion." He rattled off the house address. "What symptoms should I be looking for?" He turned his mouth away from the receiver. "Gloria, is your breathing accelerated?"

It was, but how much of that could be attributed to Zane's sitting next to her? "Uh . . . some."

"I need to take your pulse," he said, wedging the phone between his ear and shoulder. He turned over her wrist and pressed two blunt-tipped fingers to her skin. His touch ignited little firestorms all over her body.

"Her pulse seems elevated," he said into the phone.

Of course it is, she thought, closing her eyes briefly. Unfortunately, the symptoms of cyanide poisoning seemed to rival being in proximity to the love of her life.

"Are you dizzy or nauseated?"

"A little," she admitted, both of which could be explained away by the fact that Zane's thigh was touching hers, or by the Ménière's, or by the fact that she hadn't eaten chocolate in a long damn time.

He reported the information to the person on the line, asked for an estimated time of arrival, then disconnected the call. "They'll be here in two minutes. The EMT said try not to throw up." His lopsided smile was at odds with the worry in his eyes.

"It's probably just the shock of the news," she said, gulping air.

"Better safe than sorry. Hey, I thought you didn't like chocolate," he said in a teasing voice.

"I . . . was weak," she murmured, mesmerized by the concern and warmth in his gray eyes. Her lungs contracted painfully, and she was overcome with the urge to tell Zane who she was, what had happened, and that she'd never stopped loving him. If she *had* ingested cyanide and it was working its way through her system, she could be dying . . . she might have only minutes to live . . . surely she was allowed a deathbed confession to right the wrongs that had been done to them.

"Zane?"

"Yes?" he said, angling his big body closer, his eyes gentle and . . . anxious.

She faltered, the words dying on her tongue as her heart ballooned to push the air out of her lungs. Unable to stop herself, she reached forward, wrapped her hand around the nape of his neck, and yanked his mouth to hers. After his initial shock, the spontaneous kiss exploded.

He slanted his lips against hers hungrily, as if he understood her urgency. She responded with a soft moan, opening up to the flick of his tongue, thinking if she had to die, this was the way she wanted to go . . . in Zane's arms . . . wait—*die?*

She wrenched away suddenly and pulled back, touching her fingers to his mouth. "I can't believe I did that! What if I poisoned you?"

A little smile lifted his mouth, and he clasped her fingers in his hand. "I don't think a kiss would expose me, although I probably should let you breathe on your own as long as possible. But don't worry—I know CPR, and I'm not afraid to use it."

She tried to smile, but inside she was spiraling out of control. She was aching to tell Zane the truth, but was she latching on to an excuse? The lightheadedness was probably due to the fact that blood had abandoned her brain to engorge other areas.

"Zane," she said, then inhaled for strength.

"I'm here," he said, stroking her fingers with his thumb indulgently, as if she were a child. "You're going to be fine."

"I . . . I have something to tell you." Moisture gathered on her hairline.

The sound of an ambulance siren split the air. He winked and said, "Hold that thought," then rose and went to open the door. In seconds, a team of female EMTs burst in, carrying bags and equipment.

"How are you feeling?" one of them asked as she adjusted a stethoscope and pressed the end to Gloria's chest.

"Fine . . . I think," she said, trying not to make eye contact with Zane and wondering which was worse—dying of cyanide poisoning, or dying of embarrassment if her symptoms turned out to be nothing more than arousal.

"Breathe deeply for me," the woman said, her expression intent.

Gloria did as she was told, feeling more and more foolish as the EMTs took and recorded her vitals and fired questions at her.

"Does your breathing feel restricted?"

Only when she looked at Zane. "No."

"Are your eyes burning or itching?"

"A little, but that's probably because of the cat hair."

"Are you nauseated?"

"Not anymore . . . I'm not accustomed to eating sweets, so that might account for the way I was feeling."

"Dizzy?"

"Not at the moment."

"Are you taking any medications?"

She hesitated and looked up to find Zane listening.

"Ma'am? Are you taking any medications?"

She leaned forward and murmured, "Meclazine."

"Meclazine?" the EMT asked. "For vertigo?"

"That's right," Gloria said, refusing to look at Zane. Had he heard? Would he remember? Would he make the connection?

"That would explain the dizziness," the other woman muttered.

"And the nausea," the first woman said, expelling a sigh of relief. She put the stethoscope back to Gloria's chest. "Your breathing sounds fine, and your pulse has returned to normal." She removed the stethoscope and stood to include Zane in the conversation. "If the candy bar contained cyanide, it wasn't a lethal dose. Still, you'll want to have the wrappers tested."

She looked back to Gloria. "If you start to experience shortness of breath or tremors, or convulsions, call 911 immediately."

Gloria nodded, her head practically lolling in relief, but simultaneously ready to combust with humiliation. Zane probably thought she was utterly ridiculous. Her skin tingled—especially her lips, where the imprint of Zane's mouth had left a throbbing impression. When the EMTs left and Zane turned back to give her a reassuring smile, she could barely push herself to her feet.

"I'm sorry for the false alarm," she said, averting her gaze and wanting to dissolve.

"Don't worry about it," he said.

"And the, um, potentially poisonous kiss." She lifted her gaze to find him wiping away a smile.

"I'm not complaining. And I'm glad you're okay—I can't imagine losing you before I even got to know you."

The desire that darkened his eyes sent a stab of alarm to her chest and instant heat to her nether regions. The man had no idea how hard he was making this for her. She felt as if she was coming apart at the emotional seams.

"What was it you wanted to tell me?"

She blinked. "Pardon me?"

"You said you had something to tell me."

"Tell you?" The moisture evaporated from her mouth as her mind clouded with panic—she'd almost blurted the secret she'd held for nearly fourteen years. It would have been for nothing and could have led to people being hurt . . . all because she'd had a weak moment.

She swallowed, her mind racing for an explanation. "Right. I was going to tell you . . . I was going to tell you . . . that there was a half box of candy bars on Steve's desk at my office." Her relief at coming up with a legitimate lie left her breathless.

Then she was struck once again by her narrow brush with death; she'd come so close to eating one of the candy bars herself that morning before Marie had appeared with the muffins.

"What happened to the candy bars?" Zane asked.

"I assume they were thrown out in the debris. Elton the handyman might know."

Zane picked up his radio and instructed one of his officers to track down Elton and the box of candy from the office. Then he used a handkerchief to fish the wrappers out of the trash and drop them into a brown bag, which he tagged.

"How are you feeling?" he asked, his expression pensive.

"Better," she said, straightening to prove that she could hold herself up, when inside she was falling apart at the cumulative events of the day.

"Well enough to help me look around the house for other candy bars?"

She nodded, relieved to have something to do. They performed a search of the kitchen and other places where Steve might have hidden snacks but didn't find any more of the fund-raising candy. In the bedroom with the broken window, the plastic was loose, flapping in the cutting wind.

An entrance point for whoever had left the note? Gloria wondered, the piece of paper burning through her pocket into her thigh. "It looks like someone has been in here. Some of the electronic equipment is missing," she said, gesturing to shortened stacks of goods.

"Did you notice anything else missing?"

"No," she said, telling herself that she wasn't lying by not telling him about the note.

"All this equipment is just too tempting for a petty thief to pass up," Zane said. He found two boards in the garage, retrieved a toolbox from his cruiser, and nailed them in a crude X over the opening. "I'll get someone over here to fix the window," he said. "Maybe someone from the bank, since they probably hold the mortgage. And I'll warn the pawn shops to be on the lookout for brand-new DVD players." He sounded distracted, undoubtedly because he had other, more urgent, things on his mind—the cyanide poisoning was likely to cause a panic.

"If you're ready to go, I'll walk out with you," he offered.

They left the house together, and Gloria used her key to lock up. But her hand shook as the turn of events began to sink in. The only thing worse than Steve being intentionally poisoned was the thought of other tainted candy bars floating around. "Do you know how many candy bars are out there?"

"Hundreds, maybe thousands." He made a rueful noise in his throat. "Right now, Steve Chasen being targeted for murder is the lesser of the two evils that we could possibly have on our hands."

Her mind spun from all the evil "possibilities" that Zane didn't even know about . . . yet.

"The body will be released tomorrow if you're still up to planning a memorial."

She nodded. "Of course. I'll contact the funeral home."

"Gloria," he said, his eyes solemn, "now that this could be a homicide, do you know of anyone who'd want to hurt Chasen?"

Gloria bit into her lip. Guy Bishop? Ziggy Hines? Mona Black? And anyone else Steve might have blackmailed. But how could she reveal that information without exposing her own file . . . and motive? "No."

He frowned. "What about that voodoo doll?"

"What about it?"

"You said it was dressed in fabric that was similar to Chasen's jacket?"

"That's right."

He pinched the bridge of his nose, as if it pained him to say what he was thinking. "Do you still have it?"

"Yes—it's at my place."

"I guess I'll be needing it after all."

She lifted her eyebrows. "Oh, do you believe in voodoo now?"

"Of course not," he said with a scowl. "But if Chasen was poisoned intentionally, the killer might have left the doll as a calling card."

"Do you want me to bring it by the station?"

"No," he barked, making her jump. "I don't want anyone knowing about this who doesn't have to know, got it? And I *don't* want to read anything about that damned voodoo doll in the *Post*."

She crossed her arms, irritation plucking her already raw nerves. "If you do, Chief Riley, the source won't be me."

His radio blasted out a call. "I have to go," he said, the frown still marring his forehead. "I'll call you and arrange to get the doll when things have settled down." He gave her a pointed look. "*If* things settle down."

He stalked toward his car, talking into his radio. His shoulders were stiff, his expression anxious. Gloria fisted her hands in frustration. She ached to tell him that her life was just as complicated as his. And she longed to go after him, to comfort him, to tell him . . . what? That everything was going to be okay?

A hysterical laugh bubbled up in her chest as she watched him drive away. She was starting to think that okay was a place she'd never see again.

She closed her eyes and exhaled slowly. What should she do now—plan Steve Chasen's memorial? Give him up as a blackmailer? Get the hell out of town?

She pulled the crumpled note from her pocket and stared at it. I KNOW ABOUT L.L. Her cell phone rang, startling her. Private Call flashed on the screen.

Hoping it was George with good news, she connected the call. "Hello?"

"Is this Gloria?" a deep, muffled voice said.

She frowned. "Yes—who is this?"

"Did you get the note?"

Alarm barbed through her chest. A sweat broke out along her hairline as she looked around at the quiet houses next door and across the street. "Who is this?"

"I said, did you *get* the note?"

She fought the urge to snap the phone closed, to throw it as far as she could. Considering she'd always thrown like a girl, chances were she couldn't get it past the mailbox anyway.

"Yes, I did," she said past her throat, which was threatening to close. *Keep him talking,* she told herself. *See if you recognize his voice.* "You must know that Steve's dead."

"Yeah, so?"

White noise on the line hummed in the silence. Her heartbeat pounded in her ears, sending a sharp pain to her temples. "Did you kill him?" she gasped. "He was murdered, you know. P-poisoned."

A few seconds of silence passed, then he said, "Don't talk, just listen. Put five hundred cash in small bills in an envelope and leave it in Chasen's mailbox tomorrow morning before seven o'clock. If you do, no one has to know about your folder."

She wet her lips. "And if I don't?"

"Then your story will be on the front page of the *Post.*"

Fear lodged in her throat.

"I'll be watching you make the drop," the man

rasped, his voice almost unintelligible, "so don't go telling your boyfriend Chief Riley about this phone call."

The call was disconnected abruptly, and Gloria gripped the tiny handset with slippery hands, taking deep breaths to ward off a Ménière's attack. She looked around, wondering if she was being watched. Was the man on the other end of the line the reporter Daniel Guess?

Or someone even more dangerous?

Chapter 16

With the blackmailer's voice ringing in her head, Gloria drove toward the bank, her nerves jumping. She hadn't decided exactly what to do, but it seemed to make sense to have the money on hand at 7:00 a.m. tomorrow morning . . . just in case.

The Bank of Mojo was located in a former Dairy Queen and still boasted red tiled roof and dormers. It was the kind of quirky detail that Mojo residents seemed to thrive on, and, she had to admit, the conversion was appealing in a retro sort of way—although it *had* been a little off-putting to sit on a red swivel stool at a counter when she had opened an account.

She pulled up to the drive-through speaker, noting that someone had done an admirable job of covering the menu of Blizzards and ice cream cakes with certificate of deposit rates of return and the offer of free coupons to the Forever Sun Tanning Salon for opening an IRA.

"May I help you?" a woman's voice blasted into the air.

A little perplexed at this part of the transaction—except for the fact that it added to the whole Dairy-Queen-turned-financial-institution experience—Gloria looked into the camera and said, "I have a new account, but I haven't received a debit card and I'd like to make a withdrawal."

"Okay. You want fries with that?"

Gloria blinked.

"Ha! Just kidding. I'll need to see identification. Pull around."

She did as she was told. Withdrawing her wallet when she pulled up to the second window, she was surprised to see Brianna from the doctor's office.

"Hi, Gloria!" the plump girl said, leaning out and flashing a huge, lip-lined smile. "I thought that was you." Her eyelids sparkled, and her dark hair fanned out around a thick headband like a turkey's tail.

"Hi, Brianna. Are you no longer working for Dr. Whiting?"

"Oh, yeah, but the office is closed on Wednesdays, so I work here one day a week to get free checking."

"Ah. Here's a counter check and my driver's license," Gloria said, handing them over.

"Wow, five hundred smackers—are you in some kind of trouble?"

Gloria started. "No. Why would you ask that?"

"It was, like, a joke," Brianna said, deadpan.

"Oh." Gloria gave herself a mental shake. "Could you make that small bills please?"

"Wow, what's up with everyone withdrawing hunks of cash and asking for small bills? First Guy Bishop, and now you." The brunette shook her head as she turned away.

Gloria's mind raced. Was Guy still being blackmailed too? She pulled her hand over her mouth, thinking how dangerous it was for someone with Brianna's loose lips to know the medical *and* financial matters of everyone in town. Gloria shook her head—what had she been thinking when she'd moved here?

That she'd find her mojo in Mojo?

That somehow this quaint little town and its people would right the tilt of her world?

Instead she was sitting in the drive-through of the Dairy Queen Bank & Trust withdrawing money to pay an anonymous blackmailer who might have murdered Steve Chasen, and keeping it all a tidy secret from her long-lost boyfriend who had no idea they had a history together.

She thought her head might explode.

Brianna reappeared. "Twenties okay?"

Gloria nodded and watched as the woman counted out the bills and stuffed them in an envelope with Gloria's driver's license.

"Here you go," Brianna said cheerfully as she handed the bulky packet through the window. "Are you about ready for that makeover?"

"Er, maybe later," Gloria hedged.

"I was thinking I could come by the office and give you and Diane Davidson both one," the young woman barreled on. "That woman is so plain, she's transparent. It's like she doesn't *want* to be seen."

Gloria thought about the persecution that Diane had experienced and decided that Brianna's assessment wasn't too far off the mark. Diane didn't seem to go out of her way to draw attention to herself.

Brianna's eyes rounded. "Omigod, I almost forgot the big news—did you hear that Steve Chasen was poisoned?"

"Yes. Unfortunately, I heard."

"Who do you think did it?"

Gloria wet her lips. "I was under the impression that it was random product tampering."

Brianna scoffed. "My money is on that Marie Gaston, with the freaky blue hair."

Gloria looked up sharply. "Marie? Why on earth would she poison Steve Chasen?"

Brianna shrugged. "I'm just saying." A buzz sounded, and she glanced at a monitor. "Gotta go—there's Eddie Grossman to cover his child support check that bounced."

Gloria said good-bye and stuffed the envelope into her purse. She drove the short distance to the office like an automaton, pondering Brianna's comment about Marie Gaston poisoning Steve Chasen. Was it just more of Brianna's idle gossip, or did she know something?

The photograph of Marie in Steve's desk drawer popped into Gloria's mind. Had the two of them been involved at some point? Had things perhaps gone sour on Marie's end? And if so, had Steve continued to pursue her . . . spy on her? Did Guy Bishop know—is that why he and Marie had argued? Or did Marie know about Steve blackmailing Guy? Did she suspect foul play?

Gloria forced herself to breathe deeply as she parked and alighted from her car. Speculating that the voodoo doll had something to do with Steve's death was simply borrowing trouble. As she'd told Brianna, Steve's death might have been a tragic, random act.

Or just plain bad luck. After all, the man did own a black cat.

Cringing at her crudely painted Lawyer Here door, she turned the knob and walked into the office, surprised to see a stout, middle-aged man standing with Diane in front of the broken copier. Next to them, Henry snuffled at the man's pant leg as if he was on the trail of something important.

Gloria frowned at the dog.

"Tam's sent John here to service the copier," Diane said, grabbing Henry's collar and hauling him toward the bathroom. Henry resisted, sitting down and emitting sharp, hoarse barks. "John, this is Gloria Dalton—this is her law practice."

The bulldog of a man grunted a greeting, wiping his hands on a cloth as he looked her up and down.

Gloria said hello, then gestured to the copier. "Can you fix it?"

He sucked at the toothpick in his mouth. "Not on this visit. I have to order a part. Will take a couple of days."

She winced. "How much will it cost?"

"It's still under warranty," he said, gathering up his tool case. "You're in luck."

Luck? Gloria smiled at his phrasing in the context

of everything that was happening. Still, at this point, she'd take what she could get.

"I'll be back now that I know what I need," the man said, then left unceremoniously.

Diane returned, trying her best to ignore the pitiful howling and the frantic scratching from the bathroom, where she'd put Henry. She squinted at Gloria. "Are you feeling okay? You look pale."

"I have bad news—Steve Chasen was poisoned."

"Poisoned?" the woman asked, her hand to her mouth. "How?"

"The ME thinks it was a bar of fund-raising candy that he ate."

"Oh, my dear Lord."

Gloria hid her surprise at the woman's outburst—apparently Diane's Wiccan religion had not overridden the habit of muttering distinctly Southern (and Christian) oaths. "The police are going all over town, gathering up the candy bars in case there are more tainted ones out there. There was half a boxful on this desk before the accident. Did you find any when you were cleaning up?"

Diane shook her head. "No. Oh, this is terrible—and more bad press for Mojo."

From the bathroom, Henry began to bay as if his doggie heart was broken. Gloria massaged at the headache she'd been fending off for most of the day.

Diane looked sheepish. "Sorry—he can't stand being alone."

Gloria pursed her mouth. "Most males are like that."

Except for Zane . . . he seemed to be a confirmed loner, detached and distant. Did his life choices have anything to do with her disappearance when they were teenagers? Had it scared him? Made him less likely to trust people?

Or was it simply wishful thinking that she'd meant that much to him?

"Maybe you should sit down," Diane offered. "You don't look well."

Gloria sighed. "Actually, I think I'll call it a day. Will you lock up?"

"Absolutely. Feel better, okay?"

The warm sincerity in the woman's voice stopped Gloria. Diane seemed to be reaching out to her, and while the urge to reciprocate was strong, Gloria couldn't help the suspicion that tickled her neck at the woman's colorless eyes and quiet demeanor. If she responded to Diane, the woman would expect something from her in return. Friendship? Help with her case against the school board? Both things that she probably wouldn't be around long enough to fulfill. So instead of investing in one more relationship that she'd have to abandon, she simply gave the woman a professional nod and left.

Her purse, she noted as she walked to her car, was getting heavier and heavier—first with the weight of her .38 automatic, and now with the bulk of the blackmail money.

Or was that the weight of guilt dragging down her shoulders?

Clouds had gathered, low and brownish-gray, thick with the promise of rain to further dampen the spirits of the residents of Mojo. She shivered as she scanned the ominous sky, struck by a foreboding that the worst was yet to come. All signs seemed to be telling her to cut her losses (financial and emotional) and get out of town.

Her nerves were strung tight as she drove home, her hands gripping the wheel at the two-and-ten-o'clock position. She drove so slowly that an old woman driving an aged Lincoln behind her leaned on the horn. Just as she approached Goddard's Funeral Chapel, the sky opened and unleashed a torrent of rain that hammered the hood and roof of her car. The noise alone splintered her head, but the feeling of isolation and gloom was so intense that she flipped on the radio for the comfort of knowing that she wasn't the only person in the world.

Static blasted into the car until she found a station. Unfortunately, the topic of conversation appeared to be Mojo and its poisonous candy bars.

". . . the candy bars were being sold to raise money for the families of the victims of the Mojo Voodoo Museum, and now comes word that the candy itself may have led to another death in Mojo. Earlier we spoke with Chief Zane Riley of the Mojo police department about this tragic incident."

Gloria pulled into the driveway and waited for the garage door to raise while Zane's voice sounded over the speaker.

"The medical examiner's office in New Orleans has informed me that the cause of death of Steven Chasen is cyanide poisoning, most likely laced in a chocolate bar the man had consumed shortly before wrecking his car."

His baritone voice was so authoritative, so . . . safe. She pulled into the garage, and the sound of the rain battering her car was replaced with the dull thud of the rain pounding the garage roof.

"In the event this isn't an isolated incident," he continued, "we're taking the precaution of recalling the candy. If you purchased any of the fund-raising candy, place it in a plastic bag and call 911 so that it can be retrieved. We *will* get to the bottom of this."

Gloria's heart expanded in her chest. Zane sounded as if he considered injury to a Mojo resident a personal affront.

"Chief," a reporter's voice asked, "does this have any connection to the voodoo culture that has made Mojo so infamous?"

"No, it does not," Zane bit out. "That's all."

"That was Chief Zane Riley of the Mojo Police Department," the announcer said, "as we cover the latest bizarre development coming out of the little town where people go in, but don't always come out alive."

She frowned and shut off the engine. Leave it to her to seek out the Bermuda Triangle of the South.

Steve Chasen was dead, and she had evidence that people might have wanted him dead. And she was being blackmailed by his partner, who, despite his denial on the phone, also might have been involved in Steve's death. Oh, and there was a chance that Bernard Riaz was looking for her and her mother.

And she had no idea where her mother was, or if she was dead or alive.

Gloria rested her forehead on the steering wheel. What should she do about the five hundred dollars in her purse—ask for the marshal's help? Ask for Zane's help? Or try to quiet the blackmailer by giving in to his demands? Compared to picking up her life and relocating, five hundred dollars was a relatively small price to pay. Maybe the blackmailer would be satisfied and she wouldn't have to leave town.

Wouldn't have to leave Zane.

She sat until the dome light in her car timed out and dimmed. The semidarkness spurred her into action; she hated the dark and had always dreamed of living in a home that was mostly glass to let in as much sunlight as possible . . . but then windows presented another kind of security threat. And windows with bars over them were less appealing.

She opened the car door and climbed out, shimmying around stacks of boxes by the light of the bare bulb overhead.

She practically fell into the laundry room in her haste to get inside, and she scanned each room as she moved through the house. The blackmailer must know where she lived—had her security measures kept him out?

She went from room to room, checking the locks on windows and doors until she was satisfied that everything was secure. Reasoning that the blackmailer wanted money, not to harm her, she tried to relax. She needed a clear head to face the decisions before her. A stress-induced Ménière's attack would only make matters worse.

The rain landed as hard and fast as it could fall out of the sky, insulating the little house in a wet cocoon. She fixed herself a mug of tea and turned the television in her bedroom to a soft music station. Then she retreated to the bathroom and stared at her reflection, the choreographed look that she had groomed over the years going against nature. She had thinned and arched her eyebrows to a fine point, had had a small mole on her cheek removed. Zane had always called it a beauty mark, but the marshals had warned her that it was too distinctive, as her pale curtain of hair had been, and her penchant for bright-colored clothing.

Over the years she had made herself plainer and plainer to blend into the background.

It was no wonder that Zane didn't recognize her—she didn't recognize herself.

Gloria sighed. It was times like this that she missed her pragmatic mother most. In a crisis, real or imagined, her mother would allow her a few minutes to cry, then she would wipe her tears and say, "Put it behind you, sweetie. Life marches on."

"Life marches on," Gloria murmured, accepting with a tight chest that she couldn't undo the past and couldn't involve Zane in her future without putting him in danger and subjecting him to having his life uprooted again and again.

Assuming he'd even want to be a part of her future.

She groaned and shoved her hands into her hair, then leaned forward to stare at her pale roots. She couldn't solve her big problems tonight, but she could solve a little one.

From the drugstore bag she withdrew the box of hair color. In between sips of tea, she followed the directions for a root touch-up. With a towel around her shoulders, she applied the color and noted the time on her digital clock. Then Zane's green scarf, which was still lying on her nightstand, caught her eye, and she gave in to the pull of it.

Pulling its softness against her cheek, she knew how a child felt about the comfort of a favorite blankie. Somehow the velvety feel of the scarf was a substitute for Zane's touch and reminded her of all the warmth they had generated. And the fact that he'd left it in her bedroom after a makeout session made her warm in long-neglected places.

They used to lie on her bed, with textbooks open to whatever pages they were supposed to be studying, both keenly aware of the heat vibrating between their bodies. Invariably their hands or their hips would touch, and they would turn to lie face-to-face, hands and legs twining, their studies forgotten.

He would swirl his tongue around the shell of her ear and sigh as he slipped his hand under the hem of her shirt, splaying his warm fingers over her back. She would press closer to him until her tingling breasts met his wall of chest muscle, until his erection branded her thigh.

Slowly, slowly they would tease each other and undress as much as they dared. She had felt safe with Zane, knowing that no matter how high their lust ran, he wouldn't push her to have sex. When they had reached a fever pitch, they would stroke each other to climax and cling to each other, pulsing and sated. Before Zane, she hadn't known such physical bliss was possible. After Zane, she had learned that what they'd shared was rare.

"Zane," she murmured, loving the feel of his name on her tongue, then closing her eyes against the intense surge of desire to be with him, to make love with him, to finish what they'd started so many years ago.

She groaned into the empty room, acknowledging the futility of wanting Zane in light of her bizarre situation. Hanging on to memories and fantasizing about a life she could never return to was insanity. She pulled the scarf away from her face and stared at it, reeling over the power it held over her. She had to accept reality and move on, no matter how painful it seemed in the short term. She jumped to her feet, scarf in hand, and marched to the laundry room to rummage in a cabinet of items the previous tenant had left.

Before she could lose her nerve, Gloria emptied a metal trash can, tossed the scarf inside, doused it with paint thinner, and dropped a match on top.

Chapter 17

The sense of liberation that Gloria expected to feel by ridding herself of a tangible connection to Zane was overridden by a sense of panic as the green scarf crackled and began to dissolve into charred bits, sending an alarming amount of green-gray smoke into the air. She cried out and covered her nose at the foul stench—too late she realized that the yarn wasn't synthetic, and the resulting odor smelled as if she'd set fire to a yak.

Fumbling with the faucet in the utility sink, she cupped her hands to collect the icy flow and hurled it on the smoldering scarf. After a sizzle and a pop, more smoke billowed out, and the fire alarm in the next room went off, sending an ear-piercing siren wailing through the house.

Gloria grimaced and yanked open the garage door, fanning it back and forth to dispel the air as she coughed and her eyes watered. She considered crying, but when she realized how ridiculous her life was, she began to laugh—no one's life could be this screwed up.

Finally the piercing sound of the smoke alarm stopped. She disposed of the soggy, sad remains of the scarf and was seized by the wholly unreasonable feeling that she'd just destroyed whatever she and Zane had meant to each other. Gloria slid down the wall and sat on the floor, peering up through the hazy air with tears in her eyes. Steve Chasen was dead and she was being blackmailed and the one man who could help her was the only man she couldn't afford to get close to.

What now? Run? Stay? Lie?

Her mind raced, clouded with indecision. There were too many unpleasant options. She choked back a sob, yearning for a clear-cut choice that would lead her toward some semblance of a normal life.

Was a normal life even possible for her anymore? She had once thought so, when she'd moved through the paces of getting an education and throwing herself into family law. But despite her outward appearance as an involved, productive citizen, she had kept everyone around her at arm's length, rejecting the friendships of women and men who had tried to get to know her.

What had Jules Lamborne said? *You can't hide here, missy.*

Yet she had to hide somewhere. And would she

ever truly be able to have a life, to find peace, to extend herself to other people when she was in a constant state of paranoia?

She sighed and touched her finger to her forehead, feeling wet ooze—the hair dye, my God, how long had she left it on?

Would this day ever end?

She ran back to the shower, stripped, and stepped in, rinsing her hair vigorously until the water ran clear. By then the hot water heater had emptied, so she simply stood under the cold blast of water, shivering, hoping it would cool her desire for Zane, which seemed to be burning out of control, and sober her to the choices she was going to have to make within the next twenty-four hours.

When the coldness had seeped to her bones, she turned off the water, toweled dry, and changed the bandage on her hand. The eight stitches were black and angry against her skin—there would be a scar for sure.

Something that would forever tie her to Mojo, even if she left. Another episode in her life that she would have to try to camouflage so no one would be able to link her to Gloria Dalton the attorney who had cut her hand on a piece of flying glass.

She dressed in soft jeans and a brown turtleneck, thinking how she'd much rather be wearing pink, or maybe a bright blue. Maybe the next place she lived she'd try something new, like a shaved head and a hip, new wardrobe. The marshals would make sure she could practice law again if she wanted to, but it was a joke really—her fantasy of helping other people fix their lives when her own was such a shambles.

Maybe she'd change occupations altogether . . . become a teacher, work with children. Children were safe, didn't ask questions, didn't expect so much in return.

With a sigh, she scrutinized the roots of her wet hair, happy to see that they were indeed dark again. At the growl in her stomach, she padded barefoot to the kitchen and frowned when she realized she still hadn't gone to the grocery and would have to make do with another omelet. The caustic scent of scorched fibers still tinged the air. If it would only stop raining, she'd open a window. As if to mock her, the cadence of the heavy rain increased, battering the roof, the wind buffeting the little house.

The croaking noise of the doorbell ringing broke into the silence, startling her to the point of crying out. Who would be out in this weather? A stealthy trip to the side window confirmed her fears—it was Zane.

She exhaled noisily, trying to rein in her emotions. Did he know something? Had he come to confront her? After a couple of missed heartbeats, she forced herself to relax. He'd come for business, that was all . . . to pick up the voodoo doll.

Gloria glanced down at her bland, casual clothing, her bare feet, and put a hand to her wet hair—it wasn't as if she was in danger of enticing him into another kiss . . . or anything else.

After a brief pep talk, she swung open the door.

Zane stood on the covered stoop, rain dripping from his hat and dark overcoat and . . . a pizza box? Plus a six-pack of Samuel Adams bottled beer.

Zane with a pizza and beer . . . a feeling of déjà vu

swamped her. "Hi," she managed, hanging onto the doorknob to keep from falling.

He flashed one of his rare lopsided smiles that made her stomach turn inside out. "Are you armed and dangerous?"

Unnerved, she lifted her chin. "Not at the moment."

"I wanted to make sure you had something in your stomach besides chocolate bars." Then he leaned forward and sniffed. "But I can smell that you already ate . . . maybe." He grimaced. "Did you burn something?"

"Um . . . it wasn't food," she murmured.

"So do you want some of this?" he asked, holding up the pizza box.

Warning flags raised in her mind, but she was so relieved that he hadn't confronted her with her deception that she ignored them and waved him inside. "Come in and take off your clothes—" She stopped, mortified. "I mean, take off your *coat*."

He grinned as he shrugged out of his coat and hat, setting them on the mat just inside the door. "It's nasty out there tonight." He shook his head, ruffling his hair, which was almost as wet as hers.

"I'll get you a towel," she said, grateful for the chance to compose herself. She practically ran to her bathroom, then grabbed a towel and bit into it to stifle a cry of frustration and, God help her, excitement. Just like the first time that Zane had come to her house with a pizza.

Déjà vu. A sensation that cut too close to the heart.

"I can do this," she murmured aloud, staring in

the mirror to reassure herself that she looked nothing at all like Lorey Lawson. She had schooled her entire self to be different—her mannerisms, her body language. As long as she didn't have a Tourette's moment and blurt the truth, Zane had no reason to suspect she was anyone other than Gloria Dalton, attorney-at-law, newly relocated to Mojo.

Who kissed men for no apparent reason.

She massaged her temples, then took a deep breath and headed back to the kitchen.

"Here you go," she said cheerfully, extending the towel.

He reached for it with a smile. "I was about to come look for you."

His smile made her heart—and her feet—stumble. "I . . . don't have all my linens unpacked yet."

"Me neither." He wiped his bare arms and neck. "Living out of boxes makes me never want to move again."

She smiled her agreement and realized with a start that he had removed his dark blue uniform shirt. A snowy white T-shirt molded his chest and biceps. What had been the lean, lithe muscle of a teenager was now the thick, dense muscle of a man. The moisture evaporated from her mouth.

"I hope you don't mind," he said, nodding to the shirt he'd hung over the back of a chair, its sleeves dark with wetness. "Thought I'd let it dry out a little."

Swallowing past a cottony tongue, she said, "Wh-why don't I toss it in the dryer for you?"

"That'd be great. Point me in the direction of plates, and I'll serve up the pizza."

She did, her chest infused with the happy familiarity of being domestic with Zane. *Careful,* she warned herself, *this can't happen.* She turned to walk toward the utility room. "I'll pick off the mushrooms," she said over her shoulder.

After a couple of beats of silence, he called, "How did you know I got mushrooms?"

She winced—*oops.* She wasn't supposed to know that he loved mushrooms. "Uh . . . I just assumed. Everyone I know except me likes mushrooms."

"Oh . . . I thought maybe the local grapevine was at work again," he called. "It's unbelievable how nosy people are in this town."

Her shoulders sagged in relief—that had been close.

She set the dryer timer, but before she tossed in his shirt, she brought it up to her face and inhaled Zane's scent—his maleness, his musky aftershave. When her thighs began to tingle, she knew she was flirting with danger. To continue this fantasy of hers was insanity. Inhumane. Incapacitating.

All in all, wholly inadvisable.

She walked back to the living room on wobbly legs to find Zane sitting on the couch, the low, narrow coffee table set with plain white plates, a large wedge of pizza on each. He was taking a drink from a bottle of beer, and when he looked up, the sight of him took her breath away.

"I took the mushrooms off yours and piled them on mine."

Just like old times. "Th-thanks." She eased onto the couch, a good foot away from him.

He reached for his slice of pizza and gave a little

laugh. "What did you burn? The air in here smells hazardous."

"I . . . lit a candle and it . . . was bad."

"I didn't realize that candles went bad."

She nodded, feeling like an idiot, and bit into her pizza.

"This is a nice place," he said, glancing around at the craftsman-style bungalow. "Nice bones. My real estate agent didn't show me this place, or I might have bought it myself."

"I'm renting."

"Oh." He tipped up his beer for a swig. "Were you waiting to see if you'd like living in Mojo?"

She chewed slowly, then swallowed. "I suppose so."

One side of his mouth lifted. "After the week you've had, are you ready to leave?"

Gloria frowned. "Mona Black asked me the same thing. And I had the feeling that she wouldn't be upset to see me go."

"Why would your office landlord want to see you go?"

She shrugged, but her mind went to the empty folder with Mona's name on it that she'd found in Steve's briefcase. "Have there been any other reports of poisonings?"

"No, thank God."

It was a relief . . . but damning, too, where Steve Chasen's death was concerned. "I heard you being interviewed on the radio on my way home."

He made a rueful noise. "I heard that the announcer was trying to make it sound like something supernatural is going on in this town."

"What do you think happened to Steve Chasen?"

"All I know is that it didn't have anything to do with a voodoo doll." He sighed. "But that's why I came by—to get that freaky toy and try to get to the bottom of what's going on in this crazy little town."

At his dismissive tone, warmth suffused her cheeks. Then a chilling memory surfaced. "Penny Francisco told me that she thought Jules Lamborne knew something about the voodoo doll that was made in the likeness of her ex-husband, and might know something about this one, too."

"I've met the old gal—spooky, but harmless. And maybe she created the dolls, but science and common sense say that it still didn't have anything to do with Deke Black's death. Or Steve's."

Gloria wet her lips. "Except that Jules told me the other day that she wasn't sorry to see Steve gone. She said that he was spreading poison around town."

That got his attention. "Those were her exact words?"

"Yeah. Do you think she knows something?"

"I doubt it. I think she likes to pretend that she knows something."

"You don't believe that some people have a sixth sense, that some things can't be explained?"

"No," he said flatly, polishing off his slice of pizza and reaching for another one. "Everything can be explained . . . eventually. That kind of supernatural nonsense just clutters the picture."

She chewed slowly, then chased a bite of pizza with a swallow of beer. "So you think that Steve's poisoning was a random incident?"

"It seems likely. We've contacted the company that manufactured the candy, and they're cooperating. Cyanide occurs naturally in some manufacturing processes, so it's possible that it could be some kind of industrial accident. We'll know more when the candy wrapper is analyzed."

"You found it?"

He nodded. "We think so—we found a half-eaten candy bar in the wreckage of his car and sent it to the state crime lab in Baton Rouge. We should know something soon. And I requested his home phone and cell phone records."

"Really?" she squeaked, remembering that in all the commotion, she'd left the ransacked cell phone bill at Steve's house. What if the phone records led Zane to Steve's blackmailing partner, who might in turn expose *her?*

"Just covering all the bases," he said, seemingly unaware that he'd just given her something else to worry about.

"Will you keep me posted?" she asked, tamping down guilt over the fact that she was withholding information from him. Among other things, that she had a breakfast date with a blackmailer.

"I'll let you know whatever we can make public." He tipped up his beer again. "So . . . you and Cameron Phelps."

She blinked. "Excuse me?"

"At your office today. I, uh . . . I thought I saw something between you."

The air sizzled with sudden tension, in conflict with the rain that pummeled the roof and the humidity that had seeped through the seams of the old house. A nervous flush started at her neck and worked its way north.

"Cameron Phelps was at my office on business." Irritation flared in her chest—the man was way too presumptuous . . . and feeding her fantasies that he might actually be . . . jealous.

Zane wiped his mouth. "I'm sorry—that was out of line." He set his bottle of beer on the coffee table and stood. "I guess I'd better get what I came for and take off."

She stood awkwardly. "Right. I'll get the, um, doll."

"Actually, I need to bag it—the less we touch it, the better."

She pushed her tongue into her cheek. "Right this way." With her nerves zapping like broken electric lines, she led him to her bedroom, glad that this room, at least, looked moved into. She watched him take in her solid, simple furniture and wondered what kinds of things Zane surrounded himself with. Antiques? Books? High-tech equipment?

Feeling self-conscious, she walked to the lingerie bureau and slid open the drawer where she'd stashed the voodoo doll. Amidst her satiny underthings, the doll seemed to have taken on a more sinister quality since she'd last examined it. The pin imbedded in the doll's stomach now seemed less whimsical and instead made her wonder what kind of pain Steve Chasen had experienced in the last minutes of his life.

And if this doll had something to do with it.

She stepped aside to give Zane room, her skin singing with embarrassment at his bird's-eye view of her lingerie. The exotic array of animal-print teddies, beaded satin corsets, and panties trimmed with six-inch lace was a far cry from the tame, demure exterior she had worked for years to perfect.

He shot her an amused—and impressed—glance before reaching into his back pants pocket and removing a white latex glove. She brushed back her still-damp hair, wanting this to be over, wanting Zane out of her bedroom. She didn't need yet more images to torture herself with.

After snapping on the glove, he reached into the drawer and lifted the doll. Unfortunately, a leg snagged on a shiny zebra-print demi-cup bra. A hot flush consumed her as the flimsy piece of erotic fabric swung in the air. With thumb and forefinger, Zane removed the bra and held it up, his eyes shining with interest. "Nice. And unexpected."

She pulled at the hem of her brown turtleneck, mortified . . . and aroused.

"Hey," he said with a laugh, "since you know what kind of underwear I have on, it's only fair that I know what you're wearing, right?"

Gloria plucked the bra out of his hand and dropped it back into the drawer. Trying to rescue her shredded dignity, she nodded to the voodoo doll. "I think you have what you came for."

He took his time answering, his eyes going from smiling to smoldering. "I suppose."

He wanted her . . . she could feel it. Her breath caught in her chest at the realization. She wanted him, too, so much that it frightened her, because there were so many reasons not to give in . . . for both of their sakes. And how immoral would it be to make love with Zane under the pretense of being someone else?

Every cell in her body wanted to wrap her arms and legs around him and drag him to her bed, but she'd spent years denying her instincts, of being vigilant about her behavior and considering the consequences. Yet she'd never truly thought she'd be in a position to relive her fantasies with Zane.

"Gloria," he murmured quietly, then reached for her.

Hearing her new name from his lips jarred her from her reverie. She straightened and turned toward the doorway. "I'll see if your shirt is dry."

She fled to the utility room and pulled his shirt from the dryer. Unable to resist, she pulled the warm fabric to her face to fill her lungs with him one last time. Her breasts felt heavy, and a pang of desire sliced through her midsection. So many of her sexual experiences—real and imagined—were wrapped up in this man.

"It's okay if it's not dry," he said.

She jerked her head around to see him standing in the doorway. "Uh . . . it's dry."

He smiled. "Good."

She handed the shirt to him and followed him back to the living room, her pulse clicking. The voodoo doll lay on the table next to the door, encased in a clear plastic bag, its macabre features in relief under the lights. Was it a cruel joke that someone had left to frighten her or Steve, or had the little doll somehow triggered all the bizarre incidents that had happened since?

She'd come to this town hoping for a change, but

she'd gotten way more than she'd expected. She watched Zane shrug into his shirt, her chest tight with swirling emotions. She was in way over her head here. And one thing had become heartbreakingly clear: She had to leave Mojo . . . leave Zane.

He moved toward the door, not bothering to button his shirt as he reached for his raincoat. He seemed eager to leave, as if he didn't trust himself to linger over small talk. He opened the door, ushering in the pinging sounds of the driving rain, the fog of moisture hanging in the leaden air, the lush scent of wetness and earth. When he turned back to offer her a parting smile, longing welled inside her like a sob.

And something snapped.

Years of training to ignore her instincts fell away. She moved automatically, acting on impulse, allowing the moment to rule her, bowing to the emotions pulsing through her body. Fisting the openings of his shirt in her hands, she pulled him to her. Just before their lips met, she whispered, "Stay."

And from the frantic way he kissed her, it was clear that he planned to offer no resistance. With a groan, he kicked the front door closed.

Chapter 18

Zane smelled like rainwater and tasted like hops. And his hands . . . his hands massaging her lower back felt meltingly familiar and so . . . right.

She moaned into his mouth, deepening the fervent kiss and twining her hands behind his neck. He picked her up and walked them to the couch, knocking the pizza box off the table. Beer bottles and plates crashed to the floor as they sank into the feather cushions of the couch.

She pushed at his shirt, dragging it off his shoulders, smoothing her hands over the cool cotton of his T-shirt before pulling it from the waistband of his pants and splaying her hands on the smooth muscled planes of his back.

She had never been a sexually assertive person. Zane had awakened her sexuality when she was a teenager, had given her a glimpse of how heavenly lovemaking could be. When she'd been ripped away from him, she'd retreated into herself. Eventually she had lost her virginity in an anticlimactic pairing in college, and in the few physical relationships since, she hadn't been able to work up enough enthusiasm to make any of the encounters memorable.

But being in Zane's arms again, she came alive, like a starved woman having her first taste of food in years, but knowing she might never get back to the buffet. She took the lead, climbing on top to sit astride his lean hips, licking and biting at his mouth and neck feverishly, stopping only to pull his T-shirt over his head and to cast off her turtleneck to reveal a deep pink velvet bra. Her hands and mouth moved out of instinct, driven to wring every ounce of pleasure out of every second with Zane. She was determined to make enough memories tonight to last her a lifetime.

If Zane was surprised by her take-charge behavior, he wasn't complaining. His eyes were hooded, his jaw set in restraint as he murmured guttural words of appreciation. He cupped her breasts, thumbing her nipples through the soft, fuzzy fabric.

She reached around and unhooked her bra, releasing her breasts into his hands, nearly coming undone at the feel of his warm fingers caressing her, pulling at her nipples, touching her just the way she liked.

"Zane," she breathed. "That's perfect . . . yes." Under his caress, her nipples budded and her skin flushed with need. And her mind reeled over the fact that Zane was once again touching her intimately . . . she had dreamed of this so many times that it didn't seem possible that it could be happening.

She leaned forward to smooth her hands over his torso, reveling in the crisp, springy dark hair covering the wall of muscle over his abs and chest . . . the same as she remembered, only different . . . familiar, but better. Her fingers slid over a round, red scar high on the right side of his chest, and she made a rueful noise.

"What caused this?"

"It's nothing," he said, his breathing labored. "Just a scratch." Then he distracted her by lightly squeezing her breasts and moaning his satisfaction.

She wondered what he thought of her body, now lithe and lightly muscled, toned and athletic. But her doubts were erased by his caressing hands, which seemed to be in constant motion, as if he wanted to explore every inch of her.

She circled his flat, dark nipples with her fingers, then trailed down to his stomach. He inhaled sharply at her touch, his muscles contracting as she traveled lower. She unfastened his belt and fly, then smiled. "Blue boxers."

His breathing was ragged. "I wouldn't want to disappoint the gossips."

She freed his erection, sighing in satisfaction. Zane had been the first man she'd ever seen naked . . . how lucky she had been.

When she clasped his rigid cock, he groaned in satisfaction. She stroked him the way he liked it, with a firm, slow grip, until the velvety knob glistened with his arousal. He gritted his teeth and tugged on the waistband of her jeans. She stood and shimmied out of them, her heart thrashing in anticipation of being with him. He shucked his boots and pants and added the items to the litter on the floor.

Zane came up behind her, kissed the back of her neck, and cupped his hand over the lace crotch of her panties. She undulated against his hand, loving the rasp of his beard against her neck, a new sensation. She gasped when his seeking fingers found their way inside her extravagant panties, and inside her. With his free hand he palmed her breast, tugging and tweaking the nipple, jolting every nerve ending in her body. He massaged her folds, coaxing an orgasm to the surface with astonishing speed. But when her knees buckled from the abrupt explosion, she remembered that Zane had always had that effect on her . . . he knew just where to touch her, just the right pressure to apply. She cried out in ecstasy, vibrating against his hand.

But afterward, instead of feeling sated, she felt whetted and energized. Turning in his arms, she kissed his muscled chest, then moved lower to his flat stomach, and lower still to push down the boxers. She sank to her knees to take the length of him into her mouth. Her moans mingled with his as he drove his fingers into her hair. Some part of her marveled that she could be so uninhibited. But surprising him, pleasing him . . . it emboldened her. She drew hard on his shaft, again and again, until he stopped her with his hands.

"Enough," he said, through clenched teeth, then pulled her to her feet. "I don't have . . . that much self-control. I have . . . to have you."

His eyes were glazed with passion, his mouth set in a tense line. Seeing Zane nude, tall and broad-shouldered, his sex jutting, the light bouncing off his beautiful male body, made her feel loose-limbed and languid. With the rain creating an insular, staccato rhythm on the roof, it was easy to believe they were the only two people in the world.

Zane . . . how she loved him. And she couldn't wait another minute to be one with him. Drawing on a fantasy, she steered him to the long narrow coffee table and swept aside a remaining bottle. He seemed perplexed and pleased at the same time as she guided his shoulders down for him to lie on the hard surface. Then she stepped out of her pink panties and crawled on top. They kissed deeply and rubbed their bodies against each other until the friction stoked their passion to unbearable temperatures. She sat up to straddle him, finding firm footing on the floor to leverage herself over him and join their bodies in one movement that robbed both of them of their breath.

Beneath her, Zane bucked, the muscles in his stomach contracting to drive himself deeper into her. The hard table bit into her legs, but its unforgiving surface allowed them to be as deeply joined as was physically possible. The fullness, the stimulation . . . she thought she might pass out from the sensory overload and acknowledged fleetingly that this would be a terrible time for a Ménière's attack. Not that she'd noticed because she was so dizzy from Zane's lovemaking and the sheer incredulity that they were together again.

His heated skin against hers—she wanted this moment to last forever, but even as the thought slid into her mind, she felt another orgasm building from their frantic rhythm. She resisted, but her body screamed for release.

The storm inside the house rivaled the storm raging outside, rattling the windows. He placed his large hands on her hips, his thrusts growing more intense, stabbing her deeper and deeper, at last sending her spiraling over the edge into a dazzling climax. She crashed down on him, contracting around his sex, crying out his name. His body jerked, and he shouted his release as he gripped her hips and ground their bodies together.

She slumped forward to lie on him, closing her eyes against the bliss of knowing that she was the cause of his strong heart galloping like a racehorse. Their bodies flinched with spasms, recovering with exquisite lethargy.

A long, noisy sigh escaped him, and he gave a little chuckle. "Wow, that was . . . I don't know what to say—amazing."

She smiled against his skin, emotion welling in her chest. "I thought so, too."

He shifted slightly and groaned. "But I'm not sure how much longer my back can take this."

She laughed and pushed herself up, wincing as long-unused muscles twinged. She started to stand but was surprised when he caught her hand. He searched her face, his gray eyes shot with confusion. "You are one big contradiction, Gloria Dalton."

She bit into her lip, overcome with love even as her conscience plucked at her.

You're getting in over your head. This isn't fair to him—he deserves to know who you are.

The storm howled around them, a reminder that she couldn't keep the world at bay forever.

"Let's go to my bedroom," she suggested.

A mischievous smile curled his mouth. "There *were* a couple of items in your lingerie drawer I wouldn't mind seeing again."

She returned his smile, stood, and crooked her finger.

Tomorrow she'd deal with her problems . . . or run from them.

But tonight she had over a decade of fantasies to satisfy.

Chapter 19

When Gloria's eyes popped open in the predawn light, the first thing she noticed was Zane's steady breathing in her ear. She closed her eyes briefly and gave herself over to the tug of resignation in her heart, knowing the fantasy had come to an end.

The second thing she noticed was that the rain had stopped. In fact, filtered sunlight flirted with the curtains at her bedroom window.

The third thing she noticed was the clock—it was 6:40. She had exactly twenty minutes to make the money drop at Steve Chasen's house . . . or run the risk of having her identity exposed.

She moved tentatively, trying not to wake Zane, but noted with smug feminine satisfaction that their acrobatic lovemaking had apparently left the man exhausted. He sprawled nude on top of the covers, taking up his side of the bed and more, his limbs extending in all directions. She glanced at him with bittersweet pangs as she picked her way across the floor strewn with the more fanciful garments from her lingerie drawer. Last night had been wonderful . . . indescribable . . . miraculous.

And temporary.

She paused, fighting the urge to waken Zane, tell him everything and ask for his help. He would, of course—he was sworn to uphold the law.

But the U.S. marshal's words came back to her. *This guy might get it into his head to try to protect you, Gloria, but he can't. No matter what kind of supercop he is, he's no match for Riaz's men.*

The blackmailer might have nothing to do with Riaz's men, but he certainly could draw attention to her, make it easier for Riaz to find her.

She swept her gaze over the long length of Zane, his bare, muscular arms and legs twined in her sheets. Her heart squeezed painfully. She couldn't involve him in the drama that her life had become; if something happened to him because of her, she wouldn't be able to live with herself. There had been several moments during the night when she'd wondered if she seemed as familiar to him as he did to her—her sounds, her scents, her touches. More than once the look in his eyes had made her catch her breath, she had been so sure that he was about to announce that he knew who she was. And then the moment would pass, and she would be torn between relief and disappointment.

After one last look, she dressed quickly in chinos, turtleneck, and sweater, then carried socks and shoes to the living room, where she surveyed the debris they'd left last night in their haste to be together. Her cheeks warmed at the memory of her boldness, but it had felt so good to act on impulse for once in her life.

She only hoped that in the days and weeks and months to come, she would still feel as if it had been worth it.

At the last minute she decided to leave a note for Zane. On a scrap of paper she jotted *Early business meeting. Later, G.*, and left him a key to lock up.

On the way to the garage, she pulled from her purse a breath mint and a moist wipe to wash her face, then finger-combed her permed curls. Their last makeout session had taken place in the shower in the wee hours of the morning—a treat for the senses, but her hair had dried into what felt like a spongy helmet. And her eyes were scratchy from wearing the green-colored contact lenses all night.

As the garage door lifted, she had a panicky moment that she might not be able to back out with Zane's cruiser sitting in the driveway, but there was just enough room to eke by.

The streets were relatively deserted, although she passed an empty school bus. For some reason, the bus made her think of Diane Davidson. Gloria wondered why the woman would stay in a place where people persecuted her.

Mojo seemed to have a hold on its residents. As bizarre as it sounded, Gloria could feel the pull of the town as she maneuvered its quiet streets, blinking with pre-holiday lights. She passed the shopping center where her patched-up office was located and all looked calm. It was hard to believe that only a few days ago a man had driven through the window after being poisoned by a candy bar.

The town square, where she had thought someone had been shooting at her and Zane, looked as peaceful as a postcard. Dr. Whiting's office appeared quaint and dated, not the place where a witch doctor might practice voodoo.

She passed a teenager on a bicycle delivering newspapers and a lone runner dressed for the cold weather, accompanied by a dog.

Small town, USA. An observer might think she was on her way to get a cup of coffee versus making a hush-money drop.

When she turned into Steve's neighborhood, she slowed, on the lookout for obvious thug transportation: long, black sedans, military assault vehicles, souped-up muscle cars.

Instead the streets were quiet, with Ford and General Motors family cars sitting in the driveways, with brightly colored riding toys dotting the starkly dormant yards. Still, her palms were sweaty on the steering wheel as she pulled in front of the mailbox at the end of Steve Chasen's driveway.

With her heart in her throat, she reached into her purse and removed the envelope of cash that she'd withdrawn from the bank. Then, after looking all around and seeing no witnesses, she zoomed down her window, lowered the metal lid, and shoved the envelope to the back of the empty box.

Feeling like a criminal, she rolled up her window and pulled away too quickly, catching the corner of the mailbox with her car, eliciting a sickening metal-against-metal scrape.

She winced as she accelerated. Great—in addition to the expense she'd incurred to get the office up and running and replace the plate-glass window, then the cost of the clothes she'd ruined since coming to town and the cash outlay for the resident Mojo blackmailer, now she could add a car paint touch-up to her list.

At the end of the street she turned around and drove past Steve's house again. The curtain covering his living room window moved, sending ribbons of fear through her. She inadvertently tapped the brake, then relaxed—the black cat had jumped up to sit in the window, as if he knew she was there. Guilt stabbed her, but she drove on, telling herself she'd come back in a few hours to check on him. She glanced around nervously—the man had told her that he would be watching.

She hadn't realized how visible Steve's house was because his yard was free of large trees. Was the caller watching her from across the street, from the next street over from a parked car? Or could he be viewing her through binoculars from one of the big houses perched on the hills surrounding Mojo? Or from Hairpin Hill, the main road leading up into the pricey new subdivisions overlooking the town and the older neighborhoods?

Nerve-wracked, she glanced in the rearview mirror, and although she didn't spot any suspicious vehicles, she did a double take at her own reflection. In the daylight, the roots of her sleep-rumpled hair looked almost . . . *green*. She jerked closer to the mirror and cried out—they *were* green!

She clamped a hand over her hair with a groan—she needed professional help.

On many levels, admittedly, but first things first.

She drove through town back to the shopping center, praying that someone at The Hair Affair was an early riser. To her abject relief, the lights in the beauty salon were on.

Chastising herself for being so careless, she parked her car, then fished a baseball cap from the floorboard behind her seat and yanked it on her head. She hurried to the door of The Hair Affair, shivering in the early morning cold, missing the warm bed and the warm body she'd left.

How would things have been between her and Zane this morning if she had stayed? Would it have been awkward and fraught with small talk, or would they have enjoyed a morning romp?

A bell tinkled when she opened the door to the hair salon and walked in. In the rear of the shop, four women sat in a semicircle having coffee: Marie Gaston, Cecily Knowles, a middle-aged woman whom Gloria didn't recognize, and a pleasant-faced young woman wearing a pink lab coat who obviously worked there. She stood and walked forward to greet Gloria at the front counter. "Good morning. May I help you?"

"I hope so," Gloria murmured, then removed her hat.

The girl winced. "Yowza, those corkscrew curls are just awful."

"Uh . . . I was referring to the green streaks."

"Oh. Right." The young woman came closer, squinting. "Actually, it's kind of cool—are you sure you want to change it?"

"Quite sure."

The woman glanced at her watch. "Melissa Phillips

is our colorist, but she's running late. She should be here soon if you'd like to wait. Or you could come back later and we'll squeeze you in."

"Actually, I'd rather wait," Gloria said, then glanced at the gathering of women. "Unless I'm imposing."

"No, join us, Gloria," Marie piped up.

The woman in the pink lab coat smiled and motioned for Gloria to walk past the counter. "I'm Jill Johnson."

Gloria tucked her hair behind her ears—she must look a fright. "Hi, Jill. I'm Gloria Dalton."

"Oh, the new attorney."

Gloria nodded and greeted Marie and Cecily.

"Have a seat, Gloria," Marie said, pouring an additional cup of coffee from an odd-looking ceramic pot. "This is Hazel Means," she said, gesturing to the plump, middle-aged woman. "Hazel works at the Looky-Loo Bookstore a few doors down."

"For now," Hazel added, then nodded a greeting.

"We're talking about the town's economy," Cecily offered, taking a sip from her cup. "With the museum being closed and all the bad publicity, there are rumors that a lot of businesses in town might close, including the bookstore."

Gloria accepted the cup of dark liquid from Marie and took a sip, surprised at the unusual flavor.

"Apricot and cardamom," Marie murmured to her unasked question.

Gloria nodded. "It's good. Who owns the bookstore?"

"Mona Black," Hazel Means said. "She hired me to work there after the voodoo museum closed and I lost my job."

Mona didn't strike Gloria as the bleeding-heart type, so she assumed that Hazel was a good employee. "If you worked at the museum, you must know Diane Davidson."

Hazel smiled and gave a little shrug. "As well as anyone can know Diane. She's an odd bird."

The other women nodded, and Gloria had to cover a smile by sipping the spiced coffee. That was quite a statement coming from the motley crew assembled. "Because she's Wiccan?"

"No," Jill said, pulling up another chair. "Because she hangs around with that mountain man, Jimmy Scaggs."

"And apparently she has an arsenal of guns in her house," Marie said conspiratorially. "Penny and BJ saw them when they were investigating Deke's murder."

"Maybe that's because people were vandalizing her home," Gloria said, compelled to defend the woman in her absence.

"That's right—she's working for you now," Marie said.

"Yes . . . and she's a good employee."

"I heard on the police scanner that her house was spray-painted again last night," Jill said. "The cemetery was vandalized, too—headstones turned over, graffiti everywhere."

The women shook their heads, and Gloria sipped from her cup. "Sounds like a bunch of kids looking for trouble—maybe some of her former students."

"Maybe," Hazel agreed. "But you're right, Jill. Diane Davidson isn't doing herself any favors by hooking up with the likes of Jimmy Scaggs. Did you hear that Jimmy said he found a body in the woods?"

Jill rolled her eyes. "If he did, he probably put it there."

The women all chorused their agreement and drank from their cups in unison.

"How are you liking Mojo, Gloria?" Hazel asked.

Gloria patted her wiry hair and weighed her words. "I'm afraid I've been out of sorts since I got here."

"That's understandable," Cecily murmured. "Do the police know any more about how Steve Chasen was poisoned?"

Gloria casually cut her glance to Marie to see if the woman's demeanor changed. Marie fidgeted and didn't make eye contact, but Gloria knew the blue-haired woman was listening. "No. At this point it looks like a random accident, or possible product tampering."

Cecily shuddered. "When I think about how many of those chocolate bars I sold in the dry cleaner's . . ."

"Us, too, right here in the salon," Jill said. "Penny sold them at the health food store, too, didn't she, Marie?"

Marie nodded. "But not too aggressively, since selling candy bars sort of runs counter to selling health food."

"I've heard that chocolate has antioxidants," Hazel said.

"Not milk chocolate," Marie said with a laugh. "But nice try." She looked at Gloria. "Did you find a home for Steve's cat?"

"No," Gloria responded, then glanced around the circle of women. "Would anyone be willing to adopt a cat?"

Hazel frowned. "What color?"

"Black," Gloria said reluctantly. "He seems very well behaved."

But they all lowered their eyes and murmured no.

"So what happened to your hair?" Marie asked with a grin.

Gloria grimaced. "I tried to touch up my roots with a kit I bought at Webber's pharmacy."

Groans and guffaws sounded all around. "Everything on their shelves dates to prehistoric times," Cecily said.

"But the expiration date on the package was good," Gloria argued.

Marie gave a dismissive wave. "The owner probably stamped it himself."

Gloria frowned. "Isn't that illegal?"

"Probably," Marie said with a smile. "Maybe you'd better report it to Chief Riley the next time you see him."

Jill giggled. "Like over breakfast."

All the women chuckled knowingly, while Gloria's face grew hotter than the cup of coffee she held.

"Come on," Marie cajoled. "His cruiser was in your driveway all night. You should've known that it would be all over town."

Jill pointed to a small black device that looked like a radio on a shelf. "Actually, it was on the police scanner."

Gloria squirmed, mortified to be at the center of town gossip. And if the fact that Zane had spent the night at her house had been broadcast on the police scanner, that odious reporter Daniel Guess knew about it, too. Feeling obligated to offer some kind of argument, she said, "Chief Riley came by to get . . . something . . . that someone left at my office the day that Steve Chasen died."

"I told everyone about the voodoo doll," Marie offered unapologetically.

"Did you ever find out who left it?" Jill asked.

"No."

"Well, when the chief stopped by, you must have put some kind of voodoo spell on him yourself," Cecily said slyly, eliciting more laughter.

The bell on the door tinkled, diverting attention away from Gloria, thank goodness.

"There's our colorist, Melissa, now," Jill said to Gloria with a wink. "She'll get your hair back to normal."

Gloria stood and followed Jill to greet the bustling Melissa, who seemed harried as she shrugged out of her coat and hung it on a rack nearby.

"You're later than usual," Jill said with a laugh. "Is everything okay?"

The brunette with the wildly teased hair turned to Jill, her mouth curling down in a frown. "Everything's fine! Besides, it's not like I had an appointment."

Jill bristled. "I just meant that we missed you for coffee," she murmured, then gestured to Gloria. "This is Gloria Dalton. She needs an emergency color correction."

Melissa peered at Gloria, still preoccupied with putting away her purse, then frowned. "Let me guess—a victim of the kitchen sink salon?"

Gloria flushed. "Something like that."

The woman adopted a surly expression as she jabbed a finger toward an empty chair. "That's my station. Have a sit down."

Gloria eased into the chair and cringed at her reflection in the oval three-way mirror. She looked like she was wearing a clown's wig. She lifted her cup to her mouth but missed, spilling her coffee when the chair tilted slightly. She caught herself and closed her eyes, breathing deeply to ward off the dizziness . . . in . . . and out . . . in . . . and out.

It was no wonder her body was rebelling. Sleeping with Zane, giving in to a blackmailer, trying to ignore the fact that someone living in Mojo might have poisoned Steve Chasen intentionally.

A snapping sound made her eyes pop open. Melissa was shaking out a vinyl cape, which she draped around Gloria and fastened behind her neck. The woman still seemed distracted, and Gloria remembered that when she'd been in Dr. Whiting's office, Brianna had mentioned that her friend "Melissa" had dated Steve.

Hm.

"Sorry for the trouble," Gloria said, flashing a friendly smile.

"It's my job," the woman said in a clipped tone. "What color do you want it? Brown or blonde?"

Gloria blinked. "Brown, of course. That's what it was before I made such a mess out of it."

Melissa leaned forward and parted Gloria's hair with her fingers. "Yeah, but it was blonde before that." She squinted at Gloria in the mirror. "Are you sure you don't want it back to your natural blonde color—that would look better with your complexion."

Gloria sent a nervous glance to the women, who had paused from their coffee drinking and conversation.

"You're a natural blonde?" Marie called across the room. "Wow, who covers up blonde?"

"Melissa is right," Jill offered. "Blonde would look better with your coloring."

"N-no, thanks," Gloria said. "I like it brown."

Melissa shrugged. "Suit yourself. How often do you get a perm?"

"Every couple of months, I guess."

"It's ruining your hair," the woman said flatly. "Your hair is too fine to take that kind of abuse. Keep it up and you're gonna be bald."

Marie stood and walked across the room to stand behind Gloria and angle her head. "You normally have straight blonde hair?"

"N-not that straight," Gloria stammered. "Or that blonde. I just like it darker."

"And curlier," Marie said, sounding thoughtful.

Gloria met the woman's curious gaze in the mirror, then glanced away, trying not to think of anything incriminating in case the woman could actually read her mind. She was glad when Melissa leaned her back to wash her hair.

"See y'all later," Marie called, and over the rush of water, Gloria heard the bell on the door tinkle.

A few minutes later, when Melissa had toweled her hair dry and applied the hair color, Gloria said, "Someone told me that you used to date Steve Chasen."

The woman's hands stopped, and her mouth went pensive. "For a while."

"What happened, if you don't mind me asking."

The hairdresser resumed her ministrations, then wiped her hands and set a timer next to the sink.

"I don't mind. The man was a conceited asshole with a two-inch-long dick, that's what happened."

Gloria's eyebrows went up.

Cecily gave a little laugh. "Gee, Melissa, tell us how you really feel about him."

Gloria got the feeling from the woman's expression that she did want to tell more, but suddenly Hazel hushed everyone.

"Something's coming over the scanner . . . there's a fire!" She adjusted the knob, and in between static bursts, a woman's voice calmly repeated the address where a Mojo house was ablaze. In the distance, sirens sounded.

Hazel repeated the address. "Wonder where that is?"

Gloria froze. She knew that address . . . she'd been there just this morning, to make a money drop. "It's Steve Chasen's house," she said, scrambling to remove the plastic cape and grab her purse.

"But the hair color," Jill called behind her. "Gloria, you can't just leave!"

"I have to," she shouted over her shoulder, her heart pumping like a piston. All she could picture was the black cat sitting in the living room window. If it perished, it would be her fault.

And in the back of her mind, she had a bad, bad feeling that a fire at the poisoned man's house was just too damned coincidental.

Chapter

20

Gloria's heart threatened to come out of her chest as she swung into her car and retraced the path back to Steve Chasen's house. She wasn't a pet person, but the thought of the black cat succumbing to smoke and fire made her nauseous.

As did the thought that someone might have set fire to Steve's house out of revenge . . . or to get rid of evidence.

Cold wetness seeped under the white towel loosely tucked around her neck as the strong chemical odor of the hair-coloring product filled her lungs. She held a corner of the towel over her nose and wondered if she'd have a hair left on her head—blonde, brown, green, or otherwise—by the end of the day.

She turned into the neighborhood on two wheels, but a short distance later, the road was blocked by various vehicles and a volunteer fire department engine. She parked the Honda at a haphazard angle and jumped out to run toward the house. A crowd had gathered to gape at the spectacle, some neighbors in their bathrobes, a few with cameras. Firefighters shouted to each other as they rolled out equipment.

Steve's house was engulfed in flames, the brick exterior and the lawn around the house charred black. The roof had burned away in the center, releasing dark pillars of smoke into the air. Gloria's breath caught in her chest as she pushed her way through the crowd, registering the fact that Zane's cruiser sat near the taped-off perimeter.

Suddenly a man caught her arm. "You can't go any closer, ma'am."

She turned to see Guy Bishop dressed in fireman garb. "Guy—Steve's cat was in the house. Have you seen it?"

He winced. "No, sorry, Gloria."

"What happened?"

"I don't know."

"Where is Chief Riley?"

"I don't know—I can't talk now. Please stay behind the tape."

She stepped back, hugging herself in the early morning cold, feeling helpless as little pieces of charred paper began floating down to settle in the grass. She picked up a piece that landed near her foot—it was a tiny burnt portion of a phone bill . . . perhaps the very one she'd opened . . . illegally.

She looked up and saw Marie Gaston roll onto the scene straddling a red bicycle with a wire basket, her expression pensive. And was it Gloria's imagination, or did the woman exchange a worried glance with Guy Bishop, who was still trying to keep the crowd at bay?

Gloria studied other faces on the scene and recognized Elton Jamison as a volunteer firefighter. B. J. Beaumont was there, too, and his brother Kyle, plus Cameron Phelps, all dressed in plainclothes and obviously taking a break from their sobering task at the voodoo museum to help the small community deal with another crisis.

It seemed, however, that there was little to do other than contain the fire. The house appeared to be a total loss. Two enormous streams of water kept the flames from spreading to trees and rooftops of other houses and slowly began to tame the blaze. Her eyes grew moist over the loss of the cat, the swell of grief surprising her. She wondered if the pet had inadvertently done something to start the fire, or if a burglar or vandal had set it. . . .

Then her gaze darted to the mailbox. Or if the blackmailer had started it.

Had he been watching her from inside the house?

She made her way through the crowd to the mailbox, glancing from side to side, trying to be as inconspicuous as possible. She leaned on the mailbox, shifted to stand in front of it, and when she thought that everyone's attention was elsewhere, she nonchalantly lowered the metal lid and leaned down to peer inside.

"Looking for something?"

Gloria straightened and spun around to find Zane staring at her wryly. Black soot stained his face.

"Hi," she stammered. Relief to see him safe mingled with guilt, but it was immediately overridden by happiness when she saw the black cat in his arms. "You saved him!"

She reached for the cat and it went to her, eyes wild and traumatized, his singed whiskers twitching, she realized, at the odor of the chemical in her hair.

"He was sitting in the window of the living room when I noticed the smoke."

She looked up. "You were . . . here . . . when the fire started?"

He adopted a wide stance and put his hands on his hips. "Yeah. Before I forget, here's your key."

He produced the key to her house and she took it, her pulse ratcheting higher at the intimate exchange. His gaze was suspicious, his body language rigid, nothing about him hinting at the animated lover he'd been last night in her bed. Gloria glanced at the mailbox, then back to Zane, tamping down her panic. "Wh-why were you here this morning?"

"I was about to ask you the same thing."

Her throat constricted. "I don't know what you mean."

He pulled a hand over his mouth, then looked back to her. "Look—I know you were here this morning, Gloria. I followed you."

Her eyes bugged. "You *followed* me?"

"Who has a business meeting at seven o'clock in the morning?"

Her back stiffened as anger sliced through her chest. "I . . . had a hair appointment, as you can see," she lied, pointing to her wet head. "I came by here first . . . to feed the cat."

"Oh?" He reached into his jacket and withdrew the envelope of cash that she'd left in the mailbox. "Want to change your story?"

As she stared at the envelope, her mouth went dry. "I . . . that's not mine."

"Then why is your driver's license in the envelope?"

She blinked, then remembered she'd had to show her driver's license to withdraw the money. Some criminal she'd make. While her mind raced for an explanation, a soot-faced firefighter came jogging up to Zane, his breathing ragged. "Chief Riley."

Zane turned. "What is it?"

"I think you need to call the medical examiner." The man looked anguished. "We found a body in the fire."

Shock reverberated through her. She tightened her grip on the cat, who responded in kind by digging its claws into her shoulder.

Zane's jaw hardened, then he swung a steely gaze back to her, as if he were looking at a stranger. "Don't even *think* about leaving town."

She blanched and watched him stride away, his shoulders set in an angry line. Was he a mind reader, too?

Because she'd been considering doing just that.

When she looked up, she was surprised to see Daniel Guess standing on the far side of the taped-off area, lowering his camera and staring at her. How had he gotten to the scene so quickly from New Orleans? And had he observed the exchange between her and Zane?

Of course he had. And from the police scanner,

he knew that Zane had spent the night in her bed.

The reporter inclined his head to her, then lifted his camera and resumed taking photos of the house, fire engine, and the crowd.

Gloria bit down on the inside of her cheek as scenarios ran through her head. Was Daniel Guess on the scene so quickly because he happened to have been in Mojo on another assignment?

Or because he'd come to pick up an envelope of blackmail money?

Chapter 21

Gloria made her way back through the crowd to her car, coughing in the hazy, smoke-filled air, feeling as if she'd been run over by a truck. A body in Steve Chasen's burning house? And Zane thought she might have something to do with it?

Granted, his finding an envelope of cash with her driver's license in the mailbox looked suspicious, but she hadn't murdered anyone! On the other hand, he didn't know her—or rather, he didn't *realize* that he knew her, so why wouldn't she be a suspect?

She swung into her car with jerky movements. Getting the cat inside proved to be a little harder. After much wrangling and yowling, she held him on the passenger side seat with one hand and closed her door with the other. Then she laid her head back and closed her eyes, trying to make sense of things. She'd come to this little town to try to make a life for herself, and so far, all she'd made for herself was a big, fat mess.

Complaining loudly at being cooped up in her car, the cat scrambled for a foothold, then clawed its way up her sweater and buried its head in the towel draped over her shoulders. It clung to her, trembling, with no apparent inclination to ever let go.

"Great," she murmured. "I have a hairy fifteen-pound tumor." Utterly defeated, she started her car and drove back to the hair salon with the cat as a neck muffler, her mind churning. How was she going to explain the money to Zane without telling him everything?

Worse, if the blackmailer was responsible for the body in the fire, what might he do to *her*?

Then another possibility slid into her head: What if the body in the fire *was* the blackmailer? And if that was the case, who could have killed him?

She remembered the strange glances between Marie and Guy, as well as the fact that Brianna had mentioned that Guy had withdrawn money in small bills. Had he met with the blackmailer in a rendezvous that had turned deadly?

The notion sent a lump to her throat. Surely the man wasn't that desperate to keep his sexual orientation a secret. (Such as it was—the man apparently was oblivious to the fact that he was a full-blown queen.)

What about Mona? Her file had been empty, but what secrets of hers had Steve been privy to? And there was Ziggy Hines in New Orleans, who, from the photos in his file, was having a clandestine relationship with a much younger—perhaps underage—girl. Was he involved?

Gloria closed her eyes, conscious of the utter panic that hovered just below the surface of her self-control. How had she landed in the middle of all this craziness? She dragged herself out of the car, still wearing the cat, and slogged back into the hair salon. Jill and Melissa were the only ones there. Both women looked up when the bell sounded, and it looked as if Melissa had been crying and Jill had been consoling her.

The implication hit Gloria like a slap: Melissa had been late to work, snippy, preoccupied.

Had she set the fire at Steve Chasen's? And if so, why? Revenge?

Jill straightened and tried to smile. "I see you got the cat."

Gloria tried to smile back. "I think it got me, actually. Is it too late to do something with my hair?"

Melissa bolted from her chair and grabbed her coat. "I have to go." She shot past Gloria and ran out the door.

Jill shrugged apologetically. "Sorry about that."

"Is something wrong?" Gloria asked carefully.

"Melissa hasn't been herself lately, and even though she says bad things about Steve Chasen, they spent a lot of time together. I think his death has affected her more than she wants anyone to know. And the fire . . ."

"The fire?" Gloria prompted.

Jill fidgeted. "The fire just stirred it all up again." She waved Gloria closer. "Have a seat and let me take a look at your hair."

Gloria tried to extricate the cat, but he fought her, scratching her and tearing holes in the sweater she wore over a mock turtleneck. With Jill's help, she lifted the sweater over her head and set the entire cat-and-sweater caboodle in a corner near a floor heater, stroking the cat's fur to calm him. Then she settled into the barber's chair that Jill stood next to. "Are you sure you don't want to adopt a cat?"

Jill winced. "Sorry—I'm a little superstitious. Why don't you take him?"

Gloria looked at the black mound hunkering in the corner and sighed. "I guess I have no choice now." As if she needed another complication in her life. At the rueful noise Jill made, Gloria's gaze swung back to the mirror, where the hairdresser held up a dark hank of hair.

Gloria sighed. "Just do the best you can."

Jill leaned her back to wash her hair. "We, um, heard over the scanner that there was a body in the fire. Is that true?"

Gloria nodded.

"Do they know who it was?"

"No."

"Who would have been in Steve Chasen's house?"

"I don't know—a vagrant, maybe. Or a burglar." Or a blackmailer.

Jill's expression looked pinched, and Gloria guessed what was going through the woman's head—had her friend set a fire and accidentally killed someone?

As Jill washed and rewashed her hair, Gloria tried

to surrender to the relaxing scalp massage, but her mind continued to agitate like a washing machine, tossing around all the events of the past few days. Amidst the poisoning and the fire and the blackmail, the most unsettling incident of all had been making love with Zane last night and the suspicious way he'd looked at her today.

The way his steely gaze had sliced through her still cut to her marrow. But he had every right to distrust her. Hadn't she been deceiving him since the minute he had walked into her office and introduced himself?

"Okay," Jill said, wringing out Gloria's hair and turning her away from the mirror. "Let's see what color of the rainbow we have here." With apprehension wrinkling her brow, she picked up a hairdryer and diffuser and began to gently dry Gloria's hair.

With the dryer buzzing in her ears, Gloria's mind fast-forwarded to her next meeting with Zane, how she would act, and what she would tell him. Disclosing what she suspected about Melissa's involvement in the fire might distract him from her own dirty deeds . . . or would it simply make her look spiteful . . . and more guilty?

The dryer shut off abruptly, and Jill made a disapproving noise. "The ends are fried, so I'll have to cut off about an inch."

Gloria nodded absently as the woman went to work with her shears.

Jill clipped and tucked and patted and sprayed . . . and sprayed some more. Finally she sighed. "That's about as much as I can do for now—the dye was on for way too long. In a few weeks, when your hair has had time to recover, we might be able to adjust the color."

Gloria held her breath. "How bad is it?"

Jill turned Gloria around to face the mirror, and she gasped. Dark violet-hued curls bloomed riotously around her head. "I can't go out in public like this."

"I think it's kind of cute," Jill said, angling her head. "Why don't you just have fun with it?"

Gloria laughed, aware that it had come out sounding a bit hysterical. Wasn't this the reason she'd moved to Mojo? To try new things, to loosen up, to have fun? In truth, her hair wasn't completely awful, she thought as she touched the plum-colored curls; in fact, the color was very trendy and played up her fake green eyes. But it guaranteed that she'd get attention anywhere she went, and that went against a lifetime of training.

She removed the baseball cap from her purse and stuffed as much of her hair under it as she could. "Thanks, Jill. What do I owe you?"

After settling up with the woman and leaving a generous tip, Gloria sidestepped the purple hair cuttings on the floor, gathered up her cat/sweater bundle, and headed to the car. "It's just a short drive," she promised the cat, then pointed to the other end of the shopping center. "See, just down there."

The cat looked at her as if she was crazy, and she put a hand to the bridge of her nose. "I *am* crazy, talking to a cat as if you can understand me." God, she was starting to act like one of those pet-demented people that she mocked.

But at least the cat didn't freak out this time, settling instead into the passenger seat, even disentangling from the sweater and standing up to rest its paws on the dashboard as she drove across the parking lot.

Gloria couldn't help but laugh—it *was* cute.

And Christ, she needed to laugh in light of everything that had happened. She parked in front of her pitiful-looking law office. Diane Davidson's car was already there—the woman was certainly industrious. All that for a law practice that seemed doomed.

With a resigned sigh, Gloria pulled out her cell phone and called George. After a series of connections and beeps, she left a message. "George, it's Gloria. There's been another incident, and I'm indirectly involved. I'd like your advice, and"—she swallowed hard—"and I might need your help to get out of this. Call me as soon as you can."

She disconnected the call and groaned, leaning forward on the steering wheel. Why did life have to be so hard? She should have stayed in New Orleans, where the crowds and the hubbub had allowed her to remain relatively anonymous.

Anonymous and bored, yes, but anonymous and *alive*.

Suddenly, a warm body with a cold nose wormed its way onto her lap. The cat had stopped trembling, but it seemed intent on fitting itself into every hollow of her body. Gloria pursed her mouth and considered the abandoned pet, who was undoubtedly confused and scared and in need of human contact.

Not so different from a lot of humans, she conceded.

She picked him up and climbed out of the car,

shouldering her purse and retrieving the pink gym bag full of Sheena Linder's contract offers.

"Let's go in," she said, forgiving herself this one time for conversing with a cat. "I know it doesn't look like much, but you'll be safe inside."

She juggled everything to open the door to an empty reception area. Her shouted greeting to Diane was lost in the violent eruption of barking as Henry slid into view, with a bead on the feline fire survivor. The cat yowled and clawed its way up her shoulder and cheek in an effort to wrap around her head.

"Diane!"

Diane emerged from Gloria's office, her eyes rounded as she lunged for Henry's collar. "Down, Henry! Down!" She dragged him to the bathroom, pushed him inside, and closed the door. Then she came back, her expression contrite. "I'm so sorry, Gloria."

"I said *one* day, Diane."

"I know, I'm sorry."

Flinching with pain, Gloria reached up to peel the cat off her head. She knocked off her hat in the process.

"What happened to your hair?" Diane asked with a gasp.

"Long story." Then she sighed. "Diane, why is that dog here?"

"My friend Jimmy—he's still going through a tough time. He's on a mission to find the man he saw in the woods."

"This would be the dead man?"

Diane nodded, wringing her hands. "After today

Henry is finished with his medication. I won't have to watch him anymore."

Gloria closed her eyes briefly, but she realized that in the scheme of things on her radar, having Henry at the office was merely a blip. "Okay," she said, then nodded to the shaking cat. "Do you happen to have any dog food, and will a cat eat it?"

Diane smiled and took the cat in her arms. "I'll take care of him. What's his name?"

Gloria blinked. "I have no idea. Did you hear that Steve Chasen's house burned down this morning?"

Diane looked up sharply. "No. I heard the sirens, though. What happened?"

"No one knows, but a body was found in the fire."

The woman looked stricken, nervous. "Who was it?"

"No one knows that either." Gloria watched Diane's body language carefully, alert to the extreme apprehension the woman exhibited. Then a comment from one of the women in the hair salon came back to Gloria. "I heard that your house was vandalized again last night," she added.

Diane looked up, then busied herself with feeding the cat a few treats from a plastic baggie. "That's right."

"Are you okay?"

Diane nodded. "They were teenagers. I ran outside and yelled at them. They left and I called the police—not that it'll do any good."

"I heard that the cemetery was vandalized too."

"Really? Maybe that'll give the police more incentive to find these kids before . . ."

"Before what?"

Diane's pale eyes suddenly went hard. "Before someone gets hurt."

At the woman's intensity, Gloria's throat convulsed. "I hope you have a way to protect yourself."

"I do. Do you?"

"Pardon me?"

"Do you have a way to protect yourself?" Diane gestured to Gloria's purse. "Do you carry some kind of weapon?"

Gloria didn't like the direction and tone the conversation had taken—and she didn't like sharing the fact that she carried a concealed weapon. She tried to sound casual. "I guess I assumed that Mojo was a safe place to live."

"I used to think the same thing."

In the awkward silence, Gloria moved toward her office, then remembered that Diane had been coming out of it when she'd arrived—strange, since she'd asked Diane to keep her office closed and off-limits if she wasn't there. "Diane, did you need something in my office?"

The woman straightened, and her expression cleared. "Oh, I forgot to tell you—Goddard's Funeral Chapel called. I left the message on your desk."

"The memorial service for Steve," Gloria murmured, feeling bad for being suspicious—people in glass houses and all that jazz. "I'll take the cat home and change out of these smoky clothes, then I'll stop at the funeral home on my way back."

"Take your time," Diane said, comfortable with her role as office administrator. "The only other call you've had is from that reporter."

Gloria's pulse jumped. "Daniel Guess? What did he want?"

"He said he needed to talk to you personally, and that he'd call you on your cell phone."

"He doesn't have my number," she said, even as moisture gathered around her hairline.

Diane gave her a little smile. "Then you don't have to worry about him calling."

"Right." Gloria jerked a thumb toward her office. "I'm just going to drop off these contracts."

"I'll take them in for you," Diane said, reaching for the bag. "You go ahead."

Gloria hesitated, once again struck by the sense that the woman was trying to get close to her. But whether it was because of everything that had already happened or simply because the woman was invading her personal space, warning flags went up in Gloria's mind. She pulled the bag out of Diane's grasp. "I've got it . . . thanks."

She walked into her office and set the bag in one of her visitor chairs. She felt compelled to glance around her office, although nothing seemed amiss.

"I made coffee," Diane said from the doorway.

Gloria turned. At Diane's eager-to-please demeanor, Gloria felt a rush of remorse for her earlier misgivings about the woman. "That actually sounds very good. I'll take a cup to go."

Diane held up a travel mug and smiled. "I thought you might."

Gloria took the mug gratefully, moving toward the front door. She whistled for the no-name cat, who seemed eager to leave the place where a canine sniffed and scratched at a nearby door. It followed her on foot to the car, collar jingling, and when she opened the door, it sprang up into the passenger seat.

"You're smart," she said with a frown, then closed the door.

She did not need a smart cat with humanlike qualities that made her feel less lonely. It was . . . pathetic.

When she swung into the driver's seat, she glanced over at the cat, who sat there calmly looking straight ahead.

"What, no seat belt?" she asked dryly, fastening her own. She caught sight of herself in the hat, which did little to hide her purple curls; she poked her tongue into her cheek and started the car. As crazy as it sounded, not looking like herself actually made it easier to feel as if all the weird things that had happened since she'd entered the city limits of Mojo had happened to someone else—to a purple-haired, sexually aggressive lady who mixed it up with blackmailers.

Not to Lorey Lawson, ingénue.

And certainly not to Gloria Dalton, conservative, law-abiding attorney, whose wardrobe colors ran to browns and beiges, and whose life was an exercise in understatement.

She realized with a start that over the years, the personas she'd adopted had been progressively conservative, that she had covered the spectrum of female attorney archetypes. In her early twenties, she'd been a feisty corporate attorney named Stacy Kinner. In her midtwenties, she'd been a vigilant government attorney named Benita Lance. There had been a brief stint as an entertainment attorney named

Candace Meldon, and then she'd moved into family law as Gloria Dalton.

She was now the polar opposite of Lorey Lawson, and she wondered whether she had been subconsciously moving farther and farther away from that girl all of these years. No wonder the reappearance of Zane was wreaking havoc with her psyche; half of her strained to morph back into Lorey, and half of her resisted.

Half of her was exhilarated at the thought of recapturing love, and half of her was scared to death.

When she arrived at the house, the cat followed her inside with aplomb, as if it was resigned to being relocated into a new home with new smells and new views from new windows. Gloria studied the feline with begrudged respect—she could relate to being unexpectedly displaced.

"I hope you like eggs," she said, walking into the kitchen. "That's all you'll get in this house . . . at least until I have time to go to the grocery and buy kibble, or whatever it is that you eat." After scrambling an egg and blowing on it until it was cool, she lowered the saucer to the floor. The cat dove into the fluffy meal but kept looking up at her while he ate, as if he was afraid that she might leave.

"Just don't expect much from me, okay? I don't know how to do this." She set a bowl of water next to the saucer, then made her way toward her bedroom.

The sight of the strewn living room warmed her cheeks—and other places. All morning her sore muscles and tender erogenous zones had reminded her of the physical satisfaction that she'd shared with Zane, but based on the way they had parted this morning, their one-night stand would remain just that.

Although hadn't she known it would be that way? It had to be.

In her bedroom, the reminders were even more vivid. The bedclothes were tousled, the position of the pillows striking her as particularly poignant—her pillow hung off her side of the bed at least six inches, and the pillow that Zane had slept on was tucked next to hers. He had followed her across the bed as they'd slept. The symbolism struck her like a physical blow—he was seeking her, and she, as always, was running.

Her collection of extravagant lingerie was scattered about the floor, and the scent of sex and musk hung in the air. If she hadn't left at dawn to run a fool's errand, she and Zane might have greeted the morning and each other with wonder. They would have said a reluctant good-bye, and she wouldn't be dreading their next meeting.

A lump of emotion lodged in her throat. Humming to keep her mounting panic at bay, she changed clothes quickly and found a scarf to cover most of her horrifying hair.

After a quick check on the cat, who seemed to be exploring his new space, she left to make the short drive to Goddard's Funeral Chapel, which resembled a home. It was nestled among other houses facing Charm Street. The marquee near the road read Prepaid Funerals Make Lovely Holiday Gifts.

Gloria pulled into the circular driveway that led to the rear of the funeral home and parked in the expansive lot, which had been packed when she had been here to attend Deke Black's funeral a couple of months earlier.

She sat with her hands glued to the steering wheel, staring at the angel statuette sitting next to the set of white double doors, lifting a beckoning arm. How evil was it to plan a man's memorial service while withholding information about persons who might have killed him?

Heaving a sigh, she turned off the engine and climbed out with leaden resignation. It was the one thing she could do for Steve Chasen before she left Mojo.

Chapter 22

"Open casket or closed?" Greg Goddard, portly elder son of the Goddard family, asked, his voice somewhere between that of an NPR announcer and a hypnotist.

"Closed." But as with every other decision she'd made over the past hour, Gloria second-guessed herself. Was it guilt that made her not want to look Steve Chasen in the face?

"What type of flowers?"

She had no idea. Her father had always liked lilies . . . since he'd been buried quickly and without a funeral, maybe she could get through these arrangements for a stranger by thinking of what he would have wanted. "Lilies . . . yellow."

"And do you have a preference for music?"

"Piano music, maybe a hymn or two. Nondenominational."

"Sermon?"

"Pardon me?"

"In these parts, it's common for a minister to come in and say a few words." Greg Goddard gave a little chuckle. "Try to save the souls of a captive audience."

Considering that Steve Chasen had been a blackmailer who'd been poisoned and had had his house set on fire, very probably resulting in the death of someone else, Gloria suspected that the audience would be riddled with enough sinners to keep the minister busy for a while, herself included. Still, her father hadn't been much on organized religion.

Organized crime, yes.

Organized religion, not so much.

"Maybe just a eulogy," she said.

"Would you like to read it? Or someone else who was close to Mr. Chasen?"

Gloria's mind replayed all the conversations she'd had with people who had known Steve, and the choice adjectives they'd used to describe him. "Is that something you could do, Mr. Goddard? You have such a nice voice."

He blushed and dimpled. "Why, thank you. I'd be happy to read the eulogy. What about notices of the memorial service to hand out to friends, coworkers?"

She frowned—notices? "I don't think that will be necessary—it probably will be an . . . *intimate* crowd."

"Extra mourners are available for a fee."

"Pardon me?"

"It's one of our customized options. We'll bring

in extra mourners for twenty-five dollars a head to fill in the pews, if you like. They will, of course, be dressed appropriately and will be duly grief-stricken."

"Nice to know," she said, nodding, "but I don't think so."

"Life souvenir?"

"What is that?"

"A little something for attendees to take with them to remind them of their loved one, such as engraved fingernail clippers or maybe a refrigerator magnet with the deceased's picture on it. Life souvenirs are very trendy in the big cities."

"Uh, I'll pass."

Greg Goddard nodded, noting her choices as he moved down a form. She marveled that disposing of the dead had been reduced to a party checklist: Centerpiece? *Check.* Background music? *Check.* Invitations and party favors? *Check, check.*

"Now then—clothing," the man said. "I understand that Mr. Chasen's house burned this morning with, I presume, all of his belongings inside."

"That's correct."

"No bother, I have an array of suits to choose from, if that's okay with you."

"It is."

"There's a rather nice bone-colored pinstripe that will look especially good with his tanned skin tone."

She wasn't sure that mattered, since the casket would be closed, but she appreciated the man's attention to detail. And the mention of Steve's tan made her think of Sheena Linder—she needed to finish reviewing those contracts. It was one loose end she could tie up in case she had to make a quick getaway.

Greg Goddard coughed. "And where shall I send the invoice, Ms. Dalton?"

"If Mr. Chasen's estate doesn't cover the burial fees, I'll take care of it." She handed him her credit card, thinking that if she had a new name before he ran the charge through, she'd have to get George to take care of things.

"That's very generous, Ms. Dalton."

She smiled, thinking this made her and Steve even; she would forgive him for planning to blackmail her if he would forgive her for keeping those file folders a secret.

"I appreciate you putting together a service on such short notice," she said.

"No problem—business has been slow lately," he said, sounding dejected, then he gave her a wry smile. "If it weren't for the voodoo dolls, I'd have to shut down until the casualties from the spring hunting season started to roll in."

Her stomach pitched. She understood his point of view, but still. "Voodoo dolls? Do you think they actually have black magic powers?"

He shrugged. "I've seen a lot of things in the scheme of this business—voodoo dolls aren't that strange."

"Do you have any idea who might be creating the dolls?"

Greg Goddard laughed. "Take your pick in this wacky town. Haven't you noticed that there's plenty of crazy to go around?"

She forced a smile to her face—she had noticed.

"We'll have everything ready to go tomorrow at 11:00 a.m., Ms. Dalton."

She thanked the man and returned to her car, still reeling from how clinical and orderly the procedure had been. She wondered briefly about who would someday take care of burial arrangements for her. If something happened to her, would her mother even know?

It didn't seem likely. If Maggie Lawson, aka Miranda Dobson, aka whatever she called herself these days, was still alive, she could be on the West Coast, or in the West Indies, or in West Africa. In that last phone call, she'd made it clear that she planned to get as far away from Gloria as possible.

And she had, Gloria acknowledged, rubbing her fist over the hole in her heart. Her mother was even slipping from her memory, her face and features growing dim. The thought of her mother recovering alone from injuries received at the hands of Riaz's men tormented Gloria. She wondered if her mother had found her own mojo—a new life, a new husband, maybe stepchildren. And her mother had been only in her midforties when she had disappeared. It wasn't completely out of the question that she might have had another child of her own.

Gloria's heart wrenched in anguish at the thought, but she did hope that her mother was alive and well . . . somewhere. All the more reason for her to get on with her own life.

With her to-do list scrolling through her mind, she drove back to her office, smiling when she saw Elton Jamison out front with an array of power tools, measuring and marking the opening for a window.

She alighted from her car and approached him. "Hello, Mr. Jamison. Have the supplies arrived?"

He paused from his work to scratch his lower back (she gave him the benefit of the doubt). "Folks around here call me Elton."

"Right. Elton, have the supplies arrived?"

"Yep. I'll get the window in today and come back tomorrow to finish the rest."

"Great, thanks."

She opened the door to see Diane hanging up the phone.

"How did it go?" the woman asked.

"Okay, I suppose. The service is at 11:00 a.m. tomorrow. I think we should plan to close for the day."

"That's a nice gesture."

Gloria smiled. "Have you had your lunch break?"

"No, I thought Henry and I would go now if that's okay."

"Sure. Any phone calls?"

Diane retrieved the tail-wagging Henry from the bathroom and swung her purse to her shoulder. "No, but when Elton got here, there was a package sitting in front of the door."

Gloria's breath snagged on something sharp in her chest. "Package? What kind of package?"

"A pretty gift box for you. I set it on your desk."

"You didn't see who left it?"

"No, like I said, Elton brought it in." Diane winked. "It's probably from one of your male admirers."

Gloria managed a shaky smile and waved as the woman and dog left. She raced into her office. A burgundy-colored gift box and gold bow, identical to the one she'd found the first morning she'd arrived, sat on her desk, looking sweet and innocuous.

With her heart rolling around in her chest, she approached the box and lifted the lid. Inside mounds of tissue paper, her fingers closed around a small hardcover book.

She removed the novelty book, ran her finger over the shiny, colorful cover, and read the title aloud. "*Voodoo Spells for Luck, Love, and Revenge.*" She smirked and flipped through the pages of recipes and rituals for charms and potions, then realized that something else had been placed in the box, beneath the book.

Moving aside the tissue paper, alarm flooded her limbs at the sight of a voodoo doll . . . with purple hair. Lifting the crude doll carefully, she noted other details—the round button eyes, the cloth from a jacket that she thought she had misplaced. She realized there were no pins protruding from the cloth body, but swift on the heels of ridiculous relief that she hadn't been targeted for some hideously painful impalement was terror when she realized that the purple hair glued haphazardly around the doll's head was real.

Her hair.

She dropped the doll and ran outside, startling Elton. "Mr. Jamison, did you see who left the gift box in front of the door?"

"Folks around here—"

"*Elton*—did you see anyone?"

"No, ma'am. It was sitting there when I got here."

"Did you see anyone walking around or driving?"

He scratched his groin area. "Sure, lots of people shopping and such."

"Have you seen Jill or Melissa or anyone who works at the hair salon walking around?"

"No, ma'am."

Frustrated, Gloria scanned the parking lot and shielded her eyes to see to the end of the shopping center where the hair salon was located. She saw Melissa Phillips in conversation with a man. Gloria squinted—it was Dr. Whiting.

A woman who had access to the hair from the salon floor, and a man who admitted he believed in voodoo.

She jumped off the sidewalk and jogged across the parking lot toward the odd couple, her blood pumping—how dare they try to scare her!

Before she could reach them, they entered the Looky-Loo Bookstore. She followed, her mind working furiously. Dr. Whiting knew about poisons, and Melissa had had a beef with Steve Chasen. Maybe they'd been in cahoots to murder the man. Propelled by the hope that she could get to the bottom of things, she reached the door of the bookstore, panting, then stopped to catch her breath before going inside.

The interior of the Looky-Loo Bookstore was surprisingly large, and crowded, although it seemed that most shoppers were enjoying the lunch special in the coffee shop. Long, imposing bookshelves were laden with volumes of all shapes and sizes. Hazel Means stood on a stepladder, stocking a high shelf. Gloria spotted Dr. Whiting and Melissa standing in the next aisle, their heads close in conversation, Melissa's face tense and heightened in color.

What were they discussing? Who to scare next with their creepy voodoo dolls?

"Excuse me," Gloria said, insinuating herself between them.

Melissa frowned and drew back. "Hey, we were talking."

"It's all right," Dr. Whiting said quickly. "Good to see you, Gloria. How's your hand?"

She stroked the bandage absently, but she was determined not to be distracted. "It's fine, thanks."

"You should come in soon to let me remove those stitches."

"I will. But right now I need to talk to both of you."

His eyebrows shot up. "Me and Melissa? About what?"

"About a voodoo doll that was delivered to my office today."

He glanced at Melissa, then back to Gloria. "What does that have to do with either one of us?"

"You're familiar with voodoo."

"Yes, but I don't create voodoo dolls."

She eyed Melissa. "The doll has real hair—*my* hair, the color it is now."

The young woman smirked. "Then I'm sorry for the doll, but I don't know what it has to do with me."

"You had access to my cut hair that was on the salon floor."

"So did Jill . . . so did everybody in the shop today, which is about twenty people." Melissa gave a derisive snort. "I'm out of here."

Out of the corner of her eye, Gloria saw a frantic movement—Hazel Means, losing her balance on the stepladder. The woman flailed, then fell against the massive bookshelf.

"Watch out!" Dr. Whiting shouted.

Gloria looked up to see the bookshelf toppling toward her. Frozen in place, she had a vision of a purple-haired voodoo doll lying under a book.

Er, make that *squashed* under a book.

Chapter 23

A fierce push to Gloria's back sent her airborne. She landed on her stomach, sprawling and gasping for breath.

Behind her, a sickening crash and splintering of wood sounded, followed by an unending avalanche of books. Gloria pushed to her feet; from the expressions of horror on the faces of onlookers, she realized that the bookshelf had fallen on someone.

"Melissa!" Dr. Whiting shouted, scrambling to uncover the woman buried in a mountain of thick tomes.

Gloria joined in, as did several customers, as well as Hazel Means, who had managed to land on a couch and seemed none the worse for her fall. Someone called 911. In the flurry of digging through the pile, Gloria was the first to uncover Melissa's face, and the deathly pallor of her skin made Gloria's heart stall. "Dr. Whiting!"

He was beside her in a split second, shoving aside books. Several people pitched in to lift the bookshelf from the woman's chest. Dr. Whiting checked her pulse, but the crestfallen look on the man's face told the story.

Gloria covered her mouth with her hand, stunned that she had been talking to the woman only seconds earlier, and remorseful that she had been less than kind.

"Poor thing," a bystander murmured, picking up an oversized medical dictionary. "It was the reference section—she didn't stand a chance."

Someone started to weep, and Gloria looked up to see Hazel being led away. "It was an accident," the person assured her. "A terrible accident."

Gloria found herself wanting to agree, but the words were trapped in her throat, trapped by the image of the voodoo doll she'd received and the overwhelming feeling that *she* was supposed to have been the person crushed beneath the books—and would have been if not for the quick action of Dr. Whiting.

She touched his arm. "Thank you."

"I wish I could have reached Melissa, too," he said, then turned back to the gruesome task at hand.

"Stand back," a man's familiar voice commanded.

Gloria closed her eyes briefly before making eye contact with Zane, his clothes and skin still dark with soot. Apparently he'd only recently left the scene of the fire. When he took in the scene, his gaze cut to her, and his jaw hardened. She wasn't Marie

Gaston, but she didn't need ESP to know what was going through his mind.

You again?

"Everyone, please stand back," Zane said, kneeling to confer with Dr. Whiting, his face going grim when the doctor told him that the young woman was dead. They stood, and as Dr. Whiting talked, he gestured to the bookshelf and to Gloria. Zane glanced at her, instructed one of his officers to clear the area, then strode toward her.

"Are you okay?" he asked abruptly.

She nodded.

He crossed his arms and shook his head. "You seem to be finding your share of trouble today."

"Wrong place at the wrong time," she offered weakly.

He squinted. "Did you know that your hair is purple?"

She raised her chin. "Yes."

"Was it last night?"

"You didn't notice what color my hair was?"

He hesitated, as if trying to gauge which answer was less problematic, then squared his shoulders. "So what's all this nonsense about another voodoo doll?"

So like a man to change the subject. She told him about the gift box and its contents, including the fact that the doll had been made with her own (purple) hair.

"Do you know who left the box?"

She squirmed. "No."

"But?"

Gloria wet her lips, glanced at Dr. Whiting across the room, then back. "But I saw Melissa Phillips and Dr. Whiting walking together. Melissa had access to my hair at the salon from this morning, and I know that Dr. Whiting believes in voodoo."

"Oh? How did you know that?"

"I asked him about a pouch around his neck, and he told me it was a voodoo charm."

Zane's frown deepened. "Go on."

"I thought that . . . perhaps . . . that is, I wondered if . . . Dr. Whiting and Melissa knew something about the voodoo doll."

"So you followed them here and confronted them?"

"That's right."

"And what did they say?"

"Dr. Whiting said he didn't do it, and Melissa ignored me. Then she—"

"Was killed?"

Gloria nodded. "It could have been me, except Dr. Whiting pushed me out of the way."

Zane pulled his hand down his face, then he leaned in close and lowered his voice. "Look, I'm a little fuzzy here. In case you don't remember, I didn't get a lot of sleep last night."

Her cheeks flamed. "Neither did I."

"And yet you seem to have enough energy to be on the scene of *two* crimes before noon?"

She decided it was a rhetorical question.

He glared at her. "We were interrupted this morning. Why did you put five hundred dollars in Steve Chasen's mailbox?"

"To . . . have the window fixed," she said, rather

pleased that such a plausible answer came out of her mouth.

Zane crossed his arms. "Who did you hire?"

"Elton Jamison—at least I was going to," she improvised, crediting her WITSEC training for making her a proficient liar. "He's installing a window at my office, and I thought he could take care of the one at Steve's house, too."

"That's mighty generous of you."

She forced a smile to her lips but didn't respond.

"Then why all the clandestine behavior?" he pressed. "Instead of stuffing the money into a mailbox at the crack of dawn, why didn't you just give the money to Jamison himself?"

"I . . . had to check on the cat this morning, and I thought it would be easier to take the money to the job."

Zane touched her shoulder and pointed out the window across the parking lot. "The man is working in front of your office."

She swallowed hard and nodded, then picked up her mental shovel again. "But I didn't know he'd be here—the supplies to fix my window just arrived."

His mouth tightened, as if he didn't believe a word she said, then he looked around to make sure no one was listening. "You didn't have to go to such extremes just to avoid me this morning."

She blinked. "I . . . I'm sorry." Better to let him believe a safe lie than to reveal the dangerous truth.

"So why did you deny being at Chasen's house when I asked you this morning?"

"I . . . didn't want . . . you to think . . . that I had something to do with setting the fire."

His gaze grew lethal. "Lying doesn't help your cause."

She angled her head. "If you followed me, then you know I didn't get out of my car."

He didn't say anything, although she saw concession in his eyes.

"From there I went straight to the hair salon, and that's where I first heard about the fire over the police scanner."

He rolled his eyes. "Everybody in this town has a police scanner."

"I, um, understand that you and I were the headline last night."

"Apparently so."

"Just so you know, I told everyone that you came by on official business."

His smile was dry. "Oh, yes—the voodoo doll. And now you have another one?"

"Er . . . so it seems." She chose her words carefully. "Don't you think it's a rather strange coincidence that someone sent me a voodoo doll of myself under a book, then I walk into the bookstore and nearly get squashed by a bookshelf?"

A muscle worked in his jaw. "The power of suggestion is a strong phenomenon."

She gasped. "Are you saying that I *willed* the bookshelf to fall?"

He sighed, the weariness showing on his rugged face. "I'm saying that according to Dr. Whiting, and now your account as well, this was an accident, plain and simple."

"What about Steve's poisoning? Was that an accident?"

"We still don't know."

"And his house being burned down—was that an accident?"

He looked over his shoulder, then back. "The fire chief doesn't think so."

She swallowed hard. "And the body?"

"We don't know—it could be a vagrant, maybe someone who went in and started the fire to stay warm."

The sound of a camera's shutter closing cut through the air. They turned around to see Daniel Guess shooting photos of the body as quickly as he could get into position.

Zane swore under his breath and charged toward the man. "Out!" he bellowed, stepping in front of the camera lens, then removing his own jacket to cover the dead girl's face.

The reporter snapped a picture in their direction, and Gloria panicked at the thought of the man having her face on film. Then Guess gave Zane a haughty look. "Three bodies on your first week on the job, Chief Riley. That has to be some kind of record. Was there a voodoo doll involved in this one?"

Anger flared in Zane's eyes before he schooled his face into a cool mask. He grabbed the man's camera and tossed it toward the entrance. It landed with a crash, then slid several feet.

"Hey, that's a two-thousand-dollar camera!"

"Sorry," Zane said. "I dropped it. Now get the hell out."

Guess shook his finger. "You can't do this, Riley. There's something called freedom of press in this country."

"I'm not keeping you from writing about it, just from printing disrespectful photos."

The man's face reddened, and he shot a glare in Gloria's direction, but he left, scooping up his camera on the way out.

The medical examiner arrived. While the man conferred with Dr. Whiting, Zane stepped into the coffee shop to talk to Hazel and a couple of employees.

Gloria played the scene over and over in her mind, thinking that if only she'd been less brash, perhaps Melissa wouldn't have been walking away, perhaps too distracted to react to the falling bookcase. And had the young woman been guilty of the things that Gloria had accused her of?

And if Melissa had been guilty, had her secrets died with her?

She glanced across the bookstore to see that Jill had arrived, still wearing her pink lab coat from the salon, her face red and puffy.

Gloria made her way over and offered her condolences.

Jill tried to smile through her tears. "I understand that you came close to being hurt as well."

"I might have been if Dr. Whiting hadn't pushed me out of the way."

Jill wiped her nose with a tissue. "Melissa said that Dr. Whiting is a very nice man."

"Yes, he is." Gloria tried to make her voice sound casual. "Do you know if Melissa and Dr. Whiting had a personal relationship?"

Jill looked surprised. "No—I mean, I don't think so. They were just friends."

Gloria nodded, then took a deep breath. "Jill, I received another voodoo doll today."

"No kidding?" She sniffed. "What did this one look like?"

"Me," Gloria said bluntly. "With purple hair—*my* purple hair."

Jill frowned. "Your real hair?"

"Yes."

"How would someone have gotten it?"

"My question exactly. I wondered if maybe Melissa or you—"

"I didn't do it," Jill cut in, her eyes rounded.

"Do you know if Melissa did?"

Jill shook her head. "If she did, I didn't know about it."

"What happens to the hair on the salon floor?"

"We sweep it up, bag it, put it in the Dumpster out back."

So anyone who'd seen her go into the salon would have had access to her hair waste.

Ew.

"What happened here?" a woman shouted. "Who died?"

They turned to see Mona Black making her way across the bookstore, surveying the melee. When no one else seemed forthcoming, Gloria stepped forward. "There was an accident. Melissa Phillips and Dr. Whiting and I were talking. A bookshelf fell on Melissa, and she was killed."

Mona's eyes blazed. "Bookshelves don't just fall."

Hazel Means came forward, wringing a handkerchief. "I was standing on a stepladder stocking books, and I lost my balance. I f-fell into the bookshelf and—"

"Get your things," Mona cut in. "You're fired."

"But it was an accident," Gloria said.

Mona stepped closer, looking Gloria up and down, then murmured, "Are you sure about that, Ms. Dalton?"

Gloria swallowed hard. "What else could it be?"

"What else indeed?" Mona said, her eyes cold. "A lot of strange things have been happening since you arrived. People are saying that you brought bad mojo with you."

Gloria didn't know how to answer—it was true, after all.

Mona's demeanor changed, back to all business as she leaned in to whisper, "I'll talk to the family, offer to pay for the funeral to circumvent a lawsuit."

Gloria stared after the woman as she strode away. Gloria tended to agree with Penny that her former mother-in-law had ice water in her veins. Indeed, the woman's insinuation that she was the cause of recent deadly events left Gloria feeling chilled.

Zane came over and asked Jill if she could provide contact information for Melissa Phillips's next of kin. The tearful woman nodded, saying she had the information at the salon, and left to get it.

Gloria and Zane were left alone with a flurry of activity around them, staring at each other. Her heart drummed in her chest as she remembered spending the night in his arms. She wanted to tell him how much she had enjoyed their time together, would never forget it, but the time and place seemed inappropriate. There were too many unexplained occurrences in town that had everyone, including her, spooked. Zane, too, looked torn, his eyes guarded, as if trying to figure out whether to trust her, as if there were things he wanted to say but couldn't.

His radio beeped, effectively breaking the moment. He answered, "Riley."

"Chief, Jimmy Scaggs is here again," a voice blasted.

Zane's frown deepened as he lowered his mouth to the receiver. "Can't someone there handle it?"

"He says he'll only talk to you, Chief, says he thinks he remembers where he saw that dead man in the woods and wants to take you there."

Zane heaved a sigh and pinched the bridge of his nose. "Give me a few minutes." He returned the radio to his belt and muttered, "The whole town is nuts."

Gloria knew that he counted her in the mix, and she was torn between being offended at being called a nut and feeling flattered to be considered a local.

He turned to scan the scene, seemingly satisfied to see that the medical examiner was removing the bagged body on a gurney. When it rolled by her, Gloria shuddered, overcome with the sensation that it might have been her in that body bag.

"I'm sorry you had to witness this," Zane said, his hand on her arm.

"It's just so bizarre," she murmured. "Did you know that Melissa Phillips used to be involved with Steve Chasen?"

"No." He looked at her and frowned. "Do you know something you're not telling me?"

She wanted to laugh hysterically—he had no idea. "When I was at the hair salon this morning, Melissa came in late and seemed upset. When she was doing my hair, I asked her about Steve, and she had some pretty negative things to say. When I came back from the fire, she was really distressed and left abruptly."

His eyebrows rose. "Are you saying that she might have set the fire out of revenge?"

"No. I'm just saying that she was acting suspicious."

"Like everyone else in this town," he said pointedly.

Touché.

"Where is this new voodoo doll?" he asked, sounding weary.

"I left it in my office."

"Let's go get it." He stopped to speak with an officer who was still on the scene, and to the medical examiner, then he retrieved his coat and shepherded her out the door. She had a hard time keeping up with his long stride as they crossed the parking lot, but she had the feeling that he was trying to keep some distance between the two of them.

Misery wallowed in her stomach. Whatever had been building between them last night had been razed by all the screwball happenings. Her heart went out to Zane; he'd accepted the job to help eradicate Mojo of its reputation for black magic murders, and here he was thrust directly in the middle of a voodoo investigation.

It was the story of their life, she decided: bad mojo and bad timing.

When Gloria and Zane reached her office, Elton

was using a soft cloth to polish the new plate-glass window. Despite the unpainted trim, the missing siding, and the gravity of the situation they had just left, the sight of the sun reflecting off the window made Gloria smile. It was a small sign that things could be repaired, replaced, restored.

It sounded strange, but to her that window represented all the hope that she had felt the first day she'd seen it, her name lettered across it, as if to say "I'm here, Mojo."

What a difference a week could make.

"It looks great, Elton," she said as they walked up.

He stopped to scratch his armpit. "Want me to call the guy who does the fancy gold lettering?"

She hesitated. "Why don't you hold off for now . . . but thanks, Elton."

They walked into her office, and Zane closed the door behind them, eyeing her apprehensively.

"It's in here," she said, her nerves already splintering at being in the close quarters with the imposing man. Every movement of his reminded her of some movement he'd made the night before, sending awareness pulsing through her body. Light sparkled in her peripheral vision, and a bout of vertigo suddenly struck her. She gripped the back of one of her guest chairs to ground herself—she hadn't taken her Meclazine and she needed rest. She couldn't afford to be on her back with a Ménière's attack now.

Zane glanced all around, then walked to her desk, where she'd left the gift box, book, and voodoo doll. He snapped on gloves and carefully scrutinized the items. "No one saw who left it?"

"No," she said, glad to feel the vertigo passing.

"Elton brought it in when he arrived. I asked him, but he didn't see anyone in the area."

"So his fingerprints are on the box?"

She nodded. "And Diane Davidson's . . . and mine."

He picked up the primitive doll and grimaced. "Whoever put these dolls together is one disturbed person."

"I asked Jill about the hair from the salon floor—she said they bag it and put it in the Dumpster behind the shop."

"What about the fabric on the doll?"

"From a jacket of mine that went missing a couple of days ago—from my car, I think."

"When it was parked here?"

"I don't know—maybe. But I've parked all over town."

He worked his mouth back and forth. "Do you think Melissa Phillips was our doll maker?"

"I don't know, but it's possible." Then a buried memory surfaced, and she gasped. "Wait—I remember from Deke Black's murder case that he and Melissa had had an affair."

Zane's eyebrows went up. "So you're saying she could have created that initial voodoo doll as well?"

She lifted her hands. "I don't know, but it fits."

He nodded and bagged the box, the book, and the doll, then covered his mouth to hide a yawn. He looked sheepish. "Excuse me."

But the yawn was catching, and she, too, succumbed to one and gave a little laugh. The reason for their lack of sleep hung in the air between them.

"I . . . had fun last night," she said finally.

"Me, too," he said, then averted his gaze.

"But?" she prompted.

He looked up. "But what?"

She crossed her arms. "I sense a 'but' coming on."

He pursed his mouth and nodded. "*But* right now I need to focus on my job. Daniel Guess is a pain in my ass, but he's right—three bodies in less than a week is serious. I have a hunch that they're all connected, and I have to figure out how before someone else gets hurt." He gave her a pointed look. "I can't afford to be distracted by you, Gloria, considering that you've been on the scene of every crime."

His statement hit her like a slap. She looked away and bit her lip, then looked back. "I haven't killed anyone, Zane."

As he walked toward her, his hands full of bagged evidence, his eyes were dark with fatigue, worry, and wariness. "Maybe not, but you're not being straight with me, either. You're hiding something."

She opened her mouth to refute him, but the lie stuck in her throat.

"The truth is, I'm not sure who I made love to last night," he said, then turned and strode out the door.

Gloria sat frozen. She'd changed her name and her looks so many times, and had told so many lies over the past several years, that she wasn't sure she knew who she was either.

The sound of his footsteps walking away echoed the emptiness in her heart.

Chapter 24

When she heard the office door close behind Zane, Gloria's eyes filled with recycled tears. Over the years she'd cried so many tears over him and the life that had been snatched from her that at times she felt as if she'd absorbed them all back into her skin and was steeped in salty regret. When a drop of moisture escaped and rolled down her cheek, she wondered how many times she'd cried that particular tear. A hundred times? A thousand?

When the sound of the door opening again reached her, she hurriedly dabbed at her eyes, assuming it was Diane returning from lunch.

"Gloria?" a woman's voice called. "Are you okay?"

Marie, not Diane, appeared in the doorway. Her face was even paler than usual, and she looked distraught. "I just heard what happened at the bookstore—are you all right?"

Gloria nodded. "Just shaken up."

"And you received another voodoo doll?"

Gloria angled her head. "How did you know about that?"

"Jill told me, said it had your hair and everything. Creep-o-rama, but I think your hair looks cool."

"Thanks." Gloria sank into one of the chairs and gestured for Marie to sit, too. "I'm wondering if Melissa made those voodoo dolls."

"I guess it's possible, but I've never known her to be into voodoo."

"What was she into?"

Marie sighed and dropped into a chair. "Steve Chasen."

"So I'm guessing that he ended their relationship?"

"Yes. She'd have done anything for him."

"After he broke it off, was she angry enough to poison him?"

Marie pursed her mouth, then nodded. "Yeah. She got pregnant by him but miscarried about a month ago."

Shock and sadness vibrated through Gloria. "Oh, no."

"Yeah, Steve was a real asshole when she told him. Melissa had all these fantasies that they'd get married and be a little family, but all he did was hand her a wad of cash and tell her to take care of it. She refused, but the stress took its toll, I guess. She wasn't very far along when she miscarried, so not many people knew."

"Do you think she killed him?"

"If you told me that he'd been killed with rat poison, I'd probably say yes, but cyanide? Melissa wouldn't know where to get that, and she'd be afraid to mess with it."

Unless she had an accomplice, such as Dr. Whiting. Then another thought occurred to Gloria. "Did Steve Chasen end his relationship with Melissa because he had feelings for you?"

Marie looked uncomfortable. "I don't know."

"But he was interested in you?"

The woman sighed. "It's slim pickings in this town, if you haven't noticed. Most of the girls my age are married with children. For that matter, so are most of the men. There were times when I considered going out with Steve—you know, when I was really lonely and hadn't heard from Kirk in a while."

Kirk, the superhero phantom boyfriend.

"But then I heard how he'd left Melissa high and dry, and in the end, I decided it would just create a lot of problems."

"Problems?"

Her expression grew uncomfortable again. "Melissa and I weren't exactly best friends, but I didn't want to hurt her. Plus . . . Guy didn't like Steve."

Gloria's pulse picked up. "Do you know why?"

"Typical male stuff. And Steve was difficult to get along with. When he'd stop by in the mornings to have a smoothie, he'd take potshots at Guy's masculinity, that kind of thing. And when Penny was around, Steve was always dropping little innuendos about Deke, even after the man was dead, for God's sake."

"What kinds of innuendos?"

"Little digs that he knew more about Deke than

Penny did. I thought it was cruel and pointless, but Penny handled it well. It was another side of Steve that I didn't like—he seemed to be on some kind of power trip."

And blackmailing definitely would have fed that compulsion.

"Bottom line," Marie said with a sigh, "is that Steve wasn't a very nice guy."

"So I've been told," Gloria murmured. "That reminds me—the memorial service is at eleven tomorrow morning."

"I'll be there. And I'll help to spread the word."

"Thank you. I don't guess you could help me write the eulogy?"

Marie pushed to her feet. "Sorry. Writing is not my strength." Then she smirked. "Maybe you should call Sheena Linder—I hear she's writing a screenplay."

Gloria smiled. "And I think she's casting locals."

"Not all of us peasants," Marie said dryly. "Maybe Mona Black—she and Sheena have been inseparable lately. Oh, and Chief Riley. You'd better stake your claim. Sheena looks at that man like he's a big, juicy steak and she's about to go to the electric chair."

Gloria tried to look nonchalant, but a flush blazed its way up her neck. "I . . . have no intention of staking a claim on Chief Riley."

"Funny," Marie said as she walked toward the door, "but since you two spent the night together, I would think you'd at least be on a first-name basis." She gave Gloria a sly smile and a wave. "See you tomorrow."

Gloria frowned after the woman, then brought both palms to her forehead and closed her eyes.

What an unbelievable day. Two people dead—Melissa Phillips and the poor soul in the fire.

Who?

A vagrant, as the police theorized? A burglar, tempted by all the electronic equipment, who had accidentally set a fire? Or the blackmailer?

She glanced at her cell phone. Since she hadn't heard from the man who presumably would be missing his five hundred dollars by now, maybe he had perished after all. And while she wouldn't wish *death* on the person, if someone had to die in that fire, the blackmailer would be her first choice.

Her spirits lifted half a notch—if the blackmailer was out of the picture, then maybe she wouldn't have to leave Mojo after all.

Then she winced. And then what? Stay and carry on with Zane as Gloria Dalton?

Assuming he wanted to carry on. There were undoubtedly lots of available women in town, and it sounded as if Sheena Linder was ready to pounce.

As soon as the thought materialized, she groaned—how hypocritical, considering *she* was the one who'd practically attacked Zane.

Determined to focus on something productive, she went to her desk and pulled out a notebook to write a eulogy for a man she'd never really known and, if she had, probably wouldn't have liked.

Steve Chasen, age—

She squinted—how old was Steve? She pulled out the scant information in his employee file. Twenty-eight. Heartbreakingly young.

Steve Chasen, age twenty-eight, was a resident of Mojo—

She stopped—maybe a "longtime" resident? She checked his resumé. He'd listed working for Deke Black for a couple of years, and nothing before that. So "longtime resident" didn't seem appropriate, and "beloved" was a downright fabrication.

Steve Chasen, age twenty-eight, was a well-known resident of Mojo, where he worked in a respected law firm—

She winced—"respected" wasn't a word most would attribute to Deke Black, considering his association with the voodoo museum.

Steve Chasen, age twenty-eight, was a well-known resident of Mojo, where he worked as a paralegal.

Gloria stared at the solitary sentence until her eyes crossed. What now? Wasn't it customary to tell of a person's hobbies?

He had a knack for—

Pissing people off and exploiting their personal lives for money?

—high-tech equipment and maintained a lovely home.

That had since been torched and burned to the ground.

He was preceded in death by his parents.

Gloria paused, wondering if the loss of the young man's parents had caused him to lose his moral compass. After her mother's disappearance, she had felt adrift herself, but she had eventually moored herself through the strength of spirit that her mother had instilled in her. On a very deep level, it was satisfying to know that her mother had confidence that she could make it in the world on her own.

He is survived by many friends, acquaintances, and business associates, and a beloved pet cat named—

She frowned and erased.

—a beloved pet cat.

She frowned at the abbreviated eulogy, then set down her pencil. It would have to do.

The bell on the front door sounded and she rose, picking up her coffee mug as she moved toward the reception area. The entryway was flooded with sunshine from the newly installed window. Diane Davidson walked in, with Henry in tow.

"The window looks great," Diane said, then pointed in the direction of the other end of the shopping center, where a police car sat and a crowd still lingered outside. "Did I miss something?"

Patting Henry's happy head, Gloria filled Diane in on what had happened at the bookstore. Diane looked horrified.

"That poor girl. And poor Hazel—she's such a nice lady, she must be positively distraught."

"And Mona fired her on the spot."

"Our esteemed mayor. I can't figure her out. She owns half the town, and one day, she's doing something good, the next day, she's heartless." Diane made a sorrowful noise. "First Steve Chasen, then the person who burned up in his house, and now Melissa. They say that death comes in threes . . . let's hope this is the end of it."

Yes, let's, Gloria thought.

Diane turned back to look at Gloria, a little smile on her lips. "What was in the box?"

Gloria debated whether to tell her about the voodoo doll, but so many people already knew. She relayed the contents as dispassionately as she could, but Diane gaped.

"A voodoo doll . . . of you? Under a book?" Then she looked back to the bookstore. "Were you . . . in the bookstore when the accident happened?"

Gloria nodded. "I was standing next to Melissa. Dr. Whiting pushed me out of the way."

Diane was silent, but fear lit her eyes.

"But I'm fine," Gloria said quickly, giving Henry a scratch behind his ears to prove her good humor. The dog closed his eyes and lowered his head in pleasure.

"Where is the voodoo doll?" Diane asked.

"Chief Riley took it with him. He wants to find out who's playing a prank. If you see any more boxes like that, call the police."

Diane nodded mutely.

"Meanwhile," Gloria said, pouring herself a cup of coffee, "I have a lot of paperwork to do." Gloria glanced at Henry, who was sniffing wildly at her legs.

"Sorry," Diane said, dragging him away. "He probably smells the cat on your clothes."

"That must be some snout, to be able to smell buried truffles."

"All bloodhounds are good trackers—they're made for it. When they walk with their nose to the ground, their ears swing back and forth, stirring up the scent. But Henry here is extraordinary." She smiled shyly. "At least that's what Jimmy says."

"Too bad Henry couldn't find that body in the woods that Jimmy is looking for," Gloria said lightly.

Diane looked up, her cheeks pink. "He probably could if he had the original scent to follow."

"While I was with Chief Riley, he received a call. Jimmy said he thought he remembered where he'd seen the body and wanted to take Chief Riley there."

Diane's expression clouded, then she turned to drag Henry back to the bathroom.

Gloria took her coffee back to her desk, opened the file on Cameron Phelps's divorce papers, and tried to immerse herself in the details of someone else's life. His wife's name was Megan, it was a first marriage for both of them, and the union had produced no children. It was a no-fault divorce, and the property settlement of modest holdings was split fifty/fifty and looked completely run of the mill.

A divorce didn't get any easier than this, she conceded, nursing a little pang of sadness that the man's dedication to such a noble cause had driven a wedge between him and his wife. She remembered BJ's comment about how lucky they were to have someone with Cameron's credentials join the missing persons task force. But in the process of finding others, he had lost his marriage. Pity.

She looked up the number for the Browning Motel and left a message for him that he could drop by any time Monday to pick up his file. Then she wrote a cover memo that all the papers seemed to be in order and slid the file inside an envelope with a No Charge note on the top for Diane. It had taken almost no time to review the contract, and besides, it was her very small way of indirectly contributing to the work that was going on at the museum.

Since there were no more candy bars to buy, she noted wryly.

She spent the rest of the afternoon sifting through the offers that Jodi Reynolds had received for the rights to her official story as the most publicized survivor of the Mojo Instruments of Death and Voodoo Museum. Some of the offers were simple to weed out merely from the shoddy contract or ridiculous demands on the young woman's availability. By the end of the day, Gloria had managed to narrow the offers down to the three top production companies that had the best qualifications, were offering the best overall payment terms, and whose contract language was the most accommodating. One production company wanted to shoot on-site—an impossibility, considering the museum was now a crime scene, but they were certainly offering a handsome sum for exclusive rights, which would include a documentary of

Jodi touring the actual rooms where she had been tortured.

Ah, nothing was quite as entertaining as depravity.

At least Jodi Reynolds would be a very rich woman regardless of the deal she decided to accept. The money wouldn't erase the abuse she had endured while she'd been held against her will in the voodoo museum, but at least it would give her the freedom to escape the scrutiny long enough to start to heal.

She generated a cover memo with her notes for Jodi and Sheena to reference while they made their decision, then returned the offers to the pink gym bag and called the cell phone number that Sheena had given her.

"This is Sheena," the woman answered, gum snapping.

"Hi, this is Gloria Dalton. I've had a chance to go through those offers and narrow them down to the three that seem to strike the best balance between what you and your sister want."

"Great," the woman said. *Snap, snap.* "We'll be in first thing tomorrow to meet with you."

"Actually, we're closing tomorrow to attend Steve Chasen's memorial service."

Sheena expelled a noisy sigh that said she didn't appreciate something as pedestrian as a funeral getting in the way of her movie deal. "What time is the shindig?"

"Er, the service is at eleven."

"I'll see you there."

"That's nice of you," Gloria offered, "since you didn't know Steve that well."

"I have a business relationship with Goddard's—if the family wants their loved one to have a casket tan, he hauls the body down to my salon after-hours."

Gloria blanched—that had to be illegal on some level.

"I'll swing by Monday morning to talk about the contracts," Sheena said, then disconnected the call.

Feeling like she'd been sideswiped, Gloria hung up the phone, a little jealous of people who steamrolled their way through life, demanding more than their fair share. Sheena Linder didn't hide behind colored contact lenses and bland clothing. When her time came, the woman would probably go out in a blaze of neon glory and get a gold-plated tombstone.

Gloria checked her watch and pushed back her chair. As much as she didn't want to go home, it was time to call it a day. She had a cat to feed. She'd drink the beer left over from last night and try to figure out if the possibility of a dead blackmailer improved her situation.

As she and Diane left the office, Gloria glanced down the sidewalk to see Jules Lamborne going into Primo's.

"You go ahead," Gloria said to Diane, then strode toward the dry cleaner's. She had questions, and she had a feeling that the eerie little Cajun woman had answers.

Chapter 25

When Gloria walked inside the dry cleaner's, Cecily and her aunt Jules were talking. Cecily appeared to be scolding the old woman.

"Knock it off," Cecily said, her voice gentle but firm. "You're scaring the customers." When she noticed Gloria, Cecily straightened. "Hi, Gloria. Your clothes are ready." After a warning glance at her aunt, she turned to flip through the carousel of clothing behind her.

Gloria walked up to the counter and nodded hello to Jules. The woman nodded back, then glanced at Gloria sideways, her mouth screwed up, as if she wanted to say something but couldn't.

"Did you hear that I received another voodoo doll today?" Gloria asked.

"Yep," the woman said abruptly, then turned to go.

"Wait," Gloria said, holding out her arm. "What can you tell me about it?"

Jules shot a defiant glance at her niece, then looked at Gloria and shrugged. "Dunno. What'd it look like?"

"Dressed in fabric from a jacket that I lost, with my real hair."

When Jules pursed her wrinkled lips and squinted, she looked like a dried apple-head doll. "Real hair, don't see that too often. Was it stabbed?"

"No."

"Hm. Did it have a face?"

"Buttons for eyes, I think."

"Tweren't meant for you, then."

Gloria frowned. "How do you know?"

"Eyes open, no pin—the mojo weren't aimed at you. It was meant for someone else."

"Then why did I get the doll?"

Jules looked at her, her eyes shining with an almost unnatural light. "You set things in motion for the other person to get their *punition*."

"*Punition?* You mean punishment?" The nerves along Gloria's neck and spine began to vibrate as the woman's spooky mood enveloped her. "Why would someone want to punish Melissa Phillips?"

"That's for her to answer. You should feel good that while you were here, you helped the *lwa* set things right."

"The *lwa?*"

"Voodoo gods," Cecily piped up, hanging Gloria's clothes on a rack near the cash register and eyeing her aunt irritably. "Auntie Jules, I thought we talked about this."

Jules jerked her thumb toward Gloria. "She asked." The old woman muttered something Cajun under her breath and shuffled out the door.

Cecily sighed. "I'm sorry about that."

"No, she's right," Gloria said, staring after the woman. "I asked."

"Tough day, huh?" Cecily asked, ringing up the sale.

"Yeah. By now I'm sure everyone in town knows what happened."

"Everyone is spooked, all right. Lately, things seem to have gotten weirder and weirder."

Gloria opened her wallet to count out cash and realized from the empty sleeve in her wallet that Zane still had her driver's license. "You mean since I arrived?"

Cecily pressed her lips together, looking apologetic. "It's just talk, that's all. Small towns thrive on it, the juicier, the better. Things will settle down . . . eventually."

Gloria picked up her bagged clothes and said good-bye, but Jules's words kept circling through her head . . . that she had set things into motion . . . that it was her fault that Melissa Phillips was dead . . .

She drove toward her house, so numb she nearly forgot to stop by Goddard's to drop off the cryptic eulogy for Steve Chasen. Things were hectic at the funeral home, with the impending arrival of another body—Melissa's, Gloria realized with a stone in her stomach.

As Gloria made her way back to the parking lot, a

dizzy spell descended, intense enough to put her on her knees next to her car. When the horizon righted, she stood and slowly lowered herself into the driver's seat. She pulled the bottle of Meclazine from her purse and choked down a capsule without water.

The stress, she realized, was finally getting to her.

She wasn't sure how much more she could take.

She was a nervous wreck as she drove the short distance to her house. Was there really such a thing as black magic? Could a mere *doll* make things happen?

Or was she simply losing her mind, making her vulnerable to the ramblings of a woman who was almost too old to be alive?

An overwhelming urge to call Zane and purge herself seized her. She wondered if he was still tramping around the woods with Jimmy Scaggs, looking for the alleged body that the mountain man claimed to have tripped over, or if Zane had tired of all the eccentricities of the Mojo residents and simply written the man off.

Even if she gave in to the impulse to call Zane and tell him the truth about herself and the possible danger, it wouldn't explain the bodies that Zane had on his hands. She swallowed. Unless . . .

Unless Zane concluded that she had a motive for killing Steve, to keep him from blackmailing her.

And that she had used the key that Zane had given her to Steve's house to stash a body and set the house on fire to conceal yet another murder and any information about herself that might have been in Steve's house.

And that she had set up Melissa's "accident" to

coincide with the voodoo doll to divert attention from herself for Steve's murder onto the supernatural.

And didn't all of those theories make more sense than the fool notion that *voodoo* was behind the goings-on?

Gloria swallowed hard and looked to the right. "Hello, rock." Then she looked to the left. "Hello, hard place."

By the time she opened the door from the garage to the laundry room, her head ached and her senses were in overdrive. A rustle from the bedroom sent her heart to her throat. She reached into her purse and removed the .38. It felt cold and deadly in her trembling hand. She remained still, straining to listen for the sound of an intruder over the roar of her pulse in her ears.

She lifted the gun with two hands and pulled a bead on the doorway, chest-height. Dizziness tugged at her, stealing her peripheral vision. She widened her stance to steady herself and yelled, "I have a gun!"

A blur of motion appeared at the bedroom door. She lowered the gun, then nearly wept with relief to see the black cat trotting toward her. She put the safety on her pistol and put it back in her purse, feeling like an idiot, but her relief turned to alarm when she saw that from the cat's red collar dangled a note.

Not again, she thought.

She crouched and, with shaking fingers, removed the slip of paper attached to the collar. Oblivious to her distress, the cat rubbed against her leg while she read it.

WHERE'S MY MONEY?

Gloria inhaled sharply. The violation of having her home invaded was doubly alarming because someone was using her cat as a messenger.

The ring of her cell phone pealed into the air. She fumbled for it, the sound jarring her sharpened senses to the point that each ring sounded like a scream. She glanced at the display. *Private.*

Pushing the Connect button, she said, "Hello."

A metallic vibration sounded over the line. "Where's my money?"

Her throat convulsed. "I . . . I delivered it, but there was a fire."

"I know," the muffled voice continued, unidentifiable. "I waited until everyone left, but the mailbox was empty."

"You were there?"

"What happened to the money?"

"I have it," she lied, "but this has to end. People's lives are at stake here. You don't know what you're dealing with."

"I call the shots here!" The man sounded a little desperate. "Now I want a thousand."

"I . . . I need some time to get it together," she said, stalling, hoping that something about his voice would sound familiar. He didn't sound like the man who'd called Steve's house—that guy had been casual and confident. This guy seemed a little . . . on the edge.

"Okay, I'll give you a couple of days. Take the money to the Central Cemetery Sunday morning and leave it in the mailbox by the gate before six o'clock."

"How do I know you won't call me again after Sunday and demand more money?"

The man laughed. "You don't."

The call was disconnected. The sound of the click was so final that it brought tears of panic to her eyes. She pushed to her feet and made her way around the house, checking the locks on doors and windows. Everything was secure; how had he gotten into her house? She scrutinized her bedroom for signs of ransacking, although it was so messy from her love-making bout with Zane that it was difficult to tell if the blackmailer had taken anything.

That was the upside of not owning nice, flashy jewelry, she thought wryly, rubbing the silver heart medallion at her throat—it couldn't be stolen.

She sat on the side of the bed where Zane had slept, placing a hand on the indentation in the pillow. She closed her eyes and remembered the sweet contentment of being held in his arms, of feeling safe for the first time since her life had been ripped away from her. She wanted to feel that way again.

Suddenly the bed tilted. Gloria grabbed the edge of the mattress to steady herself, but the room began to spin. She gasped for air and closed her eyes in an effort to ward off the nausea that the spinning would trigger, but she had the sensation of her eyes beating from side to side—nystagmus. Not a good sign.

A heaviness settled on her lap, and she realized the cat had jumped up on the bed. Gloria let go of the bed to hang on to the cat with one hand. Comforted by the warming vibration she felt on its plump underside, she began to stroke its silky fur. The more she petted, the deeper the purring became, and the more intense the vibration against her hand. In a few minutes, she realized that the room had ceased spinning.

She slowly opened her eyes. The cat stared up at

her through slitted eyes, its body settled on her lap in pure contentment. The calming rhythm of stroking the cat, she realized suddenly, had warded off what had promised to be the most serious attack she'd had in years.

They sat that way for a while, displaced person and displaced cat, comforting each other, until her cell phone rang again. The cat leaped to the floor, and she reached for her purse warily. Was it the blackmailer again? Had he changed his mind, wanting more money, or wanting it sooner?

She connected the call. "Hello."

"Gloria, it's George. What the hell is going on there? All kinds of weird stuff is coming over the wire about voodoo dolls, and a body in the burned house of the man you told me was planning to blackmail you?"

She inhaled deeply for strength, then admitted she had tried to pay off the blackmailer, and what had ensued—the fire, the body in the fire, and the accident in the bookstore. "As the chief of police pointed out to me today, I've been on the scene of every crime. With all this extra attention, I'm afraid my cover will be compromised, if it hasn't been already."

"Well, your chief is doing his job—he requested a background check on you yesterday. He'll receive a copy of your fabricated history tomorrow morning or so."

She closed her eyes briefly, then frowned. "You mean today, don't you? He requested the background check today." After he'd walked out of her office.

"No, I'm looking at the form—he requested a background check yesterday afternoon."

Then brought pizza and beer to her house and spent the night.

"Guess that means he hasn't figured out who you really are."

"No . . . he hasn't."

"That's a compliment to you and how hard you've worked to make yourself over. Congratulations."

"Thank you," she murmured, feeling somewhat less than successful.

"But turnabout is only fair."

She frowned. "What do you mean, George?"

"I mean, I ran a background check on Zane Riley to make sure he didn't pose a threat to you."

Her throat convulsed. "And?"

"Pretty impressive—after Riley became a cop, he moved around the country from precinct to precinct, making a name for himself solving cold cases and earning about every commendation possible before moving on. Took a slug in the chest to save a hostage in St. Louis, cracked a serial rapist case in Cincinnati that went back ten years. This guy's the real deal."

Pride swelled in her chest, misting her eyes. Of course he was.

"Not much of a personal life, though," George continued. "Never been married, no kids. Looks like he's married to his job." He gave a little laugh. "Would make a good fed. And he's just the kind of guy who would try to get between you and Riaz."

"Sounds like it," she agreed. Would risk his own life, would be distracted from his primary responsibilities. "Thanks for the info, George." And the wake-up call.

"Unfortunately, I also have bad news."

Her heart skipped a beat. "Mother?"

"No, it's not about your mother, although I am worried about her. One of the other federal witnesses in the Riaz case, the one who was missing, just surfaced today . . . in a river."

She gulped air. "Do you think they're coming for me?"

"I have no way of knowing, but this blackmailing situation really has me concerned. The guy calling you on your cell phone demanding money—is it the same guy who left the message on Steve Chasen's phone?"

"I don't know for sure."

"But the guy who called Chasen was expecting five grand for the info, and the guy who's been calling you on your cell phone asked for only five hundred, then upped it to a thousand? That doesn't make sense."

"Nothing in Mojo makes sense."

George heaved a noisy sigh, clearly frustrated. "Look, Gloria, I don't know what's going on in that crazy little town, but no matter how you look at it, it's not good. I think you need to get out of there and make a full relocation."

Her limbs turned to lead. *Full relocation.* New name, new address, new background, new identity, new occupation. Same old ghosts.

"Especially considering that you're on the radar of the chief of police and he could figure you out any day."

And this time, she'd be leaving Zane . . . under suspicious circumstances. Good grief, would he think she left town because she was guilty of killing Steve? Of setting his house on fire? Of killing Melissa?

She couldn't stay . . . but she couldn't leave. She'd known for days that a relocation was inevitable. Still, the awful finality hit her like a blow to her heart.

"We'll try to track down the blackmailer through your cell phone records—after you're safely out of town," George said, his voice sounding distant.

The faces of the people she'd met and befriended in the space of a week went through her mind: Zane, Marie, Guy, BJ, Kyle, Cameron, Diane, Elton, Jill, Brianna, Cecily, Jules, Hazel, Sheena, Jodi . . . even Greg Goddard. She'd scarcely known that many people by their first names in all the time she'd spent in New Orleans.

"Gloria, I need an answer so we can act quickly."

She swallowed past a dry throat. "You're right. I can't stay. I'll relocate."

"Can you leave tomorrow?"

She thought of Steve Chasen's memorial service and realized that it would be the best time to slip out of town, when the people who best knew her were preoccupied.

"Yes."

"Pack a suitcase and drive to the U.S. marshal's office in New Orleans." He read off the address. "They'll be expecting you."

Desperation plucked at her. "Wh-what about my things?"

"Leave them," he said. "Plan to start over, Gloria."

She disconnected the call, feeling as if her chest was in a vise. Start over? That was what the move to Mojo was supposed to have been.

Chapter 26

After another sleepless night, this time for less pleasurable reasons than the night before, Gloria stood in front of her bed with her suitcase open and her heart ajar. Her eyes were so scratchy from crying that she couldn't put in her green contacts. She'd packed a few essentials and all of her lingerie—she wasn't going to leave her collection behind.

Even if no man other than Zane ever saw it.

The blue file folders that Steve Chasen had maintained on her, Ziggy, Guy, and Mona went into her briefcase. She'd decide later whether to mail them to Zane.

Everything else, she was prepared to walk away from, even her box of keepsakes. *Especially* her box of keepsakes. This time, she really was going to start over with a clean slate, emotionally and otherwise. With trembling hands, she removed from around her neck the heart medallion that her mother had given her and returned it to the box.

She picked up the ugly back scratcher souvenir and worked up a wry smile. She would have to make do with other souvenirs of Mojo—the scar on her hand, the memory of the night in Zane's arms . . . the black cat. She reached down to stroke the head of her adopted pet, feeling a rush of affection for the comfort he'd been to her the evening before, first helping to ward off a Ménière's attack, then shadowing and entertaining her as she'd moved through the house, cleaning and straightening. The abrupt way she and her mother had left their home in New Jersey had always haunted her—dirty dishes in the sink, clothes in the hamper, mail unopened . . . her father's blood staining the carpet.

They'd had no sense of closure, no sense of being in control of their destiny.

Maybe she still wasn't in control of her destiny, but she *was* in control of her dirty dishes.

As she dried the plates that she and Zane had eaten from, she knew she was only occupying her mind, trying to postpone the inevitable. *Life marches on,* her mother had told her a hundred times.

And so it did.

She wrote a letter to the Gallaghers and left it on a table, telling them that a family emergency had necessitated that she leave, and that all of her abandoned items should be sold and, ideally, the proceeds donated to charity.

She started writing another letter, this one to Zane,

and got as far as the salutation. If she told him who she was and why she had to leave, would he try to find her? If for no other reason than the fact that she was a suspect in his crime spree?

And would she truly be able to start over if in any part of her heart she held out hope that he *would* try to find her, not because she was a suspect but because he was still in love with her?

In the end, she crumpled the unstarted letter and tossed it in the trash.

She phoned her office to leave a message for Diane Davidson to pick up when she came in. Her mind churned with a plausible story for closing the office, but to her great surprise, Diane answered the phone.

"Gloria Dalton, attorney-at-law. How may I help you?"

"Diane? It's Gloria."

"Good morning."

Gloria squinted. "I'm sorry if I wasn't clear—I meant that we'd be closed all day in honor of Steve's memorial."

"The Open sign isn't turned. I just stopped by to get caught up on some paperwork before I go to the service. I'm reorganizing all the files."

Gloria winced, dreading the announcement she had to make. "Well . . . that isn't necessary. In fact, Diane, I'm afraid I have some bad news. I've decided to close the office."

"Oh." The woman's profound disappointment resonated over the line.

"Don't worry," Gloria said quickly, "you'll be paid for this week, and I'd appreciate it if you'd come in Monday to tie up a few loose ends, give Sheena

Linder and Cameron Phelps the envelopes I left with their names on them."

"Yes, of course," the woman said. "May I ask where you're going?"

"I'm not sure." The God-honest truth. "But I've enjoyed working with you, Diane."

"Same here. I'll see you at the memorial service?"

"Um, yes," Gloria said. "Good-bye."

"Good-bye."

Gloria disconnected the call, experiencing a little pang for another lie told and another relationship that would never be realized.

Her next call was to Mona Black, and for some reason, she was nervous dialing the phone—the woman emitted a bad vibe. Mona's secretary took Gloria's name, then connected her.

"Mayor Black," the woman answered, her voice distant and hurried, as if to let the caller know that she had thousands of more pressing matters than this phone call.

"Mayor Black, this is Gloria Dalton. I'll get right to the point—I'm closing the law office and won't be fulfilling my lease."

The woman made a rueful noise. "I had a feeling you wouldn't last long."

Gloria resisted asking why and instead repeated the story that she'd written in her letter to the people renting her the house—that a family emergency necessitated that she leave.

"Whatever," Mona said. "If your family emergency disappears, your lease is paid for six months."

"Thank you . . . but that won't happen."

"That's too bad," Mona said, "because Mojo isn't

for the faint-hearted, but there are a lot of good things in this town if you just look hard enough. Good-bye, Gloria."

Gloria hung up slowly, mulling the woman's words, conceding regret for what might have been.

She would simply have to keep looking for her own personal mojo . . . elsewhere.

At 10:30 a.m., she carried the single suitcase to her car and stowed it in the backseat. Then she whistled for the cat and situated him in the passenger seat. His tail curled and uncurled in silent encouragement—at least that was how she read it.

She puffed out her cheeks in an exhale as she slid behind the wheel. Now she was reading cat body language.

She winced at the spear of sudden pain through her temples, a tension headache, for sure. And she was exhausted. The drive to New Orleans would be brief, but once she arrived at the U.S. marshal's office, she would be interviewed, and assigned a new history, birth certificate, the works.

She tested a few new names on her tongue—Betsy, Deidre, Hannah, Olivia. She could be anyone she wanted to be, except the person she wanted most to be.

Lorey Lawson.

She reached for her purse and downed another dose of Meclazine. She'd be in New Orleans before the sedating effect kicked in, although deep down, she wondered if she was simply trying to numb herself to what had to be done.

She kept her tears in check until she backed out

onto the driveway. The sight of the garage door closing with her unpacked moving boxes sitting all around made her feel as if the door on her life was closing. The door on her chance to have a life with Zane.

As she drove down Charm Street, she could feel the pull of him on her heart . . . or maybe it was the pull of this strange little town, whose quirky residents had managed to get under her skin in mere days. If not for all the bizarre happenings and Zane's uncanny appearance, she had a feeling she could have been happy here.

If only . . .

She wiped at the wetness on her cheeks, then winced when a pain barbed through her temples again, sharp enough to steal her breath.

As she drove past Goddard's Funeral Chapel, a couple of cars were pulling in. The marquee, she noticed, had been changed to read *Chasen, Sat. 11:00.*

Like a matinee.

Sending silent apologies to Steve, she drove past the funeral home and slowed to get into the left-turn lane to merge onto the interstate. She breathed deeply but was unable to stave off another rush of tears as she made the turn onto the ramp. As she accelerated, sparkles of light appeared behind her eyelids. Feeling light-headed, she tapped the brake and buzzed down the windows to flood the car with fresh air. A blip of a siren sounded. She started, then glanced in the rearview mirror to realize that the bursts of light were a reflection of the blue lights flashing behind her.

Good God, she was being pulled over!

She squinted in the mirror and gasped. By Zane!

Crazily, she had the urge to stomp on the accelerator and try to outrun him. But realizing the futility—and the danger—she slowed and pulled onto the shoulder. The cat, though, apparently had had enough of the cold wind ruffling his fur. With a great yowl, he scrambled up to the open window and leaped out.

"No!" Gloria shouted and reached for empty air. Her seat belt brought her up short. In the side mirror, she watched the black furball bound through the tall grass and disappear into the trees bordering the ramp.

She moaned, but her attention quickly went back to Zane, who had pulled his flashing cruiser behind her and emerged from the car.

Frantically wiping at her eyes, she tried to think rationally, despite the headache that was descending rapidly. Why would he be stopping her? Maybe her taillight was out, or her registration was expired, she thought frantically. She pasted on a smile for Zane, steeling herself against his effect on her senses, on her heart. If she talked her way out of this, she could be on the road within a few minutes.

"Mornin'," he said as he stepped up to the car and leaned down. He looked powerful in his pressed uniform, built for authority. He lifted his sunglasses to reveal those glorious gray eyes that were, at the moment, unreadable. He was close enough to kiss, and God knew she wanted to do just that.

"Good morning," she murmured.

"I thought you'd be at the memorial for Steve

Chasen," he said, his tone mild with curiosity.

"I . . . uh . . . missed the turn. I was coming back."

"Really?"

"Yes," she said, feeling more confident.

"Then why do you have a suitcase in your backseat?"

She groaned inwardly. "After the service, I have to go on a short trip . . . just for the weekend."

"Mighty big suitcase for a weekend trip."

Frustration ballooned in her chest. "Chief Riley, did you need something?"

He studied her with an intensity that awakened every nerve ending in her body. Her temples pounded. Her palms were sweaty on the steering wheel.

"No," he said finally.

"Then why did you pull me over?"

"Because you're driving without a license." He pulled her driver's license out of his shirt pocket and held it up.

Relief loosened her shoulders, and she laughed nervously. "Oh . . . right." She reached for it, but he pulled it back.

"Not so fast. I got the results back from the crime lab. The wrapper on the candy bar that Steve Chasen ate had definitely been tampered with."

"Oh, that's . . . terrible."

"I thought I told you not to leave town."

She moistened her dry lips. "You did."

"You are a material witness to three crimes, Counselor. You should know better than trying to skip town."

"And you should know, Chief, that you need a warrant to detain a material witness."

He grinned. "Guess you got me there."

She reached for her driver's license, but he pulled it back.

"Not so fast." He reached around and withdrew a sheath of papers from his back pocket. "I happen to have that warrant right here."

Her throat convulsed—oh, God. "Zane," she said, instinctively calling him by his first name. "You don't understand. I have to leave, and you *have* to trust me."

He scoffed, then gave a little laugh. "Trust you?"

"Yes."

"Trust *you?*"

Perspiration rolled down her back. "Yes."

"Give me one good reason why I should trust you . . . Lorey."

Chapter 27

Lorey.

Gloria's mind reeled. Zane tilted his face ninety degrees . . . no, she realized, as the car began to spin, she was having an attack . . . a bad one. She closed her eyes, but the nystagmus set in, with an intensity that made her hold her head and cry out. Her ears rang as if a bell had materialized in her head.

Through a tunnel she heard Zane's voice, fading in and out. "What's wrong? . . . Lorey? . . . Are you ill?"

She tried to lie down in the seat and clawed at the seat belt holding her upright.

Then Zane's hands were on her, his touch searing her itchy, overstimulated skin. "Relax . . . I've got you . . ."

She had the sensation of being moved . . . carried . . . of being settled on a soft, horizontal surface. She fought to drag air in and out of her lungs, willing the beating of her eyes to stop, fighting the queasiness of a confused stomach.

"Did you take . . . Meclazine? Lorey . . . take Meclazine?"

She managed to nod, which set off a series of clanging vibrations in her head that took her breath away. Darkness closed in, and she lost sense of time and space. She was spinning, floating, rolling, being tossed like a rag doll . . . a voodoo doll . . . she might have been dreaming or unconscious . . . Steve Chasen was there, alive, but his face was cherry-red . . . and the man in the black coat who had killed her father, his eyes, empty, like a zombie . . . and Melissa was there, saying she was sorry, so sorry for what she'd done . . . and Dr. Whiting was there, his voice soothing, murmuring Cajun words, addressing someone named *Gran Bwa* . . . then someone strapped her on a roller-coaster car and started the ride . . . she screamed and resisted, but when the spinning became intolerable, she surrendered to it . . .

And then all was still.

Gloria opened her eyes a millimeter at a time, afraid to breathe, afraid a mere thought might bring back the spins. Her ears vibrated, her skin hummed. Her nose stung with the pungent scent of basil and chamomile. She was lying in a dark room—the morgue? Was she dead? She risked making a tiny noise, more of a sigh, really, to see what would happen. The sound resonated in her ears, sounding hollow, but normal. She swallowed, which caused her ears to pop painfully.

A touch to her hand startled her.

"Hey."

Zane. Slowly, she cut her eyes to the side and brought his silhouette into focus. And his last words came back to her . . . he knew who she was.

"How are you feeling?" he said quietly.

She swallowed again and tried her voice. "Much . . . better."

"Good. I was worried. Dr. Whiting put you in a chair and spun you like a top—he swore it would make you feel better, but I had my doubts."

A door opened, ushering in a shaft of light before it closed again. "I heard voices," Dr. Whiting said.

"She's awake," Zane confirmed, then stepped away.

Dr. Whiting came into Gloria's sight, his face vaguely discernible as her eyes adjusted to the low lighting. "You gave us quite a scare, Ms. Dalton."

"I feel better," she whispered. "What did you do?"

"I put you in a swivel chair, then rapidly repositioned you to restore your equilibrium."

A bit unconventional, but she couldn't argue with the results. Even her nausea had disappeared. She wrinkled her nose. "What's that smell?"

He smiled. "A *paket* I made for you, with ginkgo biloba to increase the blood flow to your head, basil, celery and chamomile to reduce the wind in your ears."

"I heard you talking to someone."

Another smile. "I thought an appeal to the healing *lwa* couldn't hurt."

A voodoo prayer? Unease prodded her, but after a few seconds, apprehension gave way to gratitude. "Thank you."

"You're welcome. I want you to lie here for at least an hour before Chief Riley takes you home. You can talk, but no sudden movements. And when you get home, you have to be diligent about taking your Meclazine, okay?"

She nodded, and Zane thanked him as he left the room

She closed her eyes, realizing that the moment of reckoning was near.

"How about some water?" Zane asked.

She nodded.

He brought a cup to her mouth and held a straw to her lips. His big hands were gentle, but his mouth was set in a straight line.

"Thanks," she murmured.

"So we have an hour to kill," Zane said, pulling a chair next to the padded table on which she lay. "Do you feel like talking?"

"N-not really."

"Okay, then I'll talk. You're Lorey Lawson, aren't you?"

His gaze bore into hers, his rugged face strongly delineated in the dim lighting.

What should she do? *Lie and deny,* WITSEC had taught her. But how could she now?

"Did you find my black cat?" she asked, invoking *divert and deflect.*

"No," he said flatly. *"Answer the question."*

She counted to three . . . to ten . . . to twenty. Then, aware that she could be setting off a dangerous chain of events, she locked gazes with Zane.

And nodded.

He expelled an anguished exhale, which sounded

as if he'd been holding it for fourteen years. Then he dragged his hand down his face and drew back to stare at her. "What . . . what happened to you? Why did you just leave? And why this . . . disguise?"

Her throat was so clogged with emotion that it was a minute before she could talk, but when she started to speak, the story came rolling out. "You might not remember, but my f-father worked for an import/export business and got my mother a job at the company, too, in the accounting department. When she realized that they were really working for Bernard Riaz, the crime boss, she was furious with my father." Gloria stopped to take a few deep breaths.

"Then what happened?" Zane asked.

"Then Riaz was arrested on federal charges. My dad agreed to testify and take us all into the witness protection program, but my mother refused. Until—" Her throat convulsed. "Until the night a hit man came to our house and shot my father. He told my mother if she testified, he'd come back for us. U.S. marshals relocated us and gave us new names and identities. My mother testified, Riaz went to prison, and we went on with our new lives." She drew a deep inhale into her lungs, waiting for his response.

His eyes were wide with disbelief. "Your father was murdered?"

She nodded, and pent-up tears rolled down her cheeks.

"Where's your mother?"

"She left the program several years ago and dropped out of sight because she thought I would be in danger as long as we were in contact with each other."

"You don't know what happened to her?"

"No."

"But if Riaz went to prison, why are you still in the program?"

"Because he hadn't exhausted all of his appeals. And he's out now, waiting for a new trial."

Zane looked as if he was trying to digest what she'd just told him. A dozen separate emotions played over his face, ending in bewilderment. "Does this have anything to do with what's been going on in Mojo?"

"M-maybe."

His jaw tightened. "You're going to have to be more specific."

Her mind rewound back through the week's events—where to start? "The day Steve died, I removed some file folders from his briefcase because I thought they were client folders. Instead, it looks as if he might have been blackmailing local residents."

"Blackmailing?"

"There was a folder on Ziggy Hines, the chef in New Orleans, with provocative photos inside and a transcript that indicated Steve had asked him for money to keep the pictures quiet."

Zane frowned. "Who else?"

"Guy Bishop—in his folder there were photos of him with another man."

"And what, Guy thinks his sexual orientation is a big secret? Who else?"

"Mona Black, only her file was empty."

He pursed his mouth. "And why, Counselor, would you withhold this information from me?"

"Because . . . Steve also had a folder . . . on me."

His eyebrows went up. "You?"

"With a note inside that indicated he had contracted with someone to get information on L.L."

"But how could he know that you were Lorey Lawson?"

"I don't know, but when I was at his house looking for clues, the person he'd contracted to get my information called, and I answered. I told him that Steve was dead and to forget about the information."

"Who was he?"

"I don't know. I gave the phone number to my handler to trace, but it was a phone booth in Baton Rouge."

He put a hand to his temple. "All this time, you've been conducting an investigation with the feds behind my back?"

"What was I supposed to do?"

He looked incredulous. "How about *trust* me?"

"I . . . I was afraid if I gave you the other folders and you dug into Steve's files . . ."

"That I would find out about you."

She nodded.

He pinched the bridge of his nose. "Did you set the fire at his home to destroy evidence?"

"Absolutely not. But . . . there's more."

"Why did I know that was coming?"

She told him about the blackmailer calling on her cell phone and threatening to expose her identity in the *Post*.

Zane scowled. "The newspaper can't out someone in the witness protection program."

"The way Daniel Guess has been sniffing around

for a headline, I couldn't chance it. I didn't know what to do, but I thought it would be easier to pay the money and hope the person would simply go away."

"So that explains the five hundred dollars I found in Chasen's mailbox."

"Right. The man called again yesterday and demanded a thousand this time. He told me to take the money to the Central Cemetery Sunday morning before six o'clock."

"What did you tell him?"

"I told him I would, then my handler called. He thought it was getting too dangerous." She hesitated. "Apparently another witness in the Riaz case was murdered. Without witnesses, the prosecution doesn't have a case to retry. George is afraid Riaz's men might be trying to find my mother . . . through me."

"And that this knucklehead working with Chasen might have somehow tipped them off as to your whereabouts?"

She nodded.

"You have no idea who could be making those calls?"

"No—it's a male voice, but it's muffled, with a lot of noise on the line."

"I'll have your cell phone records pulled and trace the calls—maybe he's using a different phone than the phone booth that he used to call Chasen." Then his mouth hardened. "If it's even the same guy."

"The marshal is already tracing the calls," she said quietly.

Zane's mouth tightened. "Is he tracing Chasen's calls, too?"

"Just the number I gave him. But he did run a background check on Steve, and didn't find a connection to Riaz."

Zane's entire body went rigid. "But what if it was one of Riaz's thugs shooting at you in the square?"

"It c-crossed my mind at the time," she murmured.

He put his hand to his head. "And I've been wasting my time focusing on a trigger-happy hunter."

"You didn't know."

"That's because you didn't tell me!" He fairly shook with anger. "Where were you going when I pulled you over?"

"To New Orleans . . . to be relocated."

"Relocated?"

"As in new name, new everything."

He lifted his hands. "Just like that?"

Just like that? Hurt coiled around her chest like a steel band. Didn't he realize how difficult the decision had been for her? "I . . . didn't see an alternative."

"Your alternative," he said through clenched teeth, "was to confide in me."

His anger caught her off guard. "I couldn't . . . it was too dangerous for anyone to know."

"Is that what I am to you, Lorey—just anyone?"

"No," she murmured. "You mean a lot to me, Zane. That's why I . . . wanted to spend the night with you."

His eyes blazed. "You didn't mind picking up where we left off, except you didn't want to let me in on the secret. Jesus, I feel like an idiot."

"It wasn't like that, Zane—"

"So let me get this straight—you couldn't trust me, and now I'm supposed to trust you, when you withheld evidence that incriminates you for murdering Steve Chasen?"

Her eyes went wide. "But I just told you why—"

"Where are these files?"

She blinked at his sharp tone. "In my briefcase."

His anger was palpable. "Do you realize that if you'd come to me sooner, I might have one less body on my hands?"

Gloria bit down on her tongue to stem more tears.

Zane turned away and jammed his hand into his hair. "Why I ever came to this godforsaken town, I don't know."

"Why did you?" she asked quietly.

He emitted a dry laugh. "To be close to the missing persons task force in the hope of finding you, how bizarre is that?" And from the sound of his voice, he wished he hadn't found her.

But could she blame him?

He dragged the chair as far away from her as possible and dropped into it, his body language closed and angry.

She wanted to reach out to him, but she was awash in her own shame. Sleeping with him—seducing him—without telling him the truth . . . it was unforgivable. But one question burned in her mind like a hot coal. "How did you figure it out, Zane? How did you know I was Lorey?"

He took his time answering, staring at her as if he was still trying to absorb everything she'd told him. "Little things started adding up. I even did a background check on you, but it came back clean. I thought I might be losing my mind, until I pulled you over and saw your eyes—your *blue* eyes. And I knew."

Her eyes had been too scratchy this morning to put in her green contacts. A bittersweet thrill went through her that he would remember such a small detail.

"But you're so . . . different," he said. "Everything about you has changed."

Her heart squeezed. He sounded displeased . . . deflated . . . disappointed. Just as she'd predicted.

"I need to call my handler," she said, back to business. "The U.S. marshals' office in New Orleans is expecting me."

"What are you going to say?" he asked, his tone territorial.

"I'll tell him that you know everything."

"And then what will happen?"

"They'll come to pick me up."

"The hell they will," he said, shooting up from the chair and jamming his hands on his hips. "Not until I get to the bottom of what's going on here in Mojo."

"Wh-what did you have in mind?"

"You're going to make that money drop Sunday morning, and I'll be watching. If you're telling the truth about all of this, once I get my man, I'll let the feds have you. After that, for all I care, you can disappear again. But until then," he said, walking to the door, "you're mine."

Chapter 28

After that, for all I care, you can disappear again.

As Zane helped her into the front seat of his cruiser, his words reverberated in her head. His implication was clear—after his case was made, he didn't care what happened to her. His hands were gentle and capable on her arm and waist, but he was detached, as if an unscaleable wall had sprung up between them. She struggled with the seat belt and he intervened, but he wouldn't make eye contact with her as he leaned across to fasten the buckle.

She inhaled the masculine scent of him, miserable for the position she'd put him in . . . and strangely guilty for depriving him of the Lorey Lawson he'd been searching for all these years. He must have had his own fantasies about a reunion, she realized, which probably had involved a blonde, bubbly Lorey, with her arms wide open and a perfectly plausible—and honorable—explanation for dropping out of sight, such as one of her parents being called abroad on a secret military mission. Instead, she looked nothing like herself, was hiding from the mob, and had impeded a murder investigation that put his job on the line.

They were silent on the ride to her house. It was midafternoon, a cold, sunny December day, with a gusty wind. The town seemed quiet, the square almost empty, the sidewalk traffic light. When they drove past the Charmed Village Shopping Center, Elton Jamison was working on her office front, the sun bouncing off the new plate-glass window. The Looky-Loo Bookstore looked calm, far from the scene of a horrific accident. When they drove past Goddard's Funeral Chapel, the marquee had been changed to: *Phillips, Tues 1:00.*

She bit into her lip. Greg Goddard's business was picking up. She wondered how many people had attended Steve Chasen's memorial service for his send-off, if the yellow lilies had been a good choice, and if she should have gone with the "life souvenirs" option after all.

"How does somebody get their hands on cyanide?" she asked Zane's profile.

He dragged his mind back from wherever it had been. "By stealing it or buying it from corrupt chemical distributors, or buying it over the Internet. And I'm told that people can make it from a certain vegetable root, and from fruit pits."

"Fruit pits?"

"Yeah, like apples, apricots, peaches, cherries. It takes a huge amount, but it can be done. And we seem to have our fair share of witch doctors around here who like to dabble in homeopathic cures."

"Are you referring to Dr. Whiting?"

Instead of responding, Zane put on his signal and turned into her driveway. "I put your suitcase and briefcase in my trunk. I'll have an officer go by to pick up your car."

"Thank you," she murmured. "Would you ask your officer to be on the lookout for my cat?"

"Yep." He parked in the driveway, then walked around to help her from the passenger side.

"I'm fine," she said, but her first step toward the front door was wobbly. She felt as if she'd been at sea for days and was just setting foot on dry land. He steadied her and walked with her, his body language wooden as he used her keys to unlock the front door, where he had stood in the rain only a couple of days ago holding a pizza and beer.

When she walked in, the rooms seemed eerily lonely, and she realized with a start that she was waiting for the black cat to appear. A sad pang struck her, but she held out hope that the cat had made its way back to her abandoned car.

Zane appeared behind her, carrying her suitcase and briefcase. He set them inside the door.

"Thank you for bringing me home," she said, transferring the key to the inside lock so she could secure it when he left.

Then he gave a little laugh. "I'm not going anywhere. We have a lot to talk about." He leaned down to pick up her briefcase and handed it to her. "I want to see those files."

After a glance into his cold, accusing eyes, she carried her briefcase to the coffee table and sat down on the couch to open it. Her cheeks warmed when she recalled what had transpired there between them, but their lovemaking now seemed like a distant memory.

I'm not sure who I made love to last night.

His words in her office had stung, but they had given voice to all the questions in his head . . . all well-founded, as it had turned out.

She opened the briefcase, found the files that he'd asked for, and handed them to him. Then she retrieved her cell phone from her purse. "I need to call my handler."

He nodded, already engrossed in the files.

She made the call to George and was surprised when he answered. "George, it's Gloria."

"Where the devil are you? I was about to send someone to look for you."

"I fell ill," she said. "I have Ménière's disease, and it has a habit of recurring when I'm stressed."

"I remember that," he said. "Bad dizzy spells."

"Right. I can't drive."

"I'll send someone to pick you up."

"No," she said, her gaze darting to Zane, who was watching her. "George, the chief of police, Zane Riley . . ."

"Your old boyfriend? What about him?"

"He knows everything."

"You *told* him?"

"No, he figured it out."

George heaved a sigh. "Okay, so have him drive you to the marshals' office in New Orleans. They'll debrief him."

"Not yet. I need some time to help him get to the bottom of some things that are going on around here."

Zane strode over. "Let me talk to him." He took the phone, not waiting for her to respond. "Marshal, this is Chief Riley in Mojo, Louisiana. As Ms. Dalton has told you, I have two murders on my hands. At best, Ms. Dalton is a material witness." His eyes narrowed at her. "At worst, she's a suspect."

Gloria's skin tingled under his disapproving gaze.

"The man who's blackmailing her wants her to make a drop Sunday morning and I want her to make that drop. I'll be with her."

He was quiet, listening to the man on the other end, then he frowned and adopted an assertive stance. "You don't understand, Marshal, there are two choices here. Either Ms. Dalton stays here and makes the money drop, or I'll arrest her for murder and she can cool her heels in my jail for a while."

Gloria pressed her fist to her mouth, not doubting Zane's sincerity.

"Yes, of course I'll be with her at all times," Zane bit out. "I know how to do my job, Marshal. Ms. Dalton will call you when she's ready to . . . leave." Zane disconnected the call and handed the phone back to her, his eyes stormy.

"I guess I'm staying," she ventured.

"Damn straight. So," he said, holding up the folders, "is this it, or are you withholding any more information from me?"

Other than the fact that I'm in love with you?

She closed her eyes and tried to concentrate. "I know that Steve Chasen had a thing for Marie Gaston, kept a picture of her in his desk. And I saw Marie and Guy arguing one day outside the dry cleaner's."

"Interesting, but not necessarily damning."

"And when I withdrew the five hundred dollars from the bank, the clerk there mentioned that Guy Bishop had also withdrawn a large amount of cash in small bills."

Zane's expression turned thoughtful. "Guy Bishop was also on the scene of the fire."

"Yes, I saw him. Marie was there, too, and I observed some strange eye contact between them."

"So you think that Guy Bishop poisoned Chasen, and that Marie Gaston knew about it?"

"Or read his mind, maybe."

He frowned. "Hm?"

"Marie is rumored to have ESP abilities."

He grimaced and held up a hand. "Let's just stick to the facts, okay?"

"What do you make of the pictures of Ziggy Hines?"

"Maybe an underage girlfriend? I don't know, but I'm going to find out. As far as the photos of Bishop, I can't believe a guy would kill someone over pictures that prove what seems clear to everyone already." He looked up. "The guy *is* a flamer, right?"

She quirked a little smile and nodded.

Then Zane made a thoughtful noise. "Unless it's the man he's with that Bishop is trying to protect. Do you recognize him?"

"No, but I have to admit, I didn't study them—it

made me feel like a voyeur." She took the photo that Zane handed her and squinted at the face of Guy's partner. "You wouldn't happen to have a magnifying glass, would you?"

His eyebrows went up. "You're kidding, right?"

"Wait," she said, reaching for her purse. "I think I have one of those all-in-one tool things that has a magnifier on it." She took items out of her purse, including her .38, and set them aside.

"Whoa, I'll take that," he said, reaching for her gun, then he shook his head. "I never pictured you—er, Lorey—as someone who would carry a concealed weapon."

She didn't glance up, but she felt his censure. "Like you said, Zane—I've changed. Here it is." She placed the magnifier over the photo. "It's still hard to make out, but . . ." Her memory banks chugged through the fog of medication and the vestiges of a headache, then something clicked and her mouth rounded. "Oh, my God. It's Deke Black!"

He frowned. "The attorney who was murdered? Penny's husband?"

"Yes."

"Did she . . . know?"

"I can't be sure," Gloria said, "but I'm inclined to say no, or it would have probably come up during the divorce."

"So Guy was having an affair with his lady boss's husband?"

Noting that the date on the photos predated the divorce settlement, she nodded and winced. "Maybe that's why Guy was willing to go to such great lengths to keep it secret—because he didn't want to hurt Penny."

Zane worked his mouth from side to side. "I'll let him tell me that himself. What about Mona Black's folder—any idea what was inside?"

"No. All I know is that Mona didn't seem too distraught about Steve's passing. When I asked her if she knew anything about Steve's family, she said that she barely knew him."

Zane shook his head. "The people in this town sure have a lot of secrets." He gave her a pointed look. "Present company included."

Her cheeks flamed. "What happened yesterday with Jimmy Scaggs?"

"You mean the phantom body in the woods? He took me to the place where he said he saw it, but, surprise, surprise, it was magically gone. I humored him and looked around, but after all the rain, the ground was pretty much a swamp."

"You didn't find anything?"

"Just a man's watch in about three inches of mud that could have been there for years. The guy means well, but I think he's been smoking some of his magic mushrooms."

She managed a little smile, then suddenly, her body downshifted. She was drained, physically and emotionally. The sleepless nights, the Ménière's attack, and the medication were all catching up to her. She touched a hand to her head and leaned back on the couch. "I'm sorry . . . I'm just . . . so . . . sleepy."

As soon as her eyes closed, her body pulled her toward rest. She melted into the downy couch. Sheer physical exhaustion, coupled with her soul-deep purge of finally telling Zane what had happened all those years ago, sent her spiraling toward the sleep abyss at record speed.

He said something that was garbled by the time it reached her ears, but as she was drawn over the edge of unconsciousness into a languid state, she imagined it to be *I'm so glad I found you.*

Chapter 29

Gloria woke leisurely, flush with the feeling of having her well refilled. At the faint daylight dancing on the air, she guessed it was about 6:30. She must have slept all evening and all night. She stretched her arms high over her head and brushed the headboard of her bed.

Then she froze, and her eyes popped wide open. How had she gotten from the couch to the bed? Then she lifted the sheet and looked down at her underwear-clad body. How had she gotten undressed?

From the kitchen, she heard the sound of movement and a low, male voice.

Zane, of course.

Wasn't he the answer to every question in her head?

She took a quick shower, still marveling over the grapeness of her hair. After a quick blow-dry, she pulled jeans and a gray sweater from the suitcase she'd packed yesterday, which had been set at the foot of her bed.

Yesterday—what a blur. And what a mixed bag of emotions. Zane had seemed relieved to have a puzzle solved, but he'd openly admitted that she wasn't what he'd expected her to be . . . and hadn't hesitated to let her know that he was still skeptical of her stories and her motives. She hadn't trusted him enough to confide in him, and now he was treating her with equal reserve.

She left the bedroom and made her way to the kitchen. Zane was shirtless, standing with his back to her, talking into his phone.

"Stack up the interviews—I want to see everyone today, in this order: Guy Bishop, Marie Gaston, Ziggy Hines, Mona Black . . . yes, I said Mona Black. And I'm expecting a couple of faxes, would you put those on my desk when they arrive? Thanks. Oh, and spread the word—the next officer who broadcasts where my cruiser is parked on the goddamn scanner will be doing parking meter duty until they file for their pension, got it?" He disconnected the call and set the phone down on the counter with a bang.

"Good morning," she said.

He turned around, and she was struck by his male physical beauty—the expansive shoulders, the well-developed chest, the narrow waist. Without a belt, his uniform pants hung low on his hips, revealing the waistband of his white boxers. His dark hair glistened with moisture and stuck up slightly from his running his hands through it—no doubt in frustration.

"Morning," he said, as he reached for a folded white T-shirt on a chair and pulled it over his head.

"I assume you spent the night."

He grunted in affirmation. "I slept on the couch."

"Thank you for . . . moving me to the bedroom."

"No problem."

"Do you need for me to wash or iron anything?"

"No thanks—I always keep a change of clothes in the trunk of my cruiser."

She nodded, a forced smile on her lips.

Silence stretched between them, thick and awkward. Yet even with injured and distrustful feelings between them, she could feel his body calling to hers. Her breasts tightened, and her stomach clenched with desire. He looked away and rubbed the back of his neck. The circles under his eyes and the pinch between his dark eyebrows said that he hadn't slept as well as she had.

"How are you feeling?" he asked.

"Like a new woman," she said, then at his frown, she caught herself. Not exactly the best choice of words in light of the circumstances. "I mean, fine. Good, even."

"I made coffee," he said, nodding toward the pot.

"Smells . . . strong," she said, moving in that direction.

So this was the morning after that they hadn't gotten the chance to experience before.

"Is my car here?" she asked, pouring a cup of the blackest coffee she'd ever seen.

"Yes. One of my officers brought it by last night, and I pulled it into the garage."

"Thank you. Did he or she find my cat?"

"No. Sorry."

She nodded, wondering how the cat had fared in last night's low temperatures. "I think I'll go into my office and pack up a few things that I would've had to leave otherwise."

"I don't think so," he said, his voice low.

She looked up. "What do you mean?"

"I mean that you're sticking with me today, just in case one of Riaz's guys has tracked you down. We're going to the station. I need to conduct interviews."

"I heard you when I walked in," she said, sipping her coffee. She winced at its strength, thinking she wouldn't mind a cup of Marie's flavored coffee right about now. "What will I do all day?"

"Not get into trouble," he said curtly, then drained his cup. "Can you be ready in fifteen minutes?"

"I'm ready now," she returned, matching his clipped demeanor. "I need to stop by the bank to get more cash for . . . tomorrow."

"Don't worry about it—your five hundred is still at the station in the safe. It's enough for appearances. I plan to have the guy in cuffs before he's finished counting it." He gave her a pointed look. "Like I would have before, if you'd bothered to tell me."

She bit down on the inside of her cheek. "We've gone over this."

His jaw hardened. He reached for his uniform shirt, shrugged into it, and buttoned it with agile fingers that sent her mind wandering off in carnal tangents. To derail her one-track mind, she drank deeply of the chunky coffee, then picked up her purse. "What did you do with my pistol?"

He tucked in his shirt while he moved toward the door, inserting his own weapon into a small holster. "It's in your bedroom, in the lingerie—uh, in the bureau."

In her lingerie bureau, now empty. She turned toward the bedroom, but he clasped her arm. "Leave it, Counselor. You'd only have to check it when you got to the station." He opened the door and stepped outside, scanning the area before waving her outside.

She emerged, her breath a white cloud in the cool morning air, and locked the door, easily shielded by his big body.

"Stay close," he said.

It was an order, not an endearment. They moved to the cruiser casually, but swiftly, and were soon underway without incident. "It wouldn't make sense for Riaz's men to try to kill me," she reasoned aloud, if only to calm her own fears. "If they think I know where my mother is, why would they want to hurt me?"

A muscle worked in Zane's jaw. "Maybe to smoke her out."

She blanched. "You mean . . . at a funeral?"

"Or at a hospital. But the marshal doesn't have any direct proof that they're looking for you, right?"

"Right."

"Does the government have moles in the organization?"

"I assume that's who my handler refers to as his 'sources.' "

"I did some research last night on my laptop while you . . ." He coughed, as if he didn't want to reference that they'd been in intimate quarters. "Bernard

Riaz's organization actually grew while he was in prison."

She shuddered at the implication that the man couldn't be taken down. She inched closer to Zane, wildly comforted by his presence. It felt good to know that he would protect her as long as she was in town, although the thought of him being in danger because of her was just as scary.

During the short drive, she scanned both sides of the street for the black cat but didn't see him. She sent a hope skyward that he hadn't fallen into the hands of someone who might use a black cat for some kind of evil perversion.

They arrived at the Mojo police station and entered through a back door. It was a small, but bustling, office, busier than when she'd been there while Penny had been questioned for Deke's murder. She remembered that night with a shake of her head—she'd been scared silly for Penny, and she'd advised her to call someone other than her divorce attorney. Gloria had never defended anyone in a murder investigation. But Penny had insisted that Gloria be present while she was interrogated, and Gloria had been baptised by fire.

She'd heard that the police force had been beefed up since the voodoo museum scandal. And a quick glance around proved that Zane had instigated equipment upgrades in the short time that he'd been in charge. A couple of young men were installing what looked like a high-tech scanner in a common area. One of the men looked up and waved to her. She squinted in confusion, then recognized the teenager from Tam's Electronics—Mike? No . . . Mark.

She lifted her hand and thought of the little things that she'd left undone—the repairs to her office, the broken copier, the unlettered plate-glass window.

Pieces, perhaps, that would help launch someone else's dream after she'd been relocated to a place far away from Mojo . . . far away from Zane. She glanced sideways at him, noticing how the officers and other personnel perked up when he approached. She suspected he was a demanding boss, but fair. And from what George had told her about his achievements in law enforcement, it was clear that he was highly respected. He smiled at a couple of employees, sending jealousy spiking through her chest, because he hadn't directed one of those amazing smiles in her direction since . . . since he'd confirmed who she really was.

B. J. Beaumont came walking down the hall toward them, powder-sugared beignet in hand. He slowed to talk to Zane. "I might bring you in on a conference call later if you don't mind."

"Glad to help," Zane said. "I'll be in and out of interviews today, so have someone track me down. You remember meeting Gloria Dalton."

"Yes, of course, Penny's friend," BJ said, wiping his hand on his jeans before extending it to her. He looked sheepish. "Um, if you see Penny, you don't have to mention the donut."

Gloria smiled. "I won't."

Zane led her farther down the hall into a corner office with glass on two sides and his nameplate on the door. "You'll be staying here today," he said, then gestured to a couple of stiff-looking upholstered chairs. "Sorry that it's not more comfortable."

"It's fine," she said quickly.

He shifted awkwardly from foot to foot. "Do you want something to eat? Coffee? There's usually something up front."

"I'll take some coffee."

"How do you take it?"

"Cream, if you have it."

"Have a seat and I'll see what I can do."

She watched him walk toward the reception area, her chest swelling with pride at the man he had become—doing good things, making a difference. She wanted to ask him a thousand questions about his life, but he seemed determined to stay behind the wall that he'd erected since her confession.

He came back shortly, carrying two cups of coffee. "I promise this is better than mine," he said, handing one to her.

She smiled. "Thanks."

He studied her face but didn't return her smile. "Stay put. Guy Bishop is here. I'll check in with you after the interview if I have a chance." He picked up the blue folders and headed toward the door.

Gloria pressed her lips together. "Zane."

He turned back, his expression impatient.

"About those pictures of Guy and . . . Deke. No one has to know about them, do they?"

Zane's mouth twitched downward. "Only if Guy Bishop committed murder to keep them hidden." He stepped out of the office, then closed the door behind him.

She expelled a long sigh, then turned to take in the details of Zane's office. The furniture was simple and functional—a desk, an upholstered swivel desk chair, the two chairs that were on her side of the desk, and waist-high cabinets on two walls. There was no artwork or other personal touches on the walls, but on his desk sat two small picture frames. She picked them up and stared at them greedily.

One was of Zane's parents—his father had died before she'd known Zane, but she recognized his mother's shy smile and, in fact, remembered seeing this picture in Zane's home, on the china cabinet in the dining room.

Warm nostalgia infused her chest, and she could almost smell the yeasty goodness of the pastries his mother had always had in the oven. "You must be so proud of your son," Gloria murmured. "I know I am."

The second photo was of his younger sister, Lisa, and, Gloria presumed, Lisa's family—a congenial-looking young man and two boys with impish eyes, who looked as if they were barely contained for the few seconds it had taken to get the shot.

Gloria smiled, picturing Zane swinging his nephews to his back for an impromptu pony ride, like he used to give Lisa when she wasn't feeling too grown-up for it. Remembering the affection in his voice when he'd told Gloria about them, she was sure he was a terrific uncle.

There were no other personal items on his desk, no hint of the inner workings of the man. She started to turn away when she noticed another picture frame, this one much smaller, and turned facedown. Thinking it had fallen, she lifted it, then gasped.

It was a photo of her and Zane sitting under the tree in her parents' backyard—or rather, of *Lorey* and Zane sitting under the tree in her parents' backyard.

She hadn't seen a picture of herself in so long that she could scarcely believe she'd ever looked that way. Long straight blonde hair and bright blue eyes. Fresh-faced and open, exuding sex appeal in her bright pink T-shirt stretched over generous curves. Next to her, Zane looked heartbreakingly young and handsome, with one arm around her, as if he'd been hanging on.

Except she had slipped away. . . .

Bittersweet longing filled her for that girl in the picture, the young woman who had just been awakened sexually and was blooming under Zane's love and guidance. *That* girl had mojo to spare.

She set the tiny frame back on his desk, then realized with a start that the picture hadn't fallen over—more likely, Zane had placed it facedown sometime after he'd suspected her true identity. She put it back the way she'd found it and eased into one of the extra chairs.

Gloria sipped her coffee, grateful for a private, safe place where she could think. Her mind worked like a Rubik's cube, turning and twisting pieces of the puzzle before them to see which ones aligned and which ones had to be put back into the mix.

What was Guy Bishop saying in his interview? Had he denied everything, forcing Zane to reveal the photos?

Thirty minutes later, she saw Marie Gaston arrive, the woman's face pensive as a female officer led her out of sight. A little while later, she caught a glimpse of Guy Bishop striding toward the exit, his face equally brooding.

She saw them come and go, in the order that Zane

had requested. After Marie came Ziggy Hines, a barrel-chested, dark-haired Cajun who was markedly less exuberant than he was on his syndicated cooking show, and Mona Black, whose anger was a tangible thing that sent people scurrying out of her way as she plowed through the station.

Two hours later, Gloria had long since emptied her cup. Her back was stiff, and her bladder was full. She stood and craned her neck, looking for Zane in the milling bodies, but she didn't see him. She shouldered her purse and stepped out into the hall, then asked for directions to the ladies' room.

The helpful clerk sent her down a quiet hallway near the rear entrance. She passed supply rooms and a janitorial room, then located the women's restroom sitting opposite the men's.

She knocked discreetly, then pushed open the door to find a large bathroom with two stalls, one of which was occupied. She entered the second stall and relieved herself, but just as she was righting her clothing, the overhead light went out.

"Excuse me," she called. "Someone is still in here." She unlatched the stall door and stepped out, feeling her way.

Suddenly two hands grabbed her and pulled a plastic bag down over her face and head. She tried to scream, but a drawstring was yanked closed around her neck, leaving the sound gurgling in her throat. Gagging, she fumbled in her purse, instinctively trying to get to her gun. But when her hand hit nothingness, Gloria was paralyzed with fear.

No gun . . . no chance.

Chapter 30

Gloria thrashed against the binding at her throat and clawed at the plastic bag over her head as the attacker dragged her. She threw her weight against the bigger, more solid person holding her, but to no avail. She gasped for air, but the plastic bag collapsed on her face, creating a vacuum. Her lungs were aching and she could feel the energy draining from her body. With her last bit of strength, she used her arms and knee in a kickboxing move to knock the person off balance. They didn't relinquish their hold completely, but enough for her to loosen the drawstring and drag a bit of air into her lungs.

And scream.

Like she was on fire.

Suddenly her attacker was gone, so quickly that Gloria lost her balance and went tumbling to the tile floor in the dark, landing hard on her hip and shoulder. She cried out as pain lit up her body, then she ripped open the bag to gulp fresh air. She was sputtering and tearing at the plastic ties around her neck when suddenly the door burst open and the overhead light erupted, momentarily blinding her.

"Gloria!" Zane shouted. His gun was drawn, but he reholstered it in one movement.

She felt his hands freeing the ties while he bellowed instructions to his officers to lock down the station and canvass the perimeter for anyone who didn't belong. "What happened?" he asked, helping her sit up.

"I . . . was attacked," she got out before a coughing jag took hold of her. She could feel his urgency, his panic, in the way he touched her, but his voice remained calm.

"Did you see who attacked you?"

She shook her head.

"Man or woman?"

"Man . . . or maybe a strong woman. But I think . . . they were . . . waiting for me."

"What do you mean?"

In halting breaths, she told him about the first stall being occupied, that she hadn't heard anyone leave or come in, and that she was grabbed when she came out of the second stall.

"It would've been nice to have my gun," she muttered.

Anger darkened his face. "I told you to stay put."

Disbelief flooded her. "You're blaming me? I sat in your office for two hours—I had to *pee*. I thought I'd be safe in the ladies' room of a police station."

His mouth tightened, and a vein protruded from his forehead. "Do you need to go to the hospital?"

"No," she said, pushing to her feet with his assistance. "I'm okay, just a few bruises." But she was still trembling from the abrupt adrenaline surge and retreat, and the skin on her neck was raw and painful. She leaned on him, breathing deeply. The plastic bag that had nearly suffocated her lay on the floor, a generic drawstring kitchen garbage bag. A lethal weapon in the right hands.

She remembered George's comment that the mob had traded in its old-fashioned gun-and-run tactics for more subtle, less traceable ploys. Was it the handiwork of one of Riaz's men, or did someone in Mojo think she was getting too close to the truth?

"I want this room printed," Zane commanded. "Concentrate on the first stall and the garbage bag. See if the bag came from our supply room." He continued to bark orders, and everyone scurried to follow them.

Gloria crouched down to gather the items spilled from her purse. When she stood, Zane's expression was tight. "Are you sure you're okay?"

She nodded, touched by his concern, even if it was only professional.

"Do you remember anything else about the person—maybe a sound or a smell?"

"No, the bag was over my head before I realized what was going on. But I think the person was trying to . . . remove me from the bathroom."

"You mean kidnap you?"

"I don't know, but I had the sense that they were

trying to move me toward the door. Maybe they were hoping I'd pass out."

He nodded, digesting the information. "We need to let your handler know what happened."

She balked. "But . . . he'll insist that I be relocated right away. He'll send someone to get me."

Their gazes locked, and her heart fluttered with panic at the thought of being separated from him so suddenly, before . . .

Before what? her mind mocked.

"Make the call," Zane said quietly. "Or I will."

She pulled out her phone and punched in George's number with a hand that shook. When he answered, she told him about the incident in as calm a manner as possible.

"Sounds like the mob," he said flatly. "You need to get out of there, Gloria, now. Put Chief Riley on the phone, please."

She looked up and handed the phone to Zane, whose jaw hardened as he listened to the man on the other end of the line. "It was a mistake," Zane bit out, "but it won't happen again. The minute Ms. Dalton is ready to leave, I'll escort her to New Orleans myself. Have you been able to trace the calls to her cell phone? Dead end?" His frown deepened. "I'll let you know if we get a print from the scene here. How can I reach you?" Zane pulled out a notebook and wrote down a number, then disconnected the call and handed the phone back to her. "You heard what I said?"

Gloria nodded.

"It's your call, then. I can take you now if you want."

The safety of a relocation . . . the heartbreak of leaving Zane. Several gluey seconds slid away. "Not yet," she said. "I've made a mess of your investigation . . . I want to help you find out who the blackmailer is."

He nodded curtly.

"Chief," said an officer, sticking his head inside the room. "The area is clear."

"No clothing, no vehicle, nothing?"

"No, sir. Sorry, sir."

"I'm taking you home," he said to Gloria, then tossed his keys to the officer and asked him to bring his car to the door. He left her with another officer, then returned with a second handgun on his belt, this one of a serious caliber.

She didn't object to being ushered home, and as he was helping her into the car she realized that she simply wanted to be with Zane, especially since she knew their time was so short. Even if he was angry with her and didn't feel the same, she wanted to be able to soak him up so she could later wring the most memories out of their time together.

They didn't talk on the short drive to her house. Zane was on his radio, giving orders for leads to follow up on—ticketed vehicles, ask merchants in the area if they'd noticed anyone suspicious. He also forbid anyone to talk to the press at the risk of their job.

When they arrived, he hustled her into the house and checked every entrance point. A few minutes later, she was settled on her bed, leaning against the headboard with a heating pad under her shoulder. From a first-aid kit, Zane withdrew a tube of ointment and applied it to the welts on her neck with gentle strokes.

"Does that hurt?" he asked.

"No," she croaked. His nearness sent ripples of awareness to every part of her body. It was impossible to be in proximity to him and not want to touch him back. "Did your interviews yield anything?"

Zane frowned, still focused on her injuries. "Since Chasen died, Guy Bishop is also being blackmailed by the Mailbox Blackmailer. He seems to have picked up where Chasen left off."

"The Mailbox Blackmailer—is that what you're calling him?"

"Seems to be his preferred mode of delivery."

"He doesn't have any idea who it could be?"

"None. Ziggy Hines, on the other hand, hasn't received any calls since Chasen died. He says the girl in the picture is his daughter, but the mother's husband doesn't know, which is why he paid to keep Chasen quiet."

"How did Steve even know about the girl?"

"Because Hines hired Deke Black to draft an agreement between him and the mother for support and visitation."

She made a rueful noise. "I didn't know—Ziggy Hines isn't in the client files that I inherited."

"Chasen must have made sure of that. Anyway, Hines has been on the West Coast filming his cooking show since before the candy bars were distributed, and he returned yesterday, so that takes him out of the picture."

"What about Mona Black?"

"Says that Chasen never contacted her about anything other than her son's business, that she barely knew the man."

"Do you believe her?"

His mouth flattened. "I don't know, but the woman is unshakable."

"What about Marie Gaston?"

"A total fruitloop, in my opinion. Of everyone I talked to, she seemed the most capable of actually poisoning someone."

"But what motive would she have?"

He shrugged as he put the cap back on the ointment. "Maybe she wanted to protect Guy—and Penny—from those photos getting out. Maybe she and Chasen had a side thing that went wrong. Maybe she has suppressed feelings of rage that manifested into homicidal urges, and Chasen seemed like a good target." He glanced up, his expression wry. "Sometimes there is no motive, except to make the murderer feel powerful."

"Do you think she and Guy could be in on it together?"

"It's possible," he conceded. "I asked them both about the argument you witnessed. Guy said they were arguing about their work schedule, but Marie admitted she confronted Guy about seeming so happy that Steve was dead. She said he confessed he wasn't sorry, but said he had nothing to do with it."

"So she didn't mention the photos of Guy and Deke?"

"No, but I gave her every chance to tell me if she knew about them."

"Did you ask them about the voodoo dolls?"

He pursed his mouth, then nodded. "I did. No one admitted to knowing anything about them, or who might have made them. I'm wondering if Melissa Phillips might be our culprit—both in the poisoning and the doll-making. Her family is cooperating, and we're sifting through the items in her apartment, so maybe that avenue will provide a lead."

She drank him in, loving his voice, the way he put words together, the fact that he had dedicated himself to law enforcement. She studied the planes of his mature face and mourned the fact that she hadn't been with him to experience the things over the years that had given him tiny crow's-feet and worry lines in his forehead.

"Tell me about your life, Zane."

He seemed surprised and drew back slightly, hesitant to respond. "Nothing too exciting to report. After high school, I drifted for a while, then went to college and got a degree in criminal justice. I stayed close to Jersey for the first couple of years, then moved around the country, then . . . landed here."

"Then landed here," she repeated. "Don't you think it's bizarre that we both landed here at the same time?"

He busied himself with closing the first-aid kit and wiping his hands on a handkerchief. "I've given that some thought over the last couple of days. But when it comes down to it, we were both drawn to Mojo because of what was going on with the missing persons identification project. So there really is a reasonable explanation for . . . this."

Their gazes caught, and her heart quaked. She loved him, but she quelled the urge to reach out to him. She had breached his trust and complicated his job exponentially. She understood why they shouldn't be together—at least her mind understood. Her body, however, was not convinced.

His Adam's apple bobbed, then he moved closer, his eyes angst-ridden. "On the other hand," he murmured, his mouth hovering over hers, "there's nothing *reasonable* about . . . this."

She opened her mouth to receive him, flush in the knowledge that this time he not only wanted it but also knew full well who she was. She shifted on the bed to make room for him, and they kissed like the long-lost lovers they were, twining hands and legs. He speared his tongue against hers, moaning into her mouth, giving her his breath when hers ran out.

Before, their lovemaking had been hurried, fevered. But this time, as if by mutual consent, they moved slowly, savoring every kiss and every inch of skin revealed when they peeled off each other's clothes, the way they used to when they were teenagers, stretching out each touch to prolong the pleasure as long as possible.

The difference was the knowledge that they would be able to fully experience each other's bodies. He laved her breasts with his warm tongue, bringing the tips to hard peaks, sending pleasure pulsing to the far reaches of her body. She moaned and drove her hands into his hair as his mouth trailed fire down her stomach and across her thighs, her muscles clenching in anticipation of his tongue finding the most sensitive part of her. He teased her, kissing and lapping at her tender folds until finally latching on and sending her soaring.

"Zane," she murmured, straining against the silky

pressure of his tongue. The hum of a thousand bees started deep in her womb, then climbed higher and spiraled wider until her entire body vibrated for release. She begged and resisted at the same time, caught in a whirlpool of pleasure-pain that drove all other thoughts from her brain. Then with one last stab of his tongue, she went into free fall, the explosion of her orgasm so powerful that her back arched and she cried out, pulsating against his mouth until the spasms dissipated into delicious little tremors. She inhaled deeply, then heaved a sigh of satisfaction that went all the way to the tips of her fingers and to the ends of her toes.

Zane kissed his way back to her mouth, his expression smug with male satisfaction. He had always taken great pleasure in her pleasure, saying it made his release that much more intense. She reached down to cup his raging erection, intent on returning the favor, but he stilled her hand.

"All I want is to make love to you, to make up for all the times we wanted to and didn't."

He clasped her hands in his and held them over her head. She opened her knees to give him full access to her body, rising to meet him when he probed her wet channel. With one thrust, he plunged deep into her, moaning his pleasure to be sheathed in her body. She undulated against the exquisite feeling of fullness of having him inside her, marveling over the way their bodies seemed perfectly tuned to each other. They found a long, slow rhythm that maximized the mutual pleasure of each stroke. She squeezed his fingers between hers and surrendered to his deliberate, leisurely kisses, his tongue dipping, probing to mimic his body dipping into hers, sampling her sweetness.

Another climax coiled inside her, this one deeper, tighter, more controlled. He coaxed it to the surface with measured thrusts, urging her to come with him, his jaw clenched in restraint. Her orgasm rolled to the surface and burst, sending fragments of ultra-concentrated pleasure spinning through her body as she contracted around him. "Zane . . . Zane . . ."

His hips rocked forward in a massive thrust, then he groaned his release, burying himself into her, his face tense with abject satisfaction. "Lorey . . . oh, yes . . . Lorey."

His sex pulsed inside her as their perspiration-slick bodies recovered. He caught her mouth in such a profound kiss that tears gathered in the corners of her eyes. Because while Zane had been making love to her, he'd been thinking of another woman—the woman she used to be: fearless . . . fun-loving . . . free.

And she didn't know if she could ever find that woman in herself again.

Chapter 31

Wake up, Gloria. You can't push the rewind button. Life marches on.

"Gloria, wake up . . . wake up."

She started awake, desperately clinging to the sound of her mother's voice, which had seemed so clear in her dream. Zane was standing over her, illuminated from the light streaming in from the hall. He was fully dressed in his dark uniform, just as he had been since he'd climbed out of her bed yesterday after they'd made love.

"Do you still want to do this?" he asked in the tone of professional detachment she'd grown accustomed to.

"Yes," she croaked, thinking tomorrow she'd be waking up in a safe house in New Orleans.

"Forty-five minutes," he murmured, then left her room.

She pulled herself upright, flinching at the pain that shot through her shoulder and hip from her fall yesterday. The skin on her neck was tender and taut, although it felt as if the swelling had gone down. She limped to the bathroom and turned on the shower. When she stripped out of her pajamas, she grimaced at the sight of the large purple bruises on her upper hip and her shoulder blade.

At least they matched her hair.

She stepped under the spray of the shower and tried to isolate the cause of the stone of apprehension sitting in the bottom of her stomach. Was it the money drop at the cemetery? The thought of relocating . . . again? Or the awkward disconnect between her and Zane?

When he'd left her bed yesterday, he'd reverted to all-business, spending the afternoon on a conference call with BJ and his team and going through a stack of faxes that an officer had brought to him when two of them had arrived to pick up Zane's cruiser.

"No use announcing to the blackmailer that I'm with you," he'd said.

The evening hours he'd split between checking the doors and windows to make sure they were secure, and cross-referencing a kitchen table full of phone records. When she'd offered to help, he'd given her the brush-off. The only communication he'd had with her had been establishing an escape route in the event someone broke in and he was incapacitated.

And on that cheery note, she'd gone to bed. Alone.

She turned off the water and toweled dry, her

mind turning to the identity of the blackmailer. Who in town had had a close enough relationship with Steve Chasen to simply pick up where he'd left off?

Dressing quickly for warmth, she dried her hair and took a few minutes to try to conceal some of the marks on her neck with the lotion and foundation samples that the multi-tasking Brianna had given to her. She opted to skip the green contacts. With a wry frown at her reflection, she left the bedroom and walked toward the kitchen and the scent of coffee.

"Good morning," she said, not sure what to expect.

"Morning," he said, not looking up from a fax that he was studying. The familiar bank envelope of cash lay next to his cup. "I made coffee."

"Thank you." She poured herself half a cup, then filled the rest of the cup with milk and took a deep drink, watching him over the rim. "Did you get some sleep?"

"Uh-hm."

Meaning, of course, that he hadn't. After yesterday's debacle at the police station, she suspected he had sat up on watch. "Did you have any luck with phone records?"

"Not with yours," he said absently, still rifling through papers. "The call was made over the Internet and routed through too many servers to trace."

"But Steve's?" she prompted.

"A couple of promising leads. I passed them on to Marshal O'Connor."

"You've been in contact with George?"

"Yes."

"Does that mean you got a fingerprint from the bathroom?"

His jaw hardened. "No, we didn't."

"Oh." She drank from her mug. "Is there a general game plan this morning?"

He dragged his attention back to her and stood, gathering the papers. "The plan is that I'll be in the car with you, out of sight. Two plainclothes officers will be nearby, one on foot, and one in an unmarked car. When the guy stops and takes the money, we should have him covered."

"Sounds simple."

"Let's hope so." He checked his watch, then downed the rest of his coffee.

"Zane," she said quietly, "are we going to talk about what happened between us yesterday?"

He swung his gaze in her direction. "No. At least not now. Are you ready?"

She pressed her lips together, then dumped the rest of her coffee in the sink. "Let's go."

He walked to the window, parted the curtain, and looked out into the predawn darkness. Apparently satisfied, he moved toward the garage.

She put the money in her purse. In the garage, Zane swung into the backseat of her car, and she slid into the driver's seat. When she hit the button to raise the garage door, he lay down, folding his big body into the small space.

"There is one problem," she said, starting the car. "I don't exactly know where the Central Cemetery is."

"Drive through town, it's just past Steve Chasen's neighborhood, on the left. You have plenty of time, so drive slow."

She backed down the driveway in the dark. "You still have my driver's license."

"I figured you wouldn't be needing it," he said mildly. "Considering you're going to have a new name soon, right?"

Her heart twisted. "I guess so."

"That must be bizarre . . . one day to be one person, and the next day to be someone else."

"It is," she agreed, pulling onto Charm Street. "It messes with your mind. You don't realize how much of your identity comes from the way you look, your name, your personal history. And when all of that changes . . ."

"I nearly went crazy looking for you."

She bit down on the inside of her cheek. "I'm so sorry, Zane. I nearly went crazy myself. I wrote you a letter so you'd know I was safe, and I gave it to my handler. He said he'd mail it to you, but I found out only this week that he hadn't."

"He knows that we used to know each other?"

"I had to tell him." Although she'd taken her time.

After a few minutes' silence, he asked, "What did you think when I walked into your office?"

She smiled. "I couldn't believe it. I was stunned . . . then I was scared that you'd recognize me. You probably thought I was neurotic because I was so jumpy."

"I assumed it was because of the accident."

"You got so angry when I mentioned the voodoo doll."

"I'm trying to bring this town into the new century. You have to admit, it's pretty far-fetched to think that a voodoo doll can cause things to happen."

"I would have said the same thing a few weeks ago," she said thoughtfully. "I was Penny's counsel when she was questioned about stabbing the voodoo doll that looked like her ex-husband Deke. I thought it was nuts. But now . . ."

"Don't tell me that now you're a believer?"

"Now I'm . . . intrigued. I talked to Jules Lamborne about the second voodoo doll."

"The one that's supposed to be you?"

"Right. She told me that I wasn't supposed to be hurt, that I was only supposed to set things in motion for someone else to be punished."

"Uh-huh. While the old gal was rambling, did she happen to mention why Melissa Phillips was being punished?"

"No."

"Exactly. It's all smoke and mirrors, spooky scenarios that fit the circumstances. And I won't have it influencing my police force."

Feeling chastised, she changed the subject. "Has Melissa Philips's apartment yielded any information about her relationship with Steve?"

"We found a box of diaries that we're hoping will tell us something."

She moistened her lips. "Zane, when did you start to think that I was . . . Lorey?"

He took his time answering. "At first, it didn't cross my mind that you were Lorey . . . there were just some things about you that reminded me of her—I mean . . . you."

But his slip didn't go unnoticed. Her . . . you. Two different people, and he had feelings for only one of them.

Alarm bled through her veins, pervasive and profound. Had she so thoroughly changed herself that she had, in fact, betrayed herself? Rendered herself unrecognizable inside and out? Changed the trajectory of her life away from happiness and self-actualization? Splintered herself into so many personas that it was impossible to put herself back together?

"Where are we?" he asked, breaking into her disturbing thoughts.

"I s-see the turn," she said, slowing to give her signal.

He radioed his officers, checking their location. She pulled into the cemetery, the gravel road meandering among the tombstones and crypts barely wide enough for one car. She was immediately assailed by the eeriness of the place. A dusk-to-dawn light in the center of the graveyard left the outer edges in complete darkness. The narrow scope of her headlights made her feel as if she was in a tunnel. Heavy frost covered the ground and the ancient grave markers, giving the impression that this morning, the dead were even more dead—they were dead and frozen. A full-body shiver overtook her.

"You all right?" he asked, as if he sensed her fear.

"Fine."

"Look for an old stone building."

She spotted the silhouette of the structure and turned toward it. "Someone lives here?"

"Caretaker used to, but the building is used for storage now."

She maneuvered carefully, noticing that some of the headstones were broken and toppled. Through the veil of frost the outline of graffiti was clear—and jarring. "Is this the cemetery that was vandalized the other night?"

"Yes."

"Do you think there's a connection?"

"It's a theory," he said, his tone clipped. "Do you see the mailbox?"

"I'm pulling up now." She buzzed down her win dow, wincing against the cold blast of air that entered the car as she lowered the lid to the battered mailbox and stuffed the envelope inside. She looked around as she pulled away, but all was deadly quiet. "Okay . . . now what?"

"Now you leave and drive home. Tell me if you see anything suspicious, cars that look like they might be waiting, that kind of thing."

She glanced around as she drove back into town, but the only activity at this hour on a cold Sunday morning was a paperboy on a bike and a man sweeping the sidewalk in front of Benny's Beignet Shop, which appeared to have just opened.

They were almost back to her house when Zane radioed his men. "Anything?"

"Nothing yet, Chief. Wait . . . here's something . . . no, it's just a paperboy on his bike, probably cutting through."

"That could be our guy," Zane responded. "Keep an eye on him."

"He's veering toward the mailbox—we're going in."

Zane sat up and leaned forward. "Pull over and let me drive."

She did, and soon they were zooming back toward the cemetery.

Zane's radio crackled. "Chief, the subject took the money. We're in pursuit on foot."

"I'm on my way," Zane responded.

They were there in a matter of minutes. Zane pulled into the mouth of the cemetery and slammed the car into park next to a plain sedan that had been parked haphazardly—the undercover car, she assumed.

"Stay here and lock the doors," he ordered, then bounded out, his radio to his mouth, quickly disappearing into darkness.

Her heart racing, she locked the doors and sank down in the seat until she could just see over the dashboard. In a rare quiet moment, she reflected on the events of the past few days, conceding that she'd lived more life in the past week than she had in years . . . maybe her entire life. Zane was right—she'd been attracted to Mojo because of the missing persons identification project that was underway. And within days of arriving, the things that were missing in her life had been exposed: truth . . . trust . . . courage . . . support . . . friendship . . . love.

She couldn't spend the rest of her life like this, running from herself. If Riaz was determined to find her, he would eventually. And if he did, she'd simply tell the truth—that she had no idea where her mother was. If they wanted to hurt her or kill her to try to flush out her mother, there was little she could do about it.

But she would not relocate again.

And as much as she would like to think that she and Zane could rekindle their relationship, she was realistic. Their lovemaking yesterday had been a fulfillment of unrealized guilt and fantasy that the man had carried with him for almost fifteen years, a chance to be with Lorey before she disappeared again. Both of them were guilty of confusing the present with the past.

Hadn't she wanted to be Lorey again?

She closed her eyes, bittersweet feelings flooding her chest: It hurt to realize that up 'til now, she'd been swept up in the nostalgia of loving Zane. But he was different . . . angry at times . . . suspicious . . . as suspicious of people as she was, born of the same situation. Her disappearance had taken its emotional toll on both of them.

Could she love Zane now for the man he was? Was he truly the man who could help her overcome her past, or would he simply keep her steeped in it? And would she be able to deal with his occupation, with the knowledge that every day he placed himself in danger, dealing with people like the criminal who had destroyed her family? And more important, could she keep from simply being absorbed into his life? On the heels of her decision to take back her life, she couldn't afford to love Zane if it meant giving up herself all over again.

She bit into her lip. Now that she was staying, maybe they could be friends. And in time . . . who knew?

Suddenly Zane came into view with his two officers, one pushing a bicycle, one leading a young man in handcuffs. Something about the man seemed familiar, but she didn't recognize him until he drew closer—draggy jeans, overlong shirt . . . Mark, the teenager who worked at Tam's Electronics.

The little shit.

She unlocked the door and scrambled out. Zane jerked his thumb toward Mark. "Know this kid?"

"We've met," she said, crossing her arms and frowning at the surly-faced boy. "He works at the electronics store a few doors down from my office. His name is Mark."

"He won't talk—was he friends with Chasen?"

"They knew each other—he told me that Steve had bought things there." But frankly, the kid seemed too . . . *insignificant* for Steve to have befriended enough to go into the blackmailing business with. Then a piece of the puzzle clicked into place, and she put her hand to her head. "The photocopier."

"What?" Zane asked.

"The photocopier in the law office was broken, so Steve used the one at the electronics store. I'll bet he left something there when he made a copy—a file, perhaps? More than one?"

Mark pretended as if he didn't hear her, but she knew she was right. The notes he'd left attached to the cat's collar—he'd known from Steve's handwritten note that somehow Gloria Dalton was connected to L.L., and that had been enough to make her think he'd known more. And he'd probably used some kind of electronic device to activate her garage door opener and gain entrance to her house to leave the note on the cat's collar.

Zane turned to face the young man. "Taking over a blackmailing business, I guess that's good enough motive for murder."

That got Mark's attention. "Murder?"

"Yeah, from the serial number on the poisoned

candy bar, we know it was sold by one of the businesses in the shopping center."

Gloria's head pivoted—that was news to her.

Mark scoffed. "Every store in the shopping center sold those candy bars, dude."

"Open those panniers," Zane directed the officer holding the bike, pointing to the storage compartments on either side of the bike.

Mark bolted from the officer holding him and managed to run four or five steps before the man overtook him and slammed him facedown on the ground.

"Looky here," the other officer said, removing cans of spray paint. "I think we found one of our vandals."

Zane walked over to where the officer held Mark down. "If you know something about a body, you'd better be talking."

The teenager looked defiant. "I want an attorney."

Zane made a rueful noise. "We haven't even arrested you yet."

"Chief."

Gloria looked back to the officer by the bike. He'd opened the second pannier and was peering inside. He reached in carefully and removed a roll of drawstring garbage bags, exactly like the one her attacker had used.

Her throat convulsed at the memory. "He was at the station yesterday," she said. "I saw him working on a piece of equipment."

Zane fisted his hands, his expression lethal when he looked back to the teenager. "You're under arrest for extortion, murder, assault, vandalism, and arson—for starters. Now you can call your attorney. And if I were you, I'd be thinking about which one of my idiot friends I was going to rat out." He motioned for his men to take the youth away.

Gloria stood shivering in the cold dawn, watching the young man being placed in the sedan, his body language pure defiance.

"Let's get you home," Zane said, walking back to her car.

Numb, she followed him and buckled herself in. "You said something back there about a body? Were you talking about the body in the fire?"

He nodded. "The crime lab hasn't gotten back to us on their findings yet, but one of our theories is that when the cemetery was vandalized, a body was removed from one of the old graves."

She winced. "Is that possible?"

"Unfortunately, yes. Many bodies are buried aboveground here because the soil is so wet. But older graves are vulnerable to erosion and floods."

"So you think a group of teenagers robbed a grave, put the body in Steve's house, and set it on fire?"

"After they stole all of the equipment inside," Zane said. "A pawn dealer in the city responded to our bulletin about stolen electronics—said a couple of kids came in to unload some upmarket equipment still in the boxes. When we get the pictures of the sellers, I suspect one of them will be Mark."

She shook her head. "I don't get it. Why would he attack me in the bathroom yesterday?"

"Who knows? For the thrill of it? He probably felt invincible since he'd gotten away with so much already."

She puffed out her cheeks in an exhale. "He seemed so . . . normal."

He emitted a dry laugh. "Don't let that fool you about people."

He radioed for his cruiser to be brought to her house, then they lapsed into silence as he pulled into her driveway.

"Thank you," she said finally.

"For what?"

"For . . . everything. For protecting me and for putting that kid in jail where he belongs." She smiled. "And for trusting me, when I'd given you every reason not to."

He gave her a flat smile. "Just doing my job."

"You're very good at it. I'm so proud of what you're doing with your life, Zane."

"Your disappearance had a lot to do with that. Looking for you is what made me decide to go into law enforcement, so I guess I should be thanking you."

She smiled. "You're welcome."

"So . . . do you want me to take you to New Orleans now?"

"Actually, I've decided not to go."

His eyebrows raised. "Not to go?"

"Right. I'm tired of moving around, starting over. I actually like Mojo, with all its voodoo and eccentricities, and I've decided to stay."

"But Steve's phone contact is still unaccounted for—what if he's working with Riaz? You could still be in danger."

"We both know that's a long shot." She lifted her hands. "And it's a risk I'm willing to take. I'm not leaving."

He averted his glance, and a pained expression came over his face. Finally he looked back. "Look . . .

Gloria . . . I don't think a relationship between us is going to work."

"I know that," she said quietly. "And that's not why I'm staying."

He pressed his lips together. "I need to get my head around the fact that Lorey—that *you*—are still alive. I've spent so much time looking for you, I think I became a little obsessed. And confused."

"You don't have to explain, Zane. I don't want either of us to feel like we're simply trying to recapture the past. We're different people now."

He nodded, his gray eyes remorseful. "I need to rethink some personal decisions in light of what's happened."

A cruiser pulled up at the end of the driveway.

"There's my ride," he said. "I'll let you know if you need to come down and make a statement."

She nodded and watched him leave, wanting to run after him and convince him that they could still be good together—Zane and Gloria this time. Not a relationship rooted in teenage yearning and sex, but a grown-up relationship that was unpredictable . . . bewildering . . . frustrating . . . volatile . . . problematic . . . erratic . . . crazy . . . magical . . . unexplainable . . .

And rooted in great sex.

But after he'd devoted so much of his life to finding her, she owed him his space to allocate that part of himself to another pursuit . . . to another person.

And she could use some space herself to figure out in which direction she should expand her life first.

So, instead of going after him, she pulled the car into the garage.

Trying to focus on all the good things that had happened this morning—her personal epiphany being one of them—she walked into the house, feeling better about the future than she would have thought possible. She looked around at the packing boxes lining the walls and gave a little laugh. She couldn't put off unpacking any longer. She walked toward her bed room, rolling her shoulders. The bruise was bothering her, her skin itching in a place she couldn't reach.

Feeling philosophical, she dug out her City of Mojo back scratcher and used it to find relief.

Chapter 32

Gloria smiled at the plain plate-glass window and the Lawyer Here sign as she unlocked the door to her office. She walked into the entryway and inhaled deeply. The smell of freedom.

Her nose wrinkled. And drywall, paint, and carpet.

But it was all good, she decided as she flipped on the coffeemaker and set down her things.

She thought of Zane and smiled wistfully—not great, but good.

A glance at her watch gave her pause. Diane was usually here by now. Maybe the woman had decided not to come in for just one day. She'd call her later to tell her that she'd decided to keep the law office open and ask if she'd like to stay on.

The phone rang and she picked up the extension in her office. "Gloria Dalton, attorney-at-law."

"Gloria—Daniel Guess here. What can you tell me about the arrest of Steve Chasen's murderer?"

She frowned. "Nothing, I'm afraid, Mr. Guess. You'll have to talk to the police."

"But I heard you were there."

"Good-bye, Mr. Guess." She hung up the phone just as the bell sounded on the front door.

Diane appeared in the doorway, her expression confused. "I saw your car in the parking lot. I thought you were leaving town."

"I changed my mind," Gloria said with a smile, coming out to pour herself a cup of coffee. "Can I convince you to stay on for a while?"

"Um, sure." But the woman still seemed uncertain.

"Good." Gloria gave her an encouraging smile.

"I missed you at Steve Chasen's memorial service."

Remorse stabbed Gloria. "I hated to miss it, but . . . something came up."

The bell on the door sounded again. A stout man whom Gloria recognized as the copier repairman stood there holding his black tool kit.

"Hello, John," Diane said. "I wasn't expecting you back so soon."

"The part came in," he said with a shrug.

Gloria nodded hello, then returned to her office, closing the door behind her. Her window, her copier, her life—all seemed to be on the mend.

She pulled a handful of client files in various stages of completion and rolled up her sleeves. But as soon as she opened the first folder, her cell phone rang. She sighed and retrieved it from her purse. The display read Private.

She pushed the Connect button. "Hello?"

"Gloria, it's George."

"George," she said with a little laugh, "you're not going to talk me into relocating. I've made up my mind."

"Don't talk, just listen." His voice was grim. "I don't know how much range I have on this phone. I just got a tip that someone in Mojo is working for Riaz."

Fear seized her. "In Mojo? Who?"

"It could be anyone, someone trying to get close to you, even a woman. And our source double-crossed us—we think whoever is after you might have been tipped off that we know they're there."

"Meaning?"

"Leave now . . . police . . ."

His voice petered out, then the connection dropped. But she'd gotten the gist of his message: *Leave now and go to the police.*

With shaky hands, she grabbed her purse and was walking toward her office door when a knock sounded.

Her heart catapulted to her throat. "Yes?"

Diane's voice sounded on the other side. "Gloria, could you come out for a minute, please?"

Gloria's mind raced. What had George said? The person could be someone trying to get close to her, even a woman? Her mind flashed back to all the personal questions that Diane has asked about her family, where she was from, if she carried a gun . . . and then there was the arsenal of weapons the woman had at her home.

My God, the person working for Riaz was right under her nose, trying to cozy up to her. But if George was right, and she'd been tipped off that the agents were on their way, her timeline would have accelerated.

Gloria swallowed hard. Ergo the attack in the bathroom Saturday? After she'd told Diane that she would be closing the office and leaving town?

"Gloria? May I come in?"

Terror paralyzed her. Earlier she'd been cavalier about coming face-to-face with someone who worked for Riaz, but now she was absolutely terrified.

"Gloria?"

She removed the .38 from her purse and turned off the safety, then, with her finger on the trigger, she stuck her hand back into her purse, the gun aiming straight ahead. Gathering all the internal strength she could muster, she opened the door, expecting to see a gun barrel leveled at her chest.

Instead, Diane stood there with a form, smiling apologetically. "The repairman needs for you to sign this release."

"It's so I can charge it to the warranty," he offered in a bored voice.

Gloria breathed through her mouth, willing her pulse to slow. She eased off the trigger and withdrew her hand to take the pen that Diane extended.

Diane smiled. "Ms. Linder and Mr. Phelps are here as well."

Gloria cut her gaze to Sheena and Cameron sitting in two of the new reception chairs. Sheena was preening, holding a Big Gulp in one hand and touching Cameron with the other. The man looked as if he was in pain.

As Gloria signed the form, she glanced under her

lashes at the copier repairman. Stout, athletic. Perspiration trickled down her back. She handed the form to him and waited, her heart pounding. He shoved the paper in his pocket, turned, and walked out the door whistling.

Gloria exhaled in relief.

Diane looked at her purse. "Were you leaving?"

"Yes—I have to run an errand."

"What about Ms. Linder—"

"I'll be back shortly," Gloria cut in, eyeing Diane carefully. The woman had always conducted herself so shyly that Gloria had never gotten a good look into her eyes. They were . . . colorless. She'd wondered why someone who had been so persecuted would stay in Mojo; maybe it was a good cover for her . . . a good home base for her *occupation*.

A hysterical laugh caught in her chest—*welcome to Mojo, Louisiana, home to folks in the witness protection program and hired killers.*

"Oh, I'm so clumsy!" Sheena shrieked, holding out the front of her blouse, now soaked with cola. She leaned forward to give Cameron an up-close view. "Look what I've done to my shirt!"

"We're looking," Diane muttered. "I'll help you with that," she said, tugging Sheena toward the bathroom.

Cameron stood as Gloria stepped forward, a faint blush on his cheeks. "I got your message—my forms are ready?"

"Yes. Unfortunately, I have to step out for a few minutes."

"Sure. But I'll just take the forms if you have them. I need to get back to work."

She hesitated, then nodded and turned to retrieve the envelope from the credenza. "Here you go."

Cameron extended his hand, and it took her a few seconds to process the fact that he was holding a gun. Pointed in the general vicinity of her broken heart.

Chapter 33

"Don't say a word," Cameron said, holding the gun level, "and no one will get hurt."

Gloria swallowed hard and tried to believe him.

"Hands up."

She obeyed, although her shoulder throbbed. He turned the dead bolt on the front door, then turned the sign to Closed. Then he shoved her toward the bathroom, where Diane and Sheena's voices could be heard over running water—Diane's low and soothing, Sheena's high and piercing. With his free hand, he turned the key in the lock, then used the butt of the gun to break off the key.

"Hey!" Sheena yelled. "What the *hell* is going on out there?"

"Gloria?" Diane asked, then the doorknob rattled. "Are you okay? Gloria?"

"Shut up, both of you," Cameron yelled, "or I'll kill her!"

Sheena yelped, then all was silent.

Cameron looked back to her. "Let's make this quick, *Lorey*—where's your mother?"

"I don't know," she whispered, wondering why someone with Cameron Phelps's credentials would work for someone like Riaz. Then it hit her. "You're not Cameron Phelps, are you?"

He smiled meanly. "Nope. Nice guy though, hated to kill him."

Bile backed up in her throat. The phantom body in the woods that Jimmy Scaggs had been ranting about? "How . . . how did you find me?" She hoped his ego would keep him talking.

It did.

"Friend of mine who knows what I do for a living said he was digging up dirt on some lawyer chick and found out she was in the program, thought I might find the information . . . *useful*." He smiled again. "I didn't, but Bernard Riaz sure as hell did. Now . . . where's your mother?"

She shook her head. "I don't know, I haven't heard from her in years. And your friend is playing both sides—the U.S. marshals are on the way here," she said, getting braver. "Why do you think I was trying to leave?"

He fired the gun into the wall behind her, and her courage went to hide behind her survival instinct.

"Next time," he said, "I won't miss. Where's your mother?"

"I don't know where my mother is," she said

through clenched teeth. "It was you who set fire to Steve Chasen's house, wasn't it?"

"Yeah," he said, looking smug. "My friend got panicky, thought there might be something inside that would lead back to him. I had a body to get rid of, so it killed two birds with one stone . . . so to speak."

It occurred to her that he wouldn't be telling her all of this if he expected her to walk out of there.

He shoved the gun into her rib cage. "One more chance. *Where* is your mother?"

Tears rolled down Gloria's cheeks. "I don't know where my mother is!" she shouted.

His face screwed up, and she tensed for a bullet to tear through her body, wondering if Greg Goddard would have to hire mourners to fill up the pews at her funeral.

"Stop!" Diane yelled from the other side of the door. "I'm here! Tell Riaz that I'm *here!*"

Gloria froze. *What?*

Confusion crossed the man's face.

Then a terrific explosion of glass sounded and his body jerked, blood spurting from his neck. He fell hard, his gun sliding across the floor. Gloria screamed, scrambling backward. A kick to the front door splintered it, then it flew open. Zane stormed inside, his expression hard as he glanced at the man's still body.

She had never been so glad to see anyone in her life.

With his weapon still trained on the man, Zane crouched to check for a pulse. "Was he alone?"

Gloria nodded.

He stood and reholstered his gun, then crossed to her in two strides. "Are you all right?"

She went into his arms and clung to him, shaking. "I'm okay. That's not Cameron Phelps."

"I know."

"He told me everything—he set fire to Steve's house."

"I know."

She pulled back. "How? How did you know I was in danger? Did George call you?"

"No." His face was grim. "The watch that Jimmy Scaggs found in the woods led back to a Cameron Phelps in San Diego whose physical description didn't match the Cameron Phelps I'd met. I knew something was wrong, so I came straight here and called the U.S. marshals in New Orleans on the way."

Her heart swelled with awe and gratitude. "Zane . . . I love you so much."

She wanted the words back as soon as they left her mouth. In a heartbeat, his expression went from grim to guarded.

A frantic pounding sounded from the bathroom. "Gloria!" Diane shouted. "Gloria?"

"Get us out of here!" Sheena screamed. "I'm freaking out!"

Zane pulled away and yelled for the women to stand back. Then, with a couple of well-placed kicks, he breached the lock. The door bounced back, revealing Sheena standing on the toilet, her eyes as big as eggs, and Diane flattened against the wall.

Zane helped Sheena down. Even in her traumatized state, she managed to shimmy down him as if he were a dancing pole.

Then Diane walked out and stopped in front of Gloria. Eyes shining, she pulled off the wig of mousy brown hair to reveal the shock of pale blonde hair that Gloria had inherited. Then she removed the contacts that had rendered her vivid blue eyes almost colorless.

Gloria's eyes filled with tears of disbelief. "Mom?"

Diane bit into her lip and nodded. "It's me, honey. I look different, I know. I . . . had to have some surgery."

George's words came back to her. *Riaz's men left her for dead.*

Gloria's chin quivered as she reached forward to touch her mother's new face. Within the new features, she recognized old ones—her mother's eyebrows, with the mismatched arch, the slight sprinkling of freckles across her nose, her short, spiky eyelashes, the sparkle in her eyes.

"Mom," Gloria breathed and pulled her into a fierce hug, her heart expanding in her chest. "Where have you been?"

Diane pulled back and wiped her eyes. "All over. It took me a while to recover from my surgeries, then I made my way to New Orleans."

"I went there, too," Gloria said. "I remembered that you'd always wanted to live there. I thought I might find you."

"It wasn't fun living there alone," Diane said. "It just made me more lonely for you. I came to Mojo one year for a voodoo festival, and I liked it here—it made me wish I'd raised you in a small town."

"But the people here . . . they harassed you."

"Just a few bad apples," Diane said. "Besides, I met

Jimmy here, and then I couldn't bring myself to leave. And I'm so glad I didn't."

"Then you knew it was me all along," Gloria said with wonder.

Her mother nodded. "As soon as you walked into the doctor's office, I knew. I was dumbfounded . . . and ecstatic. And when I heard on the news that Bernard Riaz was out of prison, waiting for a new trial, I knew I had to stay close to you."

Gloria laughed. "So you applied for a job?"

"Yes. Brilliant, I thought. Lot of good I was when his guy showed up."

"You saved my life," Gloria said earnestly, then remembered they had an audience and a dead man at their feet. She turned to Zane, who was ending a call on his radio. "Zane, this . . . is my mother."

He blinked in surprise. "Ms. Lawson? Good to see you . . . again."

She smiled. "Call me Diane."

He nodded and shepherded them all outside as the crime scene techs arrived to process the scene. Holding hands with her mother, Gloria watched the activity, feeling Zane's watchful gaze upon her from a few feet away. She squeezed her mother's hand, unable to remember a time when she'd been so happy.

Zane came over with his professional mask in place. "Whenever you're ready, I'll need to take a statement."

She nodded, cringing when they brought the body out on a gurney. "He told me he put the body in Steve's house and set the fire, so that's two charges that Mark won't have to face."

Zane pulled his hand over his mouth. "Maybe three. It's starting to look like he might not have poisoned Chasen."

She frowned. "Then who did?"

"I'm still working on that."

A black SUV pulled into the parking lot and two suited men emerged, flashing badges at Zane when he stepped forward. They identified themselves as U.S. marshals. "Is Lorey Lawson here?"

Gloria stepped forward. "I'm . . . Lorey."

"Ms. Dalton, Marshal O'Connor asked me to give you a message."

"What?"

"Less than an hour ago, Bernard Riaz was shot and killed in his home by a member of his own organization."

She never thought that the announcement of someone's death would cheer her, but knowing that the man responsible for destroying her family could no longer hurt them was the equivalent of having a tank lifted from her chest.

"You are officially being released from WITSEC," the marshal continued. "And if you ever are in touch with your mother, let her know that the same applies to her."

Diane squeezed her hand and Gloria squeezed back. "I have a feeling that she knows. Thank you, and give my best to George."

She stole a glance at Zane to find him staring at the marshals with a look of barely suppressed rage that she well understood—the senselessness of how criminals tore through people's lives was staggering. And there were usually more victims than met the eye.

Zane turned his back and strode away. Gloria broke away and followed him. "Zane."

He turned back, his gray eyes angry, his mouth tight. "What?" he bit out.

"Don't be bitter. What happened to my family, what happened to us, was really horrible and unfair, but it happened. Let go of the anger."

He scoffed and looked away, then back. "What if anger is the only thing that's kept you going for the past fifteen years?"

"That's not the Zane I remember."

"Well, like you said, we're both different now." He straightened, his professional demeanor back in place. "I wanted to be the one to tell you—I've decided to leave Mojo."

Her heart stalled. "Leave?"

"I've been offered a job in New Jersey that will be closer to my mother and to Lisa and her family."

She tried to smile. "That's . . . wonderful."

He lifted a hand and gestured vaguely to the businesses, to the town. "I just don't fit in here with all the voodoo weirdness and the small-town gossip."

"I understand."

He wet his lips. "Plus . . . I feel as if I've finally closed a door on my past, and now it's time to move on."

She stood there nodding like an idiot, wanting to laugh at the irony of her deciding not to relocate and now Zane was leaving. They seemed destined to be on different timelines, different paths.

"When do you leave?" she asked.

"End of the week."

"So soon."

"I haven't unpacked yet, so it'll be an easy move."

Easy for him. "You do what you have to do, Zane. Be happy. My place is here, with my mother, and I think these weird people are just what I need." She smiled. "I've found my mojo."

She turned to walk away, chin high.

And she was finding more every day.

Chapter 34

"Chamomile?" Penny asked, poised to scoop tea leaves into a diffuser.

"That sounds wonderful," Gloria said, easing into a chair at the counter.

Penny smiled. "I like your hair."

Gloria touched her grape-colored curls. "Thanks. So do I."

"So . . . what do you want to be called now—Gloria or Lorey?"

She smiled wistfully. "I'm Gloria now . . . with a little bit of Lorey in there to keep me inspired."

"BJ is still devastated over how much he and Kyle trusted the man who passed himself off as Cameron Phelps." Penny shivered. "I can't believe he stood right here and flirted with you, all the while thinking that he was planning to kill you."

"Or at least kidnap me," she said, thinking of her close call at the police station.

"Wow, what a wild couple of weeks you've had."

"I know. Isn't it ever boring around here?"

Penny thought for a few seconds. "No."

The door opened and Marie rushed in. "I got the last one!" She held up a copy of the *Post* with its headline, CANDY COMPANY EMPLOYEE ADMITS TO POISONING CHOCOLATE BAR.

"Daniel Guess is loving this," Gloria murmured dryly. The man had been calling her nonstop for an exclusive interview about her life in the witness protection program. "Although I am happy that Mark won't have to stand trial for murder."

"Steve's death just seems so . . . random," Penny said.

"Jules says that nothing is random," Marie piped up. "That everything happens so that everything else can happen."

"She told me that about the voodoo dolls and Melissa Phillips," Gloria said.

Marie leaned in conspiratorially. "Melissa's diaries revealed that she and Steve both participated in what was going on at the voodoo museum."

Gloria frowned. "How do you know that?"

Marie's mouth rounded, as if she'd been caught. "I . . . heard."

Penny made a thoughtful noise as she poured Gloria's tea. "I think it's interesting that there have been three voodoo dolls, and all of the residents who died afterward were tied to the bad things going on at the museum."

"Yeah," Marie said. "It's almost as if the evildoers

are getting what's coming to them, one by one."

"Makes you wonder who could be next," Penny mused, looking sideways at Marie. "It almost makes you wish you could see into the future."

Marie seemed engrossed in the paper, but Gloria and Penny exchanged smiles.

"Marie," Gloria said nonchalantly, "you wouldn't happen to know where my cat is, would you?"

Marie glanced up. "Why would I know where your cat is?"

Gloria shrugged. "If you had to guess, where would you say it is?"

"Well, if I had to *guess,*" the young woman said, heaving an inconvenienced sigh, "I'd say it's rolling in something . . . green." Then she made a rueful noise. "Sorry, that's the best I can do."

Gloria squinted, then glanced at her watch and pushed to her feet. "I have to run. My newest window is being lettered this morning."

"Oh, nice," Penny said. "Say, doesn't Chief Riley leave today?"

Gloria's stomach dove. "Does he?" she asked, trying to sound indifferent.

"Left," Marie said.

"What?" Penny asked.

"Left, as in already gone." Marie nodded toward the street side of the building. "He drove by about a minute ago."

Gloria pivoted her head to look at the blinds covering the windows facing the street. "You were standing here a minute ago, reading the newspaper. How do you know?"

High spots of color appeared on Marie's cheeks.

"I . . . heard him drive by. His vehicle makes a very unique noise."

"It's called having an engine," Penny muttered. "Bye, Gloria."

Gloria waved and left the health food store, telling herself as she drove to her office that she shouldn't feel so wounded that Zane hadn't come around to say good-bye. It had simply spared them another awkward conversation.

And her, more painful memories.

The sight of her office front cheered her up. Elton had finished repairing the siding, and he'd replaced the door, and the window—again. When she pulled up, he was "supervising" the application of the gilded lettering spelling out her name . . . and scratching his ass.

She smirked and climbed out of her car. "Good morning, Elton."

"Mornin'," he said, beaming. "Almost finished."

"It looks terrific," she said, nodding with approval. "Elton, I brought you a thank-you gift."

He turned a hundred shades of red. "What is it?"

From her bag, she pulled the City of Mojo back scratcher. "Enjoy."

He gave her a goofy grin. "Hey, thanks."

"Don't mention it." He needed it more than she did, even if it meant that she had to rub herself against door facings for the rest of her life.

She unlocked the sturdy new door and walked into the chilly lobby, warmed by the cheery items her mother had put on the desk—new photos of the two of them, one of them taken after Brianna had given them a complimentary mother-daughter makeover.

On her way into her office, Gloria flipped on the coffeemaker and grabbed a fax that had come in since she'd left the evening before. When she set down her things and glanced at the fax, her eyebrows shot up. "Last will and testament of Steven E. Chasen."

The cover letter was from a New Orleans bank, with a note reading that Steve had kept the will in a safety-deposit box, with directions to have a copy faxed to this number upon his death.

The bell on the front door chimed and she moved back toward the lobby, reading the will. She looked up, expecting to see Elton or the lettering guy . . . and instead it was Zane, dressed down in jeans and a navy sweatshirt, looking achingly sexy.

And holding her black cat.

"I found something you were looking for," he said with one of those lopsided smiles she thought she'd never see again.

"Hi," she breathed, setting down the fax and reaching for the cat. It came to her and licked her face, purring happily. She snuggled the cat and looked back to Zane. "Where did you find him?"

"Next to the interstate, about the same place he ran away."

"Oh. On your way out of town."

"Yeah. But I know how much you love that cat, so . . . I had to come back."

She smiled. "Yes, I do love this cat."

He cleared his throat. "I even thought it might be . . . some kind of sign."

Her eyebrows went up. "Sign?"

"That I was supposed to come back."

"Except you don't believe in stuff like that."

"Right," he said quickly. "Well, mostly I don't, I guess."

Gloria gave a little laugh. "Since when?"

He sighed. "Since I got sucked into this weird little town." From his back pocket he removed the front section of the newspaper. "I thought you might need a copy of this article for your lawsuit."

"Thanks. But since the candy company has admitted culpability by ignoring the employee's threats to kill someone randomly for the thrill of it, I think it'll be a slam-dunk case." She set the cat down and picked up the fax. "Speaking of Steve's estate, I just received a copy of his will."

"You found it, huh?"

She frowned. "Actually, it found me."

"Did he leave everything to a relative that we couldn't find?"

"I don't know," she said, flipping through. "I didn't get a chance to look." When she found the wording, she gasped. "I don't believe it."

"What?"

She laughed through her fingers. "I, Steven E. Chasen, being of sound mind and body, do hereby relinquish all my worldly possessions to my beloved *cat*."

Zane's eyes widened. "Can he do that?"

"Sure. The bank will choose someone to be executor on the cat's behalf." Gloria touched her palm to her forehead. "Oh, my God! I asked Marie just now if she could tell me where my cat was, and she said he was 'rolling in something green.' Get it? Green—cash! He's rolling in cash! She was right!"

Zane winced. "If you say so. That woman scares

me. What will you do with the money if the bank chooses you as executor?"

She reached down to scratch the cat's ears. "If the bank chooses me, then I think we shall donate all the money to the families of the victims of the voodoo museum."

He smiled. "Nice." He turned and gestured awkwardly to the window. "Your window looks great."

"Thanks," she said with a laugh. "I was starting to think that it was cursed or something."

"I love you, too, Gloria."

She looked up and blinked. "What?"

His gray eyes were clear, the little pinch between his eyebrows gone. "I love you, too."

Her heart did a little jig, but she wasn't about to set herself up for another fall. "Where did that come from?"

He captured her hand and folded it over his heart. "Here. Did you know that the reason a person's first love is so strong is because your brain is actually developing chemical pathways—you're literally learning to love?"

"No, I didn't know that," she whispered.

"I don't know how to love anyone but you, and I want to get to know you all over again," he murmured, lowering his mouth to hers for a sweet, thorough kiss.

When they parted, she sighed in satisfaction, her body turned to the "on" position. A small part of her brain pushed a big worry to the forefront, however, and she whispered, "I don't want to leave Mojo."

He heaved a sigh. "Guess that means I'll have to get my old job back."

She grinned. "Really?"

"Really." He stood behind her and put his arms around her, tucking her head beneath his chin. "There's something about this place," he murmured. "I don't know what it is, but you're right. It sucks a person in. Besides, the town needs someone sane to sort through all this mess with the voodoo dolls."

She smiled against his chest. "And that's you?"

His laugh was short and dry. "This could be my toughest assignment yet." Then he made a rueful noise. "We do have one immediate problem, though."

"What's that?"

"I don't know if that window is big enough to be able to add 'Riley' to your name."

She bent her head back. "Isn't that being a little presumptuous?"

"Marry me."

"Okay," she breathed, feeling herself expand and bloom under his kiss.

The chime sounded as the door opened. Sheena Linder and Mona Black stood there, the odd couple of the moment, from all the gossip.

Sheena sniffed as they disentangled. "Guess I'm going to have to find me a new leading man."

Gloria straightened but couldn't keep the happy smile off her face. "Can I help you, ladies?"

"We just stopped by to tell you the good news," Sheena said, snapping her gum. "We're going to make a movie."

Gloria frowned. "Who's 'we'?"

"The town," Mona said. "We've worked it out. Mojo's incorporated, and we've sold the rights to the town's story to a major production company to film right here in town."

"For a truckload of cash," Sheena said, her eyes shining.

"We're going to use it to rebuild the town," Mona added.

"Oh . . . right," Sheena agreed, sounding less enthused. "It's the only way Jodi would agree to participate."

"That's . . . great," Gloria said.

"We want you to handle all the paperwork," Mona said, and something in her eyes made Gloria think that she'd passed some kind of test by staying. Then Mona gestured between the two of them and gave Zane a pointed look. "Does this mean you want your job back?"

"Yes."

"Okay," she said, then turned and left.

"We'll be in touch," Sheena said, then looked at Zane and made a sorrowful noise. "Such a waste."

When the door closed behind them, Gloria and Zane burst out laughing.

"A movie production company coming to Mojo?" he said. "Do they know what they're in for?"

"The movie company, or the town?"

"The movie company, of course."

They kissed a long, full-body kiss, with promises of heated nights of catch-up to come. Suddenly, Gloria pulled away and squirmed.

"What's the matter?"

"It's that bruise healing. It itches like crazy."

"Here, let me get it." He slipped his hand under her blouse and scratched the skin lightly.

"Higher," she said, arching her back with pleasure. "Higher . . . higher . . . found it. That's . . . *perfect*."